According to

to a

Source

ABBY STERN

. . . .

According

to a

Source

Thomas Dunne Books

St. Martin's Press

New York

THOMAS DUNNE BOOKS.
An imprint of St. Martin's Press.

ACCORDING TO A SOURCE. Copyright © 2017 by Abby Stern. All rights reserved. Printed in the United States of America. For information, address St. Martin's Press, 175 Fifth Avenue, New York, N.Y. 10010.

www.thomasdunnebooks.com
www.stmartins.com

Designed by Sue Walsh

The Library of Congress Cataloging-in-Publication Data is available upon request.

ISBN 978-1-250-10679-7 (hardcover)
ISBN 978-1-250-10680-3 (e-book)

Our books may be purchased in bulk for promotional, educational, or business use. Please contact your local bookseller or the Macmillan Corporate and Premium Sales Department at 1-800-221-7945, extension 5442, or by e-mail at MacmillanSpecialMarkets@macmillan.com.

First Edition: May 2017

10 9 8 7 6 5 4 3 2 1

For my mom and dad, who never encouraged me to be "realistic." I love you.

AUTHOR'S NOTE

No actual celebrity names have been used, and all blind items are fictional. This note is not intended to protect the innocent, because in Hollywood, *no one* is innocent.

Hollywood's a place where they'll pay you a thousand dollars for a kiss, and fifty cents for your soul. I know, because I turned down the first offer often enough and held out for the fifty cents.

—Marilyn Monroe

You can't find any true closeness in Hollywood, because everybody does the fake closeness so well.

—Carrie Fisher

According to a

to a

Source

One

· ·

want every major moment of my life to occur at the Chateau
Marmont. I want to get married here. I want to conceive my first child
here. I even want to die here—preferably not of a drug overdose, but
when in Rome. . . .

I can't pick my favorite thing about the Chateau Marmont. The smell
on the dining patio—or the garden, as it's known among Hollywood's
elite—is definitely in the top three: floral yet masculine. And it is decorated with the world's best eye candy. The tent that was erected over the
patio during the chilly awards season recently came down, and the hedges
are, as always, perfectly groomed.

I come here at least once a week.

I feel my phone vibrate, but I ignore the text, because my heart has
nearly arrested. A mousy, brunette, makeup-free waitress just delivered our
check with a Hercule Poirot–esque inquisition.

"Excuse me, Miss Warren," she says, and I notice some of her hair has
loosened itself from her terribly unchic side braid, "why doesn't the first
name on your credit card match the name on your reservations?"

Across the table, my friend Jessica looks up, amused.

My mind is racing faster than it ever has on Adderall. *Breathe. Namaste.*
This waitress is clearly new, and probably having a hectic night. And in
fact, I've held in my arsenal the answer to her question since my inaugu-
ral visit to the infamous hotel and restaurant, because when I first started
dining at this notoriously exclusive landmark, I lived in fear of the day
my secret would inevitably be uncovered.

My identity exposed.

In my early days dining at Chateau Marmont, I was only offered a
reservation (yes, you're *offered* reservations here) at 6 P.M. After months of
regular visits, my standing was raised and I was given a coveted 8 or 9
P.M. slot. Now I'm a regular. In fact, one of the veteran waiters—i.e., not

this inquisitive fresh-off-the-boat Pollyanna—once mentioned that other than myself, only America's Sweetheart-slash-Most Beloved Victim of Infidelity's stylist and the West Coast Head of Burberry have their own regular tables in the garden.

I flash my most confident smile. "People ask me that all the time," I recite, lasering my eyes into hers. "My full name that you see on my credit card was already taken in the Screen Actors Guild, so I chose Bella. It was my childhood nickname. I don't want casting directors to get confused, so now I use my SAG name for everything."

Across the table, Jessica gives me a nod, impressed. In Los Angeles no one would question that answer, because *everyone* else here is an actor—even this waitress, I'm guessing.

I feel my phone vibrating again but I can't risk looking down. I maintain eye contact with the waitress, staring down any further inquisition. But the waitress doesn't bother to search for holes in my explanation. "Oh, okay," she says, and leaves the leather-bound bill in front of me. I smile widely until I can see she's cleared the lobby and is out of sight.

My real name is Ella Warren, or Isabella Warren, as it says on said credit card in question. I am an undercover reporter for the celebrity gossip magazine and Web site *The Life*. I'm aware "Bella" isn't exactly the most discreet alias, but when I started this job, I didn't think celebrity reporting needed a CIA-worthy nom de plume. Now I know better—the majority of the time, my job does indeed feel like a black-ops mission. This waitress was relatively easy; but what if another, smarter waiter caught on? The Chateau Marmont has a strict "no media" policy on the premises, and if I am discovered, I'll be banned. I get a byline, "Ella Warren," on my stories and sightings, so I created Bella the first time I made a reservation.

Sometimes, I wish I actually *were* Bella. She's the girl that has the confidence to own any room she enters. She's the one on the lists to the most exclusive parties and restaurants around town. She's the one that glides past the velvet ropes and receives the texts with addresses for after-parties before the lights in the club come on at the end of the night. In reality, Bella is a mere figment of everyone's imagination—and it needs to stay that way.

I grab the goblet holding the remainder of my rosé and chug it. After I annihilate mine, I reach across the table and grab Jessica's.

"Do you think she bought it?" I ask.

Jessica is my oldest friend in Los Angeles. She is a Venice Beach bon vivant—the soul of casual essence. Though you'd think she and I would clash, we've always clicked. We were English majors at college together and have known each other for eight years, which is the equivalent to twenty years in this town.

"You're fine," she says. "I wouldn't worry about it." She's the sane friend I can always count on to talk me down when I'm on the verge of checking into the hospital for "exhaustion."

This is why Jessica is one of my ride-or-die friends. She always has my back and I never have to question her motives. Because we met before I worked for *The Life* or she was a blogger extraordinaire, our friendship is genuine, and unless she's at work with me, we never talk about celebrities. Our conversations always have and still do revolve mostly around boys. Who we like. Who we used to like but now hate. Which ex's picture we bet we would see on the news. Who we secretly wish would send an out-of-the-blue text saying they missed us and beg to get back together. In college, we had a standing date every Sunday night so we could recap our weekends. We'd open a bottle of the best wine we could afford and sprawl across my living-room couches, clad in our velour track suits eating greasy pizza and watching as much reality TV as my DVR would hold. We'd talk until one or both of us passed out. Jess was a sport, and even though she didn't like pepperoncinis she let me order pepperoncinis on those pizzas. There are very few people I like enough to consume a food that isn't appetizing to me, but I'd do it for Jess and she did it for me.

Jess has parlayed her degree into the lifestyle blog *Martini Olives Count as Dinner,* which has gained her a fair share of local notoriety. She's one of the few people who's always liked me for Ella, and I trust her.

In Hollywood, the only thing more difficult than getting cast in a Netflix pilot is finding *real* friends. It's almost impossible to meet people that don't have an agenda. Sadly, many friendships here are like celebrity relationships. Despite promises and social-media proclamations to the contrary, more often than not they last for a finite period of time. As friends aren't required to sign confidentiality agreements, you can imagine that after an acrimonious split, gossip about both parties spreads faster than a fire in the Hollywood Hills. A few years ago an ex-friend of mine started blabbing about how I was escorted out of the Dior store on Rodeo Drive by security (through no fault of my own), and the story even made it all the way around town to my aesthetician.

My arm is still shaking from my encounter with the waitress when I pull out the bill. I have a generous expense account that's enough for dinner and two glasses of wine—well, three glasses, if my guest and I decide to skip dessert. I'm not supposed to surpass it, even for the tip. But since I was cross-examined only moments ago, I'm going to leave a bonus. I purposely ignore the line on the check that indicates that a 15 percent gratuity has already been included. This is really for the barrage of European diners they accommodate. Tonight I'm going above and beyond.

I show Jessica the final amount.

"How are you going to explain that one on your expense report?" She glances at her empty wineglass, begrudging my drinking her beverage.

"I'll tell Maggie the truth. I know she'll have my back," I reply, and I playfully shake my head at the fact that this millennial waitress almost deep-sixed my mission tonight.

While I sign the bill Jess kicks my foot under the table.

She knows the drill.

Former A-List Hot Mess Actress (the main reason I am here tonight) is walking my way. It takes a special skill to pretend like you aren't looking at someone while you're practically committing every detail about them to your memory.

"Well, she's in a mood," Jessica says after the actress passes.

"I would be too if I was in my twenties but looked forty-five. All of that money and access to free facials and fillers, such a shame."

Jessica is purposefully ignoring Former A-List Hot Mess Actress now, as is the rest of the garden around us. The mood has shifted; they all know she is walking toward the exit, but no one wants to look as though they noticed. Rubbernecking would be a huge faux pas. "I think they're only free because she refuses to pay," she says.

I chuckle. "How about the way she was stumbling?" I add. "I'm surprised she could even walk after all of those 'vodka sodas.' Wait, does keeping the bottle of vodka underneath the table instead of on top of it and sipping Diet Coke publicly constitute a vodka soda?"

"Only in LA," Jessica says with a smile.

My phone buzzes . . . again. "Will you excuse me?"

"Bathroom time?" Jessica looks at her watch. "Has it already been twenty minutes?"

I wink. I go to the bathroom every twenty minutes. Most of the waiters probably think I have a raging cocaine problem, but that's honestly better than if they knew the truth. It doesn't exactly take Alan Turing to crack my code, but it's secret enough for the Chateau Marmont. I saunter away from the table and into the lobby, acting so much like I belong here that sometimes I feel like I actually do. Luckily one of the two stalls is vacant and my heartbeat speeds up as I enter and pull my phone out of my purse. My fingers are sweaty and I fumble over the wrong keys while I type in my pass code. After three frustrating tries I wipe my right hand against my skirt and get a better grip. Finally. Open sesame.

I let out a deep breath. Who the hell keeps texting me?

It's my sister, Robin. I open the first message: a photo of her and my niece making funny faces.

Robin: Marianna wants to remind you about her birthday party this weekend. She's so excited to see her favorite Aunt and that Grandma is flying in to celebrate!

Robin: Aunt Ella, let us know if you're still coming and send us a funny face back!

Robin: Is Aunt Ella busy tracking celebrities? Where in Hollywood is she ☺?

I can't help smiling—Marianna is mugging shamelessly for the camera, just like I taught her! But I'll respond later. Right now, I need to rush and record my . . .

NOTES:
- *Former A-List Hot Mess Actress*
- *Vodka bottle hidden under table*
- *Wasn't able to walk straight*
- *Entourage left with her*
- *Reeked of cigarette smoke*
- *Designer clothes appeared to be in shambles with unintentional visible holes and rips*
- *Left around 12:30am*

I put my phone back in my purse, relieved that the stressful part of the night is over, and return to our table. "Let's get out of here?" I ask, ready to bolt, as if I were running toward higher ground after a tsunami warning.

"Yes, ma'am." Jessica grabs her purse. "You get what you needed?"

I do a furtive 360-degree survey of the patrons on the patio. "Yep. Let's go." But then the small of my back receives a jolt of electricity.

"Hi, Bella."

I'd recognize that inimitable masculine pitch anywhere. It's Sexy Indie Film Actor—where did he come from? And he's talking to me!

I take note of what he's wearing, not even for work purposes, but because his perfection appears effortless: Navy-blue T-shirt, distressed jeans, and combat boots have never complemented each other quite like they do as components of his ensemble. It's not even so much the outfit as his charm and aura.

I regain my normal stance and clear my throat in an attempt to keep my voice from trembling.

"Hi! How are you?"

He kisses me on the cheek, and even Jessica's jaw is agape. "Pretty good," he says. "Just meeting some friends. " He turns to Jessica, extending his hand. Even people who don't really care about celebrities, like Jessica, have one person that gets them starstruck, and I'm secretly delighted to have found hers. Sexy Indie Film Actor has her reaching to collect a response.

"This is Jessica," I interject.

"Nice to meet you," he says. Jessica fervently nods back. Then he smiles at me. "I'll see you around, babe." He continues to a discreet table in the back corner of the patio and joins two male friends.

Jessica's grin has inexplicably multiplied in length. I am loving her mutation into a total fangirl. "He just called you babe! How do you know him?" she whispers.

"From the clubs. He's friends with a promoter I know, so we end up at the same table sometimes."

"I can't believe he knows who you are!"

I sigh. "He doesn't know me. He knows Bella," I correct. "You know Ella. Everyone else here knows Bella."

Not that I'm complaining, of course.

. . . .

I finally walk through the front door of my West Hollywood apartment a little before 1 A.M. and kick off my Brian Atwood stilettos before my second foot even crosses the threshold. I'm like Cinderella and the ball is over. As soon as the shoes come off and both big toes touch the carpet, Bella is Ella again. The fibers comfort my soles, and even though it's not exactly reflexology, it helps alleviate the tension Bella endured earlier that evening.

All of the lights are off as I tiptoe to the bedroom to grab my laptop. Ethan is asleep with his back facing me. I love staring at his back. For some reason it's a comforting sight. When I'm there with him, the outside world melts away. I'm struck by how much I miss him. Even though we live together, I barely see him outside of this bed anymore, which is sadly not as kinky as it sounds.

I lean down to give him a soft kiss in our spot, the crevice where the neck and shoulder meet. We discovered it the first time we spent an entire weekend in bed having a movie marathon. He'd been spooning me and when he lost interest in his hundredth viewing of *Back to the Future,* began kissing my neck. He continued down and when he got to what would become "our spot" I let out a giggle.

"Ticklish?" he asked. I knew he was grinning even though the back of my head was facing him.

"No," I told him emphatically.

"No? So you won't mind if I do it again?" he teased.

"Not at all." He returned his lips to the spot and I didn't laugh. I shifted my body to face his. "It just feels good. Like, really comforting and like you're supposed to be there." Ethan pulled me closer and kissed me on the lips. When he finished he stared into my eyes, which was sweet at first but started to make me self-conscious. I laughed again. "Here, I'll demonstrate," I said, placing my hands underneath him and rolling him to the side. I stared at his back and was so in the midst of the honeymoon stage of our relationship I even thought his moles were cute. I proceeded to softly kiss him exactly where he kissed me.

"You're right, that does feel good. From now on, this will be our spot," he announced. I did it again and rested my head against his back and drifted to sleep.

Tonight, Ethan smells like he's just come from the woods and built his own spice rack—although he's probably been at Starbucks working on his screenplay all day—and I inhale him as if he were a congratulatory flower arrangement. I wish I could fall into bed right now but I have to write my file for *The Life.*

"What, no hug or squeeze?" he mutters, rolling over to face me, still

more than half asleep. Kiss, Hug, Squeeze is something my dad did with
my sister and me every night before bedtime when we were little. He'd
say each aloud and then proceed with the action. On extra special nights,
he threw in Eskimo and Butterfly for good measure. Throughout the years
it became our way of showing our love for each other. Now, I do it with
everyone I love, which is why Ethan is bemoaning the exclusion of his
hug and squeeze tonight.

I wish he could see me smiling in the dark. "I was trying not to wake
you but I had to kiss you."

"I want you to wake me so badly," he says, but then he lets out a yawn
and can barely pull his eyelids apart.

When I first started this job, Ethan used to wait up for me every night
to make sure I got home safe. But now he's used to me coming home
well after midnight and his REM cycle usually remains uninterrupted
even as I open and close the front door.

"Go back to sleep. I love you."

"'Night, babe," he says, trailing back off into his slumber.

In the living room, I change into my pajamas and remove all of my
jewelry. I always have to be comfortable when I file—not even a neck-
lace or bracelet on. Keeping my jewelry on at the end of the night makes
me feel claustrophobic, like I'm in a music video and have a boa constric-
tor wrapped around me. I place my jewelry on the coffee table as I open
my laptop to e-mail Maggie. I'm required to file my stories overnight in
case the editors want to use them first thing in the morning.

I scroll back through my notes and start typing.

The Chateau Marmont March 20th
Celebrities:
Former A-List Hot Mess Actress & Sexy Indie Film Actor

FORMER A-LIST HOT MESS ACTRESS
*Though she had previously been banned from the establishment, Former
A-List Hot Mess Actress made a return visit to the garden at the Chateau Marmont on Tuesday evening. She didn't appear to be upset about
being dropped from her upcoming film as she chain-smoked cigarettes and
sipped on diet soda all night. Though soda was on the table, underneath
the table was a bottle of vodka. Whenever Former A-List Hot Mess
Actress bent down to retrieve another cigarette from her purse, she took a*

swig. As the night wore on she was more than a little bit out of it and loopy. While her three male companions all ordered food she abstained, but ate off all of their plates once their meals arrived. She was clearly trying to keep a low profile and the group stayed until 12:30 A.M. When Former A-List Hot Mess Actress got up to leave, the remaining patrons immediately took notice and it was obvious they were staring and gossiping about her. She put on a pair of aviator sunglasses (which looked like Ray-Bans) despite it being nighttime and clutched her white leather purse, which looked worn, as did her green tank dress, which was complete with cigarette burns. She swiftly walked out and her entourage followed and she stumbled on the steps up toward the lobby, narrowly avoiding a fall. It looked like she went toward the bank of elevators instead of downstairs to the garage.

SEXY INDIE FILM ACTOR

Sexy Indie Film Actor made a late-night visit to the Chateau Marmont. He was fashionably late, arriving a little after 12:30 A.M. looking effortlessly casual in a navy-blue T-shirt, jeans, and combat boots. He stopped to say hello to a petite blonde before he made his way over to a group of male friends who had a Heineken waiting for him. Sexy Indie Film Actor basically bro'd out and spent his time catching up with his friends.

Maggie always jokes she can tell when I'm writing myself into the file. "Focus on the celebrities!" she'll say, but because we're friendly outside of work she humors me and rarely cuts me out of the story. Even though we are the only two that know I'm *that* blonde, I still get a thrill from being in a story for *The Life.*

I click Send, and thank God I can sleep in tomorrow.

Time to go snuggle with Ethan.

Two

. . . .

My alarm clock shocks me awake at 9 A.M. I roll over to say good morning to Ethan, but his side of the bed is empty. I reach for my iPhone on the nightstand.

Me: Where are you?

Ethan: I had an early pitch with the studio. My agent thinks this is the one.

Me: Good luck! XO

Then, with a start, I realize—Robin! I scroll back to her texts:

Me: I'm so sorry! I was covering Chateau for work and by the time I got home I forgot to text you back.

Robin: It's okay. You and Ethan are coming Saturday, right? Marianna will be crushed if you aren't at her party.

Me: Can't wait to see her and Mom. XO P.S. Tell M her duck face is on point.

I check my e-mail to see if I have any assignment requests from *The Life*. Yep. E-mail from my boss, Maggie Kalaf.

Dear Freelancers,
There will be a mandatory meeting for ALL freelance reporters for The Life, *tomorrow at 2 p.m. at our office. Again, this meeting is mandatory. If you do not attend your association with* The Life *will be terminated, immediately.*
Best,
Maggie

I squint at the screen. Mandatory meeting? What the . . . ?

I've known Maggie for years and this e-mail doesn't sound like her at all. I met her right after Ethan and I started dating. Ethan invited me out for Taco Tuesday at LA's Mexican fusion restaurant du jour for a double date with his friend. The friend was Maggie and her date was her semi-regular hookup-slash-sometimes-boyfriend, Dennis.

Maggie and I sat across from each other drinking skinny margaritas. I was trying to make a good impression on her but she was disinterested when I tried to make conversation. Maggie's expression was blank and after she gave me the once-over she didn't look at me, even though I was in her direct line of sight. I felt like I had tried some new fad diet that made me translucent. This made me determined to try harder.

"Ethan just raves about you," I said. Maggie looked at her phone and everywhere else and still wouldn't make eye contact but I continued attempting to win her approval through compliments. "He says he wouldn't have survived high school without you."

"Uh-huh," she muttered. It was obvious she wasn't actually listening to what I said, but threw a "yeah" in occasionally to shut me up.

Her eyes continued skimming the crowd around me. Tired of my one-sided small talk, I excused myself to the restroom when I finished my entrée. I leaned against the door when it shut behind me to collect myself before I went to the sink to splash some cold water on my face. I gave myself a deep, introspective stare.

"You've done nothing wrong," I told myself in the mirror. "Maggie can't dislike you. She doesn't even know you. If she doesn't want to get to know you, it's her loss."

As I was in the midst of my affirmations, I was startled when the bathroom door swung open and Southern Girl-Next-Door Movie Star joined me. She was even tinier in person than she is on-screen. She smiled at me before she entered the stall and we both silently acknowledged that I knew who she was. I stared at myself again and took a deep breath. *Namaste.* I didn't want to return to the table quite yet so I decided to fix my hair. While I was debating between a half or full ponytail, the toilet flushed and Southern Girl-Next-Door Movie Star took her place at the sink next to me.

"You alright?" she asked, noticing the hint of chagrin on my face as she was washing her hands. They were flawlessly manicured with a nude polish.

"Me? Yeah. I'm just on this weird double date and—"

"I totally get it," she interrupted. She took more towels than necessary to dry off. "I'm here on a first date. My publicist set me up with Rugged Award-Nominated Method Actor. Between you and me, he's really boring," she confided. Was this happening? Southern Girl-Next-Door Movie Star didn't even know my name or astrological sign and she was blurting out intimate details of her life to me. Not that I minded, of course, and her venting took my mind off Maggie. I folded my arms into my chest to indicate that I was listening. "I didn't want to go out with him in the first place but my publicist says I need to show the world I'm not sitting around at home after my divorce and I need a new sexy, single image even if it is totally fabricated," she continued.

She threw her towels in the trash and sucked in as she stood with her profile to the mirror. "I was with my husband since I was twenty years old, I'm nowhere near ready to date yet." She pivoted on each foot to determine if she approved of the image looking back at her.

"You look amazing," I told her.

"Really?" She inspected herself up and down one more time to make sure my compliment was sincere. She pursed her lips and silently agreed with my assessment. It seemed to have provided her with a necessary confidence boost. "Thank you, Spanx," she joked in a more hushed tone. She returned to her normal voice. "I just haven't been able to bring myself to exercise after my split so I can't live without them." I giggled. Stars, they're just like us.

"Everyone is rooting for you. Just be yourself. That's why your fans love you."

"Thanks." She readjusted her cerulean gingham button-down shirt and khaki pencil skirt and took a deep breath of her own. "I guess I better get back out there."

"Me, too." I followed her out of the restroom and I didn't notice until I almost tripped over her that like me, she was going to the patio. When I reached my table I noticed Maggie was there alone. I pulled out my chair, and before I could process the absence of our dates Southern Girl-Next-Door Movie Star tapped me on the shoulder.

"Thanks again for the pep talk," she said with a wink, before continuing to her table. I sat down to try to make the best of my Maggie situation and salvage the rest of the evening, but my behind didn't even touch the chair before Maggie's attitude shifted. She was suddenly all over me like a fruit fly at the end of a picnic.

"Were you in the bathroom with her?"

"Yeah," I responded. "Where are the guys?" I inquired.

"The Lakers game went into overtime so they went to finish their drinks at the bar to watch," Maggie spit out. It's clear she has no concern or time for their whereabouts at the moment. She's almost foaming at the mouth. "You talked to Southern Girl-Next-Door Movie Star?"

I nodded my head and she fired questions at me so fast I don't think she took a break between them.

"What did she say? How was her mood? Did she say who she's here with? Did she seem sober or drunk? Tell me everything! No detail is too small!" Her eyes were bugging out of her head, as if I'd just told her I was an alien. This was the most animated I'd seen Maggie all night.

"Oh, she was super sweet," I told her nonchalantly. "We were just chit-chatting."

"Chitchatting? About what? Did she say what she's doing here?" she interrogated, again without taking a breath.

"Yeah. She's here on a date with Rugged Award-Nominated Method Actor," I tell her.

"She is?!" Maggie receives a surge of electricity with my information. "I had a gut feeling it might be him, but I couldn't make out his face for certain from over here. They would be such a power couple."

"Don't get too excited. Southern Girl-Next-Door Movie star told me it's a setup and that he's really boring and she doesn't want to be dating anyway, but her publicist forced her to go out with someone for her im-age." As I was talking Maggie grabbed her phone and started transcrib-ing everything I said verbatim. She nodded her head as I spoke and I wondered why she was taking notes.

"Ella, you're amazing!" When she finished typing she returned to star-ing and I realized she hadn't been ignoring me, she'd been staring at who was behind me. I turned my head to confirm that Southern Girl-Next-Door Movie Star was at a table behind me. "My boss is going to eat this up," Maggie said with a duplicitous grin. "I just sent in everything you told me. Since I got it to her ASAP, we might have the chance at an exclusive."

My mind was attempting to arrange the pieces of this bizarre puzzle together but I was coming up empty. She continued ferociously typing and when she finished placed her phone on the table and traded it for the biggest gulp of margarita she'd taken all night. She swallowed it without a trace of trouble and leaned into me conspiratorially. "I work for *The Life*," she whispered. I bolted upright.

"No way!" Mystery solved. "I can't believe you work for *The Life*! That is so cool! How did Ethan not mention this?"

Maggie looked startled but flattered by my enthusiasm.

"My mom raised me on it," I continued. Now it was my turn to bombard her with questions. "What's it like to work there? Do you meet a lot of celebrities? What's the craziest thing you've ever seen happen that hasn't been published?" Maggie smiled and leaned closer—but she was cut off by the waitress returning with the check.

I reached into my purse to pull out my wallet, not wanting to interrupt Ethan watching the game. I figured he could owe me one. Before I could get half of my wallet past the zipper of my bag, Maggie waved her hand at me, to drop it back in. She threw her American Express inside the leather-bound bill.

"Put it all on my card," Maggie instructed the waitress.

"Are you sure?" I asked.

"Absolutely. The info you just gave me was amazing. I can expense dinner as a source meal." Me, a source for *The Life*! I couldn't wait to call my mom and let her know I helped a reporter for her favorite magazine.

"Thank you," I told her. "I certainly don't mind saving a few extra dollars. Ethan is dipping into pretty much all of the money he's saved his whole life so he can try to work as little as possible and focus on writing, and I don't exactly have a diversified financial portfolio fresh out of undergrad."

"If you want to try earning some extra money, you could come work for me," Maggie suggested.

"Are you serious?" My emotions heightened and I wanted to make sure she's not messing with me.

"I could use a new undercover reporter, and if you were able to get Southern Girl-Next-Door Movie Star to open up to you in two minutes, you'll be a great source for us." Wow. Me? At *The Life*? Even if she'd been condescending moments before she was handing me the dream job. I'd get to hang out with celebrities and write for *The Life*.

"Yes! I'm in! I'd love to," I cheered. *The Life* has been a part of my life ever since that night.

So while I'm curious about this mysterious meeting tomorrow, I assume Maggie will have my back, as she always has.

. . . .

Later that day, I meet Holiday Hall at Mauro's Cafe dressed in Fred Segal. She's almost become more of a sister to me, in some ways, than my own sister, Robin.

Here's the deal with my BFF, Holiday: she's British, she's very well off, and she is *fabulous*. She doesn't like to talk about being an heiress or where her family's wealth comes from. "It's tacky, darling," she always coos. Being a reporter and nosey by nature, I've tried to find out more, but the only thing Google searches have revealed is that her family runs the largest import-export business in Europe. They are vastly successful . . . and private. Unlike me, Holiday is invited to parties because she really is part of the in crowd. She didn't slither her way in because she's working and the event's PR firm wanted press coverage. The mere mention of her name scores her and a plus-one a place on any guest list in town.

Holiday is an enviable free spirit. Somehow she always looks effortlessly flawless. Her chestnut hair is mellifluous; her skin glows even if she's hungover. She never goes to the gym yet her body is better than half the Victoria's Secret models.

And she has style. She can throw together an outfit that rivals most stylists' creations. Regardless of her comfortable lifestyle, she works part-time as a shampoo girl at the Je Cherche salon in Beverly Hills where a lot of celebrities tend to their tresses, so she surreptitiously feeds me sightings for *The Life*.

Holiday and I met shortly after I graduated from college. The country still in a slight recession, no one was exactly offering me a salary I could live on. Seeing as how I had few marketable skills, and my surprise job at *The Life* was still a few weeks in my future, I had taken a job as a barista at The Coffee Bean & Tea Leaf.

Holiday came in almost every morning. Despite the outdoor temperature, she ordered her no-sugar-added vanilla iced blended with one and a half pumps of caramel as if she was ordering the most expensive bottle of wine at a Michelin-starred restaurant, and she was always heavy-handed when it came to the tip jar. After months of being able to sustain myself at multiple happy hours due to her generosity, one morning I was able to return the favor.

"That will be three dollars and sixty-five cents," I told her. She opened her Birkin to retrieve her wallet but instead dumped the entire contents of her purse onto the counter and scavenged through it like a raccoon going through trash cans after a dinner party in Beverly Hills.

Suddenly, the chic and collected Holiday who soared in every morning like she was on a permanent vacation commenced a quarter-life-crisis meltdown. "No, no, no, no, no! It has to be here." The people in line behind her became more impatient with each second that passed. "Oh my God," she said to herself. I could see the wheels in her head spinning and knew that she figured out exactly where her money was. "I'm so bloody embarrassed," she confessed. "I left my wallet in my Clare V. clutch I used last night. You should cancel my order. Of course this had to happen in Beverly Hills of all places. I'm sure I'll be trending on Twitter as soon as I exit the premises." She looked like she was on the verge of tears and tried hard to smile self-deprecatingly. "This is humiliating!"

"It doesn't have to be."

"But it will be."

"Holiday! No-sugar-added vanilla iced blended for Holiday, ready for pickup," shouted the barista at the end of the counter.

"Don't worry about it. This one's on me," I told her. "Go get your drink and get out of my line. You're backing everyone up." I winked at her.

"Thank you. You saved me. Really. My reputation and I owe you one. . . ." She looked at my name tag. "Ella." She winked right back.

I quit The Coffee Bean shortly after that incident. Working for *The Life* at night and at The Coffee Bean during the day was wreaking havoc on my body and my relationship, and once I proved myself to Maggie by continuously turning in exclusives and never missing a celebrity sighting while I was out on assignment, she started asking me to work four or five nights a week.

I hadn't seen Holiday again until I was on one of my first assignments at The Compound, *the* Hollywood club of the moment. I was fixing my makeup in the bathroom and she emerged from the stall effervescently, as only she could. Fuck. She knows me. The real me. I looked so intensely into the mirror it was almost like I was looking through it. Maybe she won't recognize me without my uniform.

But her eyes kept glancing in my direction as she washed her hands. "I know you."

"Me? No. I don't think so."

"Yes. I do." She studied my hair and looked down at my shoes—in her Holiday way, she seemed genuinely curious, not judgmental. "I never forget a face and I mean never. I ran into Megan Parsons, who used to steal all of my crayons during nap time in primary school, fifteen years later and I recognized her instantly. You, I know. But from where?"

"I think you're mistaking me for someone else." She studied me again as if I were a sculpture in the Tate Modern, inspecting me up and down. "Ella! It is you. See, I told you I knew you." I cleared my throat to try to .stop her from talking—she was using my real name!—but it didn't work. "I fucking knew it! You clean up well, darling," she said with a wink before reapplying her Dolce & Gabbana lip gloss. "You're so chic without that cap and apron. I'm—"

"Holiday. I only wrote your name on about a hundred coffee cups."

"Well, El—" I coughed again to try to interrupt Holiday saying my name. "—I think I owe you for that iced blended. Come to my table for a drink."

I distinctly remember this being a declaration instead of a question. I couldn't say no and I *really* needed a drink, especially a free one.

"Sure. I guess one drink couldn't hurt."

"Fabulous!"

I followed her out of the bathroom through the dark hallway that almost seemed to shake from the hip-hop music being blasted so loud. We stopped at an unmarked door I hadn't noticed earlier with a security guard posted up in front. "She's okay," she told him. He dutifully opened the door to what I quickly realized was a celebrity-laden secret VIP room. I joined Holiday at her table and to this day don't think I've ever had more fun or a more successful night reporting.

I helped *The Life* break one of the biggest stories of the year. Little Miss Goody Two-shoes Country Singer was arrested for a DUI and drug possession after she left The Compound that night and I provided them with every last detail. That night cemented my job with *The Life* and began my friendship with Holiday.

Yes, I may have used our friendship to benefit my job, but I never threw Holiday under the bus. I employed a strict self-imposed code of ethics to ensure I could sleep at night without an Ambien prescription. My biggest rule? I only reported on things that happened in public places. If Holiday took me to a club, restaurant, or party it was fair game. If she invited me to someone's private home and we were guests I kept my mouth shut. It sounds easy, but it wasn't always. Especially when I knew I would most likely have an exclusive if I blabbed.

Like the night she invited me out to Malibu for an intimate, invitation-only cocktail party at Restaurateur Turned Nightlife Impresario's home. It was an informal test run of his new line of cocktail mixers that were about to hit the market, and his wife, who happened to be High-End Fashion Designer Turned Infomercial Queen, was out of town. Despite her beauty and business acumen, after the third round of cocktails— Jalapeño Margaritas—I spotted him getting cozy with a toned twenty-something redheaded cocktail waitress. He playfully grabbed her from behind and put his arms around her as she entered the kitchen to refill her drink tray. I saw him whisper something in her ear and she exaggerated a large laugh. He then raised her arm in the air and kissed it up and down, like Gomez did to Morticia Addams. I could not believe my eyes. I know it wasn't the biggest indiscretion, but trust me: Bigger stories have been made out of smaller acts of infidelity. I knew Maggie would love this story, but the party was so small it was highly possible that the gossip leak could be traced back to Holiday.

I didn't want her to be punished for inviting an interloper into the almost impenetrable group, especially when she was oblivious to who I really was. Other than Maggie, Holiday was the only female friend I'd made since college, and I wasn't willing to risk my new friendship, so I didn't turn in a file from that night and many others. I hated concealing the truth from her, but could I trust her with the secret of my double life as a celebrity spy?

She was friendly with almost everyone in the Hollywood scene, and her social circle seemed to have a larger circumference than our known solar system. But I had to determine whether she was one of *me* or one of *them*. I created a social experiment, if you will, to see where her loyalty lay. Two months into our relationship I fed her incorrect gossip items about people she knew to see what she did.

"Holiday, did you hear that Small-Screen Action Starlet Turned Rom-Com Queen Notorious for Romancing Her Costars won't let her husband hang out with any of the friends he had before they were married?"

"No! Tell me more," she begged.

"Apparently she's beyond controlling. A total Dr. Jekyll and Mr. Hyde thing. The whole down-to-earth sweet supermom thing is the public part of her persona but she's batshit crazy in her personal life," I continued. "Also, you have to promise you won't say anything but I hear that Skinny Entrepreneurial Reality Star isn't so skinny from her diet empire but she's hooked on Adderall." If Holiday were sitting down she would've fallen out of her chair. If her ears could have physically opened wider to hear more gossip they would have.

She held her right hand up as if she was being sworn into court for witness testimony. "I swear I won't say a word!" And she never did. After months of these bogus stories and no indication that they'd ever crossed her lips, I told her about Bella.

"I'm a celebrity spy. But I have a code! I've never said anything that hurt any of your friends and I've only reported on things that have happened in public places." She was silent for a good ten seconds after my revelation.

"Ella, I can't believe you've become my bestie over the past few months and you've been keeping this enormous secret from me," she said stoically. My stomach began knotting until I saw a look of pure joy and excitement sweep across her face. "This is incredible. How did I never know this job exists?"

"That's kind of the point," I told her. "If everybody knew about it nobody would ever do anything. Trust me, even if you *think* you're in a private place someone's always watching."

"I don't even know what to do with myself right now!" She was giddy and my disclosure made her euphoric.

"You're not mad?"

"Not at all, darling. This is going to be a fun game that will keep me occupied. And if celebrities are doing things they shouldn't be in public, what do they expect?" She immediately pulled out her phone. "You probably know more about some of my friends than I do." She seemed like she had just taken amphetamines. "We need to go through the contacts in my phone and you have to tell me if you've ever seen them cheating or doing drugs or doing anything else they shouldn't have been. You're like a celebrity PI! You have to bring me along next time." Little did she know she'd already been on many celebrity-spying adventures with me. Who knew that Holiday Hall needed a hobby? The girl who seemingly had everything at her fingertips was bored with her life and excited by mine.

. . . .

Hi, darling," Holiday chirps as I rush into Mauro's Cafe and over to the table where she's already seated. My eye darts over to the back corner of the café. It's the socialite, the one from the reality show . . . and the sex tape. She's Holiday's nemesis. "Gives the rest of us a bad name," Holiday always scoffs. "Not an ounce of brains between her ears or class between her legs." Socialite Sex Tape Star Turned Reality Star is finishing the last of her Caprese salad and sipping straight from a bottle of Voss water. She's with a woman that looks like she's her publicist and is paying the bill. Jackpot! I'll write this up when I sit down and send it to Maggie.

"Hey. I hope you haven't been waiting long," I apologize as I take my seat.

"Don't be silly," she says, brushing off my tardiness. Without getting up, she air-kisses me on both cheeks, and as she finishes, a waiter places a bottle of Veuve Clicquot and a carafe of orange juice on our table. Mimosas are Holiday's signature daytime drink. According to her they can heal everything from a scraped knee to a bruised ego and, of course, a broken heart. It's like the Bactine of beverages. Because they help her through the ups and downs of life she rarely trusts anyone else to create her champagne cocktail. "Drink up. I'm ready for a good chin-wag today and mimosas are on me." You have to give the girl credit. She's the most charming person on the planet. Or at least in LA—and that's saying a lot.

"I'm not sure that I'll be much of a conversationalist today," I warn. "I got called last minute to work last night."

Holiday lowers her chin to illustrate her disapproval.

"I couldn't turn it down."

She's giving me the look. The one she always gives. The one that tells me that I have free will and make my own decisions and *can* do whatever I want. She often forgets that just because she can do whatever she wants whenever she wants, not everyone else can. "Come on, Hol, cut me some slack. Don't make me hire a lawyer for my defense. You're worse than Ethan."

"It's one night. It's not like you'll get fired." When I first started, Maggie told me that their old best freelancer, Erin Beck, turned down three assignments in a month and they ended up never calling her again because they didn't think she took the job seriously. So from the beginning I've been hyperaware that declining an assignment is frowned upon and noted. Even when Ethan wanted to take time off to go on vacation or visit our families I knew I should stay behind in case I was asked to work. I've even worked on my birthday.

"It kinda *is* like that. Besides, I got a weird e-mail from Maggie this morning about some mandatory mystery meeting tomorrow. So I'm glad I didn't rock the boat."

"Have you ladies decided what you'd like?" our waifish waitress interrupts. She's clad in a white tank top that would be too tight on most thirteen-year-olds but looks like a sack on her.

"I'll have the almond salad," Holiday orders from memory, leaving her menu unopened.

"And I'll have the rigatoni with peas in pink sauce." The waitress marches away without writing down our order or inquiring if we need anything else. "Way to make me feel like a fat ass, Hol."

"Oh, shh. You know I don't eat carbs during the first three days of the week."

"Hi, Holiday." Socialite Sex Tape Star Turned Reality Star struts past toward the exit as if the dining room was a runway.

"Hello," Holiday returns with disdain and a clenched jaw.

But Socialite Sex Tape Star Turned Reality Star doesn't bother to stop as she and her publicist parade toward the door so it can sail open for the approximately twenty paparazzi waiting for her in the parking lot. Holiday grinds her teeth. In the years I've been doing my job I've learned to be a chameleon and handle myself anywhere, but the one place I still wouldn't want to be is on Holiday's bad side.

"You can't let her get to you. She's not worth it." I place my hand on Holiday's. "Look how transparent she is. She obviously called the paps herself. There aren't even that many following Former Wild Child Movie Star Turned Humanitarian. I'm sending the sighting in to Maggie but the only reason *The Life* would use it is because she's nice enough to throw me the extra cash whenever she can." Holiday takes another sip of her mimosa. "I promise you, Socialite Sex Tape Star Turned Reality Star is barely relevant anymore."

My anecdote doesn't seem to mollify Holiday's hatred. Her teeth are probably sharp enough to be an extra in a werewolf movie. Socialite Sex Tape Star Turned Reality Star is standing in the parking lot posing and pretending to get into her car until the paparazzi get a perfect, flattering shot. "At least when you get papped it's because you're a socialite with style, not a D-List diva without any sense of decorum," I add. She finally smiles.

"Hopefully her fifteen minutes of fame are ticking to a close. I think the world is ready for a new It girl." Holiday leans in to the table and changes the subject. "Enough about her. Aside from your disappearing act last night how's it going with Ethan?" She has a sparkle in her eye that indicates that she wants all of the details, the more explicit the better.

Holiday fancies herself something of a relationship expert. Her analysis and advice are usually right on point, although I've never seen her date anyone for more than a few weeks. She has entire relationships condensed into a short period of time that are never short on the drama. She falls hard and fast and her romantic liaisons run their course at an accelerated speed. Holiday can be attracted to someone, go on a date, become exclusive, go on vacation together, meet their family, discuss the future, and have a raucous breakup in the amount of time it takes most people to decide if they are going to go on a second date or not. And she is very clear, these are relationships, *not* flings.

Why should she draw them out? She's constantly being flown to all corners of the world for weeklong mini-relationships with the world's most eligible bachelors, and thanks to these travels can recommend the best Four Seasons spa services at almost any of the hotel's locations across the world. She returns with a tan one can't help but covet and a trove of *vêtements de plage*. If she weren't rich herself it would probably be considered prostitution. She never has a problem getting a man; sustaining a relationship is another story, though I'd never tell her and risk hurting her feelings, so I always play along when she wants to play relationship therapist.

"Well, we're having a makeup date night tomorrow, which is good because we haven't . . . you know . . . in a while."

"How long is a while?" she pokes.

"Five, six weeks? . . ." I trail off and purposely look to the side to avoid making eye contact with her.

"The fact that you aren't sure is more concerning than anything!" Her face has morphed from playful to placid.

"Our schedules are completely opposite right now."

Holiday leans in to me as if she's my psychiatrist and shifts to a calm tone of voice. "Be honest, is that all it is?"

"Of course! It's not like we're a new couple. Besides, we have a plan," I remind her.

"Because what's better than passion?" she says, returning to her usual frequency. "A plan!" There's no passion missing from her lecture. "Darling, all I'm saying is a fire dwindling a little may be normal but it seems like you're barely working with kindling and your sex life and relationship are in dire need of an SOS!" She's fidgeting in her seat with dismay and it's taking everything inside her to remain sitting instead of lunging across the table to shake me.

"I think you're overreacting a bit. As soon as Ethan sells his screenplay he's—"

"He's going to propose," she finishes by rote, rolling her eyes. "Ella, I know about your plan. *Everyone* knows about your plan. I can recite the details of your plan by heart and that's not something I terribly want to be taking up any of my brain capacity." I try to jump in but she's embarked on her diatribe and won't let me get a word in. "All I'm saying is plan or not, a diminishing sex life is a red flag." She cocks her head to the right, looking for me to agree with her. "I have an idea, though. . . . Call him right now and get him to meet you at your apartment. When he arrives you can greet him at the door with nothing but a smile on your face. One orgasm will melt all of your relationship woes away," she says with an impish smirk.

"How insulting and at the same time adorably cliché, Hol." God love her. She really is trying to help in her own way. But something tells me that Holiday Hall's tactics don't work unless you're actually Holiday Hall.

"Well, I won't fuck you or put a ring on it, darling, but I can help take the edge off," she says as she plays bartender and mixes me another mimosa. "Here, this will help." She proudly passes me the flute.

I begin to relax as the second serving of booze and juice coats my mouth. Holiday always creates the perfect concoction. For a girl who hates math, unless it's a sale at Barneys, her ratio of OJ to champagne is impeccable. She mixes one for herself and we clink our glasses together for our traditional toast.

"To glamour and love," we cheer in unison. The flutes seem to be filled with hope, or at least a good buzz for a few hours.

"Aside from work do you have plans this weekend?"

"It's Marianna's birthday so I have her party on Saturday and my mom is coming for it."

"That will be nice."

"Yeah." I look down at my flute. "She's adorable and I'm really excited to see my mom. It's been too long." I stop, and Holiday doesn't pry any further. She knows Robin can get under my skin, and neither of us wants to kill my buzz before it even sets in. "You're so lucky you're an only child. You get the entire inheritance, get to keep your sanity, and don't have to listen to any lectures from someone who went from wild child to holier-than-thou in a matter of months." When my sister made the decision to go pre-med in college her personality did a complete 180. Robin traded keg stands and parties with frat boys for shots of espresso and all-nighters with her o-chem study group. I take another large gulp of mimosa that's so big I barely stop myself from choking.

"Not to be totally self-involved but you need to perk up. I want you in tip-top form for my party Thursday," she says, snapping her fingers exuberantly.

Holiday's dinner parties are exclusive and infamous. The glitterati of Los Angeles all migrate to her home in the Hollywood Hills a few times a year for the social event of the season. The house is filled with Louis Vuitton, Rolexes, and hidden agendas. Holiday knows *everyone*. Her parties always start out as top-drawer catered affairs, but they seem to go from swanky to scandalous within a matter of hours despite her efforts to maintain a sophisticated atmosphere. The sordid details infiltrate the Hollywood social scene before the last guest sobers up.

Ordinarily I wouldn't miss one for the world. Holiday even condones my sending information to *The Life* as long as it doesn't defame her character. It's a win-win for me, since I end up making money while I'm there, but my energy feels off and for some reason I can't get excited about tomorrow's soiree. I couldn't help but feel like I was a charity case at her last party. Everyone else was a power broker, mogul, or a Hollywood heavyweight and I couldn't even talk about my job, since I technically work undercover and there were too many attendees who would've blown my cover if they ever knew about my real identity. Even if I could've talked about it, being a freelance undercover celebrity reporter isn't exactly prestigious, like going undercover to bring down a drug cartel. But it would be nice to be able to say something to the other guests when they ask what I do for work. I usually insinuate that I come from money like Holiday and everyone thinks I'm a stereotypical party girl hanging out at the clubs every night. If they only knew.

"You will be there, right?" she asks rhetorically. She looks at me with pleading eyes like she's one of the African orphans I can save for just one dollar a day. "I can't have a party without you. You're my best friend in the entire state of California. You and Ethan can even sneak off and naughty snog in one of the spare bedrooms." She winks again and I chuckle. "But you have to be there no matter what. Please. Promise me." It's impossible to say no to Holiday, even when you want to. Something about her eyes and the way she stares at you is hypnotic. She'd make a killing as a snake charmer in India, although I'm sure she'd replace the basket with a Birkin bag. I'd probably knock over a liquor store if she asked. I turn Bella on and flash her signature smile.

"Of course I'll be there."

Three

. . . .

You'd think that the most popular celebrity gossip magazine would have trendy, contemporary offices, but they are as bland and as corporate as an insurance office. Except for the framed covers of *The Life*'s biggest-selling issues, it would never cross your mind that the e-mails leaving the cubicles contained the inside news on celebrities, glamour, fashion, and gossip.

Despite the antiquated décor of its offices, *The Life* holds incredible history for me.

When I was eight, *The Life* became my bible and escape. While my sister, Robin, conveniently likes to forget that she had a past as colorful as ROYGBIV, I remember it vividly. My coach refusing to put me in the soccer game after I arrived late because my parents were canvassing the neighborhood looking for my teenage sister. Not being able to go to the mall because my parents were in the midst of their weekly room check to see if Robin had hidden any alcohol.

I will never forget the evening I was amusing myself in the living room when another argument between my parents and Robin broke out.

"Ella, go to your room," my father commanded. Whenever he raised his voice in the slightest, even if it wasn't directed at me, it was sobering. He was a loving, doting father even though he was strict and had no problem enforcing the severest of punishments if the rules were broken.

"But I want to watch TV."

"You can watch TV later," he said sternly. I saw there wasn't an ounce of amusement and he was losing his patience, but I didn't want to miss out on something I wanted to do because of Robin again.

"But the shows I want to watch won't be on later," I whined.

"Ella, I'm going to count to three." His facial expression didn't break but I remained in front of the television. "One. Two. Th—" My mother stepped in and bailed me out.

"Here, sweetie, go to your room and read this." She gave her newest copy of *The Life* to me. She hadn't even opened it, so I knew this was a gesture of significance. *The Life* was my mother's property and no one was allowed to touch it unless she'd read it cover to cover *and* asked permission. This never bothered me because as a child I didn't have any interest in celebrities that weren't Muppets, but that day I took the magazine and retreated to my room.

I don't know what I was expecting, if anything at all, but as soon as I flipped the cover open, I was mesmerized. I'd never seen an unauthorized photo of a celebrity before. Sure, I'd seen pictures from red carpets and press events but seeing a paparazzi shot of Talk Show Host Turned Media Mogul minus the makeup leaving her workout was new. I turned page after page looking at photos and reading about the secret lives of celebrities. On one page an actress would be photographed looking like royalty with a step-by-step guide on how to duplicate her look, and on the next page, a photo of her sobbing at an LA café with the mascara that had been carefully applied per the previous instructions running down her face after a fight with her boyfriend. I was so engrossed in the magazine that I forgot there was an argument occurring in the other room. I hung on every word I was reading and grabbed a book of construction paper and a black crayon to write down the names of every restaurant, salon, and mechanic mentioned in *The Life*. I continued creating these lists, which eventually became my personal guide to Los Angeles, even though I wouldn't end up there for another decade and three-quarters of the information inside my makeshift celebrity Filofax would be irrelevant.

"I'm sorry we had to send you to your room, sweetie," my mother said as she gradually slid my door open. "We had to have an adult discussion with your sister. Do you understand?" I nodded my head. "Good." She noticed that the immaculate copy of her magazine was now wrinkled and bent but she didn't seem upset. "Did you like *The Life*?"

"Uh-huh!"

"I like it, too. It can be nice to escape into someone else's world every once in a while. It's also a good reminder that no matter how something looks on the outside, there's usually something completely different going on beneath the surface." She joined me in bed and put her arm around me and nestled me next to her. I looked up at her, sniffing her Ralph Lauren–spritzed neck until she pointed to an article about Teen Reality

Star Turned Lifestyle Guru and her tips for a successful game night. "Have you read this one yet?"

"No."

"How about we read it together?"

From then on reading *The Life* together became the ritual we bonded over. It had everything. Fairy tales, villains, tragedies, and glamour. She skipped or censored articles that were too mature for me, but I guess you could say she taught me about life through *The Life*. Reading that magazine together certainly did more to deter me from drugs than the D.A.R.E. school assembly.

. . . .

"Ella Warren. I'm here for the meeting," I tell the receptionist. She's cold and obviously disinterested in who I am and my reason for being here.

"It's in the conference room," she says without even looking up from her computer.

I look both ways, as I have never been to the conference room before, and she finally points to the left. Once I'm in the conference room I'm met by blank stares from eight other girls I've never seen before. No one says hello or even makes an attempt to exchange pleasantries.

After sitting there for what seems like half an hour, Maggie arrives, and she isn't alone. Behind her is a statuesque woman in her fifties. She looks like an aging Laura Petrie. Her jeans are tapered, her ballet flats are scuff-free, her white button-down shirt is crisp, and her gray hair is swept into a perfect low ponytail.

"Good afternoon, everyone, I appreciate you all coming," Maggie begins. I try to catch her eye, but Maggie is all business today. She reminds me of the clipped Maggie I met that first night with Ethan, before we bonded. Strange. "For those of you who don't know me, I'm Maggie Kalaf, West Coast news editor, and for those of you who don't know the woman next to me, shame on you, but this is Victoria. *The Life*'s new editor in chief, Victoria—"

"Victoria Davis!" I blurt out.

Victoria glances in my direction and doesn't smile but raises an eyebrow, impressed that I know who she is. The other girls roll their eyes at me, annoyed that I interrupted. I'm sorry but how could I not know who Victoria Davis is? *The* Victoria Davis is going to be my boss. I'd read her name on the masthead of *The Life* every time my mom and I opened the magazine together. She was the magazine's first editor in chief and made *The Life* the institution it became. Victoria has a reputation for being ruthless and doing anything to get a story. To me, she's as famous and talented as any celebrity that's ever been splashed across its pages. She left about ten years ago after she'd made it the inimitable, number-one celebrity news magazine to helm the new fashion magazine *Haute*. While successful, she never managed to ascend to the level of success she had in the world of celebrity journalism. But she's back!

"I'm sure you're all wondering why you've been asked here today." Victoria has the world's worst smoker's voice, a detail I hadn't included in my childhood fantasies. "The announcement will be made next week that *The Life* has been sold to Patriot Media and Publishing. They've brought me on to do a complete overhaul of the magazine and Web site." I can almost hear the other girls' heartbeats quickening in unison. "For the past two years *The Life*'s numbers for both the book and online have been stagnant. As of now, that is unacceptable," she says, looking pointedly down her nose at us. "If the numbers aren't increasing, it's the same as a decline."

There's no foreplay with Victoria; not a trace of warmth in her voice. "I made *The Life* synonymous with Hollywood and celebrities and I am going to restore the intrigue and allure that this magazine was originally famous for. To do that, we need the *best* celebrity gossip out there." She takes a beat for emphasis. "Not only are we competing with other celebrity news outlets but we are also up against everyone with one of these." She scoops my iPhone off the table and holds it up as if she were a DEA agent showing us a kilo of cocaine in 1981 Miami. "Now, everyone is taking photos and even videos of celebrities and posting sightings and incidents on social media. The public has inadvertently become a group of reporters and therefore our competition." She sets my phone back down and looks at me.

"Because the circulation and Web site traffic hasn't increased in recent years, there's no other choice than to cut the budget for freelancers. I will only be able to keep four of you."

Four? I count everyone again. There are nine of us! As the news sinks in, the tension in the room rises, and soon we're eyeing each other up and down as if we're tributes in *The Hunger Games*.

"All of you ladies are good reporters. Unfortunately, good isn't good enough." She clears her throat and glares at Maggie. "This is a fun job but you need to remember that it is a job and if you want to keep it, you will need to step up and find me the juiciest, most exclusive gossip you can. I need to up the magazine circulation by 15 percent in the next three months. That means half a million hits a day."

She circles the table and looks each one of us up and down before stepping in front of me. "To determine who will stay and who will be let go, I'm implementing a points-based system. Maggie." Maggie takes her cue and quietly passes a piece of paper to each of us. She stops as she completes her lap around the table and briefly makes eye contact with me before bringing her glance back to her feet. "The first four people to reach one hundred points will keep their jobs. The other five will be let go. If you don't earn a minimum of ten points a week, you will automatically be fired. Please review the point sheet, carefully."

The Life freelance scoring scheme

Cover story: 20 points

Story on inset of cover: 10 points

Feature story in magazine: 8 points

Engagement announcement: 5 points

Marriage announcement: 5 points

Pregnancy announcement: 5 points

Birth announcement: 5 points

Rehab announcement: 2 points

Dotcom article with 20,000+ views or shares: 2 points

Dotcom article with 50,000+ views or shares: 5 points

Dotcom article with 100,000+ views or shares: 10 points

Exclusive: 10 points in magazine, 5 points online

"Using this rubric, I will be sending out a weekly update that shows where all of you stand. In two weeks, I will be making the first cut and dropping the person with the lowest score. We will continue this process until only four of you are left."

Everyone looks panicked and I wonder if my panic is as obvious.

"Prove to me how much you want this job," Victoria snaps. "Take initiative. Show me how far you will go to remain a part of this legacy. Maggie will wrap up." She looks around once more and then turns toward the door without fielding any questions. The room is left in stunned silence.

With Victoria gone, Maggie has our full attention.

"I know this new system will take some getting used to, but you guys are the best out there." The corners of Maggie's mouth turn down with sympathy. "I have no doubt you're going to bring it," she says with an awkward fist pump, mustering what little zeal she can. "I'll continue assigning clubs but any events or parties you can get into on your own will give you a huge advantage. If you see something, say something. Or better yet, send something." She picks up the remaining points sheets and clutches them as if they were radioactive. "If you guys have any questions feel free to e-mail me as always. Have a great day."

Everyone shuffles out of the conference room, still looking bewildered. I let the other girls go ahead in the hopes that I'll be able to get some insider info from Maggie.

"Hey, can we talk?"

"Sure. Follow me to my office," she tells me. She rubs her eyes—I can tell she's tired. "I still need to set up drinks with you and Ethan. I was texting with him the other day but I've basically been living at the office." We reach her office and I take a seat across from her. Given the state of disarray her desk is in, she wasn't exaggerating about living here. There are multiple Starbucks cups that look at least a few days old and various stacks of papers strewn about in no state of organization whatsoever. Victoria is clearly putting the pressure on her, too.

"Is Victoria serious about this points system?" I lean back in my chair. "I mean, you used to do this job. When there's a story to report we observe the hell out of it, but you of all people know that we can't make celebrities materialize, and even if we find them, it's possible they might not be doing anything newsworthy." How can I control something that's out of my control?

"Ella, I know how good you are but Victoria doesn't care. We're all starting from scratch on this." She reaches out to take my hand. "But you've got this, girl. You're on the inside. You've got Holiday. You're so connected. Find the stories. They're out there. You just need to get them"—she lowers her voice—"and you need to get them first. The quicker, the better."

Four

· ·

"D id you hook up with my brother, you whore?" Ethan's sister, Hattie, joked when she found me in his bedroom one morning after we went barhopping together. Hattie was my roommate freshman year in college seven years ago. We were always in sync with each other—to a fault. We both based our daily actions on our horoscopes, were terrible at cleaning, and felt it was a sacrilege to turn down a cocktail. We were scared that if we continued to live together our college careers would extend way past the normal four years and we might end up in AA instead of with our BA.

Ethan was a year older than his sister, and after he graduated he moved to LA to pursue screenwriting. He and Hattie got an apartment by the beach together. Even though the commute to school was a bitch with LA traffic, she claimed she didn't care because it was senior year and she only had class two days a week.

The first time I met Ethan was at their housewarming party.

"I'm so glad you came," she cheered as I made my way through her entryway.

"I wouldn't have missed it. But you do realize that it would've been faster for me to get to San Francisco by plane than it was to get here with traffic." Hattie hit my arm.

"But look how beautiful it is down here." She shoved an alcohol-filled red Solo cup in one hand and led me out to the patio by my other. I recognized Ethan by the back of his head. Hattie's idea of décor was an abundance of family photos placed throughout our dorm room, so I was very well aware of what he looked like from multiple angles. He was standing by himself wearing a navy-blue polo shirt and jeans, leaning out over the railing.

"It's really nice," I told her. The apartment wasn't exactly oceanfront and I couldn't see much in the dark but I could hear the waves breaking, which was soothing.

"Ethan," she called. He turned his head our way. "You have to come meet Ella!" He wandered over to us. I was immediately attracted to him. Photos did not do him justice. His brown eyes were deep and so concentrated with color that they appeared plush. He wasn't traditionally handsome but there was something about the way his features combined that was magnetizing.

"So you're the infamous Ella?" he marveled. He looked me up and down. Hattie's phone buzzed with continuous text messages.

"Ugh, excuse me. I swear it's like I might as well have moved to Africa instead of west of Crescent Heights Boulevard! Ella, he doesn't know anyone yet, so entertain him," she instructed before sauntering into the living room.

"I feel like I'm meeting a celebrity," he said, brushing his sandy brown hair behind his ears even though it was barely long enough to stay there.

"Me?" I scoffed, taking a sip from my cup to hide my smile.

"Yeah. Hattie talked about you nonstop." He seemed nervous and he looked back toward the ocean.

"I hope the real thing isn't a disappointment," I said, and he turned back to me.

"I highly doubt that's possible." He put his hands in his front pockets and smiled at me. I was hooked. Aside from being cute, he was smart. As I later learned I could talk with him for hours. He had the most random knowledge of everything from comic books to ancient Greek democracy, and he finally explained Schrödinger's cat in a way I could understand it. He was the first guy I felt liked me for the real me—not the best version of yourself that you pretend to be the first few times you're getting to know someone. As the weeks drew on, my feelings intensified but I was nervous that acting on them might jeopardize my friendship with Hattie.

One night we were debating the best movies of all time and Ethan was stubbornly adhering to his opinion that no movie will ever beat *Citizen Kane*.

"Nothing beats *Citizen Kane* except for *How Green Was My Valley*. At least according to the Oscar for Best Picture in 1942," I told him.

"You're crazy. *Citizen Kane* won," he insisted, shaking his head in disbelief.

"I swear, it didn't. Let's look it up," I challenged. We Googled it and, lo and behold, I was correct. Before I could gloat or he would have to admit defeat, he grabbed me by the back of my head and kissed me. I kissed back even harder—it made every other kiss I'd had feel flimsy and like a partial outline of what an actual kiss should be.

So that morning when Hattie asked me if I hooked up with her brother, I decided to be honest: "Yes," I answered. I scrunched my eyebrows and clenched my jaw in anticipation of the verbal beating I was surely about to receive for breaking girl code to make out with her brother.

But she just cracked a smile. "Oh, I don't want to hear about it. I'm just glad it finally happened. It took you guys long enough," she quipped as she ran a wet washcloth over her face to remove last night's makeup. After Hattie's blessing and our first real date we became inseparable. I never thought I could miss someone while I'm looking at them pump gas outside of the car window, but I missed him. After graduation, Hattie was offered a coveted job in advertising in Chicago and Ethan and I moved in together in West Hollywood.

. . . .

I feel like I haven't seen you in forever," he says, reaching his hands across the red-and-white checkered tablecloth to hold mine. He massages the area between my thumb and index finger. I'm listening to him with my ears but my eyes are bouncing around the restaurant. I want to focus on our date but I have Victoria's voice trapped in my head like I'm in some bizarre movie where someone else is narrating my life and I have to do exactly what they say. My eyes home in on the back of a couple. He's on the shorter side, in his late sixties, maybe early seventies with disheveled salt-and-pepper hair, a fake tan, and all-black suit and a white scarf worn open around his neck as an accent. His date looks like she's in her thirties at the oldest and his hand is clasped around her waist so tightly it's as if she's his hostage, though she doesn't seem to mind.

Is it him? I can't tell. Not from this angle anyway. He does have a wife, so if it is him, this could be the kind of first impression I want to make on Victoria.

"Hello? Earth to Ella."

I snap my gaze to my boyfriend. "Sorry! I thought I saw Aging Iconic New York Italian Actor being seated with a date who's not his wife." He releases my hands and takes a drink.

"Was it him?"

"I'm not sure. I couldn't get confirmation from this angle." I pick up my phone, a cardinal sin on date night, but I need to figure out if the man now seated in the dark corner drinking a martini as he pets his maybe-mistress is him. I still can't decipher if it's Aging Iconic New York Italian Actor from these photos. "I'm just going to do a quick lap and pretend like I'm looking for the bathroom." He swallows, which is his tell that he's annoyed, but tells me to "go ahead."

The restaurant is packed. Dan Tana's is famous for their traditional Italian cuisine and never having your table ready regardless of your reservation time, but nobody ever makes a fuss because it's *that* good. I make my way through the crowd.

I finally reach the corner of the restaurant, pretending as if I'm lost even though the space isn't much larger than a tennis court, but one direct glance in proximity to the man in question confirms that he's *not* Aging Iconic New York Italian Actor. I'm not sure if I'm relieved that I can focus on my boyfriend and enjoy our date or disappointed that I'm going to remain at zero points for another day. I settle back into my seat opposite Ethan.

"I'm sorry, baby. I had to check. It's my new boss, Victoria. I just want to impress her."

"You're going to be fine," he assures me.

"It's not just that I admire her. This new points system she's implemented to determine which of us will keep our jobs has me spinning out." I take a sip of my Grey Goose dirty martini and lean back in my chair.

"I'm sure Maggie will do her best to put in a good word for you." He reaches for the bread basket and savagely tears off a piece of the Italian loaf and I pour a few drizzles of olive oil onto his bread plate for him.

"You don't understand. This is *Victoria Davis*. She's like queen of the monarchy of celebrity journalism." I stare at Ethan as he chews, envious of his carbohydrate consumption. "She says find a story, I need to bring her five if I want to keep my paycheck rolling in." Not only do I want to keep my job, I want to impress her, maybe even be her one day. "You know what? Tonight it's not important. Tonight is about us. I'll figure something out. I promise, the rest of the night I'm only going to be staring at the incredible, talented man right in front of me." I place my palm faceup on the table, indicating I want him to take my hand again, and he takes the hint.

"Can you believe it?" he asks, grinning as wide as a villain in a superhero movie. "It's really happening. My agent says he'll know more tomorrow but the studio can make me an offer anytime."

"I never had any doubt, babe." I reach my other hand across the table to caress his cheek. "You're a beautiful writer." His eyes are welling up with tears.

"Stop." He's proud and embarrassed simultaneously.

"I will not. Your script is Oscar-worthy for sure and every actor and actress in town is going to beg for an audition so they can be a part of it." I remove my hand from his face and return it to the table. The way his eyes dance as they stare into mine is the closest thing I've ever seen to pure happiness.

"Next time you see an actor at a club that you know I want to be in the movie, you better talk the script up." He winks, wiping away the moisture that was previously in his eyes.

"Obviously. Although I'm sure I won't even need to."

"This is it, Ella. Everything is about to change. The next few weeks the life we've had together will cease to exist. We're going to be on a new adventure."

"And I'm going to be right there by your side, supporting you."

He releases my other hand from his grip and traces each of my fingers with his, paying particular attention to my ring finger, tracing it repeatedly before moving on to my pinky. I bite my bottom lip with anticipation as he continues to gaze at me and I take another sip of my martini.

Five

· ·

Dear Freelancers,
I was going to wait until Monday to send an update but some of you have
already accumulated points. It's going to be a tight race.
Victoria

It's only been twenty-four hours since our meeting. WTF? How are people already on the board? I know that I'm not, without even scrolling through the rest of the e-mail, but I need to find out how many people are. Three. There are three people that have already found something she's using. My adrenaline kicks in even though I don't have the luxury of having the time for a full-on anxiety attack. Holiday will kill me if I show up at her party and act like Debbie Downer.

Ethan casually strolls in at 7:38 P.M. for our preplanned 8 P.M. departure and throws himself down on the bed while I complete my metamorphosis from Frankenstein with hair extensions into blond bombshell. I peek my head into the bedroom and he's still sprawled out on top of the bed.

"Babe, how long will it take you to get ready? I don't want to be late," I tell him.

"El, I think I'm gonna pass on the party tonight," he mumbles, getting under the covers.

"What? Really?"

"We're supposed to hear by midnight if the studio is accepting our counteroffer and buying my screenplay. If I go to the party I'm going to want to look at my phone every five seconds, which you know I can't do there." He pats the bed, motioning me to come lie next to him.

"I understand." Of course I wish he was coming with me but if I give him any guff for his decision to stay home I might as well get out of journalism and into politics because I'd be the biggest hypocrite ever. I reach the bed and prop myself up next to him.

"Yeah?"

"Yeah." He pulls me from my seated position and spoons me. I have a few minutes to spare, so I cuddle against him.

"You know, you could stay home with me. We can order a pizza and watch a movie. Have another date night at home to keep my mind occupied." He kisses me in our spot and his hand begins to travel down my torso, lower, lower, trying to seduce me into staying. I smile at his attempt, but I remove his hand.

"I'd love to, babe, but I swore to Holiday I'd be there tonight. Plus it's perfect timing. I need to find a story. Three people are ahead of me and the only thing Victoria cares about is points. I have to get some damn points. Something will happen at Holiday's party. It always does."

"Right." His voice lowers and his embrace loosens.

"I'll get out of there as soon as I get a story and come home to you. I love you." I turn around and kiss him. "Keep me posted if there's something to celebrate, okay?" He nods and rolls over as I order an Uber. I'm definitely not driving tonight. With my job on the line I need more than a few cocktails to maintain any sort of equilibrium. Besides, I don't want to end up in the Lynwood jail with a DUI like a lot of the celebrities I spy on.

. . . .

As I wind through the hills on the drive to Holiday's house all I can think about is trying to get my exclusive. I step out of the car, making sure to keep my legs together so I don't flash anyone like Former A-List Hot Mess Actress.

I step out wearing an Elizabeth and James dress and Aquazzura shoes, and before I can knock on the front door it sails open. I'm greeted by the maître d' of the event. He looks like he came straight out of an old movie. He has an elegantly trimmed mustache, not a hair on his head is out of place, and his suit is perfectly pressed. He takes my coat and asks for my phone. Because of the high-profile guests, Holiday always takes extra precautions to ensure that no photos of her parties float around the Internet. If you refuse to surrender your phone, you have to turn around and go home. She enjoys gossip, but in her mind selling photos takes it a step too far.

Luckily my job never includes taking photos (observations only), so even when I send info to *The Life* I have no reason to cling to my phone.

I remove my phone from my sleek black Rebecca Minkoff clutch, and he takes it in exchange for a glass of 2003 Dom Pérignon. Holiday wouldn't be caught dead serving any other champagne at one of her parties.

I take a few sips to relax. My stomach feels hollow and I realize I forgot to eat all day so I'm on a mission to find some hors d'oeuvres. Food is always hit or miss at Holiday's parties. Sometimes she orders enough food to feed a small country and other times she subscribes to the theory that food is more of a decoration for your plate than fuel for your body. Lucky for me, Holiday isn't in Hollywood anorexic mode tonight.

Uniformed waiters pass around Gorgonzola-stuffed dates wrapped in prosciutto, mini crab cakes, and everyone's secret favorite: *pommes frites.* Apparently, if you wrap french fries in wax paper and make them into a cone shape, the normally abhorrent American snack turns into an international delicacy.

I grab some nibbles and survey the guests. The attendees range from celebutants to legitimate actors to entertainment executives, with even a few high-powered people from the finance world sprinkled in. It's an eclectic group, to say the least.

"Hi, darling," Holiday squeals as she scampers over and gives me a hug. "You look *gorgeous.*"

I do a twirl for her. "I should, it's your dress." Holiday is nothing if not generous and lets me borrow a few of her high-end garments at a time. I almost always have to be dressed up for work, and being in designer clothes helps me blend into the social scene. Unfortunately my taste is Tom Ford but my budget is Target. Holiday understands my plight and has opened her closet to me. It's like my own personal Rent the Runway, minus the fee.

"Where's Ethan?"

"He's waiting to hear back about his movie and wanted to stress out about it at home. I hope we didn't mess up your seating arrangements."

"Not at all. We must have a drink for good luck! Listen, darling, even though he isn't here I want you to have a ball. Come mingle with everyone," she insists. She pulls me to the center of the living room, which is the focal point of the party until dinner is served. I don't see anyone here that I know and am anxious about finding a story. I need to collect myself before the mingling mood can strike me. This glass of bubbly and a trip to the bathroom should help me unwind.

"I have to run to the powder room, Hol. I'll be right back." I turn

around before she has a chance to stop me and make my way to the closest of her many bathrooms. After attending a few of Holiday's parties I've
learned everyone else is way too stuck up to have a conversation with
someone they don't know and who can't help them with their career. Once
they get a little tipsy it's another story, so I've invented a little game to
keep me occupied until their BAC levels rise.

I call it the Cocaine Game. I won't dance around the political incor-
rectness of this game, but let's face it, *a lot* of people in Los Angeles en-
gage in extracurricular activities and most of the time it involves "going
skiing." *Skiing* is the universal moniker for cocaine when referenced in
text messages, e-mails, or any other potentially incriminating mediums
of communication. Here's how it's played:

RULES OF THE COCAINE GAME

1. Pick an appropriate venue. A nightclub, entertainment industry
   house party, or the bathroom at the Chateau Marmont are always
   guaranteed to provide a successful game.
2. Enter the bathroom at the venue of choice.
3. Sweep your fingertips across the top of the toilet tank.
4. Estimate (as best you can) how much, if any, cocaine you've accumulated on your fingertips. Make sure to differentiate regular dust
   from the Colombian candy.
5. You are automatically disqualified if Former A-List Hot Mess Actress,
   or any Hollywood train wreck du jour, was in the stall prior to the
   start of the game.
6. NOTE: This game can be amended for multiple players, and
   whoever picks up the most cocaine wins.

Confession: You don't actually win anything when you win the Cocaine Game, only the satisfaction of knowing that people in your current
venue are as fucked-up, if not more so, than you are. I do not condone
substance abuse or booger sugar as a dietary supplement—though that last
part usually falls on deaf ears.

The party has just begun so I doubt I'll have any luck right now. I
lock the door immediately after I enter the bathroom. No need to let
any strangers in on my party game. Against my better judgment I once
taught my friend Angela the Cocaine Game when I took her to a party at

the house of Romantic Comedy Actress Who's Had Bad Luck with Men. She got a little overzealous and checked every bathroom in the palatial Pacific Palisades mansion. She won the game and her nose started bleeding all over the starlet's new Stark rug. It wasn't easy explaining that one to the security team. Needless to say, we haven't been invited back.

Holiday's bathroom is magnificent. She never leaves any detail undone. There's a huge orchid sitting atop the mirrored vanity and half a dozen Tocca candles emitting their signature Cleopatra scent throughout the room. This bathroom is nicer (and almost bigger) than my apartment. I run my fingers against the back of the toilet. Clean as a whistle. Tame crowd so far. I haven't been this surprised since I discovered shopping at sample sales is more invigorating than a day of beauty at Kate Somerville.

Since there is no snow I will kill some time by giving my makeup a touch-up. No amount of Clé de Peau concealer or eye cream can take away the dark circles from all of my late nights and early mornings at work. Somehow I've convinced myself that if I coat my lashes in more Dior mascara the sleep deprivation becomes less noticeable. Hair, check. Lips, check. Tummy, sucking in.

As soon as I turn the handle and step out of the bathroom I collide with Hugo Boss Classic Two-Button Business Suit and spill both of our glasses of champagne all over his chest.

I look up and the first thing that runs through my mind is "Agent!" Only an agent wears a suit 24-7. Seriously. Whether they have the option to change into comfortable clothes after work or not, they don't. At least it makes them easy to spot in any social situation. I have to admit, while they tend to have a lousy reputation in the female community they secretly turn me on. I love their unabated ambition and sharklike quality. In that split second I can't figure out if he represents talent or literary clients.

The second thing I notice is the man in the suit is gorgeous, so he's probably an asshole—a hot asshole, but an asshole nonetheless.

"I'm so sorry!"

I expect him to bark at me, but he just smiles. "It's fine. Don't worry about it. I would've needed to take it to the cleaners after tonight anyway," he insists as he uses his cocktail napkin to soak up the mess I've made. I join his efforts to dry his suit and as I press his chest with my napkin, I notice he smells delicious. His confident azure eyes meet mine with such extreme intensity that I feel weightless. For a moment, I think not having a date tonight might not be terrible after all.

"No, I'm really sorry." I'm talking with my hands, swinging around the wet napkin. "I've only had half of a glass of champagne, so sadly I can't even blame it on being a little buzzed—I'm just a klutz," I admit.

"Really, it's okay," he reiterates and shoots me a million-dollar smile. This guy shouldn't represent movie stars; he should be one! I feel a slight shiver run through my body and notice I have goose bumps on my arm. I can't even remember the last time I had this reaction to someone within thirty seconds of meeting. I don't even know if I felt like *this* with Ethan.

"I think it's adorable. Nick Williams." He extends his hand and I think he's reaching out to shake mine, but in fact he's handing me his business card. I scan it quickly. Nick Williams, Epic Agency . . . talent agent. God, I'm good. Too bad it doesn't list his relationship status and tax ID number. The way he's staring at me, as if he wants to throw me up against a wall, makes me, yet again, momentarily forget that I'm not single.

"Ella Warren. Nice to meet you." Ugh! I didn't mean to introduce myself as Ella, especially since colliding with him is bringing out the Bella in me. Nothing I can do about it now.

"So you're the infamous Ella. Holiday loves you. She talks about you all the time. Now I can see why." He looks me up and down but he seems more intrigued by me than to be imagining what I look like naked, and I don't feel objectified or uncomfortable at all.

"How do you know her?"

"I'm hip-pocketing her." *Hip-pocketing* is a term used in the acting world when talent agents don't sign a client but they send them out on auditions to see how they do and what feedback they receive. If they book a role they are eventually offered a contract with the agency. If the feedback is poor, sayonara, sucker.

"Oh!" I pause. I'm a little taken aback that she didn't mention anything at lunch yesterday. Miss "I'm fine washing hair" has a secret or I guess now not-so-secret life complete with Hollywood aspirations. "I had no idea she was even acting," I confess. While enjoying mimosas, we dissected every intimate detail of my life but she artfully hid hers. I don't know why I'm surprised, though. Everyone from dermatologists to nutritionists to nail technicians in this town all want to be famous. But I never thought that bug would bite Holiday. She's usually an open book, not one to omit interesting details or information about her life. I mean, she usually Facebooks, Instagrams, Snapchats, and group-texts about stubbing her toe. I'm going to have to grill her about this omission at a later date when she's not in hostess mode.

"Is there anything Holiday doesn't do?" he asks.

I look down toward my Aquazzura-clad feet.

Nick diffuses this awkward moment with a joke and offers to get us drinks. "In case you run into someone else, then you *can* blame it on the alcohol."

I can't help but smile. God, Nick is charming. I feel like I've reverted back to being the bespectacled freshman sitting alone in the courtyard during lunchtime, when the captain of the football team finally notices me.

"Let's," I reply. He holds out his arm, and we link together like the stars of a George Cukor movie, or like Bogie and Bergman. I feel like a million bucks.

I have to ingratiate myself with men for work all the time. A little flirting to be taken to the celebrity's table for a cocktail and a scoop is innocuous. Alcohol, sex appeal, and celebrity can be a dangerous trifecta, so I'm careful not to cross a line. Let me be clear, I've never cheated on Ethan. Nick graciously escorts me into the living room and grabs two flutes of champagne from a waiter's tray.

"Shall we toast?" Nick asks.

"Sure. But to what?" Our flutes are hanging in midair.

"How about to an ally at this party?" he suggests.

"Perfect." I raise my glass a few more inches.

"Cheers to meeting someone at this party whose smile could light up the whole city," he toasts. I'm not going to pretend like his line isn't cheesy, but my luminous smile widens as we clink glasses. "This is the first of Holiday's functions that I've attended. It's . . . interesting," he reveals.

"Tell me about it. Last time some girl locked herself in the bathroom all night after she found out that Holiday wears a smaller-size dress than she does."

"Seriously?"

I nod yes.

"Some of these people seem a little bit crazy. I guess you really will have to stick by my side all night," he insists. He grabs me and pulls me toward him and I feel like I might faint if I get any closer to him. Just in the nick of time, the maître d' rings a bell to signify the commencement of dinner. Talk about saved by the bell.

Nick puts his hand on the small of my back as we file into the dining room, and I feel my heart flutter until we reach the table. Ugh. I hate it when Holiday puts out seating cards. It's not so much that I care whom I sit next to as I do about whom I'm not sitting next to. At one of her previous soirees, Holiday thought it would be nice for me to get to know her astrologer. I'm no better than anyone else; I certainly wait up until midnight the last evening of the month so I can read Susan Miller's Astrology Zone forecast for my sign for the new month as soon as it's posted. It's cheaper than therapy and she makes me feel like my life will be okay. While I usually love astrology, this woman was not my cup of organic chai tea. She kept on talking about Pythagoras and destiny and claimed to be clairvoyant. I wanted to know if she could anticipate me snatching the ten-carat emerald-cut Cartier diamond ring off the woman on my left and using it to slit my wrists at the table. I already had to be concerned about what Former Singer Turned Fashion Designer Turned Yo-Yo Dieter is eating daily for work. I couldn't deal with that brand of crazy, too.

I search the table for my place card, hoping I'm next to Nick, but no such luck. I am smack dab in the center of the nineteenth-century Victorian dinner table and completely landlocked. I've never met either of the people whose names are placed next to mine, and Nick is a few chairs away on the opposite side of the table. As soon as he sits down, a German model, Anaeliese, slides in next to him. It only takes her about thirty seconds to completely drape herself over him as soon as she finds out he's an agent. *Great,* I think, disappointed.

"I'm not just a model." She sits up straight, as if to make clear she is about to enlighten him. "I'm a classically trained actress."

"Oh, are you?" He takes a sip of wine and tries to politely escape the conversation by turning his face in the opposite direction, but she's either not responding to his social cues or refuses to let opportunity pass her by, so she continues. She taps him on the shoulder until he looks back at her. "Nobody takes me seriously because my lips make me look exotic—" She briefly pauses and purses them for effect. "—And I've been told that my eyes are as captivating as watching a high-speed police chase on the news," she says, trying to entrance Nick with her deep gaze, but I can tell he sees right through her.

Anaeliese made sure to speak loudly enough so everyone within earshot would hear her. I want to throw up. She's so self-absorbed and ego-maniacal she doesn't even notice that Nick isn't listening. He mouths *help* to me and I can't help but smile and shrug my shoulders. My seat companions are fairly painless although I have to listen to a debate between them about the prestige hierarchy of *The New Yorker* versus *Vanity Fair.*

"How can you even attempt to construct an argument to dispute that *The New Yorker* is not superior? You're smarter than that," the guest seated to my right cajoles. He places his fork and knife onto his plate so the act of eating won't distract him from making his point. "Malcolm Gladwell is one of the most ingenious writers of our time. He's made people question the way they think. He's the Old Hollywood equivalent of writers, full of substance." Though his opponent at this point is staring around the table, blinking as if she's signaling SOS in Morse code, he's transfixed on making his point and continues his tirade. "*Vanity Fair*'s writers are always entertaining. I'll give you that, but my position remains the same. As a whole *The New Yorker* is a more creative and cerebral publication."

"I suppose it's true what they say, there's no accounting for taste. And I'll take your Malcolm Gladwell and raise you Krista Smith any day. She's an inspiration and an aspiration for female journalists and her influence far exceeds that of most entertainment writers."

Neither of them would concede their point.

Tonight's five-course meal consists of once-again-legal foie gras, filet mignon, and English trifle, among other vegetables and side dishes I've never seen before. I am relieved when the waiters clear the last set of plates because I'm stuffed and the tensile strength of my borrowed LBD is being tested. The end of dinner would usually indicate the end of a dinner party in most circumstances, but when it comes to Holiday, the night is just beginning. It's time to move to the conservatory for after-dinner drinks. I have to hand it to Holiday: She knows how to keep her guests happy and liquored up. I barely finish my first sip of port when Nick grabs my hand.

"Hide me," he begs, pretending to hide behind my back.

"Oh you mean you don't want to spend any more time with Fräulein Crazy?"

"You're really enjoying this, aren't you?"

"Yeah. I am. It must be really difficult to be so good-looking that supermodels are throwing themselves at you," I tease, playfully pushing him.

"You think I'm handsome?" he asks, taking a step closer to me. Now he is undressing me with his eyes.

"Good-looking. I said good-looking. Not handsome. But that's not the point," I say, trying to change the subject and taking a step back. Holiday interrupts our aperitif and calculatedly prances to the center of the room while she clinks a fork on her glass to quiet the crowd and get their attention.

"Friends." Holiday doesn't have to use a loud voice because she naturally commands attention. "I want to thank you all for joining me tonight. It's been lovely seeing you all, especially those of you I haven't seen in a while. Everyone knows that I love a fabulous party 'just because,' but there *is* a reason I invited you all for dinner." She pauses to make sure everyone is paying attention for her big reveal. "I have an announcement."

Announcement? This makes twice that I'm caught off guard. I saw Holiday twenty-four hours ago and she didn't have any announcements for me.

"The official announcement comes out tomorrow, but I've recently taken to acting, and I'm thrilled to announce that I've booked my first role in a television pilot called *Benedict Canyon* and we are shooting it in Canada next week! Because what better place to shoot a show set in Los Angeles with a plot focusing on characters in Los Angeles than Canada?" The crowd chuckles with Holiday at the absurdity. "Usually I don't have an audience when I'm being groped by a federal officer, but immigration, here I come!"

I shoot Nick a look, since he'd also conveniently omitted this piece of information from our earlier conversation. He shrugs his shoulders apologetically and winks at me. The crowd cheers and claps.

"I'm so excited to start this new journey and I'd like to invite my costars and the writer-director to join me so we can all do a group toast to the success of the show."

A group of incredibly attractive twentysomething guys and girls including Recently Divorced British B-List Comedian–Sex Addict, the swoon-worthy up-and-coming actor, Tristan Thompson, and a dashing thirtyish sandy-haired man in a suit I don't recognize join her. Waiters appear, seemingly as if from nowhere, with refreshed trays of champagne and pass them out to each guest. "To the success of *Benedict Canyon*. I'm so grateful to be working with this gorgeous, talented cast and our brilliant creator, Seth Rubin, who will also be directing the pilot." Holiday looks to her new *Benedict Canyon* family and raises her flute. "Here's to six seasons and a movie! Cheers!"

"To six seasons and a movie! Cheers!" the crowd screams back. Holiday's face glows even more than usual.

"Cheers," Nick says, turning to me.

"You knew the whole time," I assert.

"I did. Sorry I couldn't say anything. I have to keep a lot of secrets with my job." If only he knew how much I understood.

"Well, she seems really happy, so thank you for giving my best friend a chance."

"If all goes like I think it will I'm going to be the one thanking her. I think she's going to be Hollywood's next It girl. The public is already fascinated with her, and with the amount of buzz she's going to generate for the show, I think it has a real shot at being picked up." He raises his champagne glass to the sky, as if he's asking God himself to pick up the TV pilot.

I notice from the corner of my eye that Anaeliese has found a new mark. She pulls almost the identical move that she used with Nick and is draped all over Recently Divorced British B-List Comedian–Sex Addict. Is there anyone this broad won't fawn over?

"I guess you're old news," I say, nodding my head toward Anaeliese and the Recently Divorced British B-List Comedian–Sex Addict, who of course, already has a new girlfriend.

"Great," Nick mumbles. "He's my client. It's my job to know about their personal lives, too, and shall we say he has a little problem being faithful? And his girlfriend is the jealous type. I'm talking the volatile jealous type."

"Yikes. I'm pretty sure she's in the bathroom," I tell him, scanning the crowd.

"Let's hope she stays there." As soon as the words leave Nick's mouth, Recently Divorced British B-List Comedian–Sex Addict's hand travels down toward Anaeliese's butt and simultaneously his girl du jour enters the conservatory.

"Are you fucking kidding me?" she screams, quieting the entire room. "Seriously? Are you fucking kidding me?" She continues to bellow as she drunkenly stumbles over to her boyfriend and the model-slut. It's clear she's had way too much to drink and the other guests watch with bated breath.

Recently Divorced British B-List Comedian–Sex Addict unsuccessfully tries to mollify her. "Sweetheart, it's not what it looks like. We were talking about the show because there might be a role for her." This is about to get ugly. Victoria is only going to keep the reporters that have their own sources and can find stories—BOOM! I'm committing every detail of the altercation to memory.

"Do you think I'm stupid? The only role she can accurately play is an international whore," she screams. Anaeliese is now irate, too. She may be gorgeous when she poses for the camera but she definitely has the ugly-angry thing going on—and *Style & Trend Magazine* wouldn't photograph this look for any season.

"Oh, and who are you? Some slut from the valley?" Anaeliese howls.

She and Recently Divorced British B-List Comedian–Sex Addict's girlfriend lunge for each other at the same time, and I feel a slight breeze as Nick rushes toward the reluctant threesome to diffuse the situation. He pulls Recently Divorced British B-List Comedian–Sex Addict and his girlfriend to one side of the room and mollifies them, but Recently Divorced British B-List Comedian–Sex Addict's girlfriend then starts in on him, and Nick pulls his client away, and after he successfully diffuses the situation, returns to me.

"Crazy, huh?" Despite jumping in the middle of that brawl not a hair on his head is out of place.

"You know . . . actors," I joke.

"I certainly do. You're not an actress?"

"God no!"

"That's a shame. You're gorgeous. You could be," he tells me. I almost choke on my champagne. There it is. The agent is coming out again.

I lean closer to him and whisper, "Does that line really work?"

"All the time," he whispers back with a smile. I think that part of him is kidding but I'm not sure. I want to write down every detail of this argument before I forget a single foot stomp.

"Would you excuse me for a minute?"

I bolt toward the atrium, pull my claim ticket out of my clutch, and hand it to the maître d'. He exchanges the ticket for my iPhone but scrutinizes my every movement to make sure I'm not taking pictures of anyone. I have a text from Ethan from an hour ago.

Ethan: El, I sold it!

Oh my God! Oh my God! Oh my God! Ahh!
I text him back immediately.

Me: I'm so proud of you baby! I knew you could do it!

Ethan: Not without you. Come to the Hotel Bel-Air!!! Meet me and my
agent for celebratory drinks!

Before my excitement gets the better of me and I forget these details
I write them down before I reply. I open my e-mail to send a message to
myself with all of the info but before I can create a new e-mail, I see I
have one from Maggie titled, "Tonight? ASAP?"

Hi Ella,
Sorry so last minute but can you cover Ambiance? The girl that was assigned to
cover had to go to the ER. Wanted to help you get some points on the board.

I respond.

Hey Mags,
No problem! I'll take all of the opportunities I can get. I'm at a party and have
an exclusive. Was going to leave soon anyway. I'll send a file shortly. Hope
Victoria is ready to rearrange her score sheet Monday!

I feel terrible but I can celebrate with Ethan once I get home.

Me: Wish I could ☹ Maggie just asked me to cover a club for a girl who
got sick. #Points Have one for me and I'll see you at home. We'll
celebrate like we did last night! Wink. XX

I don't bother returning my phone back to my bag and rush over to
Holiday and interrupt her conversation with some of the people from her
show. The maître d' trails me like I'm wearing a million dollars' worth of
borrowed diamonds and he's been charged with guarding them.
    "It's okay," Holiday says, calling him off. He nods and retreats to his
position. She's with Gwendolyn Ross, famed and feared editor in chief of

the only fashion and lifestyle publication that matters, *Style & Trend Magazine*; the creator of her show, Seth; a woman I don't recognize but of course looks like she could have been or still could be a model; and her costar, Tristan. Holiday giggles at everything Tristan is saying, and it only takes me about two seconds to recognize the look in her eye. She has the hots for him, and any man that Holiday wants, Holiday gets. "Ella, I want to introduce you. This is the inimitable, fearless fashionista Gwendolyn Ross." Gwendolyn avoids making eye contact and is less than interested in being introduced to a plebeian like me. "And this is my costar, Tristan."

"Hey." He shakes my hand.

"Hi. Nice to meet you." He doesn't have to say anything. I notice the sparkle in his eye and know that he's smitten with her, too.

"And this is Seth and his wife, Maya. Everyone, this is my best friend, Ella." Maya looks away, as if she wasn't spoken to and I wasn't standing inches away from her. She's lucky she tricked someone into marrying her. Coming from someone who used to work with coffee, I can say she's about as warm as an iced latte.

"Hol, can I talk to you privately for a sec?"

"Of course, darling. Please excuse me. I'll be right back." Tristan leans in and kisses her on her cheek and her sweaty hand grabs mine and she skips to the corner with me.

"I'm so happy for you." I notice Holiday's eye is still fixated on Tristan even though she's fully listening to me.

"I'm sorry I didn't tell you yesterday, but you know me, I wanted to make my grand announcement and wanted to surprise everyone, including you. What do you think?" Her eyes are desperate for my approval.

"It's amazing. . . . I don't know what to say."

"Neither did I. I didn't actually expect to book a role so soon." Her eyes are now dancing with Tristan's as if they're in some kind of optical lovers' tango.

"I'm really proud of you." I don't know how to tactfully transition from congratulations to my departure so I decide to bypass a segue. "Please don't hate me, I just got asked to work and things went down at *The Life*. I have a new boss and we have to earn points now and I will fill you in later. Ethan sold his script tonight and I can't even meet him to celebrate because I have to take this assignment."

Holiday is on cloud nine, glazed in bliss. She's not really paying attention to any of the words that are coming out of my mouth. I could probably tell her that I needed to leave to go murder puppies and kittens and her smile wouldn't shrink. But it's to my benefit that she's so elated: she spares me her usual monologue about the subject.

"Dahhhhhhhhling, don't worry about it. Go be Bella. And tell Ethan congratulations for me." She kisses me on both cheeks.

"Thank you. I promise we'll have a proper celebration before you leave. I'm going to send in an item on Recently Divorced British B-List Comedian–Sex Addict and his girlfriend's fight, too, if you're okay with that?"

"You better! I need my name out there as much as possible to promote the show. Now get out of here." She shoos me away and beelines back to Tristan. The maître d' is still surveying me as I order my Uber and the only thing that interrupts his scrutiny is Nick approaching me and blocking his line of vision.

"Where'd you go?" Nick puts his hand on the wall behind me, leaning in so close that I can tell that the stubble on his face is approximately thirty-six hours old. "I was getting bored attempting to make small talk with those other people." He definitely gets an A+ for his flirting skills.

"I went to say good-bye to Holiday. I have to go." I try to push my back farther into the wall even though that's obviously impossible.

"Go? Now? Where could you possibly have to go?" He leans in farther.

"That is a long story," I tell him. He has no idea.

"Would you like some company?"

"That's a really nice offer, but—"

"Another time." He removes his hand from the wall and straightens his posture.

"It was really nice meeting you, Nick Williams."

"You too, Ella." I move toward the door. "Can I have your number?"

If I were in any other situation on the planet I wouldn't have been able to resist his request. "I'm sorry. I actually have a boyfriend."

"Now I see why you don't want company. I wish you had told me earlier so I wouldn't have developed such a crush on you."

I laugh. Does he really say things like this? I mean, obviously he does, but somehow he totally makes it work.

"Can we be friends?" he asks. He's still smiling, and walking away from him is one of the hardest things I've ever had to do in my adult life. I figure his is an empty request, since men and women are rarely just friends and one, if not both, generally have an ulterior motive, but it's easier and faster to give in.

"Sure. I'd like that," I say. The maître d' opens the door for me.

"I need your number," he calls out.

"You gave me your card. Have a good night, Nick Williams," I call back. While I wait for my car I write up a quick file on the incident with British B-List Comedian–Sex Addict and send it to Maggie. This might not be the big scandal *The Life* is looking for, but hopefully it will buy me some time.

Six

· · · · · · · · · · · · · · · · · · ·

"Just you, sweetheart?" Gus asks as I approach the velvet ropes at the entrance of Ambiance.

"Yep." I always use my saccharine, flirtatious voice with doormen. He opens the rope and motions me toward the ID checkpoint. Ambiance happens to be one of the nightclubs that use a scanner. They appear to be hard-core, but I always see a bunch of eighteen-year-old actor–reality stars from MTV running around belligerently drunk. The scanner, like most of the rest of this industry, is all for appearances.

I take a quick survey of the room and notice Jessica hanging out at the bar.

"Hey, girl!" I squeal as I approach. She throws her scrawny boho arms around me and I try not to choke from the overwhelming scent of patchouli emanating from her.

"Hi, Ella! Or should I say Bella?" Jess winks. "I was going to text you but I had a feeling I'd see you, and here you are."

"Here I am." Relieved. "What are you doing here?"

"My friend Mark is getting a table and he invited me. He isn't here yet."

"I wasn't supposed to come tonight. I was at Holiday's party, but the girl who was covering got sick. I was asked last minute and I couldn't say no. I have a new boss and I need to fill you in on all of my work drama."

"Tell me in a minute," she says. Jessica pulls my iPhone out of my hand. "What are you doing?" I scrunch my face, irritated that she's taken my phone and is intensely typing away. She holds a finger up to shush me, which surprises me. After two minutes of typing she holds my phone in my direction, offering it back to me. I snatch it away before she has a chance to change her mind. What has gotten into her? I look down at the screen to see what she was so intent on writing.

NOTES:

- *Not-So-Innocent Oversexualized Pop Star made an early appearance at Hollywood hotspot Ambiance.*
- *Arrived just before 11 pm and immediately made her way to the bar even though she seemed to already be a little tipsy when she got there.*
- *Entourage was only girls.*
- *Wore signature crop top and low-slung jeans with heels.*
- *Had playful dance-off with her friends, which she won.*
- *Took three shots of tequila in a row with her gaggle of gals and was in full-on party mode*
- *Left 30 minutes after she arrived. Left through back door and snuck out of garage to avoid paparazzi.*

"You saw all of this?" I ask Jess, my jaw agape.

"Yep!" She smiles back, well aware that she did a great job.

"She never goes out," I tell her.

"I know."

"No, I mean like never. In all of my years working for *The Life,* I've never seen her in person! I'm so jealous; she's my favorite. I've listened to her music since her debut single, dressed as her for Halloween no less than three times, and she is basically the only person I would probably ever get starstruck over. She's my celebrity white whale. I'd ask you what she was like, but you just wrote it all down for me," I joke. "Thanks, Jess. You're amazing. This should earn me some points." I release a small sigh of relief.

"Points?" she asks with a quizzical look on her face.

"I'll explain later. Part of the work drama. But you saved my ass!"

"I do what I can," she says modestly in jest, tossing her hair back, proud of her effort.

"What can I get for you ladies?" the bartender interrupts. He's gorgeous, and I think he's in the Givenchy billboard on Sunset Boulevard—either that or the Calvin Klein billboard on Santa Monica Boulevard. It could be a full-time job keeping track of LA's bartenders and their billboards.

"Two glasses of champagne, please," I answer. He slides flutes over to our side of the bar.

"It'll be thirty even." He smiles at me, pretending to flirt in the hopes that I'll leave him a bigger tip.

"This is on me, Jess. Well, on *The Life*. You earned it!" *The Life*'s new policy may be stories in exchange for points but no one said anything about cutting down on our expenses so I can still treat my sources.

My phone buzzes and I have a text from the reason why I can't stand to be around these degenerate "club" guys.

I'm waiting up for you.

"Everything okay?" Jess asks.

"Yeah. More than okay. Ethan sold his screenplay today."

"Shut up, that's great!" She jumps out of happiness for me and accidentally spills a few drops of champagne. "The plan is finally gonna happen!"

"I know and he just texted me that he's waiting up for me which he *never* does anymore. You know what that means!" I might be gaining points with Victoria to save my job but I'm definitely losing cool points as each second passes because I can't contain my excitement.

She furrows her brow. "You don't think he's going to propose to-night?"

I shrug my shoulders. "I don't know. I mean . . . he might."

"Congrats, El. To you and Ethan." She raises her glass for yet another toast tonight.

"To me and Ethan," I echo as we clink our glasses.

"I love you, but please don't ask me to be a bridesmaid. You know how I feel about the commercialization of love."

I hold my hand up like a stop sign in the name of love. "I wouldn't dare."

I maneuver my head around to try to see if any celebrities have shown up, but the club has filled up considerably in the past few minutes so my eyes are having difficulty scanning the crowd. Jessica nudges me and I instinctively turn my head. She's spotted Boybander Turned Solo Artist Turned Actor who also happens to be Not-So-Innocent Oversexualized Pop Star's ex. Maybe she got word he was en route and that's why she only stayed for a half hour, something to note in my file.

"Ella, you're about to love me." Jessica giggles. Jess rarely giggles so this must be good.

"Why?"

"Because my friend Mark is at Boybander Turned Solo Artist Turned

Actor's table," she whispers. I feel a smile emerge on my face and this time it's an expression of legitimate joy that my job will be a little easier tonight and make my bosses happy, which is more important now than ever.

"How do you know Mark anyway?"

"I buy weed from him," Jessica confesses.

"You still have a dealer for weed?" With the plethora of medical marijuana dispensaries they seemed to be antiquated—not that I'm complaining.

"Are you kidding? I don't want to be on some government list!"

She does have a point. And I'm assuming neither do the celebrities, since we all know that for celebrities there really is no privacy. I'm living proof. "I knew he had celebrity friends and clients, but I had no idea they were this A-list. I mean, they're no Sexy Indie Film Actor but what can you do?"

"Let's go over to the table. I need good observations on Boybander Turned Solo Artist Turned Actor. Never have I been so glad you're a pothead," I joke as I put my hand on her shoulder.

"I'm one of Mark's most loyal clients," she boasts.

I reapply my Stila lip gloss and we parade over to the table. Mark and Boybander Turned Solo Artist Turned Actor are the only ones there right now. As we approach them, a suit-clad security guard turns to the group inside the table to determine if we're cleared for entrance. Mark nods and the security guard steps aside to allow our passage. Once we're in, Jessica gives Mark a hug but I have my eyes focused on Boybander Turned Solo Artist Turned Actor, who's glued to his phone texting and doesn't even glance in our direction or acknowledge our presence. There's nothing that makes you feel more invisible than being in someone's presence and having them completely ignore you.

"Yo, Jess. Glad you could come. Haven't heard from you in a minute," he says after their embrace.

"I know. Things with my blog have been overwhelming and I haven't had a chance to call you and replenish. I'll definitely hit you up in the next few days."

"No worries. Sit down. Have a drink."

We accept his offer and Boybander Turned Solo Artist Turned Actor is still staring at his phone and hasn't said a word to us. Ugh. Stop looking at your phone and *do something*. I'm not going to get any points for boring. I reach for the scoop in the ice bucket and play bartender. I'm nowhere near as skilled as Holiday, but I make do. Vodka soda with a splash of cran isn't terribly complicated and I doubt it would be recommended after Dom, but it's free.

"I'm Bella. Thanks." I sip my cocktail.

"No worries. How do you two know each other?" he asks, adding a little more vodka to top off his drink. Jessica jumps in before I have a chance to answer. She wants to keep my identity secret as much as I do. I know she doesn't want to arouse any suspicion about my job or me with Mark because she doesn't want to be blamed for bringing a reporter into a celebrity's inner circle.

"Bella and I were both English majors at college together and ended up staying in LA," she explains.

As she's talking, I notice Boybander Turned Solo Artist Turned Actor get up and walk away. I pretend to still be listening to Jessica while trying to keep one eye on him and determine where he's wandered off to.

"You a fan?" Mark asks. He's clearly caught me staring at Boybander Turned Solo Artist Turned Actor despite my efforts to be surreptitious. This is so embarrassing but I have to play along.

"Yeah. Big fan." This is another one of my generic cover stories. I'm a drug addict at Chateau and fangirl at the club. What and who will I be next week? I play any role I need to get my story. I look down at my feet, pretending to be shy.

"It's cool. Most girls around your age are."

The worst was when I had to cover a small club on Melrose last year and my friend Monica happened to be one of the cocktail waitresses. I was there at least twice a week every week for six months and she told me that I came up regularly at the staff meetings. Everyone thought I was a groupie for the club because I was there so consistently.

In Boybander Turned Solo Artist Turned Actor's ten-minute absence I manage to down a second cocktail. He finally returns with a gaggle of male pals in tow that he actually does acknowledge, and the energy at the table completely changes. I move around the table, haphazardly dancing, to get an unobstructed view of Boybander Turned Solo Artist Turned Actor. After a brief chat with his pals, he returns to his iPhone, texting, while he intermittently sips on multiple vodka cocktails. He refrains from dancing or smiling or displaying any emotion or acknowledgment when the DJ spins his first solo single, which took his status from teen heart-throb to icon.

He finally perks up around 1:45 A.M. when he notices someone at the edge of our table and whispers to a male friend sitting next to him before approaching the man just outside of our table that's around Boybander Turned Solo Artist Turned Actor's age, height, and build. They are dressed almost identically in jeans and hoodies with leather jackets as their outer layer. At first glance it looks like the Boybander Turned Solo Artist Turned Actor and the non-celebrity mystery man are catching up, but within seconds their conversation becomes heated. Before I know it, Boybander Turned Solo Artist Turned Actor throws a punch and the mystery man reciprocates. Luckily the security guard stationed in front of the table jumps into action seconds later and the fight is broken up before it could progress into something much worse. A second burly security guard joins the first and they escort the unidentified participant out, and a cocktail waitress takes an ice-wrapped towel and cleans up a small amount of blood from Boybander Turned Actor Turned Solo Artist's mouth and right knuckles. Multiple guards surround the circumference of our table and I know it's time for me to *really* do my job.

"Oh my God, what happened?" I ask Mark. Any detail on why Boybander Turned Solo Artist Turned Actor might've started this fight is essential.

"That guy is the worst," Mark scoffs. "He dated Boybander Turned Solo Artist Turned Actor's girlfriend before they got together and he was being a jackass, provoking him, so he punched him in the face, rightly so, if I may add. I would've done the same thing."

Jessica and I turn to each other, knowing that I'm getting gold, when Boybander Turned Solo Artist Turned Actor calls out to Mark as he hustles his entourage toward the exit.

"I gotta run. Nice meeting you," he says to me. "See you later, Jess."

He rushes to catch up to his group and when they are all accounted for they slip out of the exit to try to avoid the paparazzi. This is why I can't ever leave work early. Boybander Turned Actor Turned Solo Artist may have seemed boring, but if I had left at 1:30 A.M. because seemingly nothing was happening, I would've missed the story. With two stories tonight I should earn a decent amount of points. If I keep this up, I'll hopefully be able to save my job at *The Life*.

Seven

....

Death Dog ingestion is usually reserved for when you are so drunk you need to get any sustenance in your stomach ASAP to help absorb the alcohol or else you'll puke. The dogs are sold on mobile grills outside of nightclubs all over Los Angeles and cost four dollars, which is a bargain when you've been drinking all night. The bacon-wrapped Death Dogs have a twofold affect. One, the fat, grease, and carbs help sober you up so you wake up with a less severe hangover, and two, in the morning you're so disgusted with the sausage sitting in the pit of your stomach all night that you eat healthfully the next day, if you eat at all.

But tonight is a special occasion and these Death Dogs are not a Hail Mary to prevent alcohol-induced illness.

"Babe!" I call out as I come into the apartment. "I'm sorry that I missed the celebration cocktails but I brought congratulatory Death Dogs!"

"I'm in here," Ethan calls from the bedroom. All I want to do is take off these Aquazzura heels and jump into Ethan's arms. He's sitting at the foot of the bed and is not in the jovial mood I'd anticipated, but maybe I can cheer him up now that I'm home.

"You have *no* idea how hard it was for me to keep myself from taking a bite of these in the Uber, but I wanted to share this moment with you. Congratulations!" I lean in to kiss him and he pulls away.

"Share this moment with me?" he winces.

"Of course. This is huge. It's official. I'm so proud of you!"

"Could've fooled me."

"What are you talking about? This is an amazing night. . . ."

But he folds his arms like a child about to throw a temper tantrum for not getting his way. "You weren't there, Ella."

"Come on, Ethan—"

"No. No excuses. You weren't there and said yourself that this night

was a huge milestone for me. It just sucks. This really meant a lot to me . . .
to us," he sighs.

"I'm so sorry, honey. You're right. I should've been there. I should've
told Maggie no and gone out and hustled for points over the weekend." I
place the Death Dogs on the dresser and sit on his lap, wrapping my hands
around his neck. "Can you forgive me?"

He sighs. "I was really hurt you weren't by my side."

"I totally screwed up. I'm really sorry. I promise that won't happen
again," I assure him. I give him a peck on the lips and he softens.

"I know. Once you start working less this isn't even going to be an
issue, so there's no point in ruining what's left of our night and making it
a big deal."

Excuse me? What did he just say? I get up from his lap, baffled.

"What do you mean, 'working less'?"

"Now that I sold the script we will have plenty of money so you
don't have to be so worried about taking every assignment or being threat-
ened with being fired if you say no, once. I thought you'd pull back a
little."

I'm shocked. I get up from his lap and pace around the bedroom trying to make sense of this. "Why would you think that?"

"We talked about it."

"We absolutely did not," I insist.

"Yes, we did, on date night. We said everything was going to be changing and we'd be moving forward with our future plans."

I scan back through last night as if my brain was a DVR and try to find
the moment to hit the Play button so I can remind myself of this conversation, but we never discussed anything even close to this. Do I have some
extreme case of early-onset Alzheimer's disease? Nothing is even close to
ringing a bell. I stop pacing and take a deep breath to calm myself and
to hopefully prevent me from saying something that I won't be able to
take back.

"Where did me essentially quitting my job figure in to that conversation?"

"I never said *quit* your job. We just talked about cutting back. You
know I hate you running around at all hours of the night stalking celebrities."

"I knew you weren't obsessed with it but you've never asked me to
stop."

"I didn't think I'd have to if we can afford you not doing it. I thought you'd move on to something else."

"Move on to something else? Ethan, I love you but I love my job, too. It would be like if I'd asked you to give up writing because you hadn't made it yet. But the difference between us is I would never ask you to give up something you love." I know that Ethan isn't confessing that he slept with another woman, but this admission feels like a betrayal. "I didn't think the plan was for me to quit my job once your career got going. I'm sorry but I can't do that for you."

"Well then maybe I can't do this anymore."

"What?" When did this go from an argument to a split? How can everything change in five minutes?

I realize I'm uncontrollably crying but Ethan doesn't come over to comfort me or even bring me a Kleenex. "I thought you were going to propose. I thought *that* was the plan."

He looks genuinely surprised. "Who am I supposed to propose to? Ella or Bella?" he says callously. "I'm done with both of you."

Who is this person? Has his body been invaded by aliens? How can the man who wrote and just sold a love story about a couple who transcend obstacles like distance and societal pressure and illness just discard someone he claimed to love?

Even though everything is happening quickly in actual time, it feels like time is at a standstill, and I feel every fracture and crack tearing my heart into pieces.

We're both silent for a long time.

Finally he says, "I'll stay with a friend tonight. You can keep the apartment. I'll come back for the rest of my things in the morning."

I don't hear Ethan leave. I'm lying in our bed, still. But after what feels like an eternity, I get up and look around the quiet room. He's gone.

I put on my pajamas and take off all my jewelry.

I hope this will all blow over and Ethan will call later and we'll work it out, so I take out my laptop and I start working on my file for Maggie. I barely know what time it is, but it's still dark out, and I need to send it before the morning.

Eight

· · · · · · · · · · · · · · · · · · · ·

After I finished my file I couldn't sleep. I crawled into bed, numb, and couldn't stop myself from nuzzling my face into Ethan's pillow and inhaling his scent. It was comforting but heartbreaking at the same time. I got to feel like he was still there with me, but it only emphasized that he was in fact gone. I couldn't decide if closing my eyes and running through all of the "what ifs" in my head was worse than keeping them open to stare at his empty side of the bed. I never got to sleep that night, but I did zone in and out a few times, which I was thankful for. I got a text from him first thing in the morning, but not the one I was fantasizing about receiving. The text informed me he'd rented a U-Haul and would be at the apartment at ten to collect his things. I went into shock all over again, and in meltdown mode I wrote Holiday a novel of texts. She immediately rang and insisted on taking me to the Chateau Marmont for breakfast so I wouldn't have to watch Ethan move out of our apartment.

And, more important, so we could drink.

I text Jessica on the way over to meet us. I thought this was a good idea at first but now I'm not so sure that I'm emotionally stable enough to be in public. "Fuck Ethan," I'm hissing when I catch my favorite Pixie Hair- cut Hostess gawking me as she escorts Former Stripper Turned Academy Award–Winning Screenwriter past me.

"And now I'm crying in front of an Oscar winner," I sob.

I should be ashamed that I'm causing a scene at my holy place, drunk well before noon, but my sadness and anger from Breakupgate are over- taking the rational part of my brain. Besides, everyone here is so self- involved they won't notice anything going on short of an earthquake. If Ethan and I were celebrities, next week's cover of *The Life* would be a picture of the two of us with a zigzag down the middle and the headline "Split: Screenwriter Leaves Celebrity Journalist Blindsided." My whimpers become whines and my sobbing turns into bawling as my outburst escalates.

"Keep it together, darling. I know you're in pain but this is still the Chateau," Holiday councils. "Now that you're single, the last thing you want is anyone thinking you've bought a one-way ticket on the Hot Mess Express." I scowl at her even though I know she's right and drown my sorrows in my Bloody Mary. In stark contrast, Holiday leisurely savors her mimosa. I look up between slurps to see Jessica being escorted to our table. She kisses Holiday on each cheek.

"How's she doing?" she asks, as if I just got out of surgery. I wish some Beverly Hills plastic surgeon would invent an outpatient procedure to repair the internal scar on my heart.

"Let's just say I'm glad you're here for reinforcement. Her perspective and faculties are eroding faster than the Malibu coastline."

"I'm right here, you guys," I yell. Their gazes both shift to me, giving me a look that says, "Lower your voice."

Jessica kneels in front of my chair and gives me an Earth Mother hug. "It's going to be alright, El." Her laissez-faire attitude is usually eccentrically charming but it's not helping today.

"How?" They're giving me nothing so I reiterate my question. "How am I going to be alright?" The girls stare at me, still speechless, so I ask a third time. "I'm really asking you, how? The person that knows me best in the world walked away. What does that say about me?"

"Much worse has happened between these walls and you know it," Holiday contends. She's right and although it may feel like it, no one has died, if you don't count my pride or my ego. Jessica gives Holiday a look, thanking her for tranquilizing me, even if it only provides momentary relief. As hard as I try to implement every rule of *The Secret* and attempt to stop my mind from wandering back to my circumstances, I fail and the tears drop down my face again.

"I just can't believe he's moving out *right* now. That he just got a U-Haul and is moving ASAP."

"Rip off the Band-Aid. It's a cliché for a reason," Holiday reminds me.

"And at least it will be easier for you to move on. You won't have all of his things lingering around conjuring up memories," Jessica figures.

"That's because I don't have anything! The only things that are mine are the bed and the dishes."

And now it hits me. I can't believe I've been so preoccupied that I haven't thought about my finances until now. Fuck! *Fuck* isn't even a strong enough expletive.

"Oh my God, you guys, I'm going to have to move. The only way I can afford that apartment and all of my expenses on my own is if I go on a cleanse. From food. Entirely. For a while." Ethan was always very conscious about budgeting and made sure he worked enough for us to never worry about necessities. But I'm beginning to calculate the expenses in my head, and despite my lack of sobriety realize that only having one income now, I'm screwed. I continue adding numbers to my monthly tab after I've surpassed the amount I earn in a month.

"Seriously. I'm either going to have to move in with Robin or a Craigslist killer and with our track record, I'm leaning toward the murderer!" Holiday and Jessica laugh but this isn't a joke! I'm about to really lose it. Like, put-me-under-a-5150-psychiatric-hold lose it.

"I know you're in pain but catastrophizing the situation won't do you any good," Jessica says.

My breathing is increasing exponentially by the second. "I feel like I'm going to pass out!"

Jessica hands me my glass of water but I shake my head, refusing the beverage.

Holiday takes the opposite approach and steps in with the tough love, gently slapping me on the face. "You have to calm down, darling!" I take one more large exhale and my blood no longer feels like it's going to bubble over and explode out of my skin. It worked. My breath returns to its normal rhythm. "You won't have to move in with your sister. But having a roommate isn't necessarily a bad thing." I roll my eyes. "Look, you clearly need to be on suicide watch for the next few days—"

"I don't need to be on suicide watch. I need to be on homicide watch," I correct.

"You made your first postbreakup joke," Jessica says, clapping for me like I'm a toddler that was recently potty-trained.

Holiday's wheels are turning and I never expected what she said next. "I have an idea. Why don't you move in with me?" For the first time in eight hours I feel a slight twinge of hope.

"Really?" I hope my Holiday-prescribed breakup cocktail of Xanax and Bloody Marys isn't making me hallucinate.

"Absolutely. You're like a sister to me and I'm going to be in Canada filming the pilot. It would be great to have you watch the house while I'm gone."

Jessica jumps in. "My boyfriend broke up with me last year, can I come, too?"

"Sorry, Jess, there's a six-month statute of limitations for heartbroken roommates," she quips. "So, what do you say?"

"Hol, that's so generous, but sometimes when friends live together things can get tense."

"Darling, that only applies to people that live in apartments, not twenty-thousand-square-foot houses. There's enough room for you to have your own wing." It's true: I've gotten lost in her house before and almost needed a docent to guide me back to the front door. "I'm going to be away for a bit and we rarely run on the same schedule anyway." I'm debating the pros and cons and both Holiday and Jessica are looking at me like I'm nuts for considering any possible alternative. Holiday comes in with the Hail Mary. "Do you really want to chance becoming a story line on *Law & Order: SVU* when you can live on top of Mount Olympus?"

How can I say no to this? I don't want to say no to this. Usually when something seems too good to be true it probably is—especially in LA, where there are usually invisible strings attached—but I know that's not the case with Holiday.

"You're positive?" I ask one last time, hoping my initial hesitation hasn't led her to change her mind.

"One hundred and ten percent." She gets up from the table and gives me a big hug, even though I should be the one bowing down at her feet and chanting her name in a prayer circle while offering some kind of sacrifice in her honor. Jessica, never one to miss an opportunity for some "free love," joins our embrace. My life: subtract one boyfriend and add luxury residence. It doesn't equal happiness but it equals a slight sense of relief for the time being.

"You can start moving your stuff in whenever you want, but that's where I draw the line. I don't do moves."

"Thank you! I'll give notice at my place and get started ASAP." For the first time since Breakupgate I feel like I don't want to die. Good-bye, West Hollywood; hello, Hollywood Hills. Our roommates' rejoice is interrupted by Holiday's phone beeping consistently.

"Geez, how many notifications do you get?!" I say. I don't think I even get that many messages on my birthday.

"It's my Google alerts," she explains.

"Who do you have Google-alerted?" Jessica asks.

"Me, of course," she says with a cheeky grin. Holiday opens every article about her, reading each with care and scrutiny, digesting every detail.

"Between the *Benedict Canyon* announcement and Ella's story about Recently Divorced British B-List Comedian–Sex Addict's fight at my party on *The Life*, my name is all over the news. I can't believe you were able to file last night with everything going on," Holiday comments.

"I'm impressed," Jess says, pulling out her phone to read the story as well.

"I didn't really have a choice. Who I *need* to impress is my new boss," I explain.

"Yeah, what's the deal with that? You said you were gonna fill me in last night but then it got crazy with Boybander Turned Solo Artist Turned Actor—"

"And then the conclusion of the Ella and Ethan saga," Holiday adds. I shake off the harsh reality of her comment and commence a new anxiety attack about the future of my employment status.

"To give you the Wikipedia version of events, *The Life* was sold to a new publisher. They hired Victoria Davis to come back and run the magazine—"

"That's so funny, Gwendolyn mentioned something about her last night," Holiday interrupts. "I made a mental note to talk to you about it, but the champagne sort of erased that memo."

"What did she say?" I ask.

"Well, darling, I wasn't particularly sober or paying explicit attention by that point in the evening but I think it was something along the lines of Victoria throwing your old editor under the bus to get this job because *The Life* is the only magazine that would even consider hiring her today. . . ." She trails off.

"What?" That can't be. Victoria Davis is not a has-been. She's a legend. "Are you sure that's what Gwendolyn said?" I ask.

"No," she squeaks. "Listening to Gwendolyn's venomous gossip about the editorial world was not where my head was at last night," she reminds me as she takes a double sip of her mimosa. "I'm sure I either misheard or she was being her usual catty self."

"I swear the gossip magazines should really be about the people running them and the reporters," Jess marvels. "Your incestuous media circle is bursting with more drama and is far more interesting than celebrities. No offense," she attaches to the end of her suggestion to keep Holiday's feelings intact. The thought of someone being more interesting than she could be is far more offensive to her than an actual insult. Holiday lets it slide but playfully gives Jess a glance to know that while she's letting this one go, Jess has been warned.

"Well, apparently now that Victoria is in charge she has the budget to keep only four of us. To determine who stays and who gets fired she's pressuring us into finding exclusives that will sell magazines and drive traffic to the Web site. We'll receive points for any of our reporting that gets used, and the better the story, the better the placement and the more points we get. She's going to fire the person with the lowest score at the end of each week until she's down to four reporters."

"Well, that's no pressure at all," Jess remarks with her trademark dry wit.

"Tell me about it," I concur. "That's why I went to Ambiance instead of going to celebrate with Ethan."

"At least you got something while you were there. If it had been a bust this whole breakup would be even more devastating," Jess says.

I nod and slurp down the rest of my Bloody Mary.

"Anyway," Holiday quickly pivots the conversation in another direction, "thank you for the story and mentioning my party. Right now all press is good press, for both of us it seems."

I grab my phone from my purse and quickly find the story and screenshot it, then throw the phone back in, so as not to arouse any suspicion.

"*Almost* all press is good press," I correct. "Trust me."

"You want another Bloody Mary?" Holiday asks.

Is she kidding? I wish this stuff was coursing through my veins. "What do you think?"

"That's my girl."

"I'll have one too," Jess chimes in with a grin. "My blog is called *Martini Olives Count as Dinner.* Can't 'write what I know' unless I partake."

. . . .

As we're leaving the Chateau, the alcohol is hitting me all at once due to the lack of real food in my system. I wish I'd had the foresight to scarf down one of those Death Dogs last night. I was too nauseated to eat after Ethan left and I couldn't stand to look at what was supposed to be a congratulatory snack that inadvertently turned into a parting gift. Right about now I'm regretting my decision to throw them in the trash. We walk down the driveway, and the paparazzi begin to swarm Holiday. Jessica waves good-bye and quietly dips out, narrowly avoiding the slew of photographers.

"Holiday, tell us all about your new show!"

"Holiday, what's it like to be Hollywood's up-and-coming It girl?"

"Holiday, what's going on in your love life?"

She's never been papped to this extent. She's like a deer caught in the headlights about to be slammed into on Mulholland Drive instead of her usually composed self. I don't know if it's my buzz or my intuition, but my something is telling me to jump in and save her.

"She's really excited," I interject. The paparazzi stop their camera clicking for a moment to see who's speaking on her behalf. "She loves the script and couldn't have asked for a better supporting cast."

Holiday regains her composure and turns it on for the cameras, but the paparazzi frenzy is diffused by hotel security, who ushers them out of the driveway as Holiday's car pulls up. Before she leaves she turns to me.

"Thanks for saving me. I don't know what happened. I've been so focused on you that I wasn't prepared for that."

"Well 'darling,' you better get ready because this is only the tip of the iceberg, and if you handle them like you just did I'm going to be more Googled than you." She hugs me and proceeds to her car.

"Get home safe," Holiday instructs.

Home? The home I know is gone. The home I know I shared with someone who now doesn't exist to me. When I stumble into my apartment my stomach drops. He really did it. Ethan moved everything out. I knew he was going to, but there was some part of me that thought while he was removing everything he would have a change of heart. The only evidence that he ever lived here are the indentations from the legs of the furniture on the living-room carpet. Half of the bedroom closet is empty and the naked hangers with all of the empty space between them somehow make me feel like I'm about to become the next victim in a horror film that is now my life. It seems almost impossible to remember what it looked like only twenty-four hours ago or what it smelled like when he lived here. The feeling of emptiness overwhelms me.

I check my phone. No texts from him saying "I miss you" or "I made a mistake." The only thing I can do is focus on myself and my new beginning and keeping my job, which I need now more than ever. My phone buzzes. It's Maggie.

Hey Ella,
I wanted to check on you. I heard about you and Ethan. I'm so sorry. If you
need anything, don't hesitate to ask. XO
Maggie
PS If you can find another story before Monday I think it would help you get in
Victoria's good graces.

I don't know why I'm surprised she knows. She was friends with Ethan first and she works in the gossip industry. Why wouldn't the news about my breakup travel through our circle of friends before I run out of tears?

And then my phone buzzes again. It's a picture of Marianna, giving me the peace sign, and then a text from Robin:

Hey El! Don't forget—birthday party tomorrow. You and Ethan are still coming, right? And you're bringing cupcakes!??

Nine

· · · · · · · · · · · · · · · · · · · ·

"Aunt Ella, Aunt Ella! It's my birthday!" I barely make it into the foyer before my rambunctious, towheaded, four-year-old niece, wearing a tiara that perfectly complements her blush-pink leotard and tutu ensemble, runs and attacks me with hugs. She grabs onto my leg as if it's a life vest and we're drowning.

"Hmmmm . . . Are you sure it's your birthday?" Her excitement turns to a look of worry. "I'm only teasing. Happy birthday, Miss Marianna. Such a big girl now! How old are you today? Huh?" She giggles. I hold up two fingers. "Are you this many?"

"No!"

"Hmm. Are you this many?" I say with three fingers this time. "Well, that can only mean one thing." I hold up four fingers. "You've got to be this many!" I grab her off my leg and kiss her all over her face and tickle her. "Happy birthday, silly goose tickle monster!" There's something about how pure and truly happy my niece is that's beautiful, especially in contrast to the current darkness I feel inside. But Marianna's hugs and jumping make me feel nauseated, and Robin notices as I close my eyes and breathe deeply in and out in an attempt to settle my stomach.

"Marianna, why don't you go in the kitchen and help Daddy with the balloons?"

"Okay, Mommy." She scampers off without the slightest clue that even though this house is still standing I feel like the world is crumbling on top of me.

"I'm glad you made it. It's been too long since you've been over." Robin leans in to hug me. It's kind of awkward. Like as if we're acquaintances from core-curriculum classes in college instead of sisters. She sniffs me. "Ella, you reek of booze. Are you hungover?"

I swallow a burp. "Technically I'm still drunk. I don't think you can call it a hangover unless you've been to bed."

She rolls her eyes at me, unamused. "You didn't drive here, did you?"

"Of course not. I Ubered."

"Well, thank God for responsibility. Did you bring the cupcakes?" she asks, noticing my empty hands.

"No, I—" She throws her hands in the air, as if I just told her I wrecked her new car, but before she can get a word out, I cut her off. "I don't need a lecture, Robin." She folds her arms and is all too eager to scold me for what she considers to be my irresponsible behavior, though she has no idea that there are extenuating circumstances.

I think back to the days when Robin was out partying past curfew and tried to escape the wrath of my parents by sneaking in through *my* bedroom window. Mine was the only window accessible through the backyard, if she stood on the patio table. She knocked until it woke me up. Whenever she snuck in, the alcohol she'd consumed that evening seeped out of her pores, more potent than perfume, and her hair was a complete mess, which, as I figured out during my own adolescence, was disheveled from a romantic tryst. She plied me with candy to coerce me to lie and insist that she'd been home before curfew. I've never forgotten her reckless days, but she has. . . .

"Clearly you do or you wouldn't have shown up to my daughter's birthday party—"

"Robin, please don't start with me today!"

"I just want this day to be perfect for Marianna," she explains as she moves her hands to her hips. Lucky for me my mother interrupts and diffuses the moment.

"And I see my perfect daughter." She comes over to hug me. I immediately notice that she is gaunt. Her face isn't as soft as I remember. It looks worn but fragile at the same time. Despite that, her makeup is impeccable and her face is illuminated by a smile as soon as she sees me. Of course her caramel-brown hair has a perfect blow out. I'd expect nothing less. She looks much thinner than usual and my suspicion is confirmed when my arms feel like they've multiplied in length as I hug her because she's gotten smaller. "Hi, sweetie!"

"It's good to see you, Mom. And also I want your diet secret. Where did you go?" I look her up and down in her black sweater dress and I briefly wonder if she's discovered the Cocaine Game.

She looks around. "Where's Ethan? I want to say hi."

"We, um, broke up." I can't help it. I lose control and the tears come out in a wave.

Robin uncrosses her arms. "Now I understand the alcohol," she acquiesces.

Mom shushes her. "I'm so sorry, Ella. Why didn't you tell me?" She holds me close to her, and the fragrance of her Lauren by Ralph Lauren–infused clothes is comforting.

"It *just* happened like a day ago," I squeak out.

"You're going to be okay." She hugs me tighter then pulls away to look me in the eye. "You are a strong, kind, charismatic young woman and don't you ever forget it."

"Thanks, Mom."

"Jeff!" My mother calls for my brother-in-law even though he's only a few feet away. "Will you show me where the vodka is? I need to make Ella one of my famous Bloody Marys." My mom is famous in our family for exactly two cocktails, Bloody Marys and piña coladas, but she makes the latter only on Thanksgiving. I'm not exactly sure how piña coladas became part of the Warren tradition of giving thanks, but ever since I was a kid, a can of cream of coconut and the blender resting on the countertop symbolized Thanksgiving to me more than turkey and pumpkin pie. Even my father looked forward to them, but he was never a big drinker, hence the reason there was always leftover alcohol available for Robin to steal.

I'm surprised that Robin even keeps alcohol in the house. She's militant about not having any of her senses impaired, even if she isn't on call. Calling her rigid would be an understatement. Because she's Miss Perfect, she keeps a bottle of everything on hand for guests and for the one or two nights a year she allows herself to relax and indulge in an adult beverage. Jeff gives Robin a confused look. He doesn't make a move without her approving it first and hasn't since they met sophomore year of college. He worships Robin. It isn't enough that being a doctor gives her a slight God complex—Jeff encourages it. He's always been secure with the fact that she's smarter, better looking, and more successful than he is. He adores taking care of Marianna and being by her side.

"Why don't you stay the night?" Robin offers. "The party is going to get hectic and I was thinking we can have a family breakfast tomorrow morning." This option sounds far superior to my original plan of packing my apartment and torturing myself with the memories of my failed relationship.

"That'd be nice. Thank you."

She smiles, and we stand there awkwardly. If this were a Lifetime movie, she'd say, "You don't have to thank me, El. We're sisters." But it's not and we just look around the kitchen in silence. My mother-turned-mixologist interrupts our not-so-Hallmark moment.

"I made it extra strong," she says, handing me a cocktail that's almost pink instead of red due to the ratio of vodka to tomato juice.

"Thanks." I gulp it down as if it's water. She takes a sip of her more pigmented drink and Robin shoots her a disapproving glance.

"Mine's virgin, don't worry," she concedes.

"I'm going to help Jeff set up the piñata. Why don't you guys relax and catch up?" Robin says, giving us some time alone. My mom glances at her watch.

"Perfect! I didn't realize what time it was. There should be a Wendy rerun on!" "Wendy" to my mother means *The Wendy Williams Show,* and she rushes to the living room to turn it on.

"Come sit down with me, Ella. I love Wendy's hot-topics segment." I slide beside her, burrowing my head in her side as she struggles to figure out Robin's remote. I lift my head and help her out. "Oh, the guest is Sexy Indie Film Actor. Have you ever met him?" I nod yes with my head still buried in her lap. "That's who you should date next." My mother pets my hair, and even with all the hectic party preparations going on in the other room, I can already feel myself starting to relax.

· · · ·

I wake up on the sofa when the doorbell rings and my mother brings me a second round. "I can't believe I fell asleep. Has the party started?"

"It's okay. You've been through a lot and my baby needed the rest. I bet you haven't had a good night's sleep in a long time. You didn't miss anything. The children are arriving now."

"Good." I sip my beverage and walk over to the kitchen counter, where my purse has been resting, too. I pull a napkin out of it and call my niece over before she gets wrapped up in her friends.

"Marianna, this was Tween Superstar Actress's napkin. I know she's your favorite so I wanted you to have it." Her face lights up like I told her Christmas would now be 364 days a year instead of the other way around. Robin isn't impressed but that's never stopped her from instilling good manners in her child.

"What do we say to Aunt Ella?"

Marianna's face is still ecstatic. "Thank you, Aunt Ella!" She hugs me tightly and I'm marginally worried the compression won't agree with all of the alcohol I've consumed.

"You're welcome, sweet pea," I tell her.

"Why don't you go show your friends the bouncy castle and I will put this somewhere safe for you?" Robin suggests. Marianna grabs her friends and they run outside.

My sister is practically glaring at me. "A used napkin? Seriously?" She sighs. "Ella. She's a child. You couldn't have gone to Target?"

"It's a memento."

"A memento with a smeared fuchsia lip stain and God only knows how many species of germs," she grumbles. "Who knows where her lips have been? Besides at Ambiance," she says, reading the club's name off the napkin.

"You told me how much she loves Tween Superstar Actress and I grabbed it at a club before the busers threw it away. It's not a big deal. Besides, I'm sure the alcohol on her lips killed anything airborne or contagious."

Robin cracks a half smile and when she realizes I've noticed, she reverts to the expressionless condescension she does so well. "I don't want her becoming obsessed with this Hollywood stuff—" She cuts herself off.

"I thought it was a nice gesture."

Robin opens her mouth to speak but decides against whatever it is she was going to say and holds her tongue. Seeing as how I'm already in a fragile state, she made the right call.

She nods. "You're right. Thank you. I'm sure we'll be framing it. Let's just enjoy the party, okay?"

Enjoy the party, it turns out, was a little bit of an overstatement. Marianna passed out an hour into it because she ate every sweet in sight. It's one of the three days a year (Halloween and Easter being the other two) that Robin lets her eat candy, so the poor kid's sugar high turned into an overdose faster than she could say *Disneyland*.

Later, I help Robin and Jeff clean up, even though I'm almost as exhausted as Marianna looks.

Once the wrapping paper has been bagged, the dishes loaded into the dishwasher, and the minefield of toys cleaned, I tell Robin, "I'm going to head to bed."

"At six-thirty P.M.?" Jeff asks. "Hollywood's number-one party girl couldn't handle our blowout party. Alright!" He raises his hand for Robin to high-five him and she does. They laugh together at his cheesy joke.

"Good night, guys."

"Good night, El. Mom is in the blue room so take the yellow room. There are clean sheets on the bed and there are some T-shirts in the dresser drawer you can sleep in. I'll wake you up for breakfast tomorrow." I give Marianna a quick kiss, grab my purse, and make my way upstairs. Before I reach my room, I notice that the light is creeping out from underneath the door of my mom's room and knock.

"Come in," she answers. She's in bed reading this week's issue of *The Life.*

"I just wanted to say good night. I'm tuckered out."

"See you in the morning, sweetheart. Kiss, hug, squeeze," she says, performing each action in that order. "I love you."

. . . .

Unfortunately, my much-needed slumber doesn't last as long as I'd hoped. My iPhone starts buzzing relentlessly at 5 A.M. and does not stop. Whenever my phone rings early in the morning or late at night my body seizes up in terror. I know it's *The Life,* I feel it in my bones. The question is, what do they want? The e-mail titles include but are not limited to: "Emergency Back Reporting," "SOS," and "Breaking News."

I open the first e-mail to ascertain what's going on even though my brain is functioning at a more infantile level than Marianna's right now.

Uh-oh. A story broke overnight.

Not just any story. *The* story. Definitely the story of the year, possibly the story of my lifetime.

Okay, it's not as big a deal as a terrorist attack or a presidential assassination, but everyone is going to remember exactly where they were when they saw these photos. It's that big.

Not-So-Innocent Oversexualized Pop Star went crazy last night. And not in the "crazy" diva archetypal I-only-bathe-in-Evian celebrity kind of way—legit, needs-a-straitjacket insane.

She left her house at 1 A.M. with a paparazzi caravan in tow, went to a bar, had a few drinks with some girlfriends, and made a detour on the way home to a barbershop, where she shaved her head. She doesn't look drunk in the photos. Was she high? Did she have a psychotic break?

According to these e-mails, we have eyewitnesses who claim she started speaking in another language when she was asked a question and locked herself in the bathroom and refused to leave until the door was kicked in by EMS. The ambulance took her to the hospital and she was placed under a 5150 seventy-two-hour psychiatric hold. Thank God Jessica happened to spot her at Ambiance the other night and gave me all of her observations. She's been on so many assignments with me, her observations and details were as good as if I'd done them myself.

Maggie and Victoria are beside themselves. They know people will freak out when they wake up and read the news. Not-So-Innocent Oversexualized Pop Star is one of those celebrities that is universally loved, which only means people will love her meltdown even more. I admit, as a fan, I'm dying to know what happened.

The Life is frantically trying to construct a timeline of Not-So-Innocent Oversexualized Pop Star's activities for the past forty-eight hours and Maggie and Victoria's e-mails are asking if anyone has a source close to her, no matter how small.

Dear Freelancers,
Your new number-one priority for stories is Not-So-Innocent Oversexualized
Pop Star. We have her at Ambiance two nights ago, but we need more details!
No detail is too small. Anyone who can provide a source with accurate informa-
tion as to what might have caused Not-So-Innocent Oversexualized Pop Star's
breakdown or an exclusive story relating to this incident will have immunity
from the points system and will automatically keep their job. If you know
anyone that's seen her out and about recently, contact them ASAP.

Aside from her rare appearance at Ambiance the other night, I'd never heard of Not-So-Innocent Oversexualized Pop Star hitting the Hollywood club scene. She was not someone that I regularly wrote about in my files. In fact, she seemed to run in a different circle in Hollywood and before this meltdown kept her personal life shrouded in privacy. I can't fall back asleep so I log in to Facebook to see if I know anyone that has even the slightest connection to her. I'm down a social-media rabbit hole, lurking on profiles that are so far removed from mine that I don't even remember how I came to click on them. It's like I was on a social-media drug binge and don't realize that four hours have gone by until . . .

I smell my mom's famous French toast wafting through the house.

I hop out of bed and race downstairs. The kitchen is immaculate, sterile almost. The countertops sparkle and the table is set as if an etiquette expert were coming to breakfast to test Robin's proficiency. Being the perfectionist she is, there isn't a napkin ring out of place. There's no evidence that twenty toddlers were here hours ago. There's barely any evidence a toddler lives here now. I honestly don't care where I eat or which fork I eat it with as long as I can get my hands on my mom's meal ASAP!

"Yes!" I'm so excited for this French toast. I honestly have dreams about it. "Thank you, Mom."

"Nobody's French toast is better than Mom's," Robin adds. It's true. I don't care if I'm at the nicest brunch restaurant in town and they use locally sourced, organic ingredients and cage-free eggs from chickens that get daily Reiki healing, it will never be as good as my mom's secret recipe, and she knows it. I've long speculated that she adds crack to the egg mixture she uses to coat the bread because it's so addictive.

"Sit down, Ella, it's ready." This is the best surprise ever. I plop into the closest seat so I don't have to waste any time before dousing my French toast in syrup and devouring it.

"Where are Marianna and Jeff?" I ask. "If they don't get in on this soon I'm going to eat it all."

"They went out for a father-daughter breakfast," Robin says.

"Why would they do that? Oh well, more for me!"

"Actually . . ." My mom takes my hand. I feel my heart stop. A person taking my hand has not been working out well for me recently, so I'm dreading whatever is going to come out of her mouth next.

Robin and Mom are looking at each other. Mom continues. "They went because I wanted to talk to you. I'm not here for Marianna's birthday or for vacation. The truth is I'm here for a while. I have an open-ended ticket."

"Are you moving here?" I ask.

"Sort of." My mom stares at Robin.

"It's okay, Mom. Tell her." My mom takes Robin's hand as well.

"Ella, you know how much I love you," she begins. She takes a breath.

All thoughts of French toast are gone. I feel my rabid appetite completely dry up. "Mom, you're really scaring me."

"I've been diagnosed with acute myeloid leukemia," she says quickly.

There's silence in the kitchen. I don't know what to say. I don't know if I could speak if I knew what to say.

I squeeze her hand so hard she has to remove it because I might break one of her bones. Aside from my death grip on her hand I'm paralyzed. I don't know if I could move my body if I wanted to.

I realize Robin is speaking: "Mom is going to see an oncologist at my hospital who specializes in blood cancers. He's a friend of mine and he's going to do everything he can for her. This can be treatable."

I still can't speak and probably look like I've had a stroke and am in need of medical attention myself. I throw my arms around my mother and hug her tighter than I ever have in my life. Cancer? How can this be happening? She kisses the top of my forehead and rubs my back, but I refuse to lessen my grip.

"I'm going to be fine. I know Robin's colleague is going to give me the best care possible." My mother is the one diagnosed with a potentially terminal disease, yet she's trying to give me reassurance.

"I love you so much," I manage to muster.

"I know you do, sweetie." She pushes me back a little and wipes a tendril of hair out of my face.

" I don't know what I'd do if—"

"If nothing. I'm going to be fine and we're going to get through this together. The Warren women are strong. Every single one of us. Never forget that."

"We have an appointment with the oncologist next week if you want to come with us," Robin says. Her voice is softer than I've heard in a long time. "He'll be able to answer any questions you have and you can learn about Mom's treatment and what we can all do to make her more comfortable." Knowing that Robin has a plan, I feel my tears finally beginning to subside.

"Yes. Of course. Tell me when and I'll be there."

I stare at the remainder of the French toast on my plate. I can't stomach the thought of eating another bite. I feel nauseated and dizzy and like my heart is about to explode out of my chest.

"It will all be okay, Ella. I promise. Have I ever broken a promise to my baby girl?"

"No," I say, shaking my head back and forth.

"I'm certainly not starting now," she tells me.

Robin drives me home after breakfast. The drive is silent and not because we don't have anything to say but because we have too many things to say that neither of us want to actually say out loud. I get out of her car, despondent, realizing that another set of problems is waiting for me inside. Before I shut the door, Robin breaks the silence.

"I'll text you the doctor's appointment info later, okay?"

"Yeah. Thanks."

"Are you gonna be okay by yourself?" she asks. "I know breakups aren't ever easy and—"

"Trust me, Robin. Ethan is the last thing on my mind right now. All I care about is Mom," I tell her. She gives me a single nod.

"Call me if you need anything, El. Really, anything. And I promise I'm going to take good care of Mom."

"I know you will." I wave as she pulls away.

I walk inside my apartment and collapse on my bed. It's not like there's anywhere else to sit. My anxiety is skyrocketing and my mind is overanalyzing every potential scenario of my mother's illness. There are about 33 million search results for "what to do after you find out your parent has cancer" online. I Googled it in the car. But no one can tell me how to make the combination of impending doom and apathy go away. The more daunting thought is that if Ethan were here, I know he'd use his prowess with prose to concoct a comforting speech. But he's not here. I'm all alone and I don't want to be. Not right now.

I call Holiday. Each ring that passes without an answer draws a new tear from my eyes. Voice mail. I hang up without leaving a message.

I try Jessica next. Same thing. It's not their fault they have lives. And I'm sure that they're convinced that I hit rock bottom the other day so the only direction for me to go was up.

The only thing I want to do right now is not think and the only thing mindless enough to get everything off my mind is packing, so I start throwing my clothes in boxes.

. . . .

I'm sure Holiday did something fabulous last night and I don't want to wake her even though it's the early afternoon, so I quietly retrieve the spare key from underneath the flowerpot next to the front door. We're going to need to find a more discreet hiding spot once I'm moved in.

I'm exhausted. I can't wait to get this box of clothes through the door. As soon as I'm inside, I set it down so I can grab some water.

I walk into the kitchen and Holiday and Seth Rubin are making out like they are on a nature show.

She's sitting on top of the kitchen counter straddling him like he's the prey in a National Geographic special. Holiday is in a robe and luckily he's in a pair of boxer briefs, but I have to do a double take to make sure that one of my best friends is in fact getting busy with a married man and that I'm not still drunk or hallucinating. I can't unsee this!

My feet feel like they're glued to the ground so I can't move, even though my head is telling my body to bolt in the opposite direction. Seth catches me out of the corner of his eye and immediately pushes Holiday away from him. She turns to see why and stares at me, terrified. We are all looking at one another slightly embarrassed and not sure who should speak first or what to say.

"I'm going to go get dressed," Seth says for all of our benefits after a good thirty seconds. "Holiday, I'll see you in Canada in a few days," he says, trying to sound professional and like he wasn't caught with his hand in the British teakettle. He retreats upstairs and Holiday hops off the kitchen island. She opens the refrigerator and grabs the orange juice without uttering a word.

"You want some?" she asks as she pours a glass like nothing had just happened.

"Okay . . . so just to be clear, we're not going to talk about this?"

"There's nothing to talk about," she replies with a mixture of adamancy and tranquility, as if I'd asked her if she felt like having Italian food for dinner.

"Got it." I may need to pour my feelings out like an erupting volcano anytime my personal life hits turbulence—especially if I was having an affair with the married creator of my TV pilot—but she's entitled to handle her own life however she wants without judgment from me. She slides my glass of orange juice across to me. "I'm here if you do," I tell her.

"Ella, I only want to say this once. I *never* want to talk about this ever again with you or anyone. It never happened. Do you understand?"

"Understood."

"Good. I should probably get dressed as well. Lots to do before I head to Vancouver," she says, rushing off like the kitchen was on fire.

I did not see this one coming. First of all I thought she was into Tristan. Secondly, I've never known Holiday to go after another woman's man. Seth, now fully dressed, rushes out of the house without another word as I'm finishing my juice.

Ten

· · · · · · · · · · · · · · · · · · · ·

We're going to a party at Foreign Born Supernatural Superstar's house tonight.

Holiday texts me, even though my room is only 1000 square feet away from hers.

It will be the perfect bon voyage LA party! Plus the party is technically "public" so you can do some reporting without breaking your code. Be ready for 8 pm.

Foreign Born Supernatural Superstar is at the top of the A-list, which hopefully means his guests will be A-list and I will get a good scoop for *The Life* and show them that I'm taking initiative and using my own sources to try to get a story for them. Even though they've used everything I turned in online, I need a magazine-worthy cover story if I want to beat out the other girls and save my job.

"I got us an Uber. You've been through a lot lately. You deserve a night to get a little bit tipsy while you search for your story," she says as we are leaving the house that evening. This is the second time in a week that I want to officially convert my religion to Holi-tology.

"Thank you."

"Shut up and get in," she says, holding the door open for me. The party is in the Bird Streets, not too far away, and as we both finish applying a final coat of lip gloss I come to find out that Holiday has another agenda when she asks, "What's your game plan?"

"Game plan?"

"Yes. Game plan." She stares at me in disbelief that I have not calculated every move tonight already. "This party will be a great place to meet guys."

"I don't know if I'm quite ready for that, Hol."

"Life doesn't care if you're not ready. In fact that's usually when you end up meeting someone." She pulls a pack of violet candies from her purse and offers me one. "You may be in the hustle and bustle of the Hollywood nightlife scene but you've been out of the dating scene for a while. You have to use technique to navigate your way through the crowd to find the right guy, now that you're on the pull."

"Holiday, are you trying to be my friend or my pimp? I won't find a good story if I'm off trying to be a ho."

"Bollocks." It is. I acquiesce. I'd rather listen to her than obsess over my mom's doctor's appointment. I haven't told Holiday yet because if I say it out loud, it's real and I'm not ready to face that yet.

"Alright, I'm listening." Her face shines and at first I can't tell if it's from the makeup or if it's her excitement about educating me on how to triumph in the battle of the sexes. It becomes clear that she's more enthusiastic about being able to impart her wisdom than she was when Armani launched a makeup line.

"The first, and in my opinion, most important step, is eye contact."

"Make eye contact," I repeat.

"No. Not *just* eye contact. It's not that simple." Of course it isn't. "It has to be quick. A pouty, seductive smile and a glance directly into the eyes and then immediately divert your attention back to whoever you were talking to before."

Holiday turns her head and gives herself a moment of preparation before she whips her head around using me as her subject and demonstrates her well-researched tactic. I have to admit that I'm impressed. She's so convincing that I can't help but let out an uncomfortable laugh. She continues.

"You can't let it linger or the eye contact turns into full-contact eye-fucking and that is far too aggressive. You want the man to be the alpha and feel like the hunter."

"Eye contact, don't eye-fuck," I reiterate.

"If, and when, the eye-contact guy, or any other guy for that matter approaches you—and always let them approach you, let him speak first," she commands. I nod in agreement. "During your conversation, make sure to ask questions about him. Men love nothing more than talking about themselves . . . and sports." I nod. "Next, casually interject the most fascinating facts about yourself without seeming self-absorbed or egotistical.

This is a delicate balance that you will have to find through trial and error. Whatever you do, don't play dumb," she emphasizes.

I may not have been out on a date in a few years, but Holiday is acting like I have the etiquette and social skills of someone who's just been released from prison—although in some weird existential way I guess I am. With every rule and tip she enjoys educating me on her guide to seduction more and more, so I play along and keep my mouth shut. Her tutelage concludes as we pull up at Foreign Born Supernatural Superstar's house. My phone vibrates and I better check it because if it's something that needs a response there's no telling if there will be service at Foreign Born Supernatural Superstar's house.

El, wanted to remind you about Mom's doctor's appointment tomorrow. 9 am. I know she's really happy you're coming. We'll see you then. Love you.

I swallow as I read the text.

"Everything okay, darling?"

I fight back the tears I know are dying to be released. "Yeah." My meek tone isn't convincing either of us.

"You can do this, El. I think you're ready but if you don't want to go, we don't have to." She thinks I'm nervous about interacting with men and I would honestly trade anything for my nerves to be occupied by sexual politics instead of leukemia logistics. Holiday bats her sympathetic puppy dog eyes at me.

"I'm okay," I assure her. Holiday nods. "It will take my mind off everything for the night and earning some points wouldn't hurt."

Before getting out we do one final makeup check in the car mirror and quickly swipe a lint roller over our dresses as we exit the car. As we approach the front door I notice that there is a security guard in a black-on-black suit and an earpiece checking the list as Holiday and I confidently stride up to his post.

"Holiday Hall, plus one." He checks his list without even the trace of a smile and he's paying more attention to his task than any TSA agent I've ever come across at LAX. He returns from his list and glances at us sternly. He pulls two sheets of paper from behind his list on the clipboard and hands them to us with Montblanc pens.

"If you'd like to enter the party each of you must sign nondisclosure agreements. I'll also need to take a photo of you with your driver's license and the completed NDA," he tells us.

He's staring at us as if we're ex-cons here to case the joint, and his humorless demeanor is mildly terrifying. I feel a shooting pain in my foot. If I sign this NDA and I give information to *The Life* and they use it I could theoretically be sued—not that I have anything for Foreign Born Supernatural Superstar to take. If I don't sign I can't go in and there's no chance of me getting any gossip and my job will still be in jeopardy. I make the split-second executive decision to roll the dice and sign. As I'm about to take the pen to paper I'm interrupted.

"Holiday! How are you?" It's Foreign Born Supernatural Superstar.

"Good, and yourself?" They double air-kiss each other.

"Algernon, they don't need to sign these. This is Holiday Hall! She's one of us." Algernon, whom I've now gathered is his private security guard, winces before retrieving the blank forms from us. I know that he wants to roll his eyes at us but he's required to keep his stone-cold face stoic.

"*Grazzi.* Don't you look dashing," Holiday flirts.

"Foreign Born Supernatural Superstar, this is Bella." She winks at me as she calls me Bella, enjoying the secrecy of our inside joke.

"Nice to meet you, Bella. Ladies, follow me."

We make our way through the house. We can both instantly feel that this party has a different vibe and energy from any of Holiday's parties. Her parties feel elegant and extravagant from the moment you walk in. Holiday is able to give her guests the sensation that they are at an exclusive affair while still providing a comfortable atmosphere. While this party has attempted to emulate that feeling with elements like waiters offering guests both champagne and cigars, other additions like the ice luge next to the bar make it feel fratty. We continue to follow Foreign Born Supernatural Superstar as we navigate our way through the large living room that is surprisingly already full, seeing as people rarely show up when a party actually starts—except for me.

"Enjoy yourselves. Will you ladies please excuse me?"

"Nice to meet you," I call out as he mingles and greets his other guests.

Aha! My first sighting of the night. Former Supermodel Turned Actress Turned Jersey Chaser is here. A jersey chaser is a woman that exclusively dates professional athletes. Without needing to say anything we turn in the direction of the bar and make that our destination.

After we grab our champagne we plant ourselves right next to Former Supermodel Turned Actress Turned Jersey Chaser. We pretend to have our own conversation, which I must say we've gotten very good at, while I'm surreptitiously listening to her. She's complaining to Triple Threat Pop Music Diva about her new boyfriend's teammates branding her as a curse.

"I know they're trying to convince him to break up with me," she whines. "They think this losing streak is all my fault but maybe if they concentrated more on practice and less on me they would actually win a game and realize I'm not the problem!" Triple Threat Pop Music Diva nods her head and takes a large gulp of her drink. "I mean I can't be bad luck. I've always been the best at everything I've ever tried."

Holiday and I look at each other and roll our eyes. We continue our faux conversation and I pull out my phone while Holiday purposely rambles on so we can continue to listen inconspicuously. I take note of what Former Supermodel Turned Actress Turned Jersey Chaser and Triple Threat Pop Music Diva are drinking and what kind of moods they are in—narcissistic and disinterested. Triple Threat Pop Music Diva is scanning the crowd, trying to find an exit strategy, and looks like she'd rather stab herself in the ears than talk to a woman whom most men in America fantasize about daily. Not cover story–worthy but it might earn me a few points. If this is how the night is starting off I'm sure it will get better as it gets later. I do like it when I spot at least one celebrity at the beginning of the night. If I don't have any notes on celebrities and the night is beginning to come to a close I get anxious that I might have missed someone.

As I'm transcribing the details I've just seen I try to elbow Holiday, but I seem to miss and catch air instead. I return to eye level and notice that she's found Tristan and has begun flirting. With "the thing that we are never going to discuss and in her mind never happened" I witnessed the other day, I hope she knows what she's doing. Her pilot shoot could get messy if Tristan and Seth find out about each other, and for all of their sakes I hope they don't.

I return to my iPhone and as I tilt my head down I notice a dark shadow standing over me. Fuck! Have I been busted by security? I've barely been here for twenty minutes. I pray that I'm not about to be removed from the premises in an embarrassing scene, and then the figure towering over me speaks.

"Do you ever put that thing down?"

Oh. My. God. Nick Williams! I fumble my phone and nearly drop it. Nick catches it and hands the phone to me.

"I was wondering when I was going to run into you again," he says.

"Oh? Really?" I try to seem coquettish like Holiday instructed, but I'm pretty sure almost dropping my phone ruined any sex appeal I may have had.

"It seemed like only a matter of time before you showed up somewhere with Holiday. I'm glad it's tonight." Nick's making eye contact with me, a good sign according to Holiday, and the sexual tension between us is palpable. I know that Ethan just broke up with me like a minute ago and technically I'm on the rebound, but between that and the news about my mom I've received an unwanted reminder that things can change in a moment and I need to live my life instead of wallowing in some sort of glamorous despair. Besides, Nick is smart and easy to talk to and I was more than attracted to him when I wasn't single so I might as well go for it now that I am. As I'm imagining what his stubble would feel like when his face is pressed against mine during a passionate kiss I realize it's been seconds since I've said anything.

I take a sip of my drink for courage. "What are you doing here?" Not a home run but not bad for my first at bat in a few years.

"I represent Foreign Born Supernatural Superstar." Duh. "How've you been?" he asks as he kisses me on the cheek. His stubble feels exactly like I'd just imagined it, rough with a hint of tenderness. When his lips connect with my face I feel the physical manifestation of our chemistry as a tingle inside of my cheek.

"That's a loaded question." I'm trying not to mumble and I'm *really* trying to pretend like I'm a normal person. He's gorgeous and I'm losing my nerve. I remember Nick being hot, but was he *this* hot when I first met him? I'm around handsome celebrities almost every day but none of them make me jittery.

"Yeah?" I've piqued his curiosity. Holiday didn't remind me in her tutorial, but I happen to remember that mystery and intrigue are key components in attraction.

"Yeah." I let his interest linger. "Anyway, how are you?"

I'm trying to focus on his response but my brain is running in circles trying to figure out how to let him know that I'm single now. If I come right out and say it I'll look like I'm desperate, or it might come across like I only want to sleep with him. While both may be true, I don't want him to think either of those things. If I don't say anything, he'll think

I'm still with Ethan. Maybe he'll ask? Come on, Ella, why the hell would he ask? Or maybe I can go back to sixth grade and have Holiday casually slip it into the conversation when she talks to him? Oh my God, this is ridiculous. I try to center myself so I can go with the flow of conversation and stop trying to manipulate it. No wonder Holiday insisted her lecture was mandatory.

". . . By the way, you look fantastic tonight." That I heard! "I see your glass is empty. Should we go to the bar and get you another drink?"

I nod my head. He takes the lead and guides me through the party, which I notice has doubled in size while I was entranced with Nick.

"Another champagne?" he asks.

"Yes, please."

Holiday sashays up to us with Tristan by her side. "Hi, Nick! Any feedback from the movie audition I put on tape?"

"They said that you have a great look but you need to work on your pacing."

"Oh well, fuck them. What do they know?" Holiday says with a wink and her charismatic smile.

"Well, they are Warner Bros., so a lot." Holiday disregards his comment. "I'm sure the *Benedict Canyon* pilot will be picked up so don't worry about it. Once it premieres the offers will be pouring in. You ready to shoot?"

"Beyond ready. I can't wait to get out of LA for a little." She gives another wink, this time to Tristan, and both Nick and I notice as he hands me my drink.

"Some of us are going to miss you," I tell her.

"Darling, it's only two weeks. Nick, will you keep Ella company for me while I'm gone so she doesn't get too lonely?" He turns to me.

"I'd be happy to but I'm not sure how her boyfriend would feel about that."

"Something tells me he wouldn't be bothered," Holiday says. "Besides we'd have to find him first."

I bite my lower lip.

"Oh, I see. So no boyfriend anymore?"

I shake my head.

"Well, then I would be happy to help keep Ella occupied." I nervously laugh. Nick places his hand on the small of my back like they are magnets drawn to each other. "Would you excuse me for a moment? Non—

Drug Addict Former Child Star Turned Entrepreneur is here and I've been trying to sign her for weeks. I'll be right back." In full-on agent mode he makes his way through the crowd.

"Holiday! What was that? That was so embarrassing. You really are acting like my pimp."

"I know you, Ella. I could see the look in your eyes. You want him but you weren't going to make a move. I was just helping you along."

"Was it bad?" I ask Tristan.

"Nah. He's totally into you too," he says.

"Really?"

"For sure," he affirms. At a party like this where all there are is options, no guy is going to spend that much time talking to one girl unless he's into her.

"Sorry, Hol. I'm just stressed out. You were right. This sexual-politics stuff is hard."

"That's why I helped." She winks. "I know you didn't ask for my opinion but I think he'd be perfect for you. He's really ambitious and successful and takes no prisoners in business, but he's also just a good guy. He's real. Nick doesn't do bullshit. Definitely not the kind of guy that refuses to commit because he's waiting to see if someone better comes along. He's the perfect nice guy with asshole potential."

Holiday and I always joke that is the quality we want most in our ideal mate. You don't want to actually date an asshole but you don't want to be with someone who is so nice he lets you get away with whatever you want.

As we chat I scan the crowd again. I see someone that I know I've seen before but I can't place her. Blond, preppy, nose seems like it has surgically been turned up.

"Hol, do you know who that girl is?" I ask, nodding to the corner.

"Which girl?" she wonders.

"The one in the Lilly Pulitzer dress."

"Never seen her before in my life," she says.

"Are you sure? She looks so familiar to me." I continue studying her. My gut is very rarely wrong, but I don't think she's a celebrity.

"I'm positive. I'd remember her face and snotty attitude. She needs to have about five cocktails and loosen up." Holiday is right. That sourpuss is pretty unforgettable. "You must've seen her around town."

"Yeah, that must be it."

"Don't worry, darling. I won't let you miss anyone," she says with a wink. Tristan doesn't seem to think our conversation is anything out of the realm of ordinary Hollywood party gossip.

Holiday raises her glass.

"To glamour and love," she says. We clink glasses and Tristan laughs, amused at our ritual. I see Sexy Indie Film Actor in the crowd. I need to stop paying so much attention to Nick and focus on my job but Nick returns moments later and my attention returns to him.

"You want to go sit down?" he asks.

"Sure." I follow him. It's one of those walks that you know is going to change your life even if you aren't quite sure how yet. We sit and stare at each other. "So . . ."

"So . . ." He brushes a rogue piece of hair out of my face. "I'm glad I get to see you again."

"Me, too." I can feel my cheeks heating up and turning bright red. I'm never this bashful with celebrities but he makes me nervous.

"I was hoping we'd get to know each other better." He takes a sip of his scotch and stares at me again.

"Were you?" I flirt.

"I was. Ask me anything." He gestures with his hands that nothing is off-limits.

"Okay." I tap my finger to my chin. "Why did you want to become an agent?"

"Well, I was born and raised in LA. I've been in the business since I was a kid. I was a child actor—"

I can't stop myself from interrupting. "Wait, a child actor! Excuse me. Anything I may have seen you in?"

"My television work wasn't exactly stellar, but I did some commercials you may have seen. I was in these commercials for this soup company when I was about nine."

My eyes widen. "Which ones?" I'm hanging on his every word and analyzing his features, trying to determine if he could be any of the child actors I remember from my childhood.

"Sawyer's Soup." It *is* him.

"Oh. My. God. You were the Sawyer's Soup kid! 'It warms the tummy and the heart,'" I mimic.

"Yes. That was me," he confesses, slightly embarrassed, finishing his beverage.

"You were so adorable!"

"I don't think I turned out that bad." He smiles to show off.

"You know what I mean. Kid adorable. Wow, I didn't know that you were a bona fide celebrity," I gush, brushing my arm against his.

"In this crowd you're calling me the celebrity?"

"Oh, yeah. You have the nostalgia factor going for you. I mean, who doesn't remember those commercials? You have to do it for me." I can tell he doesn't want to. "Please? Please, say it? Are you going to make me beg?"

He hangs his head for a moment to "prepare" and when he lifts it back up he has transformed right back into the Sawyer's Soup spokeskid. He raises his voice. "It warms the tummy and the heart."

It's exactly the same as when he was a child. I cheer and clap and can tell he's enjoying the attention much more than he is pretending to let on.

"That was amazing. I cannot believe you are the Sawyer's Soup kid. Shouldn't there be a special about you on VH1 or a Where Are They Now? photo on TMZ? Is it weird that I'm kind of turned on?"

"Definitely weird. But I like weird."

I playfully roll my eyes. "There's a lot of money in commercials, you clearly did well for yourself as an actor, so why the switch to the business side of the entertainment industry?"

Nick sighs. "Acting is so fickle and I wasn't a huge fan of the spotlight. I wasn't even planning on staying in the industry at all but I'm good at it and it's great money."

"Yeah, it's hard to turn down good money," I say under my breath. Another thing we relate on.

"My dad split around the time I did those commercials. I think my mom got me into them to make me feel special after he left. It's a good thing I did and we had that extra money." He pauses. "A few years later my mom was diagnosed with ALS and couldn't work as much so we used my commercial money to live on and put me through school and take care of her." I feel tears welling up and I do everything I can not to cry. I want to say something but I don't know what. Why did he have to bring up his mom? And his sick mom at that. I want to escape the reality of mine for a night and now she's all I can think about. "I wanted to do something that I thought would make her proud so I decided to go to law school and become a health-care advocate." I realize my hand is covering my mouth and I quickly remove it. "While I was in law school my old agent offered me an internship in the mail room at Epic Agency. One thing led to another and after I passed the bar the agency offered me a job."

"Wow." I'm thoroughly impressed but Nick is modest.

"My connections from my acting days helped me build a great client roster and I was good at it and I liked it and my mom encouraged me to follow my newfound passion. In terms of being an agent, I guess it chose me." He stares at his empty glass. "I try and justify the career transition by doing pro bono legal work for the Los Angeles chapters of ALS organizations to honor my mom. It makes me feel less like another Hollywood sellout."

Maybe this is the alcohol settling in, but it feels like his warmth is surrounding me. Nick is a good guy, I realize, and not in that colloquial kind of way. He is a *really* good guy. Those other "good guys" feel like they exist only in the movies and not in real life, especially in Hollywood.

"I bet she's incredibly proud of you," I assure him.

"She passed away while I was in college."

' That's it, there's no holding back anymore. "God, Nick, I'm so sorry," I manage to get out.

"It's okay. I'm okay. It was a long time ago."

My lips quiver and I am on the verge of an unexpected outpouring of emotion. "Are you okay?"

"I just found out that my mom has leukemia." He grabs me without another word and kisses the top of my head. I know that I barely even know him but for some reason he's comforting. He caresses my cheek. "I haven't even told Holiday yet," I confess. "I didn't want it to be real and if I told someone outside of my family it would be." He won't let go of me and I don't want him to.

"If you need anything, to talk or to get your mind off it, I'm here," he tells me, massaging the back of my head.

I look up at him with gratitude. "Who are you?" He pauses, confused, and I have to admit the truth. "I had this preconceived notion that you were this completely other guy."

"You thought I was just another asshole agent," he says with a nod of the head.

"No, I . . . well, maybe a little. You're just so handsome and charming and persuasive I figured you had to be—but I was still totally attracted to you."

He laughs. "Well as long as you were still attracted to me." We both let out a small laugh and he stares at me like he wants me but in a sweet way, like he wants to hold my hand and be there for me and give me an orgasm at the same time. "Would you still think I was a nice guy if I ask you if you want to get out of here? Maybe go somewhere a little quieter for another drink?" There's nothing I want more than to be whisked away with Nick but there's no way I'm going to let the opportunity to rack up points for Victoria pass me by. I *need* to stay here. Quick, Ella. Think of something.

"I'd love to but I feel bad since Holiday is leaving for Canada and I'm supposed to spend time with her." He looks over at Holiday, who's making out with Tristan in the middle of the room as if they were alone and in an R-rated movie. Not my most thoroughly researched excuse.

"I think she's okay." He smirks.

"Even so, hos before bros." I pound my chest like a frat bro and he laughs and is still as amused by me as he was the night we met. "I'd love a rain check sometime, though." He leans in and kisses me. His kiss is like a defibrillator and after the past few days I feel like I've been shocked back to life after only going through the motions.

Eleven

. . . .

Oh no! It's 8:30 A.M.! I don't know how I'm going to make it to the hospital in rush-hour traffic on time, but I will. I have to. I throw my hair in a ponytail as I leap out of bed. I catch a glimpse of myself in the mirror as I hurriedly brush my teeth and look less like Caring Daughter and more like Singer Slash Infamous Strung-Out Widow of World's Biggest Rock Star with the crusty mascara smeared across my face and my foundation now in only clustered patches. I grab my phone from the charger as I scurry out of the house. Robin will never forgive me or let me forget it if I'm late to meet my mom's new oncologist.

I throw my disorganized Cuyana leather tote on the passenger seat and rush to the hospital. I floor it and refuse to heed all of the traffic signs and signals, and pray that my reckless driving won't result in my being a patient at the hospital where I'm going. I race against the clock and decide to valet my car when I reach the hospital and somehow by the grace of God I manage to make it through the gargantuan maze to Dr. Jacobs's office with two minutes to spare.

When I arrive in the waiting room, I find my mother is reading this week's issue of *The Life* and Robin is updating her patients' charts.

"Hi." I go in to hug my mom, then Robin.

"You look lovely, El," my mom compliments. I know that I don't and she's being polite, a trait Robin opts not to mimic at the moment. Instead, she glances me up and down with the perfect combination of contempt and judgment. Even though I'm technically here on time, in Robin time, I'm late. She continues charting. My mom returns to *The Life,* enamored, and I search through my e-mails.

Nice work, Ella. I had other reporting from this party but yours is much better
and we'll use your observations online. You'll see your points reflected in the
next scoring e-mail.
Victoria

Nothing from Maggie. In fact, her e-mail bounced back, which is odd, but all that really matters is that Victoria received my file and it will calculate into my points for the week. My mother's pointy elbow pokes me to get my attention and I shift my focus to her. She moves her finger to the bottom right corner of her page in the magazine.

REPORTING BY ELLA WARREN

"Seeing your name in here will never get old." She beams. Robin intentionally keeps her attention fixed on her work so she neither has to argue nor feign enthusiasm for the sake of maintaining peace in an already less than ideal situation. I cock my head to the side and rest it on my mother's shoulder. I'm in a losing battle with my lethargy so I shut my eyes for a moment to recharge. I could fall asleep like this so easily right now. My body is punishing me for my lack of sleep and choosing points over my physical well-being.

"Joan Warren," the nurse calls. We march over to her single file. She looks like she's my age and motions for us to follow behind her floral scrubs and escorts us into Room Four. She lays a chart very similar to the ones that Robin has been distracting herself with on the counter. "Joan, I need to get your vital signs and then Dr. Jacobs will be in. Would you please step on the scale?" My mother complies. I study Robin and the nurse to see if any of the numbers cause concern but neither provide any indication either way. She continues taking my mom's blood pressure and temperature. "Any other physical problems?" she asks.

"No," my mother answers.

The nurse slides the chart into the holder on the door and leaves us all in silence as it shuts. I hadn't noticed the room is blanketed with posters and pamphlets for everything a layman could ever want or need to know about leukemia. My mother stares in front of her with a smile as if she's here for one of our doctor's appointments like she did when we needed our annual physical for sleepaway camp. I also look straight ahead because the reality that my mother is very sick is setting in and I fear that one haphazard glance at something might induce a flood of tears and that's the last thing she needs right now.

I'm concentrating so intently on not looking at anything that my widened eyes begin to dry out. I hear my mom's file being taken out of the holder and rifled through like it was one of those animation flip-books and the door opens. Robin jumps out of her seat to acknowledge her colleague and her entire demeanor changes. She's gone from egomaniacal know-it-all to fawning admirer with a twist of a doorknob.

"Hello, Robin," he says, shaking her hand. Dr. Jacobs is in his early fifties with dark hair that's only starting to salt-and-pepper and a sky-blue button-down tucked into his dark gray pants. I'd come to find out that his greeting is the most genial he ever gets, and while according to Robin and the American Medical Association he's the country's leading hematologist and oncologist for leukemia, his bedside manner leaves something to be desired.

"This is my mother, Joan Warren," she introduces with a newfound meek voice. I've never seen adult Robin behave in any way other than authoritatively and never timid, like she is now. Dr. Jacobs shakes her hand but quickly and is more eager to get down to brass tacks than socialize. I don't bother to introduce myself. While I most likely won't be inviting him to Holiday's next dinner party, if he can cure my mother, I will endure any form of botched social decorum he desires. Dr. Jacobs studies my mother's chart, nodding as though this is not the first time he's reviewing her case. He does that thing where he licks his index finger before he flips a page and his beady eyes absorb the information.

"How are you feeling, Joan?" he asks.

"Okay, I guess. I'm not really sure what cancer is supposed to feel like."

"It doesn't feel like anything, but if you are having any symptoms I need to know about them."

"I've lost some weight recently but that's all that comes to mind."

Dr. Jacobs makes a note. "I'd like to get you checked into the hospital and start you on chemo ASAP."

"How long will I be here for?" she asks with the first hint of fear I've seen from her.

"Hopefully about a month. If you go into remission or even if your blood counts are doing okay I will let you go home. We'll do a bone-marrow biopsy on day fifteen to see whether the blasts have been cleared from the marrow, but we need a full twenty-eight days to get confirmation of remission."

My mother takes a deep inhale.

"Joan, I'm going to be very aggressive with your treatment. Aside from your AML your body is functioning well for your age. I want to get some blood work from you today to determine what chemotherapy I'm going to give you and will be monitoring the combination and dosage throughout your treatment. We'll get you in and started within the week."

Robin is feverishly taking notes like I do for work, although in this case the devil really is in the details, since we're dealing with life and death.

"Do you have any questions for me?"

My mother purses her lips. She obviously has one but she's hesitant.

"Mom, it's alright. Whatever it is, the time to ask is now while Dr. Jacobs is here. No matter how uncomfortable the question makes you or if you think it might upset us." Robin rubs her back. "Ella and I can handle the answer to anything you want to know." I nod in agreement. Her emphatic nature is usually a nuisance, but this time it came in handy because she convinced my mom to speak up.

"What are my chances?" Instead of looking away she stares directly at Dr. Jacobs. Whatever his answer is, she's ready for it. For his part, Dr. Jacobs doesn't adjust his tone or use any flowery language for the sake of being conciliatory.

"Joan, I'm hopeful about your case but I can't make you any promises. No one can." I glance at my mom to check in and make sure she's okay. She isn't showing any emotion or sadness if she's feeling any. "Medicine isn't perfect and neither am I. But I am the best at treating leukemia and I give you my word I'm going to give you my best. I can't fight for you; I need to fight with you. I need you to want to do whatever it takes and be unwilling to give up."

"I'm ready to fight," she announces. Dr. Jacobs appears pleased that he won't need to do much coddling with her.

"Do you have any other questions?" Robin asks.

My mother shakes her head, stoically.

Dr. Jacobs returns to her chart and makes a few more notations.

"The nurse will be back and will give you the rest of the information you need for prior care and what to expect during treatments, side effects, and everything else you've never wanted to know." His eyes are still engrossed in her chart while he rattles off what I imagine is his typical Things to Know Before Chemo speech, by rote. The days after your chemo treatments will most likely be worse than any hangover you've ever had. Try to eat as much as possible in the days before you're admitted to the hospital."

"You're probably the only man in Los Angeles who says that to women," I quip. He looks up from the chart and glares at me, unamused with my attempt at humor, and returns to the chart.

"Make sure you're eating the right foods. Once you start the chemo your appetite will most likely decrease and your taste buds will change, so I want you to make sure you're eating whenever you have an appetite."

"She will," Robin interjects. "I'll make sure of it."

Dr. Jacobs is indifferent to Robin's obsequious attitude. "The nurse will get you set up for checking into the hospital and your first cycle of chemo." He scribbles the last bit of information down and closes the chart. "Call me if you have any emergencies before then." Dr. Jacobs shakes my mother's hand.

"Thank you," my mother says.

Robin once again rises as a sign of acknowledgment and chimes in, "Thank you, Dr. Jacobs. I really appreciate you taking the time to help us." He accepts her gratitude but leaves without furthering the conversation. Robin stares with esteem as he exits. She lets out a venerating sigh and I realize Robin doesn't hate celebrities; she just doesn't like the ones that come from Hollywood. I unintentionally gasp at the revelation.

"Are you okay?" she asks me.

"Uh-huh," I assure her. I can't help but snicker a little in her direction.

"What is it then?" she insists.

"You were totally fangirling over Dr. Jacobs."

"Oh come on. I was not," she argues.

"Yes, you were." I realize he's like her medical version of Sexy Indie Film Actor.

"No. Absolutely not," she maintains.

I give my eyelashes a coy flutter before I begin my imitation of her. "Hi, Dr. Jacobs."

"I did not do that," she insists. She rolls her shoulders back and puffs her chest out.

"Dr. Jacobs, if you ever need anything, and I mean *anything*—"

She cuts me off. "That's enough, Ella!" she screeches. I've never heard her yell with this kind of disdain before.

"Girls, please," my mother demands with a sharp yet calm voice. She was never one for raising her voice and now that she has I feel like I'm ten again.

"I'm sorry, Mom. I didn't really sleep last night. I didn't mean to be so combative," I explain. I feel horrible for trying to rile my sister up now of all times.

"I'm sorry too, Mom." Robin, now desperately afraid of being seen as anything less than perfect, grabs the chance to reclaim her title and changes the subject. "How are you feeling about all of this?"

"I'm fine. I wasn't expecting to have to live in the hospital for a month. I don't know why but my mind didn't register that as a possibility."

"Mom. Ella and I will come for chemo and to visit. I'm here all the time anyway, it will be just the same as if you were staying at my house. But maybe a little less disruptive without Marianna. It's going to be okay."

"It is," she says, sanguine. "I don't want either of you to worry. I will be just fine. I'm going to fight this . . ." she asserts. This was the first time I'd seen a full return of the mother that I grew up with. She's always been a positive woman who never let anyone's opinions or odds stop her from doing anything she set her mind to. ". . . Or it will kill me," she jokes. I can't help but laugh but Robin is not enjoying her wisecrack.

"Don't say that. I don't know what I'd do if—"

My mother doesn't let her finish. She doesn't want to bring our emotions to that place. "Ella, can you run and grab me a café au lait somewhere while we handle everything with the nurse?" my mom asks. Coffee? I would swim to Colombia for coffee right now. Salvation! "And a muffin too," she adds. "Might as well start increasing my caloric intake now."

"You got it. I'll be back in a few minutes."

"Go to the cart. It's much better than the coffee in the cafeteria," Robin instructs. "It's—"

"Robin, I think I can find a coffee cart." I don't mean to snap at her again but her attitude causes me to go into defense mode. She doesn't pursue her instruction any further and I'm glad I will have a few minutes to collect myself so I don't blow up at her again.

Leaving Dr. Jacobs's office, I feel lighter and my finger almost dances when I use it to call for the elevator.

As I round the corner to the plaza level to finally procure my mother's coffee I'm almost crushed by a stampede that's moving faster and with more purpose than I've seen cops busting a meth lab on the news. While the rush of people is almost moving at light speed, they don't move fast enough. It's Not-So-Innocent Oversexualized Pop Star flanked by security guards, her father, and an entourage. I can't believe I'm seeing her and that my sighting was at the hospital instead of an invitation-only Beverly Hills boutique. Despite Not-So-Innocent Oversexualized Pop Star's pace, my reporter's intuition kicks in and I immediately start looking for the small details I know *The Life* craves. First, I notice her pink wig. Then the energy drink in her hand and her now-passé navy-blue velour tracksuit. She struts down the corridor as if it were the tents in Bryant Park during NYC's Fashion Week.

I whip out my iPhone and write out everything I see, even noting that Not-So-Innocent Oversexualized Pop Star left a trail of her eponymous perfume as she sped past me. I realize that I'm shaking while typing because I know how much a sighting of her will mean to *The Life* and the points it will garner for me. As I'm transcribing my astute observations, it strikes me as odd that Not-So-Innocent Oversexualized Pop Star walked by me at all. The psychiatric unit is on the opposite side of the hospital, but perhaps they are trying to shield her from the paparazzi and there's a back door or tunnel that would provide her with a more private exit strategy. No matter, I hit Send. A Not-So-Innocent Oversexualized Pop Star sighting in addition to what I turned in this morning—this should have Victoria thinking of me as one of her best assets!

I return to my coffee mission. I don't really need caffeine anymore as that get gave me a boost of energy, but I know my mom wants one and I might as well bring one for Robin too as a peace offering.

"Three café au laits, and one blueberry muffin, please," I order.

"I'm obligated to tell you our muffins are gluten-free and made with nut-free coconut flour. Please sign this release if the ingredients comply with all of your dietary and allergy restrictions." And I thought a release for Foreign Born Supernatural Superstar's party was outrageous. What a difference twelve hours makes. I sigh with disbelief as I sign the release and while I wait for my order my phone buzzes incessantly. I feel a surge of delight because I'm pretty sure it's a response to the Not-So-Innocent Oversexualized Pop Star item I just sent in. The first e-mail is from Victoria.

This is fantastic! It's definitely going in the magazine.
Victoria

A sense of relief washes over my body and it occurs to me that though I'm here for a literal life-or-death situation, this e-mail brings me a sense of calm and temporary stability that I desperately need, even if it's a little odd. My second e-mail isn't an e-mail at all. It's an automatic message that Maggie's e-mail has bounced back—again. I better shoot her a text so she can get the IT department on it ASAP. I doubt Victoria will cut her any slack if she misses any incoming tips or stories due to a technical difficulty.

Mags, sent you 2 e-mails and they both bounced back. Wanted to give u heads up.

Xo E

"Ella, your order is ready," the barista shouts. I throw my phone in my pocket, take the order, and make my way back up to Dr. Jacobs's office, where I find my mother in the waiting room, alone.

"One café au lait and one blueberry muffin that has no nuts or gluten. I hope it has a taste." I hand her the drink and pastry. The coffee hits her lips as soon as it leaves my hands.

"Thank you, El."

I take a seat next to her. "Where's Robin?"

"Oh, you know her. She's triple-checking all of the information with the nurse."

"Of course she is." I stop myself from rolling my eyes as I usually would, because for once Robin's usually annoying neurosis is beneficial. I remove my coffee from the holder and feel rejuvenated after my first sip. I feel my phone vibrate again through my pocket and place Robin's coffee on the floor. It's probably just Maggie replying to my text, but I should check. I unlock my home screen and it's a number I don't have saved with a 310 area code.

Unknown Number: Had so much fun hanging with you last night. I want to see you again. Dinner the day after tomorrow?

It's Nick! I have a quick internal debate about whether to answer now or make him sweat it out for a few minutes but my excitement and eagerness trump the rules.

Ella: Hi you. Sounds good ☺

He clearly isn't too concerned about the game either as his response is immediate.

Nick: I'll make a reservation and get the details over to you. Looking forward to it.

Ella: Me too.

I'm brought back to the room when I realize my mother is talking to me.

"Ella, who's that?" she pries in her cute, excited voice. A stark contrast to the tone she used a few minutes ago when asking about her survival chances.

"Huh?" I'm back to reality but there's still a slight euphoria preventing me from full brain function. "Oh, just this guy," I tell her, shrugging it off. I mean I haven't even been on a date with Nick yet, what am I supposed to tell my mother? That I've already had imaginary mind-blowing sex with him no less than thirty times and I've decided I'm going to name our first daughter Evangeline and call her Evan. There's no way a girl named Evan won't be the most popular girl in high school.

"Just some guy?" She knows me better than that.

"Don't get too excited." I want to manage her expectations as well as my own. "We're going on our first date the night after tomorrow." I thought that would be enough for her but the third degree continues.

"Does this mystery man have a name?"

"Nick. Nick Williams."

"And how did you meet Nick Williams?" she inquires now, with a sparkle in her eye in addition to her smile. I wasn't planning on giving her the dossier on Nick yet but if it makes her happy it's literally the least I can do.

"We met through Holiday."

"I see." She nods her head with approval. "Well, Nick Williams made you smile for the first time since I've been here and that makes me smile." She bumps her shoulder with mine. "So he already has brownie points from your mother."

When I get home from the hospital I hurl myself backwards onto my bed as if it were an Olympic sport. If it were, that maneuver would've won me the gold medal. I'm so tired that I'm overtired and even as my back and every limb melt into my mattress my eyes won't close because they don't have the strength to do so. I'm barely lucid and all I'm seeing is the color gray but my ears work perfectly and I detect the clacking of Holiday's Jerome C. Rousseau beaded booties, which I've tried to steal no less than three times, coming down the hallway headed toward my room. I swiftly bring my hand to my mouth to make sure I didn't drool in my impotent state. I'd never live that embarrassment down.

"There you are," she buzzes as she enters without bothering to knock. "I came in this morning when I woke up to see if you wanted to get acai bowls to detox and cleanse our bodies of all of the toxins we imbibed last night but you weren't here." I don't bother trying to speak. She's on the express train of thought and I'm exhausted so I let her continue. "I figured you'd either snuck off to Nick's after how cozy the two of you were last night or you were kidnapped. I planned on texting Nick if I hadn't heard from you or received a ransom note by five P.M." I summon every ounce of energy I have to raise my head and neck up to respond to her while leaving the rest of my body viscous against the bed.

"How very proactive of you," I chime in. "Wasn't at Nick's and I'm only imprisoned by my credit-card debt. If I do ever go missing, find out if American Express has some secret lair they use to exile all of their customers that only make the monthly minimum payment; that's where I'll be. But I appreciate you looking out for me." I let my head and neck fall back to the bed.

"Then why in God's name did you get up so early? I felt like a total slug this morning. I couldn't have managed to make it out of bed before ten A.M. if Alexander McQueen himself had risen from the dead just to design couture for me." As soon as the words leave her mouth her brain catches up to them and her eyes open wider, realizing she just took the piss out of one of her idols and he still deserves her reverence. She immediately follows with, "May he rest in peace."

I told Nick about my mom last night so there's no reason I shouldn't tell Holiday now. I should probably at least sit up for a conversation this significant so I shimmy my shoulders up and scoot back so I'm leaning my back against the headboard.

"I had to go to the hospital this morning."

"To see Robin?" she inquires.

"No. Not to see Robin. She was there, well, we were there with my mom." I take a deep breath. "My mom has leukemia and we were meeting with the oncologist who will be treating her."

Holiday rushes over to the side of my bed and grabs me. If she squeezes me any harder, this hug will put me in the hospital.

"Are you okay? Is she going to be okay? Is there anything I can do? Do you need anything? Does she need anything?" she rattles off. She's still attached to me like I'm her host and the Holiday organism will die if she releases her grip even a smidge.

"It's okay, Hol. You can breathe. Her cancer can be treatable. There are no guarantees but this doctor is a friend of Robin's and apparently he's the best in the country," I manage to get out. I'm distracted by the potent fragrance of gardenia emanating from her hair. "She's going to have to be in the hospital at least for the first month but we're all hopeful, including Dr. Jacobs." I delicately remove her arms from me.

"Why didn't you tell me sooner?" she wonders aloud.

"I know it sounds stupid but it just felt like the more people I told the less I could deny that it was actually happening," I say with a shrug.

"That's not stupid," she contests. "It makes perfect sense. I just wish I had known so you didn't have to handle it alone." Her hand engulfs mine.

"I know I'm not alone," I tell her. I don't want to go through all of the emotions again right now and figure if I throw in some gossip, we can bypass the rest of the cancer conversation. "Guess who I'm going on a date with this week?" I tease. Holiday goes from empathetic to enthusiastic and looks like she wants to scream for joy.

"I don't even have to guess. You and Nick might as well have had a conjoining procedure done the way you wouldn't look at anyone else or leave each other's sides last night. I'm surprised you were even able to do your job. You were transfixed on him."

"I was not," I defend, playfully slapping Holiday's arm. She cocks her head to the left to dispute my claim. "Maybe I was a little," I admit. "Holiday, I think this is the beginning of a beautiful friendship."

Twelve

. . . .

'm surprised you had time to grab coffee in the middle of the workday," I say to Maggie, who responded to my earlier text by asking me to meet her for coffee the next day. I haven't seen her since Victoria took the reins so it will be nice to get the inside scoop from an ally. "I figured Victoria assigned an intern to be stationed at Starbucks to keep everyone on staff at their desks and make coffee runs more efficient." Maggie's lips curl like she's trying to smile but her mouth won't physically make the movement. She takes a few moments to herself and my imagination is making me more paranoid by the second, waiting for her to deliver whatever she's about to say.

"That's why I asked you here, Ella."

I scrunch my face and inhale.

"I'm not at *The Life* anymore."

I exhale. I can't believe what I hear. Maggie is saying one thing and somehow my brain is translating her words improperly.

"What do you mean?" I'm caught off guard and need her to spell it out to believe it.

"I was fired." Fired? I still can't comprehend the information. It's like she's speaking in tongues—or Dianetics. My breathing intensifies and I want to fly out of my chair and pace around as if I were going mad but trying to convince myself I actually wasn't.

"Why?" In stark contrast to my hyper reaction, Maggie is at ease. There's not a trace of anger or outrage in her voice, and since the last time I saw her she's adopted a laissez-faire demeanor.

"Victoria believes it's unacceptable that I wasn't in front of Not-So-Innocent Oversexualized Pop Star's meltdown."

"That wasn't your fault," I argue on her behalf, even though she doesn't want a defense and continues.

"*The Life* was completely blindsided and none of our reporting on the incident was exclusive." She takes a sip of her iced latte and takes a breath. "I was never able to get a source that was actually close to her."

"After everything you've done for the magazine she fired you just like that?" I'm very good at my job, and while I know that *The Life* needs freelancers and our reporting to generate a fair amount of their content I'm nowhere near as integral to the everyday operations as Maggie.

"Victoria doesn't care. She's cutthroat. With her it's kill or be killed. I'd always heard she was tough but apparently she's even more ruthless now than when she originally worked for *The Life*. Not-So-Innocent Oversexualized Pop Star is one of the celebs Victoria wants to make a priority for *The Life*. Her covers always do great numbers so she assigned me to start sourcing people close to her to give us info before any of this ever went down and she was embarrassed we didn't have any exclusive information." She studies her coffee cup like it's forensic evidence. "No one would talk to me. Not the barista she visits daily, not the girl who does her hair extensions. Boybander Turned Solo Artist Turned Actor's team wouldn't even leak any info on his ex."

"I can't believe she treated you like you were so disposable. . . ." I trail off.

"I made myself disposable. Ella, I know how good you are at your job but Victoria doesn't care about you or your track record and doesn't give any points for loyalty. To her, everyone is replaceable. She only cares about better stories and bigger numbers. If you don't want to be disposed of you can't afford to miss anything. You have to find exclusives and earn the points."

"Are you going to go to another magazine?" I ask.

"I don't think so." Maggie is one of the few people who is as consumed with the celebrity gossip world as I am, so her revelation is surprising.

"Really? I thought you love this."

"I did." She corrects herself. "I do. But I got so wrapped up in other people's lives that I lost sight of making sure I had my own. I was always in the office and the only time I went to dinner or a bar or an event was if I needed to be the one doing the reporting." I'm surprised. I thought the spontaneous nature of the job was something she thrived on. "I'm not happy I was fired but maybe this all worked out for the best for me. Besides, now every time I get a breaking-news alert on my phone I can en-joy the gossip instead of panicking that I missed something."

I stare off into space and wonder if Maggie's sermon is somehow a warning for me. She notices my detachment from the conversation and alleviates my fear.

"You're freelance. It's a totally different game for you. But if you want to win that game, you have to do it by earning points."

I nod to show her I understand. "So if you're not going to go to an-other magazine what are you going to do now?"

"I don't know. Take some time off. Reevaluate my life. Try and date now that I won't be canceling on someone at the last minute because Former Tween Pop Star Who Will Bang Any Female with a Pulse had an after-party where the cops were called or Country Singer Turned Cross-over Superstar is knocked up. Who knows? Maybe I'll end up at one of those listicle sites where every article about dating goes viral. The world can never have enough guidelines for the dos and don'ts of sexting," she kids.

"Ain't that the truth." I smile.

"I just want to feel good about whatever I do next. You know?"

My phone vibrates and I can't help but look to see if Victoria or some-one else from the magazine is calling for anything. "I'm sorry. Let me see who this is."

"It's okay. I totally understand." And she means it. She's one of the few people who realizes I'm not trying to be rude. I turn my phone faceup.

"*The Life*?" she asks. For once it isn't. It's Nick. I wonder what he wants but my curiosity is outranked by my desire for privacy and I return my phone to the table.

"No. It's . . ." I stop myself. I don't know whether or not I should tell her, since she's friends with Ethan. The phone buzzes again. I have a voice mail.

"New guy?" she assumes. She may be fired but her instincts are still as sharp as ever. I nod. It's a little awkward even though neither of us wants it to be and after a lull she jumps in. "Well, I better get going."

"Me, too." We take our empty coffee cups to the trash and it feels a little bit like *we* just broke up.

"I really appreciate you giving me the heads-up on what happened."

Maggie leans in for a hug. "No problem. Good luck, Ella."

"You too, Mags." She leaves and all I can think about is listening to Nick's message.

Hey, Ella, I'll pick you up tomorrow at 6:30 P.M. Looking forward to seeing you.

Thirteen

. . . .

H i, sexy." Nick's greeting immediately causes my cheeks to flush and I slide into the passenger seat of his Tesla. He leans in and I kiss him on both cheeks.

"Hi, you," I flirt back in my newfound seductive inflection.

"You look gorgeous." I wore my favorite pair of AG skinny jeans and mastered the effortlessly sexy look for the occasion, complete with my looks–like–I–just–had–sex tousled hair.

"Thank you." He leans in and kisses me on both of my cheeks again and plants another kiss on my lips. It feels like there's a magnetic force in our chests and we're physically being drawn toward each other. He wraps his arms around my back as I cradle his stubbly face and call on every morsel of willpower I possess not to climb over the center console and straddle him. The temptation is agonizing but I know if let my lust lead the way I will forge a pathway to my bedroom instead of building the healthy relationship I want. My brain vetoes my body and as the kiss somehow manages to intensify I extricate myself from the magnetic minefield. He smells delicious and woodsy like he always does and there's something about his suit and his style that is so sexy it makes me want to rip all of his clothes off starting with the pocket square in his Armani jacket.

"You smell amazing," he says, leaning in where my neck and ear meet to inhale another sip of my signature Marc Jacobs fragrance.

"So do you."

He kisses me again.

"Alright, if you keep this up before we leave my driveway I'm not going to want to leave at all." If there were a thermometer between our faces the mercury would explode from heat and burst the device into a thousand pieces.

"That would be perfectly fine with me," he whispers, leaning in again.

I place my hands on his chest (oh God I forgot how nice his chest is) to keep him at a distance.

"I'm sure it would be." I laugh but inside I feel torture. Be strong, Ella!

"I've wanted to grab you and kiss you like that since the night I met you," he confesses, brushing his hand across my well-kissed cheek.

"Me, too." He won't stop looking at me and I can't stop grinning like I won a kiddie beauty pageant. "Although I did have a boyfriend at the time and I am kind of a lady after all."

"Yes, you are." Our chemistry is carnal, and as each second passes we are succumbing to it. "I haven't Googled it recently but to my knowledge, making out hasn't ever killed anyone," he suggests, drawing my body closer to his.

"Stop trying to agent me." I wink. "This isn't a negotiation." If it was and it continued I would most assuredly lose in the next few critical moments but he doesn't need to know that.

"Yes, ma'am." He pulls himself back into his seat fully and we finally reverse out of my driveway. Nick's eyes spend more time intertwined with mine than they do on the road. It isn't exactly the safest transportation but I'm also not objecting. I'm just as lost in him because I don't even realize we're heading toward downtown until we approach the entrance to the 10 freeway.

"Where are we going, by the way?" I wonder if he's taking me to one of those invitation-only underground pop-up dinners in the Arts District. I haven't been to one and am of course dying to go. If you aren't a chef, restaurant blogger, or culinary influencer they are nearly impossible to attend. The culinary world might be an even tighter-knit, more impenetrable community than Hollywood.

"You'll see," he teases.

"One of the things you will come to learn is patience is not one of my virtues." Hopefully he thinks that's cute because I'm not joking.

"Understood." He stares at my face and then his eyes briefly linger on my chest before coming back to my face. "I'm looking forward to getting to know your other virtues." He doesn't expound upon his vague itinerary or destination. He's as good at keeping secrets as I am. My curiosity is getting the better of me and his reticence is sending my imagination into a tailspin. He admiringly shakes his head when he catches me using the location finder on my Yelp app to see what's around and attempting to deduce his secret agenda.

"You really are impatient." He takes his right hand off the wheel and places it on top of mine.

"I wasn't exaggerating."

"Try and relax. It's a date. It's supposed to be spontaneous and fun." He's right. It is. I put my iPhone away and enjoy our hand-holding. Nick exits the freeway at Figueroa Street and the answer to the enigma unveils itself as if it popped into my head by magic and an overconfident smirk reveals that I'm no longer perplexed.

We pull into the Staples Center complex and my hunch was correct. "Lakers game. Of course." Well played, Nick.

"My boss was supposed to bring A-List Sex Symbol Box Office Gold Turned Critically Acclaimed Actor to the game but he's still shooting so he gave me the tickets. I hope it's okay."

Nick's spontaneity is sexy and a welcome departure from Ethan's reluctance to do anything even remotely industry-related with me. Basketball is technically part of the sports realm, but in LA it intertwines with Hollywood, as does almost everything. I smile.

"I mean . . . I guess that's acceptable," I concede. We continue to wind through the streets to the parking complex and arrive in an area I've never seen where we stop at a valet I never knew existed.

"Welcome back, Mr. Williams," the attendant greets.

Nick exits and comes around the car to open my door for me. So far he's making an unforgettable first-date impression. We proceed through a private entrance and he leads me through the catacombs of the arena to the Chairman's Room, a private club for VIP patrons. Screw a pop-up dinner! This is exponentially better. Nick presents our passes to the security guard and he leads me to the bar. I'm trying to absorb everything about my surroundings and don't hear Nick the first or even second time he asks me what I'd like to drink.

"I'll have a Grey Goose martini, very dirty, please," I respond upon his third attempt and I snap out of my stupor. As he orders I return to my observation and notice that C-List Actress Turned Lifestyle Entrepreneur and her noncelebrity husband are having date night at a table in the corner sans kids. She's being flirty and won't stop giggling while he's caressing her arm. I'm glad for their sake and their children's that their marriage seems to be well intact, but a public outburst would certainly be beneficial for me right about now.

"Grey Goose martini, very dirty, for the 'lady,'" Nick announces playfully when he hands me my drink and pokes at now another one of our inside jokes. "What's that toast you and Holiday do?" he tries to recall.

"To glamour and love."

"Ah, yes." He humors me. "To glamour and love," he repeats, clinking my glass with his tumbler full of scotch. He puts his arm around me and guides me to a table. I almost feel unsettled because I'm not feeling unsettled at all. I don't know if it's all of the schmoozing I've had to do for my job, but I thought I would be more nervous going on my first date after spending years with a guy I thought I would be with forever. It's almost like Nick doesn't realize how good-looking and successful he is, but he does, and because he doesn't lead with it the absence of arrogance makes him even sexier.

"What's been going on since I last saw you?" Now that we both have drinks he's settled in across from me.

"It's actually been an eventful few days." Normally I wouldn't bring anything less than perfect up on a first date but since I already told him about my mom I figure there's no harm in being honest.

"Has it? Tell me," he leads. "Good or bad eventful?"

"Went to see my mom's new oncologist—"

"Oh . . ." Nick takes a large sip of his drink. He clearly didn't mean to open this can of worms. "I'm sorry."

"She's checking in to the hospital to start her first round of chemo in a couple of days."

He reaches across the table and places his hand on top of mine. His look is thoughtful and he's gone from the guy who desperately wants to sleep with me to the guy that desperately wants to console me.

"Yeah. Her doctor is an interesting man. Without saying he's hopeful in so many words, he said he was hopeful."

Nick takes another sip of his drink intentionally, so as not to interrupt.

"My sister says he's the best."

"You have a sister?"

"Yeah. Her name is Robin. She's ten years older, an ER doctor . . . total God complex slash thinks she knows everything about everything and couldn't be more my opposite. We've never had the best relationship but she has a four-year-old, Marianna, that I would do anything for." I take my phone out of my bag and notice a notification of an e-mail from

Victoria. It's titled "This Week's Points." I shake it off and open the photo Robin sent me not too long ago of Marianna doing her duck face and hand him my phone.

"Wow, she's adorable. A pose you taught her, I assume?"

I shrug my shoulders innocently. "I love her more than anything. And she has the sweetest, most outgoing little personality. Who knows, you may be repping her one day."

"I will keep her on my watch list," he jokes. "You were saying your mom's doctor . . ."

"Oh, yeah . . . His people skills aren't my favorite but my sister said he's the best so we have to just deal with his lack of bedside manner."

"The only thing you need from him is to help her get well. She's got you and your sister for the rest." He always knows the *perfect* thing to say and makes him even sexier than I thought possible.

"And then aside from that my boss got fired and *my* job is possibly in jeopardy, so there's that whole mess."

Nick leans back in his chair pensively and stares at me as if I were a complete stranger. "You know, I just realized that I have no idea what it is that you do."

I instantly feel a sharp pain overtaking my left bicep. Is this what a heart attack feels like? A stroke? My mind has been overwhelmed with everything else going on in my life that I hadn't done my predate due diligence to consider what I was going to tell Nick about *The Life*. I guess some part of me maybe thought that Holiday had filled him in, but as I think about it now, she wouldn't have, because from the moment she learned the truth she took a volitional vow never to discuss Ella/Bella with anyone without my explicit prior consent.

I don't want to start our first date with me lying to him or even deliberately omitting any of the truth but he is an agent and I'm nervous how he's going to react. Will he think that I'm untrustworthy? Will he think that I'm using him to get info on his clients? Will our date be over before it really even started? While the relationship between celebrities and *The Life* or any other gossip outlet is ultimately symbiotic, there are plenty of people in the industry that hold a great deal of disdain for us regardless of the exposure we give their clients. I need to tell him. It's my only choice.

"I work for *The Life*." I try to evaluate Nick's expression after the revelation but he's giving me nothing.

"I know *The Life* well. What do you do over there?" Now he's playing detective.

"I'm actually freelancing." I don't want to lie but I really don't want him to run for the Hollywood Hills either.

"Do you cover red-carpet events for them?"

"Not exactly. I'm more like one of their 'specialized freelancers.'" I give him that look, letting him know that there's a lot more to what I'm saying than the words.

"'Specialized' meaning . . . ?"

"I'm a spy," I blurt out. "Well, undercover reporter if you want to get technical." He looks at me more confused now than ever. "You know when you read gossip on celebrities out at parties and clubs and after a specific detail the article says, 'according to a source'? I'm the source. It means I was assigned or asked to go to the club or restaurant or wherever to get stories undercover or that on my own I was able to get them something that they were able to use." Nick remains reticent, and I know this isn't a favorable indication of acceptance. I have to make him understand he can trust me. "I have a code, though."

"What kind of code?"

"I never betray anything my friends tell me in confidence and don't report on things that aren't happening in public." I hope this helps my platform for why Nick should take me on a second date. He takes a moment to go over everything in his head.

"Holiday knows?"

"Yes, of course. We've been friends for years. She's one of the maybe four or five people who do." *Please don't hate me.* "I didn't want to lie to you but I also don't want you to think I'm slimy or you can't trust me."

"If Holiday trusts you then I can, too."

I give myself an internal "cha-ching" motion that I've made it past this hurdle. "It might end up being a moot point anyway. If I don't get my boss something that will break the Internet I'm going to be out of a job, too."

"You seem to be very resourceful. I think you'll be just fine." I'm glad one of us thinks so. I finish the last of my martini.

"Do you want another?" Nick asks.

"No, thank you." That martini was strong. I don't want to get tipsy and say something crazy to Nick. Plus, I need to have all of my faculties right now so in case my job did put a damper on his excitement for me my charm will counteract it.

"Good. I want you to remember everything tonight," he says, his eyes smoldering. "Plus this place is prime real estate for helping you save your job." He winks. Could this guy be any better? "We should probably get out there. It's rude to miss tip-off."

Nick polishes off the last of his scotch and he takes my hand as he escorts me to the basketball court. I think he really might be okay with this. We walk around the perimeter of the court and instead of going toward the stairs to find our seats he points straight ahead.

"Courtside seats? I hate to tell you, Nick, but you are setting a really bad precedent for yourself," I tease.

"Yeah, I just realized I really screwed myself for date two." Yay! He's thinking he wants a date two, too.

"A little bit." He pulls my chair out for me and I place my purse as far underneath my seat as possible. I would so be the girl to accidentally have one of the straps a touch into the court and have the MVP trip and fall and injure himself for the rest of the season. "Are we going to be on the kiss cam?" I flirt.

"God, no! I paid the guy a hundred bucks so we wouldn't be." He laughs and I laugh, too.

"So if I do this we won't be on the JumboTron?" I lean in and give him a peck on the lips, or what I meant to be a peck. He leans into it and places his hand on the back of my head and we are full-on making out. Courtside. At a Lakers game. I'm briefly distracted from the issues in my life.

"Ahem," I hear softly bouncing off the rim of my ear. I continue to allow Nick's kiss to consume me. "Ahem!" This time it's louder and closer and absolutely directed at us. I release my lips from Nick's and am partly annoyed that someone has interrupted our romantic interlude and partly scared that whoever it is will yell at me. I turn my head and am faced with my kiss-blocker: Older Multi-Oscar-Winning Womanizer who is also a notorious Lakers fan and apparently isn't a believer in love *and* basketball. He's wearing sunglasses despite the fact that it's nighttime and we are indoors, and even though his eyes are hidden behind the opaque lenses, I can feel him condemning me with them. Lucky for me the game is starting so he transfers any annoyance he has with me into passion for the game. I'm catching basketball fever, too.

I admit it; sports are not my thing. I'm great with recognizing and staying current on almost everyone in the entertainment industry, but with sports, I don't know anyone except its few crossover stars. Maggie even made sure not to assign me to the events or places that would be athlete-heavy because I did her no good at them. When it comes to sports I usually classify myself as a bandwagoner. I'm not invested in a team unless I happen to be living in their hometown and they make it to the play-offs. After that I'll attend any form of social function to watch and cheer for the team as long as I'm provided with booze and food. But literally sitting on the court while the game is being played is a transcendental experience.

I'm high-fiving Nick every time we score and booing every time the Knicks score. The players are running right by us and can hear everything we say so I feel it's my duty to express my happiness or discontent. My grasp of the game is basic at best but I'm screaming along with all of the other fans as if I placed my kid's college tuition as a bet.

"Yo, what up, Nick?" one of the Lakers shouts as he holds his hand out to slap Nick's as he runs by between plays.

"Keep it up, man. Stay focused and you've got this quarter." Nick is really adorable when he's being encouraging and of course now I'm imagining him coaching our children's Little League games even though there's still time for our first date to go horribly awry—not that I think it will but that's insane forward-thinking, like putting the Oscar win before the Golden Globe nominations are even announced.

"He looks familiar." I'm trying to place him and run through the work dossier in my head, since I know the one place I don't know him from is basketball.

"Yeah? He should." He muses at my basketball naïveté. "NBA Champion Scoring Sensation is one of the best forwards in the game, maybe of all time."

"No. That's not it." I wrack my brain. "Did he get a DUI last year while he was dating B-List Reality Star from A-List Reality Family?"

Nick shakes his head at me in amused disappointment. "First off, yes. Although now he's dating Former Supermodel Turned Actress Turned Jersey Chaser. Secondly, that's not why he's famous to the majority of the American public."

"Nick Williams, do you know everybody in this town?"

Nick makes a feeble attempt to be bashful. "Nah. Only about eighty-five percent," he says with a wink. "And mostly because I represent them . . . or they want me to represent them." Another feather to add to his baller cap. "But NBA Champion Scoring Sensation and I went to high school together. He was a basketball prodigy; I was a former child star. Our destiny was written in the sky," he jokes.

"You could totally pitch that idea to a studio and package it and have the next big buddy comedy on your hands," I joke. "Nick Williams, you are full of surprises."

"As are you, Ella Warren. Speaking of which, am I going to read about our basketball date in *The Life* next week?"

I playfully elbow him.

"You should be so lucky."

We return to the game and Nick's high-school bestie misses the last shot of the half. The crowd boos and the chanting gets louder when Former Supermodel Turned Actress Turned Jersey Chaser is featured on the JumboTron and fans scream obscenities at her for cursing him, the team, and the game.

"I'm going to get a round of beers for us, you want anything else?" Nick asks.

"I'm good."

"Yes, you are." He leans down to give me a kiss and I pull away after a second so I don't make things awkward with my seatmate again. Nick retreats to the concessions and I pull out my phone to check Victoria's e-mail. Come on, you got some good stuff this week.

1) *Not Me*
2) *Not Me*
3) *Not Me*
4) *Ella Warren*

Yes! My Not-So-Innocent Oversexualized Pop Star exclusive bumped me up! I breathe a very clichéd yet still very real sigh of relief and feel calm . . . a calm that Older Multi-Oscar-Winning Womanizer interrupts.

"Pretty hot and heavy for a basketball game," he notes. I detect a bit of malice in his remark but he's a legend so even if he's acting like a jerk I feel like it would be a little blasphemous and disrespectful to sass him.

"I'm sorry about that. It's our first official date and the chemistry between us is really intense." Why am I telling him this? He doesn't need or probably want an explanation, just for me to keep my tongue inside my own mouth.

"I can see why. With you around it's difficult to focus on the game." He lowers his sunglasses down his nose and leers at me. Oh my God, he's hitting on me. If he wasn't being totally creepy and didn't do it to every woman who's probably ever sat in this chair it might be flattering but that's not the case.

"Thank you," I respond, trying to brush him off without being overtly rude. It doesn't work.

"Sweetheart, why don't you ditch the suit and let a more seasoned man take you out after the game?" I laugh it off. "You're beautiful."

He continues to slather on what he considers charm. I pause to wonder if he would have been like this if he weren't famous or if the fame leads to the douche-baggery. It's the Hollywood equivalent of the chicken-or-egg conundrum. "Wearing a suit to a sporting event and sitting courtside to impress a pretty girl; let me guess, he's an agent?" I nod uncomfortably, not knowing what else to do. There's literally nowhere for me to turn and there's a house photographer a few feet away so causing a scene isn't an option. "I've been in this industry for fifty years, let me help you out and give you a little piece of advice and maybe save you some time, sugar lips. With agents, their clients will always come first. You can fall madly in love, get married, and give him children he says he loves, but his clients will still come first. You will never be his top priority."

"Thanks for the warning but he's not like the other agents." I smile even though I want to hiss at Older Multi-Oscar-Winning Womanizer. Doesn't he have a director or someone he can schmooze at halftime? Even a Laker Girl he can sexually harass? I muster up every ounce of decorum I can and am able to smile and nod.

"Let me guess, he's 'different'?" His sarcasm is starting to wear on me.

"As a matter of fact, I think he is."

"I hope that works out for you, sweetheart."

He presses his sunglasses back on his face and luckily Nick returns with our beer. As he sits down he puts his arm around me and I lean in and give him a big smooch just to spite Older Multi-Oscar-Winning Womanizer.

"Thank you," I whisper to him. He pets my hair and we stare at each other with the most pathetic smiles on our faces and I don't even care. I couldn't even tell you which team won the game.

Fourteen

. . . .

'm quickly adding the hospital to my most-frequented-establishments list. I'm anxious about my mom's first chemo treatment but I wouldn't miss being with her for anything. I make my way to my mom's room. As soon as Robin found out which room it would be she sent me an e-mail with detailed directions how to get there from the parking garage. I'll admit, I was annoyed when I received it but her directions were accurate and I made it to the room quickly, where Robin is waiting for me and my mom is having blood drawn.

"Hi, sweetheart," my mother coos.

I go to give her a hug. "Hi, Mom."

"You must be the infamous Ella," the heavyset bespectacled brunette nurse in teal scrubs comments. "I'm Nurse Richards. It's nice to meet you."

"Nice to meet you, too. You nervous, Mom?" I check.

"Not now that you're here."

Nurse Richards finishes her blood withdrawal. "I'm going to get this tested really quickly so Dr. Jacobs can determine your dosage for today. Robin, would you and your sister like to take your mom down to the treatment room and I'll meet you there?"

"Sure." Nurse Richards and Robin help my mom into her wheelchair. The walk to the treatment room is ominous. None of us really know what to expect and are all nervous inside but don't want to worry each other. I'm scared that I'm going to break down when they start and that's the last thing she needs.

"I have Joan Warren, she's a patient of Dr. Jacobs," Robin tells her.

The receptionist checks her computer.

"Yes, we're ready for you. You all can come on back." She opens the door to the lobby and escorts us to the treatment room. I don't know how to describe it and this sounds odd but it's like a sick summer camp. It feels

like we've entered a tepid rec room, and at first glance it's an amalgama-
tion of diverse people, from age to ethnicity to energy, who are all bonded
by the fact that they've all already gotten what will probably be the worst
news of their lives.

I also notice the quiet. Some people have their headphones on to
listen to music or watch something on their iPads. No one is laughing
raucously or talking on their phone.

I find my mind wanders from my mother to the other patients. I look
at each of them and wonder about their individual stories: what kind of
cancer they have, how far along they are in their treatment, what their
chance of survival is, whom they've brought as their companions, and their
mood. At first glance the chemo room appeared cold and sterile, but as I
sit here longer, it feels full of hope, determination, and spirit. It takes about
an hour after my mom's blood work for the chemo to begin.

"Joan, we're ready to go," Nurse Richards tells us. "I'm going to implant the port first and then will administer your chemo." I look away as
this is done. Robin and I are definitely the odd couple of sisters and while
she got the doctor genes, I got the squeamish ones. I hold my mom's hand
since I can't bear to look but she doesn't make a peep indicating any pain.
Robin taps my leg when it's over.

Nurse Richards says, "Just try to relax and I'll be around if you have
any questions or you need anything. I believe Dr. Jacobs is going to try
to pop in to check on you as well. He likes to do that if he can between
patients."

"What do *we* do?" I whisper to Robin.

"Anything we can to distract her." She rubs my mom's hand and my
mom tries to smile but can't seem to gather the desire for much more than
duck face.

"So we just sit here for a few hours?"

"That's the idea, Ella. Anything is better than her sitting here alone,"
she adds.

"Sorry, I'm a chemo virgin." My comment relaxes Robin, who lets
out a sound that almost sounds like it could have been a small laugh even
though she didn't want it to be.

"Does it hurt, Mom?" I ask. She's literally being poisoned right in
front of our eyes . . . even though it might save her life . . . and it's hard
to marry the incongruous pictures of what's happening internally and
externally.

"No. That implant wasn't my favorite thing but I can't feel anything now." That gives me some minor relief. "Since we have some time on our hands, I want to hear more about this new boy you've been seeing, Ella."

I know I'm blushing even though I'm trying to fight it, but it's no use.

"We have our second date tomorrow night." I don't want to sound too excited but it's hard to stifle the intonation in my voice when I'm talking about Nick, especially after our first date. "He's making me dinner at his condo."

"That's romantic." Her eyes brighten. "How did you meet him again?"

"Through Holiday," I remind her.

Robin, never one to miss an interrogation, chimes in. "Is he an actor?" I can tell that she's crossing her fingers, toes, and even strands of hair that he isn't.

"No. He's an agent. He's her agent."

"Much better." She doesn't even try to hide the snark in her judgment and I rush to defend Nick and my choice to date him.

"Yes, it is. I chose power over beauty, although I couldn't be more attracted to him."

"I want to see a photo of him," my mom requests.

I take out my phone and have an e-mail from Victoria.

Dear Freelancers,
As you know the World Pop Music Awards are coming up this week. Hydra
Water is sponsoring the official after-party and in return for mentioning them in
our coverage they have agreed to let one of our reporters inside for observation.
This assignment will be eligible for points. It will be given on a first-come,
first-served basis.
Victoria

I reply immediately and Victoria responds that the job is mine. I'm glad I didn't wait a second longer to write her back. She sends another group e-mail within thirty seconds.

Dear Freelancers,
Thank you all for your interest but the assignment has been taken.
Better luck next time.
Victoria

I close out of my e-mail.

"I don't have any photos of us yet. Let me look and see what I can find online." I go to WireImage and search for Foreign Born Supernatural Superstar and am able to pull up photos with Nick from his last premiere. I return the phone to Robin and she scrolls through the photos.

"I don't see him," she says. "All I see is Foreign Born Supernatural Superstar." I lean across my mom's lap and point to Nick standing off to the side of Foreign Born Supernatural Superstar while he's being interviewed.

"He's right there. In the black Tom Ford suit on his phone," I tell her.

Robin groans. "Do you have any real-life photos?"

"Well, he has Instagram but you can only see his profile photo because his account is private," I explain.

"So why don't you add him?" Robin wants to know, thinking that this problem has an easy solution. I know my sister has been out of the dating game even longer than I have, but you'd think that someone with her intelligence wouldn't ask a question that contradicted decades of sexual politics.

"Robin, I can't add a guy I like that I've only been out with once! Do you know how desperate that is?"

"Yeah, because your whole family is trying to stalk him online and you pretending you don't like him as much as you do paints you as the picture of sanity," she pokes, and I can't help but laugh at how this does look a bit stalkerish . . . even for me, whose most valuable skill on my résumé is technically stalking.

"I think he's very handsome," my mom adds after seeing the photo.

"He's a really nice guy too but he also has that agent thing where you know he doesn't stop until he gets what he wants. It's so hot."

Robin rolls her eyes and mimics me but gives me an amplified Valley-girl voice. "It's sooooo hot." She is on one today and laughs at her own ridiculousness. Now that the stalking is over we need something to do. "Do you want to watch TV, Mom?"

"No, I don't watch daytime TV except for *Wendy* and it isn't on yet."

Robin reaches into her tote bag.

"If you're up for it, I brought something to keep us occupied." She pulls out her iPad and after a few swipes hands it to my mother. "I had all of our old family photos converted to digital files."

I move my chair over to the other side of my mother so I can have a better look. I have to give Robin credit; my mom has gone from lethargic to lively looking through the unexpected scrapbook. We're enjoying it just as much as she is. Robin has almost every moment of our lives that's ever been documented on the tablet. The terrible school plays we were both in. Birthday parties with family, with friends, and all of the carby confections we ate along the way. She stops on a childhood photo of Robin at a fairy-princess birthday party.

"Oh my goodness, that's Christine Stone. Robin, do you remember her daughter, Sara?" she asks her.

"Sort of, I think?" Robin obviously doesn't but wants to humor mom.

"I will never forget Sara's fourth birthday party. When she blew out the candles on her cake she told the entire party she wished for a better mother. I didn't know whether to laugh or call child protective services." She giggles and the other patients stare—it's not malicious and they're not angry but they're wondering what she could find so funny during chemo treatment. After a moment they return to their companions or their solitude, but my mother stays transfixed on the iPad and never notices that they stared. "After all these years I can't believe that's stuck with me." She swipes again. "Ella, look at how adorable you were in your soccer uniform."

"You were adorable but terrible," Robin recalls.

"First of all, tennis turned out to be my sport. Second of all, I was not." I know I wasn't a champion fullback but it was a participation sport. I got a trophy.

"It's not that you were so bad, you just didn't really care about the ball being in play. All you wanted to do was gossip with your friends and then you were surprised when the other team came charging at you," she clarifies.

"Okay that *does* sound like me," I admit.

My mother continues swiping and finds a gem that I don't remember ever seeing before.

I study it. "Robin! When did you have multicolored hair? How do I have no memory of this?" The girl in this photo definitely shares my DNA.

"Probably because it lasted for about six hours before Mom dyed it back herself in the kitchen sink."

"Is that when you spent the night at Kelly Nixon's house when her parents were out of town?" My mom tries to recall the circumstances of this incident because Robin had innumerable acts of disobedience.

"Yes." Robin twinkles, recalling her youthful antics.

"I had completely forgotten about that. I never thought that your re-bellion would extend to stealing Ella's Kool-Aid to dye your hair. If I would've seen this coming I would've locked our pantry like the liquor cabinet."

"You know, Ella, you aren't the only trendsetter in the family." Robin straightens her shoulders. "Look at how many celebrities dye their hair crazy or multiple colors today, thank you very much. I was fashion-forward and way before my time."

I can't argue with her. "Yes, Robin, you were a true Van Gogh. Never appreciated in your time." Robin sticks her tongue out at me playfully the exact way Marianna is so fond of doing. My mom swipes again and we are all eagerly awaiting the next memory and it's Robin and Jeff on their wedding day.

"You were the perfect bride." Mom beams.

"Thanks, Mom. My goodness, I can't believe how young Jeff and I look. Maybe I need to pop down to the dermatologist and see what he can do for me."

"Please, you work weirder and longer hours than I do. You look great for your lack of sleep and having an energetic four-year-old," I remind Robin.

My mom turns to me. "I hope I'll be able to see you get married."

I don't like her talking about not being here even if it is a possibility and I snap at her. "Why would you even say that? Of course you will!" I catch my breath and let my emotions subside. "I'm sorry. I didn't mean to be all huffy. It was just upsetting to hear you say that."

I can see in her eyes she accepts my apology.

"Maybe things will work out with this Nick fellow . . ." she says lin-geringly. Leave it to my mother to be killing the cells in her body and more concerned about me finding a husband.

"One date at a time, Mom. Can we swipe to the next picture and get me out of this pressure cooker?" I beg.

She smiles and swipes again to a family photo from the summer we spent at Lake Champlain in Vermont in our coordinated denim shirt-and-white shorts ensembles . . . with my dad. Our last family photo.

"I can't believe how long it's been," I slip. I didn't mean to weigh down this experience even more but it just came out when I saw the photo. I always thought I was older but looking at that picture now, I realize I was just a kid when he died.

"Fifteen years next July," my mom reflects, brushing her finger over him on the iPad. Seeing our last photo together while my mother is in the middle of getting chemo . . . the emotions are a bit too much to tolerate and somehow we've managed to make cancer even more depressing.

"I brought something, too." I want to lighten the mood, and neither my mom nor Robin seems to have any objection to me changing the activity. I pull this week's issue of *The Life* out of my purse. Robin doesn't object and we huddle back around Mom.

"I need to see what her diet is for this postbaby body five weeks after delivery," Robin exclaims with a lot of doubt. My mother flips to the page with the article and Robin scoffs. "Please, there's no way that Foreign Lingerie Model Turned Business Mogul can claim she lost all that weight, 'running around with the baby.' It's medically impossible even with a superhuman metabolism. I smell a secret tummy tuck. There, El. You have a new story. You're welcome."

"Just because it took you over a year to take the baby weight off with Marianna doesn't mean that's how long it takes for everyone," I jest. Robin smiles but also looks like she sort of wants to obliterate me . . . in the most loving way possible. My mom loosens her shoulders and rests her hands in her lap. We may not be Wendy Williams but she's enjoying watching our spirited sibling sparring, and the return to a more tongue-in-cheek dynamic is making her feel at ease. "I think we would all much more enjoy the article on Self-Deprecating Clumsy Awards Season Darling's hair transformation." I flip to that page.

"I honestly don't know what I'd do without you girls. This is horrible and I know I'm going to feel even worse as the days go on but having both of you here with me makes this tolerable."

I've been trying to hold back my emotions all day. Between chemo and cancer and the photo of my dad and now her saying nice things I can't hold it in any longer.

"Excuse me, I need to go to the bathroom." I rush out of the treatment room and am able to find the bathroom without feeling like I'm navigating my way through a cornfield maze. I go into the first stall of the empty bathroom and the door swings shut behind me as I grab a piece of toilet paper and use it as a makeshift tissue. Before I leave to check the mirror for any smudged makeup, two women enter in medias res of what I come to learn is a confidential gossip session and I immediately overhear one of them mention Not-So-Innocent Oversexualized Pop Star. My ears abruptly perk up.

"I actually feel really sorry for her," the first woman says. "You can tell none of this was her idea." I stare at the women's feet through the bottom of the stall. They're wearing sensible heels that I can tell are made from expensive leather so I'm guessing they're either doctors or high up in hospital personnel. I don't want to risk leaving the stall and having them clam up, so their identities will have to remain a mystery.

"I know," the second woman agrees. "She is showing signs of improvement, though."

"Youth is on her side for that. But after this who knows if she'll ever be able to live a *normal* life?"

"Doctors can only help her heal physically. The rest is in God's hands. I'm praying for that girl every day."

One of their pagers rings and they both flee the restroom as quickly as they arrived. I grab my iPhone from my pocket.

Hi Victoria,
I'm not sure if you can use this or not but I'm at the hospital where Not-So-Innocent Oversexualized Pop Star was hospitalized and while I was in the bathroom I overheard two women talking about her. I don't know who they are but they work at or for the hospital in some capacity. They said that she's showing signs of improvement but they aren't sure if she'll necessarily ever be able to have a normal life.

Victoria responds immediately.

Thank you, Ella. I will see what I can do and will keep you posted on your points. I'm still hunting for a source that knows what triggered her breakdown. It's my top priority. If you can find that out you won't need to worry about points anymore!

I return to the treatment room a little more confident and a lot less emotional to find Dr. Jacobs with my family.

". . . I won't know anything until I know." He seems particularly stringent when I arrive. "You need to be patient and trust me," he tells them.

"We do, Dr. Jacobs. It's just our nerves and the time that's making her mind wander," Robin explains. From what I've seen, Dr. Jacobs doesn't seem like a man who's familiar with the concept of nerves or free time and with that is paged and excuses himself.

"What were you guys talking about?" I ask.

"I wanted to know when he would have an idea if I'm responding to the chemo," my mom tells me.

"You will," Robin insists. "I know he can't or won't guarantee anything, but Dr. Jacobs never lets cancer win." We return to the iPad, and I'm memory lane's next target as my gawky teen years flash before my eyes, giving me a small dose of horror and my mom and sister a nice laugh.

Even with the minor hiccups, the hours that I thought would be torturous flew by, and it feels wrong to say but I enjoyed our time there.

"Can I get you anything?" Robin asks Mom when we return to her hospital room.

"Thank you, but no. I'm exhausted." She sighs. "All I want to do is get in bed and watch *The Wendy Williams Show*."

We help my mom into bed and she immediately grabs the remote and turns on the TV.

"Can I watch with you?" I ask.

"Of course, sweetheart, snuggle in." She lifts her arm for me to find my spot.

"Room for one more in there?" Robin asks. Robin has never made it a secret that she's not the biggest fan of the show but she's doing her darn best to make an effort.

"Always." My mom lifts her other arm and her energy is waning.

"Do you have to grab Marianna from school?" I ask.

"Jeff is picking her up, which is nice because I didn't realize how tired I am."

I let out a little grunt and realize how tired I am, too. We all are because we fall asleep together for a little nap before Wendy interviews her first guest.

Fifteen

· ·

He's cooking for you? At his condo?" Jess asks with a suggestive look in her eye.

"It's not like that," I insist.

"It's *always* like that," she maintains. We roam around my walk-in closet trying to figure out the perfect outfit for me to wear tonight.

"We had courtside seats at the Lakers game on our first date, what's he going to do to top that? Charter a plane to Cabo for Taco Tuesday?" Her facial expression still asserts she's right. "I think it's sweet that he's actually putting effort into the date and that it's private and intimate."

"Oh, I have no doubt it will be intimate," she agrees.

"You know what I mean. We're both out so often that it will be nice to have some mellow one-on-one time."

"Mmmhmm." She's convinced this date is designed to get a girl into bed.

"I regret asking you to come over and help me pick my wardrobe," I joke.

"Me, too. This is so much more Holiday's domain," she comments. "You couldn't have tried stuff on for her on FaceTime?"

"I really haven't talked to her since she's been gone. A text here and there but we've both been pretty occupied. I haven't even told her I'm going on a second date with Nick. I wore skinny jeans on our first date. What do you think of this?" I hold up my black miniskirt and a plaid button-down. "Yay or nay?"

"I love it! The skirt is supersexy but the button-down says 'I'm not trying too hard.'" She reviews my choice again. "Since when have you needed anyone's style approval? I know you've always had an inner fashionista but you've never asked for assistance styling yourself for a date."

"That's because my dates were with Ethan. He didn't care if my clothes matched. Hell, he'd barely have noticed if I had worn my pajamas on a date if I threw a Maje leather jacket over them," I tell her with an all-too-familiar roll of my eyes.

"Don't hate . . . Maje leather jackets give any outfit carte blanche," she warns me.

"I'm not hating. It was kinda nice that he didn't care but it's also nice to date a guy who cares about his own appearance."

"Have you spoken to him? Ethan," she clarifies.

"Nope. Radio silence. I haven't heard a word from him since he broke up with me. It's in the past. I just want to move on."

Jess realizes she's hit a nerve and changes the subject back to a man who doesn't make me feel like the clothes even Goodwill won't accept. She navigates herself out of her ex digression.

"What's his style vibe?"

"Effortless and perfect," I muse, turning my frown upside down. She laughs over how smitten I am. In the midst of the honeymoon phase, Nick could order a drone strike on civilian targets and it would be difficult for me not to think he's anything short of amazing. "I'm not kidding," I assert. "He dresses better than I do and has more designer clothes. Hmm, is that a deal breaker?" I joke. Jess curls her lips. "No, but he's really mascu-line and rugged. Like, he may be wearing a six-thousand-dollar suit but something tells me he wouldn't mind if I ripped his shirt off and ruined it."

That description gave her a visual and she gets it now.

"So, yay or nay?" I repeat.

"Yay! With heels and make sure you wear a black bra that can peek out a little," she advises.

"I'm beginning to see why you think that everything is an advance for sex," I tease.

Jess shakes her head with a smile. "Alright, girl, I've got to get back to my blog. The Internet waits for no one. My readers are already begging for a new post after the one from this morning. You've got the outfit, you're gonna look hot. Text me and let me know what happens tonight." She turns to leave my room. "Or should I say tomorrow morning?"

"I'm not listening to you," I say. I change into the outfit we picked and am satisfied. It's sexy but not slutty and is stylish without being avant-garde. Now it's hair, makeup, and anticipation.

. . . .

Hi, sexy." Nick kisses me on my lips as he ushers me into his Sunset Strip condo.

"I brought a bottle of rosé. I hate red wine so I split the difference between red and white. I hope that's okay." He takes the bottle from me and places it on the dining-room table before returning for a more extended kiss. "I will take that as a yes?" My hands wander toward his chest, which is covered with a blue-and-white personalized Williams-Sonoma apron. I let out a giggle. It's so dorky and out of character for the Hollywood power agent that it's endearing.

"Would you like the tour?" he asks.

"Of course."

I can already tell that Nick's style extends to home décor. The condo is modern but doesn't feel uncomfortable, and he has walls full of art that would make a heist worth the risk of being caught. Original Mario Testinos and Annie Leibovitzs line the hall and he's a guy so of course he has a rare photo of the Rolling Stones I've never seen before. I'd be disappointed if he didn't.

"I love the flow," I gush.

"I was going for 'bachelor pad that doesn't scream *serial killer,*'" he jokes.

"Mission accomplished." It screams less sociopath and more *Architectural Digest.* He places his hand on my hip and lightly pushes me into the kitchen.

"And here's what I've been working on in the kitchen: carbonara and a Caesar salad." The granite countertop and stainless-steel kitchen smells how food porn looks. I take a breath deeper than I ever do in yoga and want to stick my face in the pot full of pasta.

"Stop. You did not make this." I squint, trying to detect any indication of chef deception from Nick but he's calm . . . even serene, I'd say.

"I did," he insists.

"Mmhmm. We'll just see about that." I go to his trash can to inspect the contents, ready to scream "J'accuse" when I find takeout containers he's trying to hide to pass off takeout as a home-cooked meal, but it's empty. "Okay, so you're successful, charming, and you cook . . . what the hell am I bringing to this equation?"

Nick doesn't skip a beat. "You have a perfect ass."

"Do I?"

He wraps his arms around me and lets them slide lower and lower until his hands are able to give my bum a small squeeze. "Yep. One perfect ass attached to a sexy, smart woman."

"This perfect ass will be about two sizes bigger after this meal, but it smells delicious."

"Are you hungry? We can finish the tour later," he suggests.

"Starving."

"Good." He begins to plate our dinner.

"Wineglasses?"

"Top left cabinet," he instructs. I pour the wine and put it on the table as he serves dinner. Much to my dismay, he's removed his apron. "To glamour and love?"

"To glamour and love," I repeat. I take a sip of wine for good luck but am dying to dig into his meal. I take a bite and drop my fork on my plate as the pasta awakens my taste buds.

"Oh my God. Are you serious?"

"Is it okay?" he asks, quickly tasting his creation to make sure he hasn't poisoned me with an overzealous amount of crushed red-pepper flakes or something.

"Okay? This is like the best thing I've ever eaten. Where did you learn to cook like this?" I want to know more but I'm too busy trying to daintily eat the delicious pasta (when all I really want to do is unhinge my jaw and shovel it into my mouth) to be bothered to talk.

"My mom."

Oh. I'm not sure if I'm supposed to talk about her or if it's a sensitive subject. "Is it hard for you to talk about her?"

Nick has lived through what's currently my biggest fear. His eyes fall to his plate and he takes a small breath before bringing his gaze back to me and answering. "Not anymore. It was for a long time, especially since she was the only parent I had, but I'm able to focus on all of the good memories now. The sadness is still there but it doesn't overtake the happiness I get when I think about her." I twirl my carbonara on my fork and then untwirl it and then retwirl it. "How's your mom doing?"

"We had her first chemo treatment yesterday," I tell him.

"How was it?" He puts his fork down.

"Scary and weird. I never imagined my mom would be sick like this. Sitting there with her and my sister, knowing she wasn't getting to leave after it was over killed me. But as awful as this sounds, in a totally fucked-up way it's the first time in recent memory that I had fun with both my mom and my sister," I tell him. "Trust me, my sister is usually not fun and we usually do not get along."

"I know what you mean. You feel like you're expected to be serious and somber throughout a parent's illness but you're still allowed to enjoy your time together even if it's under less than ideal circumstances."

"I never thought of it that way," I tell him.

"I hope you never have to go through what I went through and I'm sure your mom will be fine but if, God forbid, something happens, you'll be glad you have a few family memories with some levity from this time, too. You'd regret making it so intense and all about the doom and gloom of the situation later."

I pick my fork back up and take another bite. I was a little nervous about our second date since there wasn't that much to actually talk about during the Lakers game, but I didn't need to be. I feel like somehow we are connected to each other, that we flow well together. After Nick's third glass of wine he gets a little bolder with his conversation.

"Okay, I've gotta ask . . ." He pauses, pours himself another glass, and takes a sip before continuing. I feel trepidation as I wait for him to reveal his question. "You've gotta tell me more about how this thing with *The Life* works."

I'm relieved to hear it's nothing more salacious or a curiosity about why Ethan and I broke up. "What do you want to know?" I ask. "I'm an open book for you tonight."

"Really? That easy?"

I smile.

"Just like that, huh?" He was expecting a little more of a challenge.

"Just like that. I'd say you've earned it with this meal."

"Give me everything, then." He reclines in his chair, taking a sip of wine, before I begin.

"I guess I should start with my secret identity."

He leans forward and slams his elbows on the table when he hears this. "Secret identity?" I give him an evasive smile. "Now your love of martinis makes sense," he jokes. "Secret identity, please proceed. I want to know more."

"So, when I was first assigned to cover the Chateau I made the reservation under Bella because I usually get a byline and I'm sure you know they have an insanely strict no-media policy. I ended up going there at least once a week and was there so often I kept running into the same people I was running into when I covered clubs, so I had to be Bella all the time to maintain my Chateau cover." He's hanging on my every word and takes a gulp of wine before encouraging me to continue. "I was Bella so often that she kind of became my alter ego."

"What's the difference between Ella and Bella?" he asks.

"Ella is a little more grounded and responsible. Fun but not a party girl. Bella is easily convinced to have that one last drink and will slip into whatever role she needs in order to get her story."

Nick is listening intently. "That's so hot. Go on," he urges.

"Ella arranges Bella's Chateau nights with her boss, usually on Fridays since celebrities usually leave clubbing on the weekends for the amateurs. And for the nightclub stuff, you know, there's usually one or two nights a week per club that are considered the hot night for celebrities to go, so the magazine tries to divide them up between all of their freelance club girls; but if I have a particular in with a promoter on a certain night or a door guy I know who will always give me VIP access I can request a specific club or a specific night. The clubs always go through cycles of being popular to being forgotten, so they will generally try to have us cover the same club on the same night each week so we work our way into having the most access and the best coverage. Like, for example, I am pretty much always at Ambiance two nights a week right now."

"How did I not know about this?" he wonders.

"Because I would be very bad at my job if you did," I tease. "And I'm very good at my job."

"I knew that media outlets had sources, but I didn't know that they planted some of their own all over town."

"The things you don't know . . ." I tease.

"I'm intrigued and terrified." His face begs me to continue.

"One thing that can be annoying on my end is there are a lot of last-minute assignments. *The Life* has a source tip them off that a particular newsworthy celeb will be at a bar or restaurant on a certain night and sometimes it's even their publicist that gives us the heads-up. Like, if their client just had a bunch of rumors going around about him cheating they will let us know where he and his wife are going to dinner so my boss can send me to observe them and report back on how lovey-dovey they were with each other." I check in with Nick and he's fascinated. "And sometimes it's as simple as doing observation at a party. Trust me, the reporters aren't only on red carpets at parties. And that's pretty much how it works."

He finishes his wine and stares at me, still digesting all of the information I just gave him along with his carbonara. I finish my glass, too, and Nick finally snaps back to his usual self.

"I'm full. Do you want anymore?" he asks.

"That was delicious, but no. I don't think there's a speck of Parmesan cheese left on my plate. I feel like a beached whale. I don't think I can ever eat again."

"Good. You could stand to gain a few pounds. You're a little too skinny."

"Nick Williams, are you trying to get me into bed? Because saying that is pretty much pure seduction." I don't know if it's the wine or our chemistry or his compliment or my big mouth but I think my sexually charged comment just took things to the next level and I'm glad I listened to Jess and wore that sexy lace black bra.

"You know we never did finish the tour," he suggests.

"No, we didn't," I agree. He gets up and offers me his hand. Our energies pulse through each other and I feel like I could spontaneously combust any second from all of the anticipation building up in my body.

"Shall we?" I follow him to a closed door that I'm assuming is his bedroom. He pauses and is trying to figure out how to tell me something before we go inside. "There's someone I want you to meet."

Of course. This is just my luck. Here I am thinking how lucky I am and there's someone else he's hiding in the bedroom and he probably wants me to be some monogamish, polyamorous hotwife or sister wife or something. He opens the bedroom door and twelve pounds of golden fur rush over to him.

"What can I say? I have a thing for blondes?" My relief is noticeable. "What? Not what you were expecting?" He revels in the joy that he set me up.

"Thankfully, no! I've been around a lot of quirky people, clearly for too long."

"Ella, meet Lizzie."

I kneel down next to Nick and scratch her behind her ears. "Hi, Lizzie!" She licks my knees and it tickles, and she moves on to my calves and ankles. "I think she likes me."

"Did you put lotion on today? She's a lotion whore."

I giggle. "That's okay. She's so sweet." I can't stop petting her.
"She's my girl."

"How long have you had her?"

"About eight years." Nick scratches behind her ears. "Lizzie, your dinner is in your bowl," he tells her with a pat. She runs out of the bedroom and Nick closes the door behind her.

He pulls me into him and kisses me deeply as his hands travel up, down, and all around my body in no order in particular and leaving no landscape unexplored. They move from the back of my head to my butt to my breasts to my face and as they are about to charter the area between my legs, I rest my chin on his shoulder with the side of my face resting on his and take a deep inhale. I will never get enough of how good he smells.

He unbuttons my shirt and helps me out of it and does the same with my skirt. His hands on my skin are energizing. Nick picks me up and I wrap my legs around his waist and we fall into the bed.

I proceed to unbutton his shirt and I finally get to see the body I've been fantasizing about since I spilled my drink on him. I remove his shirt and his body descends on top of mine and he kisses my neck then moves on to my cheek and my décolletage before moving to unhook my bra, still kissing me.

"Wait, wait," I moan.

He takes his lips off me.

"Is everything okay?"

"Yeah. Great!" I kiss him as reassurance. "It's just, will she be okay out there by herself?"

Nick moves his lips back to my neck and between kisses is able to convince me. "We had a nice talk earlier and she said she understands that while she's my number-one blonde, I'm a man and I have needs and right now I need a different blonde," he says, continuing with his funny metaphor. He nibbles on my ear and I forget everything I was just saying. Hell, I forget the last letter of the alphabet.

Nick's kisses are delicate but passionate and my whole body is so alive. He moves down and kisses my stomach. He suddenly stops and looks up at me directly in the eyes. We share a smile that somehow manages to say everything we're both thinking. I guess Jess was right. . . .

Sixteen

· · · · · · · · · · · · · · · · · · · ·

There's a bounty on Not-So-Innocent Oversexualized Pop Star's head and the prize is our jobs. Victoria called a last-minute mandatory meeting at the office for the freelancers this morning, and ironically, if she hadn't I might've been able to get some intel, since I was supposed to go to chemo with my mom and I seem to get something on her every time I'm at the hospital. I felt horrible canceling. I called my mom and explained the situation. She totally understood. Robin, on the other hand, sent me a text message that was less forgiving.

Robin: I can't believe you're bailing on chemo . . .

I reply as I walk into the meeting.

Me: I feel horrible. My meeting is mandatory, what can I do?

I put my phone away and take a seat as I did a few weeks ago. Victoria arrives at 10 A.M. on the dot and locks the door to the conference room behind her. Seems like if any of us were late we would've had one less person we were competing with for points but unfortunately no such luck. As I look around the room I recognize a familiar face—the snobby girl from Foreign Born Supernatural Superstar's party. I knew I'd seen her before. She's my competition! She locks eyes with me and squints, in a bid to intimidate me, but it doesn't work. Victoria told me my reporting was the best she got from that night. The energy is more ruthless without having Maggie as an intermediary and all of us knowing what's at stake.

"I'm disappointed in this group." Victoria doesn't believe in foreplay. "When you fail, I fail, and Victoria Davis does not fail. I will do whatever it takes to get this magazine back to the stature I left it at." She walks around the table, as she did in our first meeting, looking at each of us as she passes. I'm not sure if she's trying to intimidate or motivate us but regardless of her intentions, from the looks on everyone's faces it's a mixture of both.

"I need the best reporting team there is and I'm not convinced that's what I have in this group. Aside from you, Ella. Your reporting from the World Pop Music Awards was some of the best I've seen recently. You went above and beyond to spot European Royal making out with B-List Chameleon Singer-Songwriter. She infiltrated the caterers' quarters. You should all be doing that," Victoria recommends. Everyone stares at me like I just brought the teacher a fresh-pressed apple juice to get on her good side. My snobby competitor gives me an especially dirty look.

"How can no one have a personal source for Not-So-Innocent Oversexualized Pop Star?" she demands to know as she pauses her walk. "This isn't a rhetorical question. Any of you are free to answer."

"She's really heavily guarded," the snobby one answers as a defense. "She's never alone and everyone who works with her has to sign an outrageous nondisclosure agreement."

This isn't breaking news to Victoria, who is appalled by her excuses and doesn't bother to tell her that she doesn't care.

"She has been in the hospital for almost three weeks. That's an inordinately long period of time for someone who had a little snap. Not-So-Innocent Oversexualized Pop Star's psychiatric condition is worse than we originally thought and we need to find out what's going on. This is your job!" she not-so-gently reminds us. "The only thing the public knows is what they see in paparazzi photos. The online message boards are rampant with conspiracy theories, and it's the mystery the world wants answers to right now and no one has any answers. Every outlet we compete with is vying for the exclusive as well but we *need* it. If we are the first to break the story of what's happening we will hit all of our goals for the year in one issue. So I don't care what you do or how you do it, but find me something and find it soon and find it first." She repeats her brusque exit again as well and after sitting in that pressure cooker, chemo feels like it would've been a breeze.

Me: Hey, meeting ended a lot earlier than I thought. Should I meet you guys at the hospital?

Robin: Don't bother. She's napping. We got the results from her bone

marrow biopsy. Her count wasn't doing as well as Dr. Jacobs had
hoped. He's going to give her a different dose of chemo for her next
treatment.

Me: I feel horrible.

Who bails on their mom's chemo for a work meeting? In hindsight I
can't help but wonder what the fuck I was thinking.

Robin: I know Mom would never say anything but I could tell she
missed you. Please make it up to her.

Me: I will! I swear.

As annoying and condescending as she can be, Robin is right. I need
to come up with something to let my mom know I wish I would've been
there today. As I'm driving home I come up with the perfect plan. I just
need to wait until my mom is awake. I wait a few hours to call her.

"Hi, sweetheart. How are you today?" she answers.

"I'm good. I'm so sorry I missed chemo today, Mom. How was it?"

"Oh, it was chemo. You've been to one treatment you've been to them
all. I told you not to worry about it." Maybe Robin was exaggerating and
it was really she who was upset with me for not coming. But she didn't
mention her biopsy results, which means she's scared, so I should've been
there no matter what.

"I still wish I could've been there. How about a mother-daughter night
out in Hollywood for some quality nonchemo time together? I'm thinking a Spago date night once your counts are high enough. Would you be
up for that?"

"That sounds lovely. Thank you, Ella, for giving me something to look
forward to." It's not a seat in a player's box at the US Open, which oc-
cupies the top spot on her bucket list, but at least I can help my mom cross
one thing off.

Seventeen

· ·

The last thing I want to be doing is working tonight. Holiday's pilot shoot wrapped and she came home this morning. We never really connected while she was away. I'm sure she was devoting 100 percent of her focus to *Benedict Canyon*, but if she were a guy I would think that she was ghosting me. As soon as she got home she scurried to her room and passed out without even taking off her shoes. I really want a proper girls' night catch-up session so I can fill her in on everything, but I have to work my usual Thursday night.

I arrive at Ambiance at 11 P.M. sharp and no surprise, Gus is at the door.

"Hey, babe," he says, kissing me on the cheek as he unhooks the rope. "Solo tonight?"

"Yeah. I just needed to get out of the house," I tell him. Another one of my regular white lies. I'm one of the few patrons here this early. In my experience it won't start filling up for about another hour. Around 12:45 A.M. is when things really get going and I have to be at my most alert. A few people may trickle in over the next few minutes who bought tables and bottle service. They come early to get the most out of their money, but since the celebrities' tables are comped I have some time to kill. I find an empty table and text Nick.

Me: Wish I were with you instead of at Ambiance xo

Fifteen minutes later I'm approached by an entitled cocktail waitress with a brunette bob and blunt bangs. I hate this girl. She's worked her way along the club circuit about the same amount of time I have. She always rotates to the hot-spot club and I can't seem to get away from her. She's always dating the up-and-coming young male celebrities so she thinks she's a goddess and she's so rude to me.

"You need to move," she snarls without so much as an "excuse me." "The guests for this table have arrived." She tosses her head back authoritatively. Unfortunately no one I know is here yet so I have to retreat from my seat with my proverbial tail between my legs. I decide to hover near the bar, since it's on the exact opposite side of the club. I feel a tap on my shoulder.

"Excuse me, you're Ella, right?" Whoever just spoke to me asked for Ella, not Bella. Is my cover blown? My saliva instantly evaporates as I turn around. I look up and am relieved when I see the reveal. "I'm not sure if you remember me. Tristan." He squints his eyes, unsure if I'll recognize him even though he's got a bigger Twitter following than the president.

"Yes, you're in *Benedict Canyon* with Holiday. We met at her party."

"And at Foreign Born Supernatural Superstar's party."

"Right. Of course." The knots release from my body so quickly I almost feel light-headed with relief. "It's nice to see you again." He shakes my hand and has a firm grip. I hate people, especially men, with weak handshakes.

"I saw you over here and recognized you. And all of her photos. And she talks about you nonstop." I smile. "Is she here with you?" He looks around, trying to see if she might be in another area of the club.

"No, I wish. She crashed as soon as she got home," I tell him.

His face loosens with relief.

"That must be why she hasn't texted me back."

"I bet you'll hear from her tomorrow," I assure him.

"Yeah. We're . . . sort of seeing each other." His entire face widens as if he just got Botox and smiling is the only expression he can make.

"Oh, are you? You better behave tonight then. Holiday has a spy here." He laughs and I'm amused that he thinks it's a joke. Tristan glances around my perimeter again.

"Are you here by yourself?"

"Yeah, I needed to get out of the house for a drink," I say by rote . . . again.

"Wow. I'd never be able to go out alone. I'm way too insecure."

"Says the smoldering TV star," I joke.

"I know, but still, I don't have *that* kind of confidence," he says. This time I smile and take the compliment. If only he knew I had no choice and I'm getting paid to be here.

"That settles it, though. You're gonna come to my buddy's table. Holiday would kill me if I didn't take care of you."

He's trying to be a good guy, offering to let me hang out at a table with bottle service but being with him I have to be much more surreptitious about my observations and can't get up and take as many laps around the club without arousing any suspicion. I'd rather focus on my job and get out of here as soon as possible but I don't want to be rude. He gestures to his table a few feet away and I follow him. The surly cocktail waitress gives me side-eye when she notices me as she drops off the first round of bottles. I give her my best fuck-you smile—only for a second so she knows I have more important matters to tend to, like Tristan introducing me to his friends.

None of them are famous, which bodes well for Tristan's character but not so much for me cultivating more points.

"We have vodka and champagne. What can I get you?" Tristan asks.

"Champagne, please."

"Of course. You're Holiday's friend. I should've known." He removes the bottle from the ice bucket and tilts the flute as he pours the bubbly from the bottle. He's no champagne novice either.

"Tristan, we will be fast friends," I say, raising my glass to thank him.

"I'll drink to that," he says, pouring some for himself as well. He raises the flute in the air. "Cheers." I clink his glass.

"Are you excited to see if the show gets picked up?" My mouth tingles from the champagne. Tristan leans his chest forward, placing his elbows on his thighs, and plays with the condensation on his glass.

"Yeah. It will be awesome if it does."

"Don't be too enthusiastic or anything," I quip.

He grins. "Nah, it's just that I've been down this road before." He takes a sip of his drink. "A lot." He takes another sip.

"I think you're going to be just fine. Nick—"

"Holiday's agent?" he wonders.

"Yes, her agent."

He stares at me now, trying to figure me out.

"Anyway, he isn't concerned and when the rep isn't concerned the talent shouldn't be." My assurance doesn't do much for Tristan's anxiety.

"Agents do have a tendency to tell their clients what they want to hear, whether it's the truth or not," he warns.

"Oh, I know," I agree. "But he's a pretty honest guy." A devious smile glides across my face. "Let's just say I can tell when he's being truthful and when he's embellishing." Tristan reads my innuendo and softens his shoulders, appearing more tranquil that his career is on a prosperous path.

I'm discreetly trying to survey the room to see if any other celebrities have shown up but so far, nothing. I excuse myself to go to the bathroom so I can make my lap. I double-check every person at a table with bottle service to make sure that my gut is correct and I'm almost looking so hard for someone to be here I feel like my mind might experience a mirage and fool me into thinking that A-List Sex Symbol Box Office Gold Turned Critically Acclaimed Actor is here, since he's still a nightclub staple even though he's well into his forties and, according to Nick, wrapped his latest film.

After my unsuccessful lap I proceed to the bathroom and check my e-mail when I'm safe in the stall. There's one from Victoria—this week's points e-mail. I close the toilet lid and sit down to prepare myself. I'm not the biggest on prayer and I get really irritated by those people who pray only when they need something, so instead I'm going to ask the universe for a dose of positive energy. I click the e-mail open.

Patriot Media and Publishing Employment Scoring Rubric
1 million hits/day-first month
2 million hits/day-second month
5 million+ hits/day-third month and on
200,000 copies/month-first month
500,000 copies/month-second month
1 million+ copies/month-third month and on

Huh? This is strange. I don't have anything to do with sales. I exit out of the e-mail, trying to make sense of it, and find a second note from Victoria.

Dear Freelancers,
Please disregard the previous e-mail. Below is the correct weekly points e-mail.
Victoria

She must have accidentally forwarded another scoring rubric the first time. The only person that rubric could be for is her. I shake my confusion off and return to my concern for my own job. Here it goes. . . .

UPDATED POINTS CALCULATIONS

1. *Not me*
2. *Not me*
3. *Not me*
4. *Not me*
5. *Not me*
6. *Ella Warren*

I'm number six?! This is not okay. I'm so close to the chopping block that my skin could be pierced with even the slightest movement. I have to get something tonight, but Tristan and his friends certainly aren't going to help me bump my way up this list. I type up the few notes I have on Tristan and leave the bathroom in a panic, hoping that a celebrity has shown up while I was in there. I do another full lap before returning to the table with no such luck.

"I poured you another drink," Tristan says, handing me a flute.

"Thanks." I take a large swig to calm myself down. I hop on top of the banquette again with my stomach in knots. My eyes move around as if I'm following the movement of the strobe light, and my desire for small talk right now is null. I look down at my phone every few minutes to physically watch the evening and my chance at earning any substantial amount of points tick away. I happen to be looking down when a text from Nick pops up.

Nick: Just got home from premiere and after-party for Former Rapper Turned Ambitious Comedic and Dramatic Actor's new movie. Exhausted and about to pass out. Will be missing our slumber party tonight.
'Night, sexy.

Nick's text makes me smile but I close out of it because I need to focus all of my attention on my surroundings. At 1:45 A.M. the bar announces last call and it's official that my night is a bust. I throw my phone in my purse and tap Tristan.

"Thanks for letting me chill at your table," I tell him.

"Yeah, sure, no problem."

"I think I'm gonna head out." I'm ready to give him a hug and call an Uber.

"You sure you wanna call it a night? My boy texted me and he's throwing an after-party at his place." His friends high-five each other at the news. "You wanna roll with us?"

Right now all I want to do is send in my short file on him and go to bed.

"I dunno . . . I think—"

Tristan interrupts my lame excuse before I can even make it. "C'mon. It's at Twentysomething CW Bad Boy Heartthrob's house. He usually throws a pretty good after-party and he's not too far from Holiday's house."

If he hadn't buried the lede he wouldn't need to persuade me at all. This after-party is my Hail Mary to save the night. Twentysomething CW Bad Boy Heartthrob! Even if I didn't need a better item for *The Life* I would go. Some people say that nothing really juicy happens in LA before 2 A.M. so it's worth a shot. I know I have a code and normally wouldn't break it to troll an invitation-only after-party for work gossip but I'm number six on Victoria's list and I'm desperate. Tristan is offering me an opportunity; I need to take advantage of it. Besides, what's the use of having a code and not reporting on people's indiscretions in certain places if I can't report on anyone at all because I lose my job?

Twentysomething CW Bad Boy Heartthrob will be a good get. Not only have I had an unrequited crush on him since his show debuted but I've never seen him out before. He has a long-term girlfriend who recently stuck by him while he made a quick trip to rehab. He's had his fair share of scandalous behavior but always manages to maintain a much lower profile than his fame or indiscretions usually allow. This could put me in the top four!

"I'm in," I tell Tristan, trying to keep my reply monotone when I want to squeal and jump up and down. My heart races and I can't stop playing with my hair. I place the locks behind my ears, then in front of them. I try one side tucked behind my ear and the other in front. I'm giddy and nervous and want to look perfect. I've gone from celebrity journalist to weak-in-the-knees fan with one sentence.

"You ready to roll?" he asks, when the rest of his crew has gathered.

I follow the boys to our chauffeured SUV. We arrive at Twentysomething CW Bad Boy Heartthrob's Sunset Plaza home and we can hear the noise from the party outside. I make my way up the steep driveway, which is almost insurmountable in stilettos; we stop in the kitchen to pour some cocktails before proceeding through the rest of the house.

A group of generically pretty girls, who dress like they came from a magazine photo shoot, and refuse to even make eye contact with me are stationed in the kitchen as well. In LA, celebrities aren't the only ones that can make you feel invisible. Girls like this only talk to people that buy them dinner, booze, or Christian Louboutin shoes, or are famous or can make them famous.

"God, those girls are awful," Tristan scoffs. I couldn't agree more. "I don't know how but somehow they always end up at every after-party."

There's a very specific art to a successful after-party. A few key elements need to be in place to convince people to hang out after the club instead of going home.

1. The first element is the same as with anything else in life . . .
   location, location, location. The more unattainable the house, the
   better. Bonus points are given out if the house has a media room, a
   priceless work of art (Warhol or Banksy are preferred), or a room
   converted into a club with its own bar and dance floor separate from
   the actual living area of the house.
2. Next, there must be an unlimited supply of booze and there must be
   an appropriate amount of mixers with a wide variety of colas, energy
   drinks, and juices. If the mixers are off-brand, points are automatically
   deducted.
3. A pool is essential as well. If there aren't any shenanigans going on
   dans la piscine, what is the point of losing out on beauty sleep?
4. The last requirement for the perfect after-party is, of course, the
   perfect host. There are two types of hosts that can make an after-
   party great. A perfect host can remain aloof and anonymous, which
   is sometimes preferable, because then they aren't pacing around the
   house hovering over guests and worried about people pocketing
   their belongings. About 50 percent of the time the guests never
   meet the host, or even know the host's name. The second type of
   host is the ringleader of the party, encouraging their guests to eat,
   drink, and be merry. The perfect host will *always* offer guest rooms
   to their visitors who have enjoyed too many spirits or "recreational
   activities," or who want to fool around a little bit. Men are generally

better after-party hosts than women because a vase that's broken by
accident isn't cause for a full-on emotional meltdown—or worse,
the end of the party.

Although, since my longtime crush is hosting this fete, I think most
of those rules are eradicated by his mere presence. I won't lie; it's my goal
to get an introduction to fulfill the fantasy of my inner-teenybopper self.

His friends disperse across the house but I follow closely behind Tristan
when we leave the kitchen. He seems to know his way around and leads
us to the backyard where a fire pit and heat lamps are keeping guests warm
during this unusually crisp Los Angeles night. We stop next to a table,
under a heat lamp, and I immediately spot Twentysomething CW Bad Boy
Heartthrob on the opposite side of the pool. He's drinking liquor straight
from the bottle and is flanked by girls. I sip my drink and scan the rest of
the backyard to see if I spot any other celebs in attendance and to distract
myself from gawking at my crush. Moments later my attempt at a cool,
calm, and collected demeanor is put to the test as Twentysomething CW
Bad Boy Heartthrob approaches us and gets close enough for me to
notice a small diagonal scar above the left corner of his lips, which must
usually be covered by makeup, when he greets Tristan.

"Hey, man. How's it going?" he asks, taking a swig from the bottle of
Don Julio 1942. He swallows his shot and gives Tristan a bro embrace
with one arm while his other hand clutches the tequila bottle.

"Not too bad," Tristan answers. "Good to see you, man. It's been a
minute."

"Yeah. The network and my publicist are making me keep things chill
after rehab," he explains, using one hand for air quotes to discredit his
treatment as he rolls his eyes, sets his tequila on the table and lights a cigarette, conjuring the image of the rebels of old Hollywood. "So I'm bringing the party to me."

He certainly doesn't look like a former junkie. He looks exactly like he's
always looked on-screen, which isn't always the case with celebrities. He's
the epitome of bad-boy chic with his easy leather jacket, black V-neck
T-shirt, and jeans that couldn't fit any better if they'd been sewn on to
him.

"This is E—," he introduces. I cut him off before he can finish saying
Ella since this is the kind of crowd where I might stumble upon someone
who knows or has met Bella.

"Nice to meet you." My voice quivers and I stutter on those four small words. Twentysomething CW Bad Boy Heartthrob is even making Bella shy. I instantly feel heat permeating my entire face and I'm sure that it's redder than a red carpet. He looks me up and down, assessing what he can see and inferring what's hidden underneath my clothes. He inhales another long drag of his nicotine, which frees his hand to meet mine. When we touch I'm almost certain that my body chemistry will be altered forever. His firm handshake coupled with him gazing into my eyes makes me feel like we're alone and the crowd blurs into the background.

He frees his hand first, which is for the best because I don't think I'd ever let go.

"Are you two . . . ?" He drops off in an attempt not to be too forward.

"No!" Tristan and I both say.

"You know Holiday Hall?" Tristan asks. Twentysomething CW Bad Boy Heartthrob searches and I realize he's the type of person who probably doesn't retain any information not directly relating to his fame or orgasm, so Tristan assists him and adds context clues. "She's in my pilot. British."

A look of recognition enters his face. "Right. Yeah, the British chick?" He continues to puff on his cigarette and isn't masking that he has no interest in Tristan's story about Holiday.

"We're seeing each other," Tristan announces proudly. When the information computes, Twentysomething CW Bad Boy Heartthrob's enthusiasm grows.

"Nice, dude. Totally fuckable." He gives Tristan a playful punch on the shoulder. Tristan's face drains and he's mortified I'm witnessing this display of misogyny but allows Twentysomething CW Bad Boy Heartthrob to continue. "I'd hit it. She's kinda cool."

Tristan sees an opening to stray from the momentum of this conversation and introduces me. "She is cool, and this is her best friend," he says, placing his arm around me.

Twentysomething CW Bad Boy Heartthrob eyeballs me again even though it's clear I don't hold his interest and he wants to move the conversation along. "How'd that pilot go, man?" He takes a deep, over-exaggerated inhale and rubs his nostrils together with his thumb and forefinger. "You're so lucky to be on a new show. I'd give both of my nuts to be done with mine. I'm so fucking bored. The thought of doing another season literally crushes my soul."

"You were never really into your show, even in the beginning," Tristan adds.

"I know but at least it was tolerable then. Now . . . Jesus Christ! I'm twenty-eight. Playing a nineteen-year-old who's trying to figure out girls and how to ace his statistics final. It's empty and makes me feel like a hack. I don't wanna be on an after-school special that airs in prime time anymore," he whines.

I wish I could unhear all of this. *Manors of Mandeville* has been my favorite show since it premiered. Jess and I watched the pilot at least a dozen times when it first came out and to this day I've still never missed an episode.

Twentysomething CW Bad Boy Heartthrob removes his cigarette from his mouth, noticing he's smoked it to the filter and tosses it on his perfectly landscaped lawn while he twists his foot over it, smearing the ash, tarnishing grass. As his attention returns, two very young-looking girls wearing bikinis emerge from the pool and drape themselves around either side of him and they steal his focus. Neither of these girls happens to be his current girlfriend but that doesn't stop him from looping his arms inside of theirs and resting his hands on their hip bones, which are exposed from their very low-rise bathing-suit bottoms. "Damn, you girls look sexy." He reeks of machismo and they giggle and revel in the fact that he's ogling their bodies. There's no attempt to hide his indiscretion and he moves his hands to their bottoms.

I'm less shocked by his lack of concern for his home or blatant infidelity and more bothered by his condescending comments about his show. I wish I hadn't heard them but I did . . . and straight from the source, but I still don't want to believe them. Twentysomething CW Bad Boy Heartthrob's first acting job was *Manors of Mandeville,* unless you count being an extra in a soda commercial. In a postrehab mea culpa interview with *The Life* he praised the show's writing staff and his fellow cast members for delving deep into the difficulties of being a millennial. He didn't mean a word of it.

I understand that a majority of what celebrities say in interviews is preplanned, heartstring-tug-inducing embellishments conjured up by publicists and regurgitated by actors, but between him being an alcohol-enthusiast, a womanizer, and ungrateful, any allure he once held vanishes. At least I have some gossip to file and because he's such a jerk I'm giving myself a pardon from any possible guilt I would feel about sending in a file from his after-party. "*Twentysomething CW Bad Boy Heartthrob ready to leave show that made him a star."* My crush has turned into disgust faster than a mudslide in the Hills decreases property value.

"It's cold. Let's get you inside," he says to his belles de jour. He not so subtly cups their butts and gently pushes them toward the living room. We all follow, allowing him to shepherd us into the living room.

I need to start taking notes before I forget anything. Aside from being an addict, Twentysomething CW Bad Boy Heartthrob is known for being paranoid, so I'm sure he's installed a myriad of security cameras all over the house. The last thing I would want is for my crush to bust me, but I can always count on one place for privacy.

"Do you know where the bathroom is?" I whisper to Tristan.

"I don't remember exactly, but I know there are plenty of them. Just choose your own adventure and you'll for sure find one down one of the hallways." I stare around the colossal living room and squint my eyes, hoping that I can find a clue that will help me determine which hallway I should investigate first. I have three choices and they are all illuminated but cryptic at the same time. I make the executive decision to try the left side.

"I'll be back in a minute." The click and clack my shoes make as I take each step on the Carrara white-marble floor echo through the hollow hall. I stop when I reach the first closed door. I knock and count three Mississippis. No response so it must be empty. My hand is clammy from shaking Twentysomething CW Bad Boy Heartthrob's hand and it makes it difficult to get a close grip on the doorknob but I manage to get it open.

The room is drab and even before I turn the light on I can make out piles of memorabilia from Twentysomething CW Bad Boy Heartthrob's career, slightly visible from the hall's glow. Scripts are piled up near the door. Framed magazine covers that have never been hung rest on the baseboards. Strewn about a desk are standard teen-idol awards and trophies in the shapes of everything from a bucket of popcorn to a remote control and even a standard regulation surfboard propped against the desk. There's one I don't recognize and my curiosity is piqued. I take a brief look-see to make sure no one is coming. By the time anyone sees me being nosey on the security footage, I'll be long gone. When I confirm the coast is clear I turn on the light and infiltrate the room. I pick up an unrecognizable award. As soon as it's off the desk I notice the place below the rectangular base is shiny and almost a completely different color. The area around the award is coated in dust and it's obvious that none of this stuff has been touched since it was abandoned—as if they were a disgrace instead of signs of distinction. I can now see that the mysterious trophy is actually a giant faux gold-plated iPhone with an inscription that reads YEAR'S SEXIEST MALE SELFIE TAKER. I chuckle to myself and place the prize back on the desk exactly where it was before, matching the base to the outline of dust. I turn off the light and quietly close the door.

I progress about fifteen feet before I find myself in front of another door. I knock again, this time simultaneously opening the door. I jump back, startled, as I see a toned masculine body clad in expensive denim and a formfitting navy T-shirt bent over the countertop whose head is moving from left to right as he snorts a rail of cocaine. I grasp the doorknob to pull it shut but the person turns his head and I recognize him before I can escape.

"Bella?" It's Sexy Indie Film Actor. He could blow my cover if he refers to me as Bella instead of Ella in front of Tristan and vice versa. Sexy Indie Film Actor opens the door to make sure it's me and ushers me inside. "I didn't expect to see you here."

"Small world, smaller city," I retort with a graceless laugh in an attempt to decrease the awkwardness of catching him mid–drug use. He straightens himself out and takes a deep inhale of air to make sure all of the powder made its way into the nostril and up his nose, checks his nostrils in the mirror to make sure the evidence of his transgression is gone, and then comes over to give me a hug and kiss on the cheek. He loses his balance a little when his lips make contact with my cheek and I put my arm around him to give him a little stability. I can smell the whiskey diffusing out of his pores. The pungent smell is so overwhelming that if I didn't know any better I would think whiskey was recently discovered to have antiaging properties and he actually smeared it all over his face instead of imbibing what I can only imagine to be a lot for the odor to be this thick.

"You want a little?" he asks, pointing to the remaining pile of powder.

"No, thanks. I'm good, I just really have to pee," I tell him.

"Sure, no problem. I'll get out of your way." He quickly plugs his left nostril and blows his last line, once again checking the mirror before he turns to leave. "I'll see you out there," he says as he passes me. I close the door and shrewdly make sure to lock it. I don't want someone busting in on me while I'm doing something I'm not supposed to be doing like I just did to Sexy Indie Film Actor. I don't have time to process the surprise of his secret drug use because if I'm gone too long Tristan might become suspicious. I close the lid on the toilet, sit down, pluck my phone out of my purse, and write down my notes. When I finish I throw my phone back in my bag and wash my hands.

I return to the living room where about ten people are gathered including Twentysomething CW Bad Boy Heartthrob and Sexy Indie Film Actor, who's sitting next to Tristan. I scurry over there, praying that neither Ella nor Bella has been or is about to be exposed. I plunk myself down between them and Sexy Indie Film Actor pats my knee while Tristan smiles. So far it seems like my secret is still safe. My lungs, not so much. I'm getting a contact high from the dense marijuana smell and notice that Twentysomething CW Bad Boy Heartthrob, who has a bikini babe on either side of him, has a psychedelically decorated bong in his lap. Clearly his postrehab clarity and sobriety, which he proselytizes about every chance he has in the press, is another lie manufactured for the public's benefit and even more so, his career. Bikini Babe Number Two reaches the bong in our direction as an offering while she continues to cough.

"No, thanks," I tell her.

"I'm good, too," Tristan says.

"You sure, dude?" Twentysomething CW Bad Boy Heartthrob asks.

"I'll hit it," Sexy Indie Film Actor chimes in. Bikini Babe Number One passes it to Sexy Indie Film Actor and he returns it to her and she takes another hit before she passes it around to Bikini Babe Number Two, who takes a hit and then returns it to Twentysomething CW Bad Boy Heartthrob, who indulges again.

"But when you think about it, lingerie is just a bikini you don't wear in the water," Bikini Babe Number One claims.

"I've never thought about it like that," Bikini Babe Number Two considers. I have my doubts that either of them have ever really thought about anything, and even Twentysomething CW Bad Boy Heartthrob is deadened by their vapid discussion from the look on his face. Sadly his brain and his genitals disagree with one another.

"Why don't you girls get to the bedroom?" he requests. "I'll be up in a minute."

They eagerly bounce up from their seats as if there is silicone in their butts, too, and without question heed his request as he takes one last indulgent bong rip. He passes it back to Sexy Indie Film Actor, who exchanges a small bag of cocaine for the bong.

Twentysomething CW Bad Boy Heartthrob grabs his keys out of his pocket for a quick key bump. He snorts the drugs and wipes his nose with a newfound look of invigoration in his eyes, passing the plastic bag back to Sexy Indie Film Actor. Now I definitely don't feel bad. It's one thing if he's smoking a little weed to relax but indulging in narcotics way crosses the line, and I have no remorse for spying.

"Enjoy the after-party, kids. I'm going to get the private party started." He goes to Tristan, shaking his hand. "Great to see you, buddy. Thanks for stopping by." Twentysomething CW Bad Boy Heartthrob winks at me before he retreats for his tacky threesome. I feel dirty witnessing his drug use and infidelity and I wallow in the despair of my dream-boy disenchantment. People warn you never to meet your heroes and tonight confirms my theory that the same goes for your Hollywood crushes.

When I signed up for this job, in addition to giving up a normal sleep pattern, I gave up the fantasy that the rest of America gets to have about Hollywood. Witnessing his self-aggrandizing, womanizing behavior is a memory I will never be able to remove.

Tristan turns to me.

"I think I'm ready to call it a night too," Tristan admits. Thank God. I couldn't leave him and Sexy Indie Film Actor alone together and knew I was going to have to wait one of them out. "The rest of the guys are gonna stay and I'm gonna send the car back for them. Do you want to stay or head out?"

"I'm definitely ready to leave." I place my hand on Sexy Indie Film Actor's shoulder. "Have a good rest of the night. Glad I ran into you," I tell him.

"Good to see you, babe," he says without getting up. I sling my purse over my shoulder and follow Tristan to the car.

There's no traffic on the way home. There's no traffic anywhere at this hour. My mouth is dry yet the taste of stale champagne continues to linger. The sky is gray even though the sun is not yet on the horizon, and it won't get much brighter because of the smog. It didn't rain but everything feels wet and I am ready to get out of these clothes and my now day-old makeup.

The morning humidity overpowered my hair on the short trek from my driveway to the front door and although I have a Brazilian blow-dry, I feel the baby hairs around my forehead frizzed. I rush to my room and slip myself out of my dress, shoes, jewelry, and thong as if they were full of toxic chemicals and throw myself across my bed to open my computer. I'm too tired to procure a set of sleep clothes and would swear my eyes are bloodshot even though a quick selfie confirms they are not. Regardless of how I look or feel I need to write my file. I include Sexy Indie Film Actor's presence at the after-party but omit his drug use. He's never been anything other than sweet to me and the trivial number of points it would garner isn't worth ruining his reputation. As soon as I finish, I drop my iPhone next to me without even bothering to place it on the charger.

Eighteen

· ·

I learned through my breakup with Ethan how important it is to maintain your relationships with your girlfriends, so even though I want to spend every waking moment we aren't working and I'm not with my mom alone with Nick, I'm trying to keep a hos-over-bros mentality. I've seen Jess fairly regularly but I haven't spent any time of note with Holiday since she came back from shooting the *Benedict Canyon* pilot. Holiday has been less of a social butterfly and more of an antisocial shut-in and spends a lot of time alone with Tristan but she finally agrees to join Nick and me for dinner night at Doheny Circle, where Nick is a member.

Doheny Circle is a members-only club. Of course you can't just apply to become a member. You must have the referrals of two current members, write an essay almost as long as your college application essay, be approved by the board, and pay a hefty initiation fee as well as monthly dues. Aside from their dining-room and bar privileges they offer various social events, film screenings, and of course scotch tastings. It's sophisticated, and being here with Nick feels very adult. It's a nice departure from my previous relationship. Ethan barely had a streaming subscription to Netflix.

"No agent-client business tonight, Nick. I'm strictly here in best-friend capacity this evening," Holiday notifies Nick.

"Understood," he tells her.

"And to warn you that if you hurt Ella, I will run you over with your Tesla and drop your body into a desolate part of the canyon where you'll never be found." Her accent makes it sound charming but her threat is intimidating. Holiday is not someone I would want to cross.

Nick takes the comment in stride and humors Holiday. "Noted. Now that the threats are out of the way for the evening, shall we order?" He laughs.

"Yes, I'm ravenous," I chime in.

"How about we start with a bottle of champagne for my favorite glam-our and love girls?" he suggests.

"Yes! I'm dying for some. I've been craving some bubbles since 3 P.M.," I confess. I really have. If there were a way for me to get an IV full of calorie-free champagne I'd do it.

"None for me. I think I'm going to stick with water tonight," Holi-day tells us, dismissing his offer.

"Water? Really, Hol?" Something must be wrong. Champagne is an essential for survival to Holiday. Even if she had to flee her home and become a refugee she would somehow find a way to smuggle splits of champagne with her for sustenance. She can survive without eating for a few days but those fermented grapes are a staple of her diet. This is a huge red flag.

"I'm trying to stay camera-ready in case the show gets picked up. I can't afford any hangovers, under-eye circles, or empty calories right now." I hope her acting is more authentic in *Benedict Canyon* because even though I'd never say it, I don't believe one word.

"That's what I like to hear from my clients," Nick boasts and puffs out his chest to exaggerate.

"I never thought I'd hear the words 'none for me' come out of your mouth when referring to champagne, Hol."

"It's what people call maturity, Ella," she teases. I'm still not buying her newfound health kick and start running through other possibilities in my head.

I can't help but notice that there are only three of us and Holiday is without a plus-one even though we told her to bring Tristan.

"Where's Tristan tonight?" I question.

"He has a film audition in the morning so I didn't want to distract him." I don't really believe her but I'm also not going to give her the third degree in front of Nick. Maybe she's a little off because there's trouble in paradise, and if that's the case our conversation should be private, though when Holiday is having problems with men her go-to coping mechanism is champagne, so I'm not entirely sure I've discovered the real problem. Nonetheless, I'm ready for my bubbly.

"To glamour and love." I raise my glass to Nick's. "And a toast to my sober friend, Holiday. None of this would be possible without you." I lovingly glance at Nick. "And to *Benedict Canyon* being picked up." We clink glasses as Holiday sips her water. I notice her widening her eyes, trying her hardest to fight back the tears from my toast.

"Thank you. Love you, too, El. You are my sister." She finishes her water. "Will you excuse me? I see Gwendolyn Ross just arrived and I want to say a quick hello. I need to make sure I stay on her good side." She leaves and as soon our trio becomes a duo, Nick leans in and kisses me.

"What was that for?" I ask.

"For making the past few weeks so amazing. You're a pretty damn good girl, Ella Warren. Your job is sketchy as all hell, but you're my favorite girl, regardless."

I wish I could take his compliment but I have a gnawing feeling I can't shake. "I may be a good girl but feel like a bad friend. This is the first time I've hung out with Holiday in weeks and we basically brought her on our date."

Nick brushes off my concern. "We told her to invite Tristan. It's not our fault if he didn't come. She wouldn't have come by herself if she didn't want to." I sigh. He rests his hand on my thigh, trying to soothe me. "You know Holiday better than anyone. Do you think she ever does anything she doesn't feel like doing?"

"That's true," I concede, but I'm not 100 percent convinced. "I can't help but think there's something else going on with her, though. She seems off."

"How do you mean?" he asks.

"She didn't want any champagne. . . ." I trail off. I know it sounds trivial to him but it's not.

"Just because—"

"Nick, trust me. That's a huge red flag . . . like not the-size-of-a-pimple-the-night-before-prom huge, but the-size-of-Mars huge. Something is wrong," I insist.

He inches closer to pacify me.

"I'm sure she's fine. She's probably exhausted and nervous to see what happens with the show." I nod. He plays with a tendril of hair behind my ear to lighten me up. "This is the first real job she's ever had and the first time she cares about the job she's doing. It's probably her way of dealing with the pressure." He's probably right but I need to hear it from her to feel better.

"I'm sure you're right and I'm overreacting but would you mind if I don't spend the night? I think Holiday and I need some one-on-one girl time."

"I think that's a good idea, El. I love that you want to be there for your friend. Plus I have plenty of scripts I need to read that have been piling up on my nightstand since you've been occupying most of my evenings . . . not that I'm complaining, of course." He gives me a sweet kiss, this time on my forehead.

"Thanks, babe."

"But since you aren't coming back there's something I want to talk to you about now." I freeze. "The past few weeks with you have been so different from what I've had with any other girl. I'm sure you have plenty of guys that are chasing you every time you're out and you have other options and I know it's soon but I want you to know that I'm all in and hope you are, too?"

He looks at me composed while I'm freaking out on the inside. It's like Pop Rocks and soda have invaded my body and exploded. Nick Williams is asking me to be exclusive!

"So, like boyfriend-girlfriend?" I check.

He reaches his hand to caress my cheek. "Yeah, like boyfriend-girlfriend," he mimics. "What do you think?"

Think? I don't have to think. "I'd love that!" I can't remember the last time I was this happy, and when I pause to try to remember, I'm not sure if I've ever been this happy.

"Good. Because I'm really falling for you, Ella Warren," he admits.

"Good. Because you're stuck with me, Nick Williams . . . I mean, boyfriend," I correct.

"Here." Nick pulls a Doheny Circle membership card out of his wallet and hands it to me. "I'm supposed to put someone else on my membership."

This is the Hollywood equivalent of giving someone a key to your apartment. I stare at the titanium card before I place it in my wallet. "I was going to give this to you anyway, but girlfriends should definitely be additional cardholders." We kiss again and our eyes lock in a silent gaze like a beam in *Star Trek* that is only interrupted when Holiday returns.

"How's Gwendolyn?" I ask.

"It was par for the course. I can never tell with her. She'll go on about the best new designer, the best wine, the best meal, the best man, the best hotel in Cannes, and she never cracks a smile or displays an emotion. She has the same mannerisms and inflections when she talks about her most dreadful list, too, so who knows. I think it's who she is as opposed to being a side effect from the Botox. I'm not sure she's ever excited about anything or anyone," Holiday says.

It's time for my proposal. "Hol, what would you say to a girls' night later? Just you and me."

"Really? Just the two of us?" Her face lights up.

"I have a ton of scripts to read and contracts to review so you'd actually be doing me a favor taking this one off my hands for the night."

I give him a look and he returns with a shoulder shrug that implies he's just trying to help. That's my *boyfriend*.

"Face masks and reality TV?" Holiday asks. She has a happy tone in her voice for the first time tonight.

"You know it, girl!" Holiday perks up once we plan our date and more of her charm peeks through our dinner conversation. Nick graciously pays the check and drives us home. Holiday jumps out of the car as soon as we reach a complete stop.

"Thank you for dinner, Nick!" She rushes into the house without her signature good-bye double kiss. I roll down the window and call out to her, "I'll be in in a minute." I lean in to kiss him good night. The taste of the spearmint gum he just chewed tingles the roof of my mouth and the sensation travels through each limb of my body. I try to pull away because I know that if I don't leave now my willpower will diminish more each second and I might not ever get out of his car, but he pulls me in even closer.

The faint sound of our breath reaching a crescendo is a harmonious duet. I'm addicted to his kiss. I run my fingers through his hair and the next thing I want to do with my hand is unbutton his shirt so I attempt to pull away again and this time he allows me to. Nick releases from the embrace and kisses my forehead. I grab the door handle.

"Good night, girlfriend," he whistles.

"Good night, boyfriend," I repeat as I close the door. I watch Nick pull out of the driveway and breathe deep before going inside.

"Holiday," I yell.

"In my bedroom, darling," she calls out. The one problem with all of the square footage in her house is that you can hardly hear anyone even if they're screaming. I follow her voice and it gets louder. I enter her room and find her sitting on the floor with a pile of junk food larger than the BP oil spill in front of her.

"What is this?" I'm shocked. Holiday peers up at me, ashamed, like a dog that rips a sofa apart even though he inevitably knows he will be caught.

"My secret stash of cookies and chips," she says between bites. It's like a 7-Eleven exploded in her room.

"How long have you had this?"

"I've collected it over time and I started on this particular assortment before you moved in," she confesses.

"I had no idea you had a secret arsenal full of gluten and glucose. I am so glad I didn't know about this sooner."

"You know I'm always prepared. There's no warning before an earthquake or an emotional meltdown." I was right—there *is* something going on with her and I will get to the bottom of it, but first I'll join her in indulging in some snacks.

Holiday eagerly tears open a bag of Cool Ranch Doritos as I plop down next to her. We stick our noses in the bag as if we're wine-tasting and dig in as if we hadn't just had a full meal.

"Oh my God! I forgot how good Doritos are!"

"They really are. They're worth every single calorie," she sings. We devour the chips and each bite is so delicious we would orgasm from eating them if it were physically possible. This is the closest Holiday and I will ever come to a threesome together. I never thought I would have a transcendental experience eating powder-covered corn chips but I am and I'm not complaining.

Once we polish off the bag we hide the remnants and take a break to put on face masks before we continue our gluttony. Our civilized girls' night is quickly deteriorating into a carb bender complete with a sugar high. I eye the rest of her stash piled in front of us and am ecstatic when I see a bag of Fun Size Snickers, hiding.

"How long has it been since you've had a Snickers?" I wonder.

"Too long." She meticulously tears the bag open as if it were a bomb she was trying to disarm, rips the wrapper off, and places the candy bar in her mouth. "Mmm." Maybe nothing tastes as good as skinny feels, but all I care about is how good this junk food is making me feel right now.

"Nick is going to be able to feel every Dorito I just consumed in my ass."

"Speaking of which, how are things going with you guys? You two seemed to be even cozier than before at dinner. I want details," she begs.

"You talk to him just as much as I do."

"Yes, but only about work, darling. Besides he's a smart man. He wouldn't confide in me knowing that we're best friends."

"He asked me to be his girlfriend tonight."

Holiday coughs on a Snickers. "Oh my God!" she squeals.

"I know."

"Nick is one of the most eligible bachelors in Hollywood and that's not a euphemism. He was on *LA Magazine*'s list." That makes me feel amazing and slightly intimidated at the same time.

"After everything that happened with Ethan, I wasn't sure that I would feel this way again, especially so soon, or that anyone would feel this way about me again. We spend the night together almost every night, and it's hard for me to sleep without him anymore."

"My little Ella. Look at you. Always working with celebrities but instead of being a star fucker you turned out to be a rep ho," she jokes before hugging me.

Holiday is genuinely excited for my happiness but she's still mum about her news.

"What's been going on with your mom?" she asks.

"You know . . . chemo. We have her bone-marrow biopsy coming up so we'll know more then about how she's responding."

"Keep me posted," she requests.

"I will. Thanks for asking. But Hol, stop deflecting. I can tell you have something on your mind. Spill. What's going on with you?" I probe.

"What do you mean?" She stares at me blankly like I just asked her to explain quantum physics in three sentences.

"You know I know you better than this. Passing up champagne, leaving your boyfriend behind to willingly be a third wheel, and now this." We both stare at the mound of colorful empty wrappers in front of us and know there's a metaphor for feeding something in this sight. She stares at her perfectly polished fingers. My instinct is telling me I'm going to have to pry it out of her.

"Ella, I'm scared," she finally admits.

"Scared of what?" She's reticent and I can tell she's engaging in an internal debate about confiding in me. I've never seen Holiday like this and I'm a little afraid for her. "Does it have something to do with Tristan?"

"Sort of." A flood of tears rushes out of her, and for the first time in our friendship I see her cry.

"Holiday, what's wrong? You have to tell me. You're scaring me."

She tries to string sentences together but they are difficult to understand through the tears and snot. I rub her back for a few minutes to calm her down until she can speak coherently. She places her head in my lap and I pet her hair. After a few minutes she gazes up at me, and as much as I can see she wants to tell me I also know there's a part of her that wishes she could keep this secret forever.

"I'm late," she whispers.

"Oh my God!"

My reaction causes her to cry harder. "At first I thought it was stress but haven't been able to stop eating and my boobs have been tender and I've been fatigued, but I started getting anxious and my brain was spinning out of control, so I Googled the early symptoms of pregnancy online and I have all of them," she whimpers.

I lean back toward her nightstand and grab a tissue and wipe away the tear residue from her face. "What if it's true . . . ?" Her voice drifts into silence.

"Shh." I try to mollify her.

"I don't even want to say the word out loud," she mutters between sniffles.

"Is this why you weren't drinking?" I ask.

Holiday nods and buries her head in my lap again like an ostrich in the sand.

"It's going to be okay." I continue petting her. "First we need to be sure and then even if you are pre—" Holiday looks up at me and her look stops me from saying the word. "Even if you are, you have options."

"That's not even the worst part," she sniffles. "If I am, I'm not sure if the father is Seth or Tristan." That is a bomb I was not expecting, but I know that I need to conceal my shock or else it will push her over the edge.

"Let's not jump to any conclusions. You shouldn't even have these thoughts running through your head yet. You need to take a test," I tell her.

"I know. I've been too scared, plus what if the paparazzi see me buying the test? I've been getting papped more now that I filmed the pilot and the last thing I need right now is a photo floating around of me buying a . . . test."

I can't help but smile. "Holiday, I love you but you're not that famous."

"Are you calling me D-list?"

"Of course not! You're just not A-list . . . yet. I mean the paps aren't waiting outside of the house to follow you. You happen to frequent the hot spots they lurk in front of. I think we can make a covert trip to the drugstore. The paps are much more likely to be out busting celebrities who are actually buying drugs." My joke doesn't resonate and Holiday continues to wallow.

"I can't be . . . Ella. Not only is this the first time in my life that I'm doing something that I actually care about, but I love Tristan and I could lose him. If he *is* the father he might not be ready for this and if he's not he'll probably leave me. He's the first guy I've loved in years and I messed it up."

"It's going to be okay," I console. "First off, there's no baby daddy without an actual baby." Holiday finally lets out a little squeal that was partially a laugh. "We aren't even positive that you're knocked up."

She scrunches her mouth at me.

"If you ever refer to my possible child's father as a baby daddy again I will kick you so hard in your ovaries that *you* will never be able to have children," Holiday warns. She smiles and follows her joke with more bawling and I know she actually isn't kidding.

"Just because you're hungry and your boobs feel extra large doesn't mean you're pregnant. You've been depriving yourself of refined sugar and simple carbohydrates for years and you've been under a lot of pressure lately. You were bound to crack someday," I point out. Holiday grins. "There's no point in jumping to any conclusions until you take a test. We're going to CVS to get you one right now."

"Right now?" She stares at me with a look of sheer terror.

"Yes, right now. The only thing that waiting will do is drive you crazy and a trip to the psych ward will be worse for your career than a potential pregnancy. Because again, you're not Not-So-Innocent Oversexualized Pop Star." Holiday glances down at her lap and I place my hand on top of hers. "Whatever the results are we're going to figure this out together."

"Ella, I don't know if I can. I'm too scared," she squeals, removing her hand from underneath mine and tucking her hair behind her ears.

"You don't have to do anything. You just have to sit in the car while I go in and buy the test—so there's not even a chance of anyone recognizing you." She begins doing the breath-of-fire technique to try and soothe herself, but her cheeks are red and she looks more flustered. "You need to do this and you need to be there. This is one of those defining moments in your life that all of those speakers in TED Talks always ramble on about."

Holiday finishes her breathing exercise and preps herself as if we're leaving the huddle for the final play in the Super Bowl, but before we break she throws her arms around me.

"Thank you, Ella. I don't know what I'd—"

I interrupt. "Let's go. Enough stalling." I wink.

"Let's take my car," she suggests.

"Okay, but I'm driving." Under normal circumstances, Holiday isn't the best driver. It's not that she's a *bad* driver but that she's careless and doesn't pay attention. She's usually off in her imagination in a fantasy world and doesn't notice traffic signs, traffic signals, or other traffic. Now that she's worked herself up into a state of mania, I'm definitely not letting her get behind the wheel and endanger two, possibly three, lives.

. . . .

I return to the car and place the bag containing the pregnancy test in the center console. Her eyes linger on it, knowing that this box is more clairvoyant than the numerous psychics and tarot-card readers she's visited throughout the years. Its contents will determine the trajectory of her future. I'd like to tell her that the hard part is over but I know that her waiting three minutes for her results will be excruciating. We begin the drive home in silence and after five minutes I have to add some levity to this drive of dread.

"I almost wish you would've come in. The people-watching at a twenty-four-hour drugstore at this hour was better than spying on celebrities. I'm pretty sure the guy in front of me was buying supplies to dispose of a dead body," I comment. Holiday continues her silence and I briefly take my eyes off the road to make sure she's okay. Her eyes are fixated on the bag and I don't think she's taken a breath through her mouth in minutes. My eyes return to the road and I need to breathe. I wasn't anticipating such an intense or late girls' night but lack of sleep is nothing new and Holiday needs me.

As we're getting closer to home I finally hear Holiday take a breath and I'm relieved. But then I hear a rustling sound and look over at Holiday again. I turn on the dome light.

"What are you doing?" I shriek. She's taken the pregnancy test out and quickly inspects the box, like she's analyzing the nutritional information on a box of cereal, opens it, and pulls a test out. "Holiday!" I shriek. Put that down!

"What's the big deal? I just wanted to see it," she explains, still holding both objects in her hands.

"You can't be so careless, Hol. I know I said the paparazzi aren't following you but that doesn't mean at *this* moment you should act like they aren't." I look to her again, to rip the box from her hands, when a bright flash appears, almost blinding me.

"Shit!" I scream. A red-light camera! I'm not paying attention for two seconds, trying to make sure Holiday doesn't dig herself into a public scandal, and instead I commit a traffic crime. "That's like a five-hundred-dollar mistake." I groan.

"I'll pay for it," Holiday insists. "I don't know what I was thinking. Thank you for always trying to protect me."

I try to shake it off and focus on the task at hand when we get back home.

"How does this work?" she asks. "I pee on the stick and if the smiley face shows up my career is over before it started?"

"No. I went for the high-end digital test. I figured this is one item you don't go generic with. You pee on the stick, wait three minutes, and either the words *pregnant* or *not pregnant* will appear in the window." She sighs, anxious over the most important 180 seconds of her life. "Now get your skinny ass into the bathroom and pee."

Holiday complies and I fall to the bed and take a brief moment to close my eyes and finally process my thoughts. What if Holiday is pregnant? I put on a brave face, acting assured and not wanting to add to her anxiety, but she very well could be with child. She's done so much for me that whatever the result, I will be there for her. My heartbeat speeds up when she exits the bathroom.

"Three minutes," I tell her as I set the timer on my phone. She lies next to me on the bed as we wait in silence. After what feels like a lifetime we hear the alarm ring. "It's time. You ready?"

"No." Her face has gone pale and is cloaked with sheer terror. "I can't do it," she cries.

"Yes, you can," I assure her.

"Will you look for me?"

"Are you sure? This is big. You might want to do it yourself. . . ."

"No. I can't. My heart is beating so quickly I feel like it's about to beat out of my chest."

"Okay. I'll look." I get off the bed and as I enter the bathroom she calls out to me.

"If it's bad don't drag it out," she requests.

I proceed into the bathroom and pick up the test resting on the edge of the sink. "Well?" she bellows from the bedroom. I know that she's in a state of panic but I don't know what to tell her. I silently return to the bedroom and extend the test to Holiday. She doesn't look. "Ella, you're scaring the crap out of me. What does it say? Pregnant or bloody not pregnant?"

"Both."

"What do you mean, both?" she snaps.

"I mean it says 'pregnant' but the word 'not' keeps flickering in and out." She finally peeks for herself. "The test must be malfunctioning," I add.

"Well, that was anticlimactic," she snaps, not at me but at the situation.

"There's another one in the box. Try again," I tell her. She repeats the process and the second time the wait is filled with more aggravation than suspense. The timer rings and she goes to retrieve her results.

"Bloody hell!" she roars. "So much for your name brand." She hands me the second test and I see the same results as the first.

"It must've been a manufacturing error," I tell her. Holiday throws herself back on the bed and I can tell she's about to commence phase two of her meltdown, so I quickly jump in.

"Do you want me to go back to the drugstore and get another test from a different brand?"

"No," she whimpers. "That was too emotionally exhausting to possibly go through again. I'll go to the doctor. I'll get a 100-percent answer that way, whatever the results are. . . ." She sighs.

"I know we wanted to find out tonight but I think that's the best solution. You'll get some much-needed sleep and I'll call first thing in the morning to get you an emergency appointment."

"I just want this to be over either way." She swallows.

"I know. But there's nothing we can do about it right now. The best thing you can do is calm down and get some rest."

Holiday crawls under her covers and I wrap her into the sheets like she's a burrito. "Thank you, Ella," she whispers. "I might not be able to have champagne right now, but having you is even better." *That* is a compliment coming from Holiday Hall.

"You're welcome, sweetie." I move toward the door.

"Ella . . . you can't tell anyone about any of this. I know you wouldn't but you know sometimes you just have to say it out loud." I can't believe that she's finally acknowledging what happened. "I'm serious. You cannot breathe a word of this to anyone. Not even Nick. If they pick up the show and I am . . . he'd be obligated to tell them before we sign the contracts. They could replace me and I could lose my dream."

"I promise." We stare at each other, both realizing what is at stake. "Rest up. I'll see you in the morning."

Nineteen

. . . .

D r. Nazari can't see Holiday until 11 A.M., so I have time to shower and make myself look like some semblance of a human being before I have to wake Holiday. We go to the same gynecologist, but that's not unusual. Dr. Nazari is the It OB/GYN. There's an It everything in Los Angeles. The one thing I have listened to Robin about over the years is that you should always try to see the best doctors when possible and to prioritize your health above all else. If I didn't, I'd have a collection of designer purses that could rival Holiday's. . . . well, not really. She has a *lot* of bags. Dr. Nazari is as well known for her bedside manner as she is for her supermodel looks and impeccable fashion sense. Every time she enters the exam room her Diane von Furstenberg wrap dress is paired perfectly with matching Louboutin pumps with fresh makeup and not a hair out of place. If you didn't know better you'd swear she's just come from a photo shoot instead of a delivery room. She understands women in Los Angeles. We like comfort and she decked out her office to meet her patients' needs. Her office is nicer than the apartment I lived in with Ethan. Every room has its own flat-screen TV and scented candles. It sounds frivolous but I need amenities when I have to spread my legs without dinner first.

When we arrive at Dr. Nazari's office Holiday can't sit still.

"Read a magazine or something," I suggest. She shuffles through the selection, which are mostly periodicals on parenting but happens to find an old copy of *Departures* toward the bottom of the stacks.

"Holiday Hall," the nurse calls out. Holiday didn't even have a chance to crack the binding.

"Everything will be okay," I assure her.

"Will you come back with me? You know how much I hate needles."

I try to lighten the mood.

"At least you weren't ever tempted by the tramp-stamp fad." She grins. "Yes, I'll come with you."

As we enter, the nurse hands her a sealed plastic cup. "We need a urine sample. Place it inside the window when you're done, then go to exam room three."

Holiday nods and goes to the bathroom while I wait for her in the exam room. She enters and the nurse follows, asking her a slew of standard questions. "How often do you drink? How many drinks would you say you have a week? Do you smoke? How many sexual partners have you been with? Have you ever had unprotected sex with any of your sexual partners?"

When the nurse places the tourniquet around her arm Holiday looks like she's about to puke or pass out. I take her hand in mine.

"Pinch me when it starts to hurt," I tell her.

"Are you sure?" she asks with her voice shaking already. "I don't want to hurt you."

"I'll be okay." As soon as the needle punctures her skin she digs her nails into me. I'm holding my pain in so she can get through hers.

"All done," the nurse tells us what feels like an eternity later. I inspect my hand, limp with pain, and the imprints of Holiday's nails look like track marks. "We'll run the test and the doctor will come in to discuss the results."

I put on the TV and there's a rerun of *The Wendy Williams Show* on. I grab a bottle of sparkling water and slink into the office chair, beat and bruised, but grab my phone.

Me: Watching a rerun of Wendy and thinking of you. See you tomorrow for your 28 day test results. I know you're gonna be in remission. I love you, Mom! xo

There's a knock on the door.

"How are we doing today, Holiday?" Dr. Nazari asks as she enters the room.

"I don't know, you tell me," Holiday answers. She shakes Holiday's hand and notices me in the corner. "Nice to see you again, Ella." Dr. Nazari flips through Holiday's chart and holds a separate piece of paper with her test results. She scans the paper and I'm waiting with as much antici-pation as if it were me who might be pregnant. Holiday looks up to the ceiling. Like me, Holiday isn't big on organized religion. She believes that Karl Lagerfeld is her messiah and his cat, Choupette, is his prophet, but I'm not sure they will be able to help her in these circumstances.

"You are not pregnant." We both shriek and when it comes to an end I let out a small uncomfortable laugh. I feel lighter and didn't realize how much sympathy anxiety I was having for Holiday until now that it's sub-sided. Not only would the decision of whether or not to have the baby have changed her life in one way or the other, but knowing her, not hav-ing the child wouldn't be an option she would've been able to live with. Though having it would've created a bit of a PR nightmare. Aside from the hazey paternity circumstances, every pound she gained and man she's been photographed speaking to in the last three months would've been scrutinized by every celebrity media outlet until she gave birth. "Since you're here, I'd like to go ahead and do your annual exam and we can discuss different birth-control options if you'd like, to try to prevent this situation from happening again." Normally Holiday wouldn't sit through a lecture disguised as a discussion given by anyone, but after hearing this news she'd listen to Sir David Attenborough narrate an earthworm's existence—she's so relieved she doesn't care.

. . . .

I've never been as terrified as when Dr. Nazari was lecturing me," Holi-day confesses when we're finally out of there. "It was all STDs this and STIs that and birth control, birth control, birth control!"

"You think she was bad? That's nothing. She's like Dr. Seuss compared to Dr. Jacobs's bedside manner."

Holiday's mouth widens at hearing the comparison.

"Do you know how much you scared me?"

"Fuck, darling, I scared myself," she admits. "I was envisioning I'd have to accessorize all my outfits with a scarlet *H*."

"Yeah, way to be a Ho-liday." At least neither of us has lost our sense of humor. "You know, spending the past hour at the gyno with you spread-eagle wasn't exactly on my bucket list."

"Yours, mine, or the Republican party's," she quips back. "Get me out of here, I need a dirty martini!"

"No champagne? Are you sure you don't have pregnancy brain?" I jab.

She places her arm around me and explains.

"Champagne is for celebrations. Martinis are for fucking miracles." She raises her hands to the sky. "Come on, I'm buying."

"Somehow, Holiday, things always work out for you." I giggle.

"They do." She tries to mask her nerves with her wit but her fear still shows through. "I know there's going to come a day when they don't."

"I love you, Hol, but after this near miss I hope to God I'm not around to see what your emotional state is when that day comes." And I mean it.

My phone begins buzzing and won't stop. It's Robin.

Robin: Mom's 28 day counts came back!!

Robin: They've improved!

Robin: She's not in remission but Dr. Jacobs is allowing her to come home!!

Twenty

. . . .

Surprise!" I yell when my mom and Robin enter her house.

"Ella?! What are you doing here?" my mother asks, flabbergasted.

"More importantly, how did you get in here?" Robin interrogates.

"You gave me a key when you first moved in," I remind her. "And I'm here to celebrate you being home from the hospital."

"That was very thoughtful of you," my mother says, embracing me.

"Do you want to stay for dinner tonight?" Robin asks. "Jeff is making lettuce-wrap tacos."

"As tempting as that sounds, I can't. I have to work tonight but I wanted to be here to welcome you home."

"We'll have dinner together soon," my mom assures me.

"Actually that's part of the reason I came by . . . to ask you if you're feeling up for that mother-daughter Spago date I owe you?"

"Absolutely!" The glimmer that's been missing for so long has returned to her eyes. "When are you free to go?"

"How about tomorrow?"

"Tomorrow?! Wait, wait, wait. Mom, I'm not sure it's a good idea. You *just* got out of the hospital," Robin reminds her.

"That's the point, Robin. I've been in the hospital for the past month and life is short. I've been looking forward to this. I could spend every night at your house resting for the rest of my life and there's still a chance this cancer could beat me. I don't want to live like that." Robin's eyes change and we all know she connected with what my mother said. "It's just dinner. It might even make me feel better. Ella, do you think you will be able to get us a reservation on such short notice?"

"It shouldn't be a problem, but I can always have Holiday make a call if there's an issue."

"Then it's settled! I'm going. Now I just need to find an outfit that hides my port."

"I'll bring your bag up in a minute, Mom," Robin calls out to her. "Ella, do you really think this is a good idea?" I can almost hear her teeth yearning to grind against each other out of anger.

"It was your idea for me to do something to make it up to her for missing chemo!" I remind her.

"And I'm glad you are, but she has cancer, not a cold. Can't you make it up to her with a little less excitement? She's doing better but she's far from cured. She still has to do outpatient chemo and needs to watch her diet." Her frustration is increasing, but I'm not gonna let her ruin this for me or my mom.

"Can you be her daughter instead of a doctor for once? You know she will get a huge kick out of this. She's been looking forward to it. She said it herself."

Silence.

"Besides, isn't a positive attitude and a high spirit proven to help people who are sick? You can't keep her cooped up in the house if she isn't at the hospital."

Robin lightly moans.

"C'mon, it's just dinner and she has to eat. I promise, I won't let her bus any tables."

"Fine, do what you want," she tells me, upset that I'm questioning her authority and her medical opinion.

"Screw cancer!" I hear my mother yell from the top of the stairs.

. . . .

It's just like how it looks in *The Life*," my mother gushes. She's ecstatic, her eyes darting around as if she's a trophy wife in a diamond mine.

"I really am sorry I missed a chemo treatment. I wanted to be there but I got caught up in work and . . . there's no excuse. I'll be there next time."

"I understand, Ella. You have to live your life. I know Robin gives you a hard time but you're there for me as much as you can be." I smile at my mom because I want her to enjoy her night out but I'm disappointed in myself and ashamed. Nothing should take precedence over my mother's health. "I can't believe I'm at Spago!" she sings.

"I know you've always wanted to come here."

"It's classic Hollywood but what's even better is being here with you." She smiles. I know that dinner doesn't expunge the fact that I missed chemo but she is so happy to be here.

"Do you know what you want to eat?"

"My appetite isn't back to full swing yet so I might not be the best food decision-maker at the moment. You're my Hollywood guide. I trust you to choose."

"How about we ask him?" Her eyes follow mine and none other than Wolfgang Puck is mingling in the dining room checking in on his guests. My mother is in heaven.

"How are you two beautiful ladies doing this evening?" he asks when he reaches our table. My mother blushes.

"Chef, what would you recommend tonight?" I ask.

"Have you been here before?" he inquires.

"I have but it's my mother's first time. It's a special occasion."

"In that case, leave the ordering to me." My mother is impressed and feels like a queen, and despite Robin's displeasure about our outing I think it could be what my mom needed.

"Thank you, Chef," I say with a grateful grin.

He brings out course after course of different delicacies. I'm normally a pretty good eater but I can't keep up, especially because my mother has the appetite of a bride before her wedding day. But she always has room for dessert, cancer or no cancer. During the dessert course of some kind of pastry that's dark chocolate with a name way too fancy to pronounce, my mother stops midbite. She tries to say something without opening her mouth, like a ventriloquist, but I can't understand anything. Finally she whispers, "Middle-Aged Self-Proclaimed Bachelor Actor is at the bar." Not only is he the biggest celebrity she's ever seen in real life but she also knows that at this moment she's the sidekick to a reporter for *The Life*. "It looks like he's sipping a scotch. I will try to get a look at the brand when the bartender pours him a refill."

"Very good eye, Mom."

She's proud of herself, and it's so cute to see her excited and get a look at what I do through her eyes. "He's even more handsome in person." We scoot our chairs a little bit around the table so we have a better vantage point. "He's a good get, right?"

"Totally!" And if I can get Victoria the right details I might have a chance at a cover story. At the very least I should be in good standing points-wise with everything I've turned in this week. We observe multiple women approaching Middle-Aged Self-Proclaimed Bachelor Actor, and while he's not inappropriately friendly, he's very polite to each of the women who thought they might have a shot at seducing the star. No such luck.

"Do you think he'd take a picture with me?"

I usually despise the idea of asking a celebrity for a fan photo but if it makes my mom happy, I'm all in. "There's only one way to find out." We make our way over to the bar. We are about to approach Middle-Aged Self-Proclaimed Bachelor Actor when my mother grips my arm like we're going down in a plane crash.

"I can't do it, Ella."

"Sure you can," I encourage.

"I'm too nervous." She's about to make a run back to the table, but I know how much a picture would mean to her and am not unnerved by his presence so I step in.

"I will ask for you." My mother nods and I break free from her grasp.

"Excuse me, I'm so sorry to bother you but my mom is a really big fan of yours and she really wants a photo with you but she's too nervous to approach you."

He looks over at my mom, who nervously waves. "I don't mean to be an asshole but if I take one with her then I have to take one with whoever else asks and I wanted to have a low-key night." At Spago? He came to Spago to stay under the radar?

Oh, hell no. I pull out the big guns. "She's in town being treated for leukemia and it would really mean a lot to her if you could make this one exception." Okay, it's not exactly kosher to manipulate him and prey on his sympathy but if I can use the cancer card to make one of her fantasies a reality, I'm going to do it. I'm really just giving her a senior Make-A-Wish moment.

"Oh, I'm so sorry," he says, embarrassed by his previous refusal. "Yes, of course I'll take a picture with her. What's her name?"

"Joan."

"Joan, get over here!" My mom rushes over. "Hi, Joan, it's very nice to meet you."

I haven't seen her this happy since before her diagnosis.

"It's very nice to meet you," she echoes. My mom is massaging her hands, which is her tell that she's anxious.

"Are you enjoying your evening?"

"Oh, yes. My daughter is so sweet to treat me to a Hollywood night." Middle-Aged Self-Proclaimed Bachelor Actor flashes that smile that made him a star.

"Let's take that picture, shall we?" He leaves his barstool and places his arm around my mom.

"You ready?" I ask. They both nod. "One, two, three." I snap a few photos on my phone.

"Are they good?" My mom wants to know.

"Take a look." She scrolls through them and the joy on her face is illuminating her spirit. Note to self: If yoga is nature's Xanax, joy is nature's Botox.

"Thank you. This was a real treat."

Middle-Aged Self-Proclaimed Bachelor Actor gives her a hug. "Enjoy your evening, ladies."

We return to the table and I begin writing notes on everything that happened during the interaction, highlighting that he "graciously took photos with fans."

"I will never forget this," she tells me, and I have to fight back a quivering lip and tears. I bury my face back in my iPhone.

As I type, an e-mail clicks through. It's the updated points sheet. Even with my info on Not-So-Innocent Oversexualized Pop Star I'm still number four? How is this possible? Where are these other girls getting their scoops and how are they getting them? Thank goodness I at least got a sighting in here because it looks like every last point is going to count before Victoria does her next round of termination. I return to my notes in a frenzy to make sure I get everything down, and thank goodness my mom has my back.

My mother, now even more enamored with Middle-Aged Self-Proclaimed Bachelor Actor than she was before, has kept her eye on him while mine has been buried in my smartphone. She clears her throat loudly like she's done this with me a hundred times before so I look up. She tilts her head over toward the bar area and I see it; well, in this case, her— Middle-Aged Self-Proclaimed Bachelor Actor's ex-wife! She takes the stool next to him at the bar, and now this has gone from a sighting to a potential story. Why is she here? Does his new girlfriend know he's meeting her? They're supposed to hate each other, having had one of the most acrimonious divorces Hollywood has ever seen.

My eyes are shifting between them and my phone as if my head was on a remote control that could only look at those two things . . . until I hear my mother release a sigh.

"Mom, are you okay?" The sparkle that has been in her eyes all night has disappeared.

"I'm feeling a little nauseated and tired, that's all." She tries to conceal her discomfort but I can see right through it.

"Coffee, ladies?" the waiter interrupts.

"Ella, that's up to you if you want to *stay*." What she really means is, do I want to drag out our meal so I can spy?

"No, thank you. Just the check, please."

"Are you sure you don't need to stay to see what happens with them? I don't mind." Her sentiment is sincere and clinches my decision.

"Not a chance. I'm going to get you home."

My mom keeps her eyes peeled to Middle-Aged Self-Proclaimed Bachelor Actor while I pay the bill. I'm glad we saw him. He inadvertently paid for our dinner by allowing me to expense it for getting the sighting. My mom remains reticent as I sign the bill and continues her self-imposed but brief vow of silence until we get in the car and are assured of our privacy. She then releases her breath and can't wait any longer to spill the dirt on our drive home.

"His ex-wife continually tried to make eye contact with him, which he denied the whole time I was watching. He seemed distant and was drinking at double the speed he was before she showed up," she rattled off. I laugh. I don't know if years of reading *The Life* gave her an innate sense of what details to key into or if she's better at my job than I am.

"Are you gunning for my job too?" I tease her. My compliment gives her smile a shimmer.

"Never. I'm just trying to help. If you get a byline, it's a win," she affirms. "His hands appeared stiff, and it seemed like he even clenched one into a fist at some point throughout their conversation." She continued providing the minutest details until I pulled in the driveway.

"You're back early," Robin comments when I bring my mother inside. My mom gives me a kiss, a hug, and a squeeze.

"Thank you for tonight. It was so special to be there with you." She starts removing her jewelry at the base of the stairs. Like mother, like daughter. "Is Marianna still awake for story time?"

"No, she's been asleep for about an hour."

"Just as well, I'm exhausted. Good night, girls." She slowly walks upstairs, holding on tightly to the railing.

"'Night, Mom," I call out. Robin and I are left alone, staring at each other.

"I'm glad you had fun." This is Robin's way of offering peace.

"We did. But I think you were right. She got really tired. Maybe it was a little too much too soon. I'm sorry. I should've listened to you." I stare at every corner in the room, waiting to incur my sister's wrath, but it doesn't come.

"I'm not trying to be a bitch, El. I just want to do everything we can in our power to make sure her body is capable of beating this disease."

"I know. I'm sorry. I won't question you again." I'm not sure if I was being selfish, bringing her out as a way for me to feel better for missing chemo. I swallow and Robin hugs me.

"She did seem like she had a lot of fun, though. It might not be what the doctor ordered, but maybe it was what she needed." I shake my head. "I better get back home. I have a file I need to turn in and I'm pretty exhausted myself." I make my way toward the door. "Give Marianna a kiss for me."

"Will do."

"Maybe I could come by soon and take her to the park or something after school?"

Robin's expression transforms into an actual smile. A feat for me.

"She'd love that." She approaches me for one last hug. "'Night."

Twenty-one

· · · · · · · · · · · · · · · · · · · ·

lla! Ella! Did you hear?" Holiday hollers and storms in, waving a bottle of Dom. I'm lying in bed attempting to take a nap but I'm so exhausted I can't sleep so I don't mind the spontaneous distraction.

"No, what?" I wiggle my way up and rest my back against the headboard.

"*Benedict Canyon* got picked up! I go back to Canada tomorrow to shoot the series!" she squeals.

"Congratulations, Hol!" I leap out of bed to give her a hug. "I'm so proud of you." I guess those glamour-and-love toasts have paid off for us both.

"You know what, darling?" She admires herself in my mirror. "I'm proud of me, too. When I got the news I literally screamed into the phone. I probably busted Nick's eardrum."

"Eh, better than anything else on him being broken," I tease.

"We *must* celebrate tonight. I'm thinking Chateau? I know you're still on your crusade for points, so if we go there we can kill two birds with one champagne bottle." I furrow my brow at her updated cliché but can't help but morph it into a smile. "We'll meet up with Nick and Tristan after and I won't take no for an answer."

"Well, then, I guess I don't really have a choice. I'll ask Victoria if she's assigned it to any of the other girls already." I grab my phone and quickly e-mail Victoria. "I'll let you know what she says . . . but be warned, if she says I'm allowed to cover, I might have to include you in my file, 'British Heiress Turned Hollywood It Girl,'" I tease.

"Darling, you fucking better." She winks. She hoists the champagne above her head as if it's a trophy, and to her it kind of is. "I know it's a bit shy of five P.M. but it *is* a special occasion. Let's pop this open!"

"I won't argue with that!"

Holiday pops the cork with her signature ease and grace and takes a swig directly from the bottle. I hadn't noticed that she didn't bring glasses but if Little Miss Classy is down to drink a bottle of bubbly like it's a forty, who am I to argue? With her wealth, social status, and soon-to-be celebrity being what it is, it's nice to know that she can let go with the best of 'em. In her own way, of course.

Holiday pauses with the bottle at her lips. "Wait! What are we drinking to?" she asks.

"*Benedict Canyon*," I say, stating the obvious.

"I know we're drinking to that but we need an actual toast. We *always* toast. Something eloquent." She's searching. "How about to everything being perfect?"

"Nothing is ever *perfect*, Holiday. But I think we are both pretty damn close."

"If life were perfect, why would we need champagne?" she adds, finally taking another swig. Oh, how true.

My phone buzzes.

"We're good for tonight." Victoria said no one else was assigned to cover Chateau yet.

"Fabulous! It will be a night we won't forget."

. . . .

I groan under my breath when we arrive at the host stand at the Chateau Marmont. Of course Pixie Haircut Hostess, my least favorite, is working tonight. Why wouldn't she be? I transition into Bella.

"Hi, reservation for Warren for two for 8 P.M." I always try to get away with only using my last name instead of getting into the Ella/Bella of everything—especially after my debacle with the waitress a few weeks ago. The hostess escorts Holiday and me to a table, but instead of leaving the lobby and leading us on my familiar walk outside to the garden, she brings us a few feet away to a table in the dining room inside. Why is she seating us here? Nothing happens inside the dining room, that's why I don't sit inside. While it's always been clearly stated that my request for a patio table is not guaranteed, I've never not been seated there. The celebrities *always* sit outside in the garden, rain or shine, through summer and winter. Pixie Haircut Hostess knows I always sit out there, too. As much as it pains me to talk to her, this is absolutely necessary. I need to address this so I can do my job.

"Sorry to be one of those annoying people but I requested to sit in the garden. Is there nothing available out there?"

She rolls her eyes and leans in to me, too close for comfort. "Follow me," she instructs. Oh good, she realizes her mistake. She's going to take us out there. Holiday and I follow her, but she turns around. "Just you," she says to me. I obey and follow her to the side of the living room next to the piano. She glares at me with an undeniable smirk before speaking.

"It's come to our attention that you work for *The Life*," she announces. Fuck! Fuck! Fuck! Fuck! Fuck! What do I do? Relax. You've got this Ella . . . Bella . . . whoever you are. It doesn't matter. Just be calm and you can fix this. You've always been prepared for this. Now is not the time to panic. Be confident and stand your ground.

"Oh, yeah. Sometimes I do some freelance red-carpet stuff for them." If they know that I work for *The Life* there's no point in denying it. But I *can* downplay it.

"We didn't know that. I've seen your real name on stories online, *Ella*." My heart stops. At least it feels like it has. Is this what it feels like to have a stroke? As soon as she calls me Ella I know that my years of duplicity have come to an end. My intuition tells me there's no recovering from this, even with the best lie, but I'm not going to let her win this easily so I proceed to my next tactic. The best defense is a good offense.

"I wasn't aware that I was required to present my résumé and tax return when I make a reservation." I know that I'm in the wrong here and getting into it with this particularly thorny hostess isn't going to make my situation any better but I can't help myself. If anyone was going to bust me, why did it have to be *her*?

"I believe you're aware that it's our policy that we do not allow any media to dine here." Of course I'm aware of it. It's printed on the menus along with a warning that there's no flash photography—or photography of any kind, for that matter—permitted on the premises without exception. "I'm sorry but you're not welcome in the garden anymore. Tonight you can still enjoy your last meal inside if you like." She turns to leave.

"Wait!"

She whips her head back around, annoyed that she has to continue speaking to me.

"How did you find out?" I blurt out. I have to know. Did someone rat me out? Was it one of the other reporters? Was it someone I thought was my friend? Did they Google me? I have a million scenarios racing through my mind.

"Well, Ms. Warren, it seems like you have your sources and so do we."

Pixie Haircut Hostess struts away, pleased with her tongue-lashing, enjoying the bomb she's just dropped on me. I've been coming here undetected for years. I can't imagine how they found out, even though it's really not important. My mind is spinning out. What if to spite me even more she spreads it around the hospitality community in LA? All of the restaurateurs and nightlife impresarios and their employees routinely mingle. Everything in LA works on a barter system. I'm sure she gives coveted Chateau reservations to club owners and promoters in return for a table and bottle service. If she exposes me to other people I won't have to be worried about being fired. I'll be blacklisted. I'm frozen for a moment and my head can't think what to do next.

Once the hostess is out of sight Holiday rushes over. "What's wrong?"

It takes me a few moments to collect myself before I can speak. Once I say the words out loud my punishment will become real. "I . . . I got busted. They found out that I work for *The Life*. It's over. I'm persona non grata. She banned me." My hands are shaking and I'm doing everything in my power to fight back tears. I've already cried here once. I cannot do it again. I won't do it again.

"How did they find out?"

I can barely get the words out. My body and mind are in a state of shock. "She wouldn't say."

"I wonder who it was," Holiday ruminates. She's missing the point.

"It doesn't matter how—they know. And what if she tells other restaurants or worse, club owners?" I'm in a haze. I feel like I'm on whatever drug is the opposite of Ecstasy. My whole body feels limp and in sharp pain at the same time, like I want to spring toward the exit with every cell of my being, yet I'm paralyzed. "I guess in a way I'm surprised it took this long, since it's been so long that I stopped worrying that I'd be outed." My body has chills running through it and not the exciting kind I get with Nick, the I-feel-like-I-could-puke-without-warning variety.

"This is completely unacceptable. Let me talk to her. I've been here longer than she has and have probably paid her salary more than once." If it were under any other circumstance Holiday's call to action would've been snobby and condescending, but she was trying to defend me against this scrawny yet powerful enemy. She isn't one to allow things to happen passively. She always fights to the very end and sometimes won't give up even after she'd been declared the loser. "Let me see if I can work my magic."

She marches over to the hostess, leaving me motionless. I look on and each second am trying to assess her progress. First she embarks on the friendly route. She places her hands on the hostess stand and leans in. Knowing Holiday and from my limited field of vision it looks like she's saying, "There has been a misunderstanding."

Holiday playfully tosses her perfectly tousled tresses in an attempt to seduce the hostess into a false sense of camaraderie. The hostess's acerbic expression remains intact, and Holiday goes to Plan B. It looks like she is saying, "It doesn't have to be this way. I'm sure we can work something out between us gals."

All of my brain functions and motor skills have decided to take a brief hiatus and I black out for a moment. When I come to a few seconds later I can see even from a distance that the hostess isn't budging. She's standing her ground, explaining herself to Holiday, and glances in my direction, giving me the evil eye. Holiday returns to me, defeated.

"She said we can take the inside table or leave. I can't believe that didn't work. No one has ever told me no before," Holiday concedes.

"Thanks for trying, Hol," I muddle, biting the inside of my cheeks.

"I did get her to agree to keep your identity a secret."

I raise my head and look into the face of my savior, yet again.

"And she knows I will make her life a living hell around town if she goes back on her word. Your secret is safe."

"I don't even know what to say," I stammer. "Thank you for having my back."

"Darling, you've always had my back and I have yours. Trust me, this is not the last she will be hearing from me." I sit facing forward, motionless, a victim of trauma. "Ella?" I continue beaming straight ahead. "Ella?" I nod my head. "Ella!" she snaps sternly.

"I'm going to get fired." I wish I were in my pajamas rocking back and forth on my bed.

"You don't know that," Holiday consoles.

"Yes, I do! I was just banned from the biggest celebrity spot in town. In fact, I was banned for the very reason it is the biggest celebrity hot spot in town. Yes, I can go to clubs or parties, but this was my most consistent way of earning points. I'm at a huge disadvantage compared to all of the

other girls. There's no way I will be able to keep up with them now."
Taps is playing in my head.

"You'll figure it out, darling. If there's one person who can creatively
get herself out of any jam, it's you. Right now you need to take a deep
breath and calm down. Let's take the inside table and we'll get you a glass
of wine and something to eat. I want you to relax before we meet Tristan
and Nick."

"I'm not in the mood to celebrate. You should go meet them, though.
You've all worked so hard on *Benedict Canyon* and deserve this. I don't
want to bring the party down."

"Absolutely not. You're my best friend and I'm making you eat here.
If they are going to treat you like this, you *have* to eat here and show them
that they didn't faze you. Show them how fucking fabulous you are," she
demands.

I know what Holiday is trying to do and I really appreciate it, but I
have to figure out what the hell I'm going to tell Victoria. This is going
to be the hardest e-mail I've had to write so far. Do I just tell her I got
busted or give her all of the details? She's not going to respond well to
either tactic. Holiday interrupts my contemplation.

"You don't have to come out afterwards but I insist on dinner."

"Hol, I'd love to but I don't think I can expense this one."

"Darling, it's on me."

I hate that she's treating me on her big night.

"Holiday, one more thing. Please don't tell Nick," I beg. If Nick and
I have one weak spot in our relationship, it's my job. He tries to accept it
but I know it makes him a little uneasy. Hearing that his girlfriend was
shunned from the Chateau won't exactly be a turn-on.

"You're not the only one good at keeping secrets, Ella. Now come on.
You need a shot of something . . . of anything," she says as she leads me
to our drafty, lonely inside table.

Twenty-two

· · · · · · · · · · · · · · · · · · · ·

I wake up the next morning and hope the whole incident at the Chateau was just a bad dream but as the minutes pass the reality sets in. I stare at my iPhone for what seems like hours. I'm trying to give myself the courage to open my e-mails. After ten minutes of purgatory I squint my eyes and press the e-mail icon. There it is, Victoria's response to my non-file file from last night.

> *Ella,*
> *I need to see you in the office today. 12 PM.*
> *Victoria*

Of course she does. My mom has an appointment with Dr. Jacobs today at 11 A.M. I could maybe make it from the hospital to *The Life*'s office in thirty minutes if I don't hit any of the prelunchtime traffic at that hour. Plus I need at least fifteen minutes to get out of the doctor's office to the parking garage and pay and this is all assuming that Dr. Jacobs is running on time with his schedule and that my mom's appointment only takes ten minutes. Today is not the day to be tardy to a meeting with Victoria and if I go to the doctor's appointment I will be cutting it very close. What am I supposed to do? I don't have any leverage to try to change the time with Victoria but I will feel awful if I miss my mom's appointment again. On the other hand if I don't go to this meeting there's no way I will be able to save my job, even though the possibility is incredibly slim as it is. I text Robin.

> Me: You're going to kill me but I can't come to the Dr. Jacobs appointment today. Emergency work meeting at noon. I'm being summoned by my boss. I'm sorry.

Robin: I'm sure I don't even need to say it so I'll just tell you to come over for dinner this week.

That wasn't as bad as I'd anticipated. One woman disappointed in me down, one woman disappointed in me to go.

The receptionist escorts me to Victoria's office. She's on the phone when I arrive and points for me to sit down and for the door to be closed. That never signifies upcoming pleasantries are about to be exchanged. I oblige and take a deep breath.

"I said I'll have it soon," Victoria says slowly, annunciating every syllable in the sentence to assert her alpha self. "You'll have it," she repeats. "Fine! By the end of the day," she screams and hangs up the phone so harshly I'm surprised it doesn't shatter.

She takes a moment to collect herself and refocuses all of her attention on me. Whether I'm ready or not, it's time to meet my fate. I glance down briefly to avoid eye-fucking her and notice a memo on her desk from the CEO of Patriot Media and Publishing. From what I can see, it looks like a warning that her job is in danger if sales don't drastically rise in the next sixty days. Victoria notices me looking at it and grabs the paper and flips it over, sternly. "What exactly happened last night?" she interrogates.

"Pretty much what I wrote in my e-mail."

"Tell me again," she instructs. "Verbatim."

"The hostess pulled me aside and told me that she knew I worked for *The Life* and I'm no longer welcome to dine in the garden." Victoria's eyes are scrutinizing me, and her demeanor is making my heart rate speed up.

"Do you know how she found out?" she pries.

"No."

Victoria furrows her brow.

"I asked her but she wouldn't tell me," I add.

"I don't mind saying that I'm disappointed in you." No, she does not mind saying that because she's completely devoid of emotion while expressing it. "The day I met you, I thought you might be special. I saw a spark. A spark I hadn't seen since I had it in myself. I was rooting for you." It's like I'm allergic to bees and ten thousand of them are stinging me. The only thing worse than being crushed is being crushed by someone that you've idolized almost your entire life. "Maggie kept going on and on about how you had celebrity friends." Her voice is bored by my apparent failure.

"I do!"

Victoria glares at me with disbelief and leans over her desk.

"There just hasn't been any good gossip lately."

"I don't see why all of my other girls come to me with stories instead of excuses." I feel beads of sweat developing in places I didn't know it was possible for beads of sweat to develop. Victoria leans back in her chair, patronizing me. "You either don't have the sources or you don't have the skills to keep up with everyone else."

"That's not true," I insist.

"Ella, this puts me in a very difficult position. I'm trying to revamp *The Life* and you're putting that in jeopardy. We can't send you to the Chateau anymore, and who knows if your detection put any of my other girls in jeopardy. We are both at a huge disadvantage. I simply don't see how you will be able to earn the points to compete."

Adrenaline rushes through me like my body is a racetrack. "Please. Don't fire me," I beg.

"Tell me what other choice I have? Aside from this I asked you to find us a big, exclusive story worthy of a magazine cover and you haven't delivered."

I feel like a criminal being coerced into entrapment. "I tried! I've been going out on my own time. I've been getting into exclusive parties on my own." I'm throwing myself on her mercy but Victoria doesn't seem to have any.

"Nothing you've turned in has had any wow factor."

"What about when I saw Not-So-Innocent Oversexualized Pop Star at the hospital?"

"That was good work but nothing earth-shattering. It's not like you were able to get details about what caused her breakdown or an update on her condition."

"That's not my fault!" Victoria's blank facial expression means she doesn't care if I would've had to convince someone to break confidentiality or their Hippocratic oath, so I try again. "What about the file I turned in on Twentysomething CW Bad Boy Heartthrob?"

"Ella, everyone knows he's an addict and went to rehab, and cheating on his noncelebrity girlfriend isn't worth mentioning. It's not like you had details on his evening and then he died. Those would've been valuable. But yours were just another weekday after-party. Hardly uncommon for him." My throat is bone dry. "Maggie told me that you have been an important asset to this company and that you are ingratiated in the Hollywood scene. The fact that you don't know one piece of gossip that no one else does is not currying you any favor."

"With all due respect, Victoria, it's not like there's some scandal out there that I'm sitting on."

"Actually . . . it is. You're friends with Holiday Hall."

"Yes," I murmur in confirmation.

"Then why didn't you tell me about this?" Victoria sharply swivels her chair to grab something off a pile behind her desk and places it in front of me. It's the red-light camera photo of Holiday and me. I haven't seen it yet. It usually takes six weeks to arrive in the mail.

"Where did you get this?" I'm barely able to get the question out because I'm flabbergasted by what I'm looking at.

"Not that it's important but I have sources everywhere, Ella. Everywhere. I have one at the LAPD who runs celebrities' license plate numbers a few times a week and you can imagine my surprise when he sent me an incriminating red-light camera photo of Holiday Hall and *you* in the driver's seat." My jaw is agape and I want to say something, but my brain and mouth are too shocked to communicate with each other and create speech. "The only place I haven't been able to penetrate yet is the hospital but I'm working on it and I'll find someone. Anyway," she continues, "I need a story to go along with this photo and if you want to save your job, you're going to help me tell it."

I'm paralyzed by fear.

"What do you see in this photo, Ella?" she prods. I swallow and take the deepest breath I can without her noticing. Victoria folds her arms. "Because I see Holiday holding a box and something that looks like a pregnancy test. Now, it's blurry and I'm not positive that's what it is but I ran it by legal and we're gonna take the chance and go with it." I gulp.

"The question is, why is she holding a pregnancy test? Now the test could've been yours, since you're in the car with her, but nobody logs onto our Web site or reads our magazine for you because nobody cares about you, so that storyline is out." She rattles on. "I suppose it's possible she was buying the test for someone else but it's around midnight according to the timestamp on the photo and the box is open. Plus that wouldn't drive traffic to our site."

My legs tremble.

"Ella, if you don't help me with the details, I'll have to figure them out on my own and I don't think you or Holiday will like what I come up with." She leans into me, piercing my body and soul with her eyes.

"So here's my working headline, 'Holiday Hall Pregnant with Tristan Bailey's Child? Spotted Drinking at the Chateau Marmont. Is She a Bad Mom-to-Be or Did She Have an Abortion?'"

"You can't do that!"

"Oh, but I can," she snickers. "The box and object look reasonably enough like a pregnancy test so the chances of an attorney advising her to sue us for negligence or libel are slim, and if she wants to pursue litigation it will be a long and expensive process. I know she can afford it but I doubt she'll want to drag this out in public any longer than she has to. Come on, Ella. Help me help you help your friend. Tell me what really happened."

I cough on the air because the shock makes it difficult for me to swallow and breathe. I feel like every cell in my body is shaking. I can't let Victoria ruin Holiday's reputation.

I blurt out, "None of it is true! Holiday never got an abortion because she wasn't even pregnant. She had a scare but it was a false alarm and she didn't even know if the baby would've been Tristan or Seth Rubin's!"

Victoria cackles and it's only then I realize what I've just said. "And now you're back in the game. See how easy that was."

Victoria is talking to me but all my mind registers is *No! No! No! No!* While trying to protect my friend, I just gave her exactly what she wanted.

"No, Victoria, you can't use this. I was trying to stop you from writing lies. You can't print that!" I plead.

"Of course I can and I will." Victoria snickers. "See, I knew you had it in you. I'm glad I gave you the opportunity to save yourself. I wasn't wrong about you."

I close my eyes as I realize what she orchestrated. The pressure of being fired combined with what I had thought was admiration for Victoria made me lower my guard, and all the words came tumbling out unchecked.

My body is shaking and I'm dizzy. I have to fix this.

"I won't go on the record and it will be hearsay and Holiday will sue you. She's litigious and she can afford the legal fees."

"Let her. We'll say that according to our source the information is factual and correct. And we legally don't have to reveal our sources."

"It doesn't matter. She'll know that it was me. I'm the *only* one who knows."

"Oh, Ella, after all of the years you've worked in this business you can't really believe that there's such a thing as secrets. You should be happy you still have your job."

I'm not exactly sure how that helps. My best friend's career is in danger and it's my fault, which means I will lose my best friend and my home and . . . Nick! I hadn't even considered how he's going to react. I love him so much it's hard for me to even allow myself to feel it because it's so great that it scares me. After Ethan and the news about my mom I find some happiness and I have to open my big mouth and burn everything to the ground. This directly affects his client and therefore indirectly affects him, I don't know if he'll be able to forgive me. It was an accident, but will that matter? I need to tell him before he hears it from someone else.

I'm not sure if my legs are ready to support the weight of my body after my self-induced trauma, but I know that I can't stay in this office or this building another minute longer if I ever have any hope of regaining my sanity. I take a breath and gather the strength to get up.

"I've gotta go," I curtly tell Victoria, careful not to look her in the eye because I might throw up if I do. I turn and walk to her door.

"Good job today, Ella," she says, stopping me in my tracks. This is not a day to be proud of myself and I resent her manipulation tactics to make me try to believe otherwise. I take another breath and quickly walk out.

I don't know what to do or where to go, and the only thing that makes sense to me is that I need to see Nick. I drive to his office, in an almost catatonic state. Maybe he can help me undo what I did somehow. I ask the receptionist to let him know I'm here. I take a seat on one of the chic off-white Jonathan Adler sofas in the lobby. A minute later, Nick's assistant, Melanie, arrives to escort me to his office.

"Hi, babe, this is a surprise. What are you doing here?" he asks as I enter his office. He looks incredibly happy to see me and my stomach turns just thinking about what I'm about to say.

"I didn't know where else to go." My voice cracks and I can feel the color drain from my face. I suddenly feel cold.

"Honey, is everything okay?" I shake my head no and he gets up from behind his desk to hold me. "What is it? Is it your mom? Is she okay?" All

I can think about is how amazing he is and that I'm not ready for us to be over. I'm terrified of how Nick will react when I tell him about what I've done.

"It's not my mom."

"Good." He leans against the front of his desk, rubbing my arms, still trying to ascertain why I'm having a meltdown in his office. He cares about me so much.

"I just had a bad day. Work stuff," I mutter, trying to find the words. "I'm under a lot of pressure." I can't hold it together any longer and begin to sob. Nick takes me in his arms again and I know I should but I can't bring myself to tell him what I did. Not right now. Especially when he's being so sweet and doing his best to console me. I don't want him to change the way he sees me and there's no way it won't. And maybe by some stroke of luck some secret fairy godmother will change Victoria's mind and I won't have to confess or maybe I can still fix it somehow.

"It's going to be okay. Come over tonight. We'll get takeout and have a night in together. Okay?" I nod. He kisses the top of my head. "Babe, I hate to do this but I have to run to a meeting with a client. I'll see you in a few hours. Okay?"

"Yeah." I sniffle.

"Whatever it is, I promise you'll feel better later. Give it some time." He kisses me again.

. . . .

I do not feel better that night. I can't help but let my mind spiral out of control wondering how he will react when I confess what I've done.

"Is there anything I can do?" he asks. His desire to make me feel better makes me feel worse.

"No," I tell him. My entire body is numb. I can't taste any of the Sugarfish Trust Me sushi he had delivered, which is usually my go-to comfort food. I can't laugh at any jokes when we watch TV, even though I'd give anything to laugh. The bath that Nick draws for me to help alleviate my stress makes me feel like I'm sitting in a pool of my own filth instead of relaxing at a spa. When it's time for bed he kisses me good night. I try to sleep but it's useless. I lie in bed next to Nick and as I watch, the minutes tick by on the clock. At 6 A.M. I grab my phone from Nick's nightstand to see if *The Life* posted the Holiday exclusive. I pray that another scandal broke out and Holiday's will be null and void, but the minute my hand touches the phone I get a breaking news alert, "British Heiress Turned Hollywood It Girl's Affair with Married Director—Now Dating Costar." And of course the subheading: "Was there a secret love child?"

I feel a panic attack coming so I slip out of bed and take my phone into the bathroom. I dial my mom, ready to spill the whole story and for her to give me some kind of reassurance that I haven't screwed up my entire life but Robin answers her phone.

"Hello?"

I can't respond. My judgmental sister is the last person that will give me any comfort right now.

"Hello? Ella?"

I hang up. I return to bed and I'm shaking. Nick rolls over to spoon me but I stop him. He lets out a moan. He tries again to spoon me and I push him away.

"El, come here," he mutters, reaching for me with his arm.

"I can't." I have to do it now. I think my skin will jump off my body if I don't. "Nick, wake up. I need you to wake up." I poke him. He rolls the opposite way and his back is now facing me. "Come on, I'm serious."

"Babe, it's too early for this. Come back to bed."

I shove my phone in front of his face. "Read this!" I shrink into the mattress as his eyes adjust and he digests the words.

"What did you do?" I've never heard him say anything with vitriol . . . until now. He continues to read the story. "Why would you do this?"

"I didn't mean to," I wail.

"You're going to have to explain that to me because I don't understand how you accidentally leaked a story like this about your best friend."

I try to gather the words but my sobs are turning into dry heaves and I begin rambling. "Victoria got me all riled up and told me she was going to fire me for being kicked out of the Chateau and then—"

"Wait, you got kicked out of the Chateau?" He's taken by surprise.

"Yes, and she was threatening that she was going to fire me because I wasn't getting her any exclusive gossip. Then she showed me a photo she got from a red-light camera of me and Holiday, and Holiday was holding a pregnancy test. She told me to give her the story behind it and after I said no she said she'd have to run whatever she thinks the story is, and her made-up version was so horrible and inaccurate I blurted out the truth in a panic, trying to defend Holiday." I throw my face into a pillow. I can't bear to look at him or even worse, have him look at me.

"So the story they printed is true?"

I nod yes with my face still stuck in the pillow.

"And no one thought to tell me that my client might either A, be pregnant, or B, could have a huge problem with both her director and costar?"

I turn my head, keeping my left cheek planted in the pillow. "She asked me not to say anything to you," I tell him. "I was trying to protect my friend's secret."

"So it's okay to tell the national media but not your boyfriend slash her agent?"

"I didn't mean to tell them! It was a horrible accident," I insist.

"And after this happened you didn't tell me so I could help you fix the situation and stop them from running it because why?" he questions.

"I don't know. I came to your office to tell you and you were so nice to me. I got scared you'd leave me and I couldn't. I thought I could handle it myself, but it's Victoria Davis. There's nothing you could've done to stop her," I say between sobs.

"You don't know that. I could've tried or at least been prepared with a plan for damage control, but now it's too late." He's so incensed I feel like I'm about to see smoke come out of his ears.

"Nick, I'm sorry." I hang my head in shame. "This is the biggest mistake I've ever made in my life," I add, still crying.

"I don't even know what to say to you right now, Ella. I was never really a fan of your job but I accepted it because I thought that it was something you did, not who you are. Apparently I was very wrong." He throws on a T-shirt and sits on the edge of the bed. From behind I can see him squeezing the bridge of his nose, trying to understand what I'm telling him. He shakes his head and stands up, moving toward the bedroom door.

Still holding mine, Nick grabs his phone and rushes into the living room where he opens his laptop and begins setting up his agent triage station. I follow him. "I'm so sorry—"

"I'm going to try to do damage control. Do you have any idea what you've done?" I'm about to answer when he answers for me. "You just put Holiday's role and the entire future of *Benedict Canyon* in jeopardy."

"How? Isn't it already picked up?"

"It doesn't matter. They've barely shot anything and don't have much money invested in it at this point. The network can either replace Holiday or pull the plug and replace the show with one of their other new pilots. They are going to flip out about her being involved in a scandal like this before the show airs and finds an audience. Maybe if this wasn't her first job and she had a loyal fan base things might be different, but the network is going to be nervous about the majority of the public potentially hating the star of their show that they're putting a lot of money into."

"Nick, I don't know what to say. I'm really sorry." I move toward him and he flinches away. "If something does happen, you'll find Holiday another acting job, though, right?"

"You really don't get it, do you? It's not just about Holiday or about the other actors. Do you have any idea how many people work on this show that aren't featured in *The Life*? Everyone behind the scenes . . . the writers, the crew that are all counting on having a paycheck to support their families? It's always about the celebrities with you. All you see is this fantasy that you help build with *The Life*. These are real people and real lives you're screwing with." I don't know what to say to him. "I don't have time for this right now. I need to get to work and I need you to leave." He isn't asking.

"Nick—"

"Ella, I'm saying it nicely. I don't want to be an asshole. Please don't make me be an asshole. Go home." He extends my iPhone to me. I sheepishly take it.

"Can we talk later?" Maybe once he has the situation under control he'll calm down.

"I'm not sure how you think a conversation later will be different from the one we're having now. You betrayed two people you care about." He looks at me with a contempt that breaks my heart and makes me wish I hadn't woken up yesterday morning. "Even if you didn't mean to, you did." He runs his hand through his hair, like he's still trying to understand the last five minutes. "Please, leave," he reiterates as he goes into the bathroom, making sure to lock the door behind him. I don't bother to get dressed and I throw my jacket on over my nightgown as I gather up the rest of my clothes and put my shoes on, ready to leave, when he pops his head out of the door. "Wait," he calls out, "does she know?"

"Not yet. I couldn't bring myself to do it until I was sure they were going to use it. I was praying that someone would announce a split or pregnancy or something and Victoria would forget about it."

"You need to tell her," he scolds. "If she hears about this from the media instead of from you, that's another catastrophe you've set into motion."

"I know. It's just . . . this isn't something you really tell someone over the phone."

"Well, unless you charter a jet up to the *Benedict Canyon* set in Canada you're gonna have to do it on the phone. And I suggest that you do it soon because I need to strategize with her about the collateral damage this is going to cause and there's no way I'm telling her for you."

"I'll call her as soon as I get back to the house," I promise him.

"You better."

"Please come by after work tonight. Please," I beg. He stares at me with the coldest eyes I've ever seen—colder than Ethan's ever were.

"I'll see." I walk through the living room and take a mental picture of everything. I don't need my reporter's intuition to realize I probably won't be here again. I notice our picture from the photo booth at Doheny Circle on his fridge. The two people in the photos don't exist anymore. It's four quadrants of us snuggling, kissing, smiling, and looking like two people falling in love. I quietly sneak over and slide it from its magnet and place the picture in my purse.

I have no idea how I'm going to tell Holiday. I think that the only thing I can do is tell her exactly like I told Nick. It's the truth. I'm terrified of how she's going to react. I know it's going to change our relationship forever but I hope that there's still some semblance of a friendship we can repair after I confess.

Despite that trace of hope I know there's a very real possibility that I could be losing my best friend the next time I unlock my phone. Holiday isn't even a best friend—she's like a sister to me. Most of the time she was more of a sister to me than Robin. Robin. Ugh, great. She's going to have a field day with this when she finds out, which she inevitably will because I'll have to tell her I'm moving and she'll ask why. The instant I mention *The Life* she will refuse to let me explain. Robin will proceed to roll her eyes, and you know how when people make mistakes they tell the people they've wronged that no one can punish them or make them feel any worse than they have already made themselves feel? They haven't met Robin. She has a supreme talent for heightening a person's guilt, remorse, and self-hatred. Contrary to Robin, I think my mother will be disappointed but understanding. In fact, she will probably try to soothe my broken spirit when right now she should only be concerned with her own well-being.

I arrive at Holiday's house but the trip home is a blur. I'm consumed with fear but I know that I have no other choice but to make the phone call. The first time I call it rings until I'm sent to voice mail. I try again. Same thing. The third time I try Holiday answers.

"Hello?" She sounds like she's still half asleep.

"Hey, it's me." I pause.

"El, is everything okay?"

Thank god she was still asleep and when she looked at her phone only saw my name on caller ID and not the breaking news alert *The Life* sent out about her story.

"No. It isn't, actually." This sobers her up and I hear in her voice that she's coming to.

"Are you alright?" she asks.

"Physically I'm fine, yes." I pause again.

"What is it then? Your mom? Nick?" I can't seem to find the words to tell her that I betrayed her. I can't say them out loud because if I do it makes it real and I will have to live with it forever. I know the story is already online and will now live forever anyway, so my rationale doesn't make any sense, but my mind is hysterical.

"Go to your computer and check the home page of *The Life*."

"Right now? It's too early for gossip, Ella." She has no idea how right she is, but she's about to find out.

"Yes, now."

"Fine. Give me a second." I swallow a gulp of air to prepare myself for whatever is about to come next. I wait for Holiday to say something, but there are no audible noises, much less a voice, on her end.

"Holiday?" I finally hear her trying to push her tears back. I've never heard Holiday cry like this, even during the pregnancy scare, and it's a worse sound than I ever could've imagined.

"Why would you do this to me?" she screams.

"I'm so sorry, Holiday. You have to know that I didn't intentionally tell them. Victoria tricked me—"

"No! Don't you dare. Don't you bloody motherfucking dare pretend like she's the villain when it's you!" she screams. Her words sting and right about now I'm wishing I were a victim recounting my harrowing experience of a near-death attack on *Shark Week* instead of incurring the wrath that is deservedly coming my way.

"I wish we could talk in person. I want to explain how this happened," I beg. "I love you, Hol, and I never meant to hurt you. It was a mistake." She has truly been family to me, and losing her is far worse than losing Nick. I don't know what I would've done without her helping me get back on my feet after the breakup with Ethan, and her antics always help take my mind off my mother and her illness.

"There is no such thing as a mistake, Ella. Do you know what mistakes are? They're the things we'd do, the choices we'd make, the way we'd act all of the time if there weren't any consequences," she lectures. "In this life there are consequences, darling."

The way she bites me with the word *darling* makes me yearn for the way Victoria says it. I take a moment to process everything she's saying and she's right, there are consequences to our actions. I may have told her secret but I didn't force her to have an affair with a married man. Those were *her* actions and they have consequences just like mine. I know that I deserve to incur some of her wrath but she has some misplaced anger with the situation as well. She can't blame this whole thing on me, but bringing this up would be cruel.

"Do you know what the worst part of this whole thing is?" This is clearly a rhetorical question, as she doesn't give me a second to answer. "You can't even own it and take responsibility for your actions. I'd have more respect for you if you said, 'Holiday, I did what I had to do and your secret was the only one I had. I'm sorry but I was in a pinch and I made a decision. It was the wrong decision but *I* made it.' With you it's never *your* fault because you were 'tricked.' Guess what? You *always* have a choice. You just always make the wrong choices and then blame everyone else." I let her continue berating me without interrupting. It's the very least I can do for her right now. "You are the most selfish person I've ever met, and coming from me I hope you take that as intended—as a scathing insult. You chose your job over everyone: Ethan, me—even your sick mother. You always joke that when you go to work you become Bella, but guess what, you *are* Bella. It's Ella who doesn't exist anymore."

I hear Tristan interrupt on her end of the conversation. "What the hell is this Google alert I just got about you, Holiday?"

"If you'll excuse me I have to deal with the mess you made of *my* life. I think that it goes without saying, but since it's you I'm dealing with I am going to just bloody well say it. I want you to move out of my house and I don't want you to leave a trace of your existence behind. Don't call me. Don't text me. Unfollow me on social media. From this moment on we are done. I'm sure your mother will be so proud of you," she shrieks, making sure to hammer that last nail into my coffin before she hangs up.

I somehow manage to make my way to my room and don't wake up until hours later to the sound of the doorbell beeping every second.

"Jesus, Ella, you look like hell." Nick gives me the once-over.

"I kind of passed out after I called Holiday." I feel light-headed and really want to go to the kitchen for some water but figure I better stay where I am and continue this conversation.

"She called me right after. She had to skip rehearsal today, she was so upset." I search his face for an iota of compassion but there is none.

"I need to move out of here ASAP and she doesn't want to be friends with me anymore."

Nick does his signature shrug. "Can you blame her?" His calm demeanor is making our conversation and me feel worse. I wish he would just yell at me and get his anger out so we could move past this. He's still standing outside.

"Do you want to come in?" I ask.

"No, I can't stay." I look down at the porch and stare at his oxfords because my intuition tells me that what I don't want to happen is about to happen. "I wanted to do this in person."

"You don't have to say anything else, Nick. I get it, we're over, too. Message received." I move to close the door.

"I don't want to do this, Ella."

"Then don't," I beg and try to throw my arms around him, but he takes a step back and takes in the hurt look on my face. He takes a breath and sits on the porch step and pats the ground, motioning for me to sit next to him. My tears haven't slowed down but I join him.

"This isn't only about Holiday. If word gets out that it was my girl-friend who gave *The Life* the story I could lose all of my clients." He looks out toward the view of Los Angeles that makes this Mount Olympus property so expensive. It's agonizing looking down at the lights of the city filled with beauty and hope when I feel empty up here.

"And they're more important than I am?" Older Multi-Oscar-Winning Womanizer's words are coming back to haunt me.

"No, of course not. El, I care about my job just like you care about yours." He stares out and I can tell he's doing it to stay composed. I desperately want him to look at me. "I never asked you to give up what made you happy for me because I didn't like it. Even if I take my clients' feelings out of the equation, tell me how I'm supposed to trust you?" He finally turns to look at me, waiting for my answer.

"You can trust me, Nick. You know me. I told you what happened. This was all a huge mistake." Why can't anyone understand? I feel like I keep yelling at the top of my lungs but nobody hears me.

"El, I believe you."

"You do?" I catch my breath.

"I don't think you're a malicious person. I believe that you didn't *mean* to tell Victoria about Holiday, but you did, and that's a huge problem. I don't feel I can trust you."

I vigorously shake my head. "You don't mean that," I tell him.

"I wish I didn't. But it's always going to be in the back of my mind. What happens one day when you overhear me talking to a client or I bring you to a business dinner where confidential information is being discussed and *The Life* gives you another ultimatum and you accidentally slip again? If you did it to Holiday I'd have to be an idiot to believe you wouldn't do the same to me." He looks down at his hands and I feel my heart plummet into my stomach.

"You said you cared about me. That you could see yourself with me in the future." I can't even look at him right now. If I looked in his eyes all I'd see is the life that we both said we wanted to share together being shattered.

"I do, but I . . . I can't do this." He gets up and places his hands in his pockets. "I'm sorry." His mind is made up. He walks to his Tesla and before he gets in, looks back at me. I watch him drive away.

Just then I realize I never talked to my mom and I feel even worse.

Twenty-three

. . . .

I called Jessica, hysterical after the dissolution of two of my most important relationships outside of my family. I'm surprised she could decipher any of what I said during my tear-fueled rambling but she managed to put the pieces together and even offered to help me pack so I can be out of Holiday's faster. Thank God I still have one friend left.

"Are you sure you don't want to stay with me for a bit while you get back on your feet?"

"That's really sweet but I think I've hit my quota on staying with girl-friends who are trying to help me out of a bind." She understands. "I love you for offering, though."

"Where are you going to go?"

"I don't know. I've looked at a few places that are okay. I'll decide soon. I have a few weeks before Holiday comes back to LA for her hiatus but I want to have everything packed up so I can move as soon as I sign a new lease. I know she's technically in another country but I can feel her hostile energy in every room in this house." I haven't been paying rent so I have enough for a basic apartment, security deposit, and first and last month's rent.

She continues folding my clothes, neatly placing them in boxes, then goes over to my closet and returns with another pile of clothes.

"This is the last of it," she says.

"Thank you." I stare at my empty walk-in closet.

"It's no problem, really. It's oddly therapeutic packing for other people and I'm procrastinating on a new blog entry anyhow."

"No. I mean thank you for still being my friend. Thank you for not hating me."

"Look, what you did was fucked up but nobody hates you."

I know Jess is trying to mollify me but I'm not buying her theory. "Yes, they do! Holiday hates me. Nick hates me. Hell, even my own sister hates me! For her own different reasons, but still . . ."

"For what it's worth, I don't think Holiday hates you."

I roll my eyes.

"She's really, really angry with you and I wouldn't count on her as an organ donor, but I don't think she hates you."

"Her internal organs are just as damaged as mine are anyway." I sigh.

Jess grabs my hand. "Good. Whenever you're going through a breakup and you make a joke it means you're starting to heal."

"What's the step after that?" I wonder.

"Actually moving on. That's the tricky part." I close my eyes and take a deep breath. "Think of it like this, you can't change anything you've already done. All you can do is move forward. Live your life. Try to find a way to make things right. She may not forgive you but at least you'll know that you tried."

I stare at my paltry boxes. "You make it sound so easy."

"Oh, it's gonna be a bitch. But once you become the person you want to be you won't punish yourself for your past mistakes anymore."

I collapse on my bed and stare at the ceiling.

"You want to grab dinner tonight?" Jessica offers.

"I can't. I'm having family dinner at my sister's house and then going to work. Later this week?" Seeing as how I have no boyfriend anymore my schedule is remarkably clear.

"Sure. Let me know if you need anything in the meantime." Jess gives me a hug and leaves. Her compassion and lack of criticism make me want to cry as much as Holiday's contempt and Nick's disappointment in me, not to mention my mother's illness and my strained relationship with Robin. I'm not sure what I'm feeling right now so I'm feeling everything.

· · · ·

Robin pulls me aside when I arrive for dinner.

"How are you holding up?" She seems genuinely concerned and I'm confused.

"I'm fine."

Her expression tells me she doesn't believe me. "Are you sure?"

I shrug my shoulders, not knowing what she wants from me. This definitely wasn't the welcome I was expecting. "What are you talking about?" I blurt out.

"Ella, come on. You text me to keep an eye out for apartment listings and Mom showed me the article from *The Life*. I put two and two together."

The only thing I can do is sigh. "I really don't want to talk about it right now, okay?"

"That's fine. I just wanted to let you know that if you want to save money and need a place to stay, there's room for you here."

"That's a nice offer but you have a full house with Mom as it is." Robin is slightly offended that I rebuff her and though we've been getting along a little bit better lately, I don't think that removing the buffer between us would have a positive effect on our relationship. It would be a horrible idea, but in an attempt to maintain the semblance of peace we've found, I lie. "It's really nice of you. I'll think about it."

"The offer is on the table." Her eyes dart to the wall. "There's something else," she adds, pausing. "Mom's counts aren't improving. If they don't show a significant amount of improvement the next time she has blood work done, Dr. Jacobs is going to put her back in the hospital. And aside from her not being here, it's not a good sign."

"How bad is it?" I ask.

"I know you're going through a lot so let's just leave it at 'really not good.'"

We may not be BFF's, but Robin still knows me pretty well and can tell that the news rustled up my emotions and I'm about to cry.

"Please don't," she pleads. "I don't want Mom to worry more than she already is or be concerned about our feelings, okay?" I nod. "If you want to talk, I'm happy to one-on-one but the only thing I want Mom focused on is herself."

Robin takes my hand and leads me into the dining room. Marianna has her favorite teddy bear, aptly named Bear, seated next to her.

"Aunt Ella, you're next to me! Bear was just saving your spot for you."

"Thank you, Bear."

Marianna moves him to her lap.

"Now, Ella, when am I going to get to meet this handsome, charming beau of yours. I'm not going to be around forever you know, I do have cancer—"

"Mom! That's not even funny," Robin chides.

"Oh, come on! If I can't have a sense of humor about it what's the point of having a potentially fatal disease." She laughs Robin's criticism off.

"Actually we aren't seeing each other anymore," I tell her.

"Why not?" She looks disappointed, and even if Robin put the puzzle together it doesn't mean I need to clue my mom in.

"It just didn't work out." I'm not offering any additional details. I don't want to relive another breakup again.

"I'm sorry, sweetheart. It's his loss. He didn't know what he had." If only she knew that the problem was that he knew exactly what he had and that's why he ended it. "Jeff, this dinner smells divine. Don't be insulted if I don't finish," my mother requests, changing the subject as he puts a whole roasted chicken and green salad on the table.

"Thanks, Joan." He places a hand on her shoulder. "What part of the bird would everyone like?"

"Mom, why don't you take the breast meat, since it's nice and lean," Robin suggests, and as soon as she does Marianna giggles. "Sweetie, what have I told you? *Breast* is not a bad word. It's a part of the human anatomy." Marianna giggles again as soon as the word *breast* comes out of Robin's mouth and my sister chooses not to fight this particular battle tonight.

My mother gets through half of her meal before resting her fork on the table.

"You got through a lot of that, Mom. I'm impressed," I tell her.

When we finish I offer to clear the plates. As I lean over the kitchen sink I want to collapse and scream, but none of those are options right now. I just want one stable thing in my life, which would usually be my mother, and even though she seems to be doing well, cancer is unpredictable. Marianna comes running into the kitchen with her favorite book about a precocious mouse that loves baked goods.

"Aunt Ella, can you read to me for story time tonight?"

I look down at her flushed cheeks and can't say no to her excited little face. "Sure."

She jumps up and down and raises the book above her head as if it were the holy gospel and screams, "Mommy! Mommy!"

Robin comes rushing into the kitchen, now in her scrubs, thinking there's an emergency. "Is everything okay?" She surveils the kitchen to make sure there are no fires or floods. She calms down (well, for her) when she sees there are no injuries or claims to make against her homeowner's insurance policy.

"Since you have to go to work, Aunt Ella is going to read to me tonight!"

Robin looks genuinely surprised. "Ella, are you sure?" Her question is almost insulting.

I roll my eyes and bite my tongue—to the best of my ability. "I think I can handle story time, Robin. But you better make sure to put away all of the matches and knives just in case."

"You don't have to be so combative all the time. Jeeze. All I meant was I thought you had to go to work, too."

I pull my phone out of my back pocket. "It's 8 P.M."

Robin stares at me, thinking she's made her point, clueless as to what time a nightclub even opens anymore.

"I think I'll be okay."

"I know you don't want to talk about it but do I need to worry about you?" she asks.

"Robin, you have a daughter, husband, and our mother to worry about. You don't need to add me to that list. I'm fine," I tell her.

"Well, then . . . perfect. I'm going to head out."

Marianna's spirit dampens. "I don't want you to go, Mommy." Her voice is almost whiny but there's more sadness than brattiness, and I bend down and hug my niece.

"Do you know how much fun we're gonna have, though?"

Robin joins my bid to put a smile back on Marianna's face. "Yeah. You get me all the time but tonight you have your cool aunt Ella to read to you."

Marianna takes this into consideration. I up the ante. "If you're good, I'll read you two stories." That sends her into hyperactive, and her jumping and cheering become exponentially more vigorous. "Why don't you go put your pj's on and I'll be right up." Marianna doesn't stop bouncing around as she dashes out of the kitchen like one of Santa's reindeer, shouting as she's en route.

"'Night, Mommy!"

Robin smiles. "Hey! Princess Marianna, get back here!" Marianna halts and her face drops, thinking she's in trouble. Robin walks over to her. "Aren't you forgetting something?" Marianna squishes her face together, trying to think, but she's definitely confused. Robin helps jog her memory. "Kiss . . ."

"Oh, yeah!"

"Kiss. Hug. Squeeze!" Robin playfully slaps her behind and Marianna zooms out of the room again and up the stairs until she's out of sight.

"Thanks for that. She's been getting really upset recently when I leave."

"Of course. You know I'm crazy about the little strawberry." Our moment is interrupted by my mom waltzing in, humming a song like she's performing on Broadway. She clasps her hands together when she notices the tender vibe between Robin and me, and for her this is like peace in the Middle East.

"Look at my beautiful girls!" She moves between us so she can curl her arms around us both at the same time. "My two working girls. I'm so proud of you both." It's almost hard to believe that us getting along can make her *this* happy. Robin looks at her watch.

"Speaking of which, I better get going." Robin kisses Mom on the cheek. "Call me if you need anything." Knowing she can handle herself, my mom shoos her away. "See you soon, Ella."

I wave good-bye. My mom hugs me again and I hear Marianna's little voice bellowing from upstairs.

"Aunt Ella! I'm ready now!"

"I'm being summoned," I joke to my mom. "Good night." I proceed upstairs and find Marianna tucked into her bed with not one, not two, but a pile of books on top of the covers. She might be little but she knows I'm terrible at saying no to her. She has the smile on her face to prove she's won me over without having to say a word. She hands me the book she wants to start with and beams, clearly proud of herself. We finish the first book and the next one comes like it's on a conveyor belt. And the next and the next. I'm losing steam and don't realize we've passed out and I still have my arm around her until my phone buzzes in my pocket with a text from Jessica.

Jess: Good luck at Ambiance tonight.

It's 10:45 P.M.! I jump out of bed and give Marianna a quick kiss on the head, careful not to wake her, and storm out. Traffic from Robin's is bad so I didn't have time to drop my car off and Uber. As each second passes I'm overthinking and working myself up into a fit of hysterics as my mind repeats the news that my mother's health hasn't improved. I have no choice, but I want to be at Ambiance about as much as I want to be in front of a Mexican firing squad. But since I sold my soul to *The Life* I better not slack on any assignments. Besides, now more than ever I can't turn down the money.

I give Gus, the bouncer, a hug after he opens the rope for me to enter. Why is it that Gus has been the most consistent man in my life throughout the years? I make my way inside and don't even do a lap before heading straight for the bar. The bartender who helped Jessica and me and who's waited on me countless times since then comes over.

"The usual? Champagne?" he asks, leaning toward me with the hope of increasing his tip.

"Not tonight. Vodka soda, please." I reach into my purse for my credit card.

"Changing it up. I like it." He's laying it on . . . thick.

"Champagne is a celebratory drink. I don't have much to celebrate right now. It's a hard-liquor kind of night." He laughs as he finishes dispensing the soda water into my glass and has no clue how sad that actually is for me.

"Keep it open, or close it?" he asks as I slide my credit card across the bar to him.

"Open." I finish my first drink standing there and do my first lap around the club and don't see any celebrities yet, so I return to the bar so I can observe from there. I don't look conspicuous standing there alone. I catch the bartender's eye again. "Can I have another?"

"Coming right up." He gives me a wink.

I pace around the bar area to stay alert and my eyes continue to scan the room but I question my gut when I spot a familiar face near the DJ—Ethan. I have to do a double take to make sure it's him. I always trust my instincts, but a club is the last place I would ever expect to see him since he was so fond of articulating his disdain for "the Hollywood scene." Not only is he here, but he's here with a girl. What the fuck? I'm over him but I'm becoming more pissed off as the seconds tick away. He had the audacity to criticize me and now here he is drunk off the Kool-Aid. This is the last thing I need right now. I chant *Namaste* to myself, trying to reach a sense of Zen. The only other comfort I have at the moment, even though superficial, is that I look like a *Sports Illustrated* swimsuit model next to the manic pixie dream girl on his arm.

I take a huge gulp of my second vodka soda while I decide on my next move. Unfortunately, I don't have the luxury of time while trying to make my decision. He catches my gaze and now the guy who broke my heart and ditched me like last month's issue of GQ is walking toward me. I want to cry. I want to scream. I want to punch him. I want to steal Harry Potter's cloak of invisibility. He's reaches me and sadly none of these are options.

"Hi there," Ethan says as if nothing had ever happened between us. He's acting like I'm someone he helped with a chemistry lab in high school instead of talking about a life together with.

"Hello." I try to annunciate every syllable so the callousness of my tone won't go undetected over the music.

"How've you been?" he continues.

"Fine."

He keeps going even though I'm being curt. "I'm glad to hear that." He looks me up and down. I cross my arms in front of my breasts hoping he takes my new body language as a cue, since he's clearly not getting the hint from me being curt.

"You look great." I'm not even going to bother replying to this. For some reason, he takes this as an invitation to continue to pry. "You working?"

"What do you think, Ethan?" This is all too much. He knows this is my night at Ambiance. My head is spinning and not from alcohol. My mom, Holiday, Nick, now Ethan is back like a Netflix TV reboot—I can't take this anymore! I never got any closure from our breakup and I have hundreds of things I've wanted to say to him. I want to ask if he ever really loved me. I want to ask if he's happy now that I'm not in his life. I want to ask him how he could walk away and never look back. I want to know why it's so easy for guys like him and Nick to walk away from me. But none of these things come out of my mouth.

"Are you fucking kidding me? That's what I get after almost four years together? Years of me supporting your dream—and you bail when you don't like something. You're a pussy, Ethan!" I shout. I have to for him to hear me over the music. It's loud but I'm louder and he heard every word. He takes a step back, rattled by my public outburst, but I'm not letting him get off this easy for a second time. He ran away before but now it's my turn to say what I need to say. The DJ drops another beat and increases the volume. So do I. "Who the fuck do you think you are that you can walk up to me and be nice and pretend like we're good and you didn't do a horrible thing?" He tries to answer but I won't let him. "You think you're the good guy? You're not. Far from it. You're not nice. You're—"

"Stop it, you're causing a scene," he says in a stern voice that some-how seems to cut through the club sounds without an increased volume.

"Oh, now that your public profile is rising you don't want to be in-volved in anything that might make you look bad, huh?" I scream at the top of my lungs when the music becomes deafening and because my an-ger has boiled over. "Fuck you!"

"That's enough. You know exactly why I left. I wouldn't have left, Ella, but I couldn't stand dating Bella anymore. Don't act like I spon-taneously walked out. You consistently chose your job over our rela-tionship."

"Excuse me?"

Ethan gets his face close to mine to make sure his point is heard. "Now who's pretending? You cared more about Bella and Hollywood than you did about us and that's fine. Just fucking own it!"

And with that, I take the remainder of my vodka soda and throw it on him as if I'm on a Bravo reality show and storm straight back to the bar since I just wasted my perfectly good cocktail. I notice Ethan's manic pixie dream girl rush to his side after I doused him with my drink. She duti-fully brings him napkins and helps him clean up. I turn my back to them, lean on the bar, and order another vodka soda.

"Bella?" Oh God, now what? Or now who, I suppose, is a more ap-propriate question. The last thing I want is another altercation. I slowly spin around, holding my breath with a clenched jaw. It's Sexy Indie Film Actor! I've never been so happy to see a familiar face. He's oozing sex appeal, and everything inside me wants him to make me feel better.

"Hi!"

"You look fantastic." He's slurring his words but I don't care that he's already beyond hammered and to him I probably look like a blur more than a beauty. Maybe tonight can be salvaged after all. I look over at Ethan to make sure he sees me with Sexy Indie Film Actor, and he does as he's in the middle of probably telling his girlfriend that I'm a sociopath, but I couldn't care less. "I haven't seen you since that after-party at Twenty-something CW Bad Boy Heartthrob's place."

"I know."

"He's around here somewhere." His search of the crowd is futile in his inebriated state.

"That's okay, I'd rather be talking to you." I smile and make sure that for him my body language is inviting and enticing.

"What do you say; shots?"

I normally don't do shots, especially while I'm sipping on a cocktail. Historically they don't end well for me, but what the hell? "Shots!" I agree, perhaps a little too overeagerly. I want to numb myself after Ethan-gate.

"Bartender, two shots of tequila." He leans on the bar and I'm not sure if it's to flirt or for stability, but either way it's hot. I mean, he is Sexy Indie Film Actor, after all. "Who are you here with?"

"I'm all by my lonesome tonight." I sweep my fingers across his forearm so there's no confusion that I'm trying to seduce him. I need to feel desired tonight. "I needed to get out of the house and let off some steam." He places his hand on my hip and pulls me toward him so our faces are only inches apart from each other.

"I might be able to help you with that." He explores my hip with his hand.

"Oh, yeah?" The bartender slides our shots in front of us and neither of us breaks eye contact when we reach for our shots.

"Cheers." He downs his shot without wincing.

"Cheers." With Holiday I used to love toasting, but now I loathe it. I cough on the straight alcohol after I swallow.

As soon as we place our glasses back on the bar we're eye-fucking each other.

"Hey, do you want to play a game with me?" I ask.

"Yeah, I would like to play with you." I pop a piece of gum in my mouth and grab Sexy Indie Film Actor's hand and lead him toward the bathrooms. "I don't know what you're thinking but I like where that pretty little head of yours is at." I open the door to the men's room and after he stumbles in I lock the door behind him. He grabs me and kisses me and our sexual chemistry is palpable. "So what's this game?" he asks. I run my hand along the top of the toilet tank and it comes up clean. I moan. "What's wrong?"

"I was trying to show you the Cocaine Game. Both of us were supposed to run our hands back there and see who could pick up the most," I huff.

"Well, why didn't you say so?" Sexy Indie Film actor reaches into his pocket and pulls out a small bag of cocaine and begins cutting it along the back of the toilet.

He finishes cutting the coke into lines. Before he rolls up a hundred-dollar bill and attempts to hand it to me, he licks his finger, dips it in the bag of drugs, and smears some of the powder over his gums.

"No, thanks. That's all you." The last thing I need to add to my already fucked-up mind is narcotics.

"You sure?" he asks.

"Yeah." I may be fucked up but I'm lucid enough to know that drugs will only intensify all of my not-so-warm-and-fuzzy feelings. He shrugs his shoulders and does both lines then grabs my hips again and gently pushes me up against the door before he kisses me again. That "drunk, sloppy, I don't care that we're both fucked up right now" kind of kiss.

The men's room wasn't my first choice for a lust-fueled rendezvous, but at a Los Angeles nightclub it's either that or the photo booth. Those are the only two semiprivate make-out options. The ladies' room always has a bathroom attendant selling perfume, hair spray, gum, and cigarettes and making sure that only one person is in a stall at a time. It's more to make sure that they aren't doing drugs together than to prevent any sort of hookup, but the attendant is vigilant and there would be no way to sneak a guy in, and clearly Sexy Indie Film Actor had both vices on his mind.

"You taste like cocaine," I moan when I briefly tear my lips away from his for the first time in what feels like hours but in reality is minutes.

"You taste minty fresh," he compliments. Our faces are only inches apart. After a short beat we both say, "Win-win?" In this moment, we are two people that are connected through unspoken pain. He takes out the bag of coke again and does another small line before shoving his face back toward mine. Everything is spinning and all I hear is rap music blaring at decibel levels that must not be safe for human ears, but I don't care.

It feels like time and energy have stopped and we are the only two people in existence. I'm sure it's just the alcohol. We return to our lip-lock that is somehow violent and romantic at the same time and starts to heat up even more. When I woke up this morning I didn't think that I would have the Sexy Indie Film Actor's hands traveling inside of my shirt and attempting to unhook my bra. As much as part of my brain is telling me to go for this, I'm not in any state to take things further with him. I once again break my lips away from his.

"We should go back in," I tell him. He hears me but instead of answering proceeds to kiss my cheek and my jawbone and continues down my neck. "Seriously, we should go back in."

"Are you sure?" Of course I'm not sure. There are about three million women who would hire a hit man to take me out and take my place at this very second and I'm nursing one broken heart and reliving another. But I have to get back inside. I nod my head. He continues kissing my neck and décolletage until I turn the lock on the door that my back is pressed up against and I leave Sexy Indie Film Actor in the stall. There's a few men waiting to use the restroom and I try to avoid eye contact as I make my way to the door.

I wait for him around the corner and he brings me to his table where, lo and behold, Twentysomething CW Bad Boy Heartthrob is seated with his harem and bottle service. As we join them, Sexy Indie Film Actor passes the bag of cocaine back to its rightful owner aka Twentysomething CW Bad Boy Heartthrob.

"You want a drink?" Sexy Indie Film Actor asks me. His are hypnotizing. I know I shouldn't but . . .

"I'll have one more." I stare at the various bottles resting in a large ice bucket on our table and the standard fruit juice mixers. It's cute that he wants to play bartender, and I do really want another drink. He gives me a quick peck on the lips before he grabs a bottle of vodka to mix me a sugar-fueled beverage of his choosing. The girls in Twentysomething CW Bad Boy Heartthrob's posse are giving me major side-eye due to the gender ratio of females to the two actors. Sexy Indie Film Actor lays his arm around me and leans back on the banquette with the drinks completed. He tries to tell me about the upcoming role that his representation thinks will get him an Oscar or a nomination at the very least. I can't make out much of what he's saying since the music has been turned up even louder and I'm also keeping an eye on Twentysomething CW Bad Boy Heartthrob, who is now brazenly doing lines of cocaine off our table without caring who sees him. He snorts line after line without hesitation, and any allure he might have been able to salvage after the incident at his house is 100 percent gone now.

I excuse myself a few times to go to the ladies' room to take notes for my file, and I also politely tell Sexy Indie Film Actor he can't join me for another rendezvous. I do a lap each time I walk back, and no other celebrities have shown up. I'm literally sitting in the middle of my story tonight. I still have my phone in my hand when Sexy Indie Film Actor grabs it and poses with me and snaps a selfie.

"We look hot," he says, admiring the photo. We take more and after we're done duckfacing and posing, Twentysomething CW Bad Boy Heartthrob is finally out of drugs but isn't done.

"Let's get out of here," he says, motioning to Sexy Indie Film Actor. "My guy is gonna meet me in ten and we'll bring the girls back and get an after-party goin'." Sexy Indie Film Actor agrees.

"You wanna come with us? With me?" He's eye-fucking me and I'm fairly certain he wants to actually fuck me but there's no way this will be a good decision. Besides, I didn't lose two of the most important people in my life to leave early and possibly miss something only for Victoria to end up firing me. Bella gives him her best answer.

"I can't tonight." Sexy Indie Film Actor looks dejected. I am probably the only (stupid) girl to reject him since he's been famous. "Rain check?"

"'Night, Bella." He leans in for one last kiss and the entourage is off, following their messiah. I leave the table to ward off any suspicion about why I'm staying when my entire group left and return to my post at the bar. I stare at my phone, wanting to text Holiday that I just made out with Sexy Indie Film Actor. I suddenly miss Nick and I torture myself by opening our text history.

Nick: Miss you.

Nick: Can't wait to see you tonight, babe!

Nick: Wish I were still in bed cuddling with your perfect sexy ass . . .

Nick: I've fallen for you faster and harder than I ever imagined possible.

I reread them over and over and over again, trying to reconcile these messages with the last few days. I know I should delete them but I can't physically bring myself to do it and continue to keep my nose buried in my iPhone.

After I've sufficiently tortured myself I get up to do another lap around the club. I'm looking but I'm not really paying attention. The reality of my life sets in. No Nick. No Holiday. My mom's illness . . . and I'm terrified. I keep asking what if's about all of them, especially my mom. I know I have to think positively, but it's natural to be concerned and this is all a little much to process while I'm staring at go-go dancers.

"You don't look like you're having any fun," a drunk guy tells me as he accosts me near the bar. I'm not. "Come on, put that thing down and come dance with me!" He tries to pull my phone from my hand.

"Get away from me!" I yell as I shove him away.

"Jesus, lighten up, sweetheart. You're at a club. You know that, right?" He turns around and mumbles "bitch" audibly enough so I could hear before he returns to his group of douche-bag friends. I look at my phone and it's 1:50 A.M. Minutes later, as soon as the lights come up, I buy a bottle of water from the bar and close out.

As I pull out of the parking lot I realize I'm a little buzzed. A little more than buzzed if I'm honest. I wanted to get out of there so badly and get into my bed as fast as possible I didn't even think about leaving my car. It's not a decision I recommend but I can do this. I've made the drive to Holiday's a million times and as long as I focus I'll be okay. I can't help but replay tonight's events in my mind as I drive, trying to make sense of them. I need to go to bed and I need to wake up tomorrow and clear my head and figure out where I'm going to live and how to move on with my life. Almost immediately after I turn onto Laurel Canyon I hear my phone go off with a message alert. At this hour it might be important so I fish it out of my purse with one hand while keeping my other hand on the steering wheel and my eyes on the road. I quickly look at the message and it's an alert from *The Life*.

The Life: Report: Twentysomething CW Bad Boy Heartthrob Overdoses on Drugs

I just saw him. I can't believe this. My mind is shaking and so is my body and I swerve as I glance down at my phone again to confirm that I've read what I think I've read and the tragedy doesn't have time to sink in because I hear police sirens and a voice directing me to move to the side of the road. My heart sinks and from nerves I feel like I could projectile vomit on my dashboard. The cop must've seen me swerve. Thanks to my love of movies and TV I know exactly what's about to happen. The officer approaches my window.

"Ma'am, I'm going to have to ask you to step out of your vehicle."

. . . .

I arrive at the police station and there doesn't seem to be any rush booking me. I'm escorted through the door and this is one exclusive back room I wish I was never escorted into.

"Klick, female DUI to book and process," my arresting officer calls out, passing me off to the female officer. Officer Klick takes a sip of her station coffee and looks me up and down. I can't help but notice she'd be so pretty if she weren't in the middle of arresting me. She's about fifteen years older than I am with caramel hair pulled into a tight bun, and her hands are delicate.

"Don't worry. This one isn't a troublemaker."

She takes another sip of her coffee before she takes the reins and takes me to the photo area. "You okay?" she whispers.

"Yes."

She uncuffs me. "Don't smile, and look remorseful," she advises. I give my best mea culpa pose, a far cry from the selfies I was taking with Sexy Indie Film Actor a few hours ago. Sadly, no amount of filters or Facetune can help the embarrassment of this particular type of photo. Though Officer Klick is no Patrick Demarchelier, I'm channeling the same somber harrowed look that I'm sure he gives as art direction when shooting models for editorials. That look where I'm glancing off in the distance, pensive and starving. She then takes me to a desk where I'm fingerprinted and she takes my purse, including my phone.

"You can make your phone call now." She hands me the receiver for the landline and I hesitate. This call is going to be worse than facing the judge at my arraignment because there is only one person I can call. I dial and almost hope she doesn't pick up.

"Hello?" Robin grumbles when she finally answers her phone. I'm sure she's confused by the caller ID.

"Robin, it's me. I know you're working but—"

"El, what is it?"

"Robin, whatever you do please don't hang up. Please. I'm at the Hollywood Hills police station. I got a DUI. I'm okay. No one was hurt, but I need you to bail me out when your shift is over." Silence. "Please. Robin?" I plead.

"My shift ends at 6 A.M., you'll have to wait," she says and hangs up. I know I have more than a lecture coming my way, which I deserve this time. I'm probably lucky that she is at work and didn't have time to draw our conversation out. I hang up and slump my head into my hands. I take in the humid smell of the station and the chipped paint on the neutral walls.

"Do you need to go to the restroom before I take you to the holding cell?"

"Yes." I want a minute to collect myself before I'm locked up.

"Right through that door." I follow her index finger and open the door she's gesturing to. I avoid looking in the mirror and splash some water on my face. It's only a few hours. I can do this. As I return from the bathroom, Officer Klick lets out a loud shriek. My heart jumps. What's going on? Are we under attack? Did Jess hear about my arrest and organize a "Free Ella" jailbreak? Officer Klick sees the terror on my face and apologizes.

"I'm sorry, Ms. Warren. I didn't mean to alarm you." She looks at her phone again. "It's a silly celebrity thing. I got an alert on my phone."

"What celebrity thing?" I'm panicked. What could it be or who could it be? I know it's not good news.

"Twentysomething CW Bad Boy Heartthrob died."

I feel woozy and like I'm about to faint.

"Can I sit for a second?" Officer Klick pulls the chair out of the desk for me. "I can't believe this. I was with him earlier tonight."

"You were?" Her eyes widen, even though I've just been arrested for a misdemeanor. Even in LA, fame is a currency.

"Yes. And you're sure that's what your news alert said?"

She holds the face of her phone up to me to look at. "That's what *The Life* said. And I trust whatever they say."

"Yeah, well, you should. I work for them," I grumble.

Officer Klick's already kind demeanor mellows even more. "Really? What was he like?" I've gone from prisoner to person of interest.

"I feel bad saying this now but he was kind of an asshole, honestly." My tears, which don't ever seem to go away anymore, resume.

"It's okay. He's in a better place now," she affirms.

"No, it's not that," I sob. "It's just . . . I have to e-mail my file on him into my boss with all of my observation on him tonight or I'll get fired. If I don't get her every detail for this breaking-news story, I'm done. I probably deserve it." I grimace. "Can you just lock me up so I can sit for a bit?"

"No. Not yet." She leans over her desk and grabs me a tissue. "I'm not really supposed to do this but you haven't caused any trouble so here's something for your good behavior." She hands me my iPhone and I feel like I'm being handed Excalibur. "Can you do it in ten minutes?"

"Yes! Oh my God. Thank you! I don't know what to say."

"Don't say anything, just type," she orders. I'm forever indebted to Officer Klick for helping me. I unlock my phone and copy and paste my notes into an e-mail and add color and additional details as fast as my motor skills will allow. I'm able to complete my file with Twentysomething CW Bad Boy Heartthrob and this time have to include Sexy Indie Film Actor, since this story is too big to omit any details. I hit Send in seven minutes and return my phone to her.

"Thank you again, really. You saved my job."

She smiles but I know it's time for me to trade my cell phone for the holding cell. She guides me by my arm and I'd give anything to hear clinking glasses toasting to glamour and love instead of my cell door clinking shut. I sit on the bench and make an effort to close my eyes and rest but it's impossible. I stare at the wall, playing out all of the possible scenarios of what will happen when Robin picks me up. I really have no idea how she's going to react. All I know is I'm in a lot of trouble, with the state of California and with her. Around 8 A.M. Officer Klick returns to my cell.

"Warren, you made bail," she says, opening up the cage to my freedom. I step out and relish the reality that I can once again walk left or right as far as I want and vow never to end up here again.

"Thanks."

Her former pleasantries become earnest. "I don't want to see you back here, Ms. Warren."

"You won't. I promise."

"No job is worth your life. Besides, you're too pretty to end up in a real jail and inmates don't look too kindly on spies and narcs." She opens the door and releases me into the lobby where Robin is waiting with my bail bondsman. She's exhausted and she looks it. She looks almost as bad as I look in my mug shot. Her mouth is so tense I can almost hear her grinding teeth. Her eyes pierce into mine with contempt and her folded arms indicate that if we weren't in a police station where she'd be arrested on the spot, she would murder me.

"Now, Ms. Warren, do not miss your scheduled court appearance or there will be a warrant issued for your arrest." She hands me a paper to sign for the receipt of my things.

"She'll be there," Robin tells her. "I'll make sure of it." She went from staring me down to not being able to look at me.

Officer Klick hands me a stack of papers. "Here's all of the information

for court and instructions on how to recover your vehicle." More important, she returns my purse and my phone. I grasp the device, ecstatic to
be reunited, and don't want to let go.

Robin snatches the papers away from me and pushes me out of the
police station with the heavyset sweaty bail bondsman following.

"Thank you so much," Robin tells him, shaking his hand. "I'll be in
touch." She turns and grabs me and gives me the biggest, tightest hug I've
ever received from her. "Are you okay?"

"I'm a little shaken up, but I'm fine. Luckily I was the only one in
holding for the evening so I didn't have to endure the uncomfortable
'what are you in for' discussions with other criminals." She rolls her eyes.

"I'm hungry," she says before going radio silent. I'm unnerved by Robin's reticence but I'm not mistaking it for compassion quite yet. I don't
know if I should be worried or feel relieved. We ride in silence until she
pulls into a twenty-four-hour diner on Ventura Boulevard. It's bustling
inside, with parents treating kids to a special Friday breakfast before school,
people fresh off the graveyard shift sitting at the counter having a meal
before they go to bed, and sprinkled in are the eccentric characters of Los
Angeles arguing with each other, one guy who's cutting his toast with a
fork and knife. These people are complete enigmas, but I find them fascinating to watch and wonder about their daily lives—usually, not today.
An older waitress in her 1950s uniform, who's clearly overworked this
morning by the very noticeable scowl on her face, skulks over to us moments after we slide into a booth.

"What'll it be?" she asks. I place my phone on the table, so happy to
be reunited, and pull a menu out from between the napkin dispenser and
the wall.

"I'm kinda dying for pancakes." I look to Robin for an iota of emotion or an opinion but her face is rigid. "Should I? I think that being arrested is as good as any excuse for a diet cheat day." Still nothing from
Robin. "I'll have the short stack. Can you heat up a little syrup and bring
that out with the order? Having hot syrup really makes all the difference,
don't you think?" Neither of them respond.

"Just coffee and toast for me," she says as she returns the menu, still
avoiding making eye contact with me.

"Great, big spenders," the waitress mocks as she scribbles down our
order. I lean my head back still in disbelief about my evening. Robin continues to stare at everything but me and I know that even though she's

probably going to yell at me, I have to express my deep gratitude for her bailing me out literally and figuratively.

"Thanks again, Robin. I know bailing me out of jail wasn't exactly on your weekly to-do list." I take a breath to punctuate my sincerity. "I really don't know what I'd do without you."

"Really? That's funny because you certainly don't treat me like that."

My filler-free forehead wrinkles at her accusation and I jump to my defense. "That's not true—" I try to tell her but she doesn't want to hear anything from me. She puts her hand up for me to stop and plows right through my attempt to explain.

"You treat me like your boring, burden of an older sister that has a stick up her ass that you tolerate only when necessary. Do you ever call me to actually do anything with me? We haven't been to a movie or out for a meal together on our own in forever." Her face moves like Silly Putty because it can't settle on being angry or hurt and keeps converting between the two. "If it weren't for Marianna I would have barely seen you the past four years and you're only around more now because of Mom."

"Robin, it's not my fault we don't do anything together. You never want to do anything fun," I tell her.

"Fun? That's all you ever think about is fun. Ella, you have to grow up," she clamors. Her cheeks tighten, which always happens when she goes into her auto know-it-all mode. "For goodness' sake, I just bailed you out of jail!" She shakes her head in all directions in disbelief that I'm not immediately conceding. "You have to stop caring about the wrong things and stop being so self-centered. The Earth doesn't revolve around you."

I know she just helped me but she's taking it too far and her accusations incense me. Despite my gratitude I can't stay mum. "You're the biggest hypocrite I've ever met. With the audacious way you revise history when it's convenient for you, you really should've gone into creative writing or been a politician." I take a gulp of air and continue. "You think I need to grow up? My mistakes aren't taking anything important away from you."

Robin releases her pointer finger from her clenched fist and it's obvious that she's going to follow it with her middle and ring fingers to make a list with a visual aid of the reasons why she believes my statement is incorrect but I refuse to let her interrupt. "When I was growing up, Mom and Dad never had time to come and watch me at tennis camp or take me to the playground or do anything with me because they were always

tending to you." I look her right in the eyes to let her know I'm not backing down, but Robin shakes her head in denial. "You can't pretend with
me, Robin. I grew up with you. This facade of perfection you've constructed
is bullshit. I know what a mess you were before you were an egomaniacal doctor. And not only were you reckless, *you* were selfish." Robin rolls
her eyes, still trying to discredit my memories and the truth. "You didn't
care that you took all of our parents' time and attention because of your
behavior. You took that from me during my childhood and by the time
you got your life together Dad was gone. You stole my time!" My face
feels like it's burning and flushed with redness. I'm screaming at her now
and thank God there aren't any other customers here.

"I'm sorry that you didn't get as much time with Dad as I did. I'm
sorry I'm older. I can't fix that, Ella. It's not like I expected him to have
a heart attack and die." I can feel tears coming again and this is why
I've always avoided this conversation. "Dad's death didn't affect me less
because I had more of his attention. I only had negative attention from
him. Do you know how that feels? I have to live with that regret every
day and nothing will ever make it better. Our father loved us both but he
only knew me as a mess, not as an accomplished doctor or the caring
mother that I am today. I will always have contrition about that but I let
it go. I had to. You have to let it go or else *we* will never have a shot at a
real relationship."

I turn my head away with purpose. "This isn't even about me!" she
shouts. "But I'm shocked you even paid attention to me, just being an
anonymous doctor. All you've ever cared about are celebrities."

"You're wrong and you know it, so you're reaching. That is not true,"
I contend. I don't want to continue this conversation so I pick up my
phone to distract myself and open my e-mails.

Robin irrately reaches across the table, grabs my phone from my hands
and browses frantically.

"Hey! Give that back!" I extend my arm in an attempt to recover my
iPhone and she leans farther back in her seat to hold me off until she finds
what she's looking for.

"Look!" She turns the screen to face me. "You don't have photos of any
real people in here. It's all screenshots of your articles and selfies with
celebrities—the only people you deem worthy of your attention don't even
know your real name. Who the hell *are* you?" I fold my arms in front of

me and my skin feels like it's about to explode as my blood bubbles beneath it. Robin notices and shifts her tactic and tries compassion. "The *Ella* I know doesn't get DUIs and need to be bailed out of jail. Do you even recognize yourself anymore?" The disappointment in her voice is heartbreaking.

I pause before I answer. I realize I have no tears left to cry, which is probably some sort of an ironic metaphor for my empty soul. "No," I answer honestly. I look down at the floor, disappointed in myself. I notice an empty container of cream and packet of raw sugar on the floor that haven't been swept up from a previous customer.

"Then it's time to make a change." She moves over to my side of the booth. "I know this has been a tough year for you but you have to start taking some accountability. Everything with Holiday, Nick, this DUI . . . these aren't mistakes. These are choices."

I feel dizzy.

"You're not the first one to tell me that."

The waitress arrives with our order.

"You still have time to make it right with everyone," she contends.

"How?" I feel helpless. I don't know how to even begin.

The waitress interrupts with our food.

"Coffee, toast, and a short stack with *warm* syrup." The waitress smirks. "Oh, goody, we're having a feel-good moment. How lovely."

Robin ignores her. "My offer still stands. You can live with me for a while until you get back on your feet. I'll help you out with your legal fees and you can help me with Marianna and you go to every single doctor's appointment and chemo treatment with Mom." She hands me a napkin to use as a tissue.

"Thank you. And I promise I'm going to pay you back." I have no idea how but I will.

"We can figure all of that out later," she says. "And Ella, I am sorry. I never meant to consume all of Mom and Dad's time or overshadow you in any way."

"Thanks. I know it wasn't intentional and you were just a teenager. I guess I just needed to know that you knew your rebellious years affected me, too. . . ." I trail off. Hearing her apologize and accept responsibility without qualifying it or adding any sort of defense is what I've been waiting years to hear.

"Maybe everything that's going on in our family happened for a reason. Maybe Mom and your DUI are the universe's way of helping us find our new dynamic."

I raise my eyebrows. I've never heard Robin, a woman of logic and science, speak like this. "Universe?"

She raises her shoulders. "What can I say, you've been rubbing off on me."

Even though moving in with Robin is the only realistic option of how I should proceed and it's certainly not how I would've orchestrated things, I want to move in with her. I want to try to make our relationship work and be with my mom and niece even if it's not under the best of circumstances. I rub the napkin against the bridge of my nose.

"God forbid her cancer gets worse and you didn't spend as much time as possible with her, you'll regret it for the rest of your life. We both have that with Dad. I don't want that for you with Mom."

"You're right." I take a breath. "It was just easier for me to pretend that she wasn't really that sick because the thought of her not being okay is too hard."

"I promise you, Ella, I'm not your enemy. I'm rooting for you. I think you're so brave to go after what you want, even if it's something I don't necessarily understand."

"Really?" I wonder if I'm still legally drunk because it sounds like she just gave me a compliment.

"Of course. I just don't want you to lose yourself in the process." She tucks a piece of hair behind my ear. "Now eat your pancakes before your syrup gets cold." Robin places her hand on top of mine and then returns to her side of the table. I unhinge my jaw and take a huge bite of pancakes.

"How are they?" she inquires.

"Not nearly as good as Mom's French toast," I review in the middle of chewing.

Robin smiles. "I could've told you that before you ordered them."

"Speaking of Mom, you aren't going to tell her about this, are you?" I plead. Most people think that when they mess up, no one could ever be as disappointed in them as they are in themselves. In my case, the thought of my ailing mother learning of my DUI and being disappointed in me would be a million times worse. "I will buy your silence with candy if that dynamic still works," I offer.

Robin finishes her coffee and takes a moment for herself before answering. "I wasn't planning on it, no." Phew. "She'll realize something is
up eventually when she notices you aren't driving but for the time being
I don't think we need to give her anything else to worry about. It's our
little secret, but a Snickers wouldn't hurt."

"Robin, I'm scared. Is Mom gonna be okay? Please don't sugarcoat it,"
I request. "Look, the worst has already happened. I need to know. I need
you not to treat me with kid gloves."

She returns her mug to the table.

"I don't know. She's making progress but cancer can be unpredictable. It could go either way and that's the truth. We have to keep Mom's
spirits up. I know that Dr. Jacobs will do everything he can but no one
can make any promises. Is that what you needed to hear?"

I nod yes.

My phone buzzes and Robin hands it back to me. I haven't checked
my e-mail since I was released from jail. It's an e-mail from Victoria.

Ella,

*AMAZING reporting on Twentysomething CW Bad Boy Heartthrob!! (And
some good stuff on Sexy Indie Film Actor too.) Between you and my source at
the hospital who tipped me off about the ambulance for the overdose and his
death we are leading the coverage on this story. Congratulations! The points
e-mail will be sent out in a day or so but I wanted to show you the current scores
first after your amazing reporting at Ambiance.*

1. Ella Warren

2. Not me

3. Not me

4. Not me

....

Twenty-four

You just can't get enough, can you, Ella?" Nurse Richards jokes. "You haven't missed a single chemo appointment with your mom for the past few months. You're a good daughter."

"Yes, she is," my mom agrees.

"Kind of a slow day in here," I say. Since my falling out with Nick and Holiday two months ago, I've been at Robin's and go with my mom to her appointments. We are the only people in the treatment center today.

Nurse Richards leans her head to the side. "You won't be alone for long. Joan, can I get you anything?"

"Not right now."

My mom continues with her issue of *The Life* and when she flips the page I stop her from flipping to the next. The headline reads, "Stars Who Shopped Instead of Adopted." There's a huge photo of Holiday and her new King Charles Cavalier puppy, Harry. "There needs to be at least one King Harry in my lifetime," she's quoted as saying in the article, while a few lines down she's ripped to shreds for purchasing a designer dog instead of choosing to rescue. "Shallow?" is printed across a family photo of Holiday, Tristan, and Harry. I release a sigh.

"She's sure been getting raked over the coals lately," my mother notices. "There was an article last week about her eating at a restaurant that doesn't boycott GMO ingredients."

"Everything she does is under a microscope now," I tell her. "If Holiday sneezes and uses two tissues instead of one, there's an article about her lack of concern for pollution and the environment, which then spins out into her not caring or believing in climate change." It sounds so ridiculous when I say it that I wouldn't believe it if I hadn't read it online yesterday. At least she has Tristan by her side.

"It's too bad you can't use any of your connections to help her," she says, turning the page to something less controversial: noninvasive plastic surgery. My phone buzzes. It's a text alert from *The Life.*

The Life: Report: Sexy Indie Film Actor Completes Rehab

Talk about adding insult to unwanted infamy. My heart sinks. He lost a key movie role because of the notes I turned in on that night about Twentysomething CW Bad Boy Heartthrob.

Just then, three burly men with walkie-talkies burst into the room. Both my mother and I are stunned. One of the men walks over and inspects my mom's IV and gives me a long glance up and down. He then takes her magazine and puts it facedown on the table next to her.

"We're clear," he speaks into his walkie-talkie.

The door is hurriedly opened and in walks Not-So-Innocent Oversexualized Pop Star!

"Thank you," she tells the three men. I have so many thoughts running through my head I'm having trouble choosing one. What is she doing here? Why is she in the chemo treatment room? What the hell is going on? I realize my jaw has been agape since the moment she walked in, and I close it.

Not-So-Innocent Oversexualized Pop Star surveys my mom and me just like I'm scanning her. Once she assesses us and is comfortable, she nods to her bodyguards, who retreat to the other side of the door. To my surprise, she unzips and removes her hoodie, revealing her port, and takes off a wig and exposes her bald head. Nurse Richards preps her exactly the same way she preps my mother. I still can't believe one of my idols is in front of me. It's taking everything inside of me to stop myself from asking for a selfie. I glance at her head again and realize an autograph is more probable but still not appropriate.

"How are we doing today?" she asks Not-So-Innocent Oversexualized Pop Star. In this moment, she's not the most legendary pop icon in the world, she's just . . . human. "I'm sorry we couldn't get you your usual private room. There's been some plumbing issues in the wing and space is limited."

"It's alright. It actually feels nice not to be so isolated for once," she muses. "Even while I was living here I rarely had contact with anyone else."

"How are you feeling, sweetheart?" Nurse Richards asks with a hint of pity in her tone.

"Terrible," Not-So-Innocent Oversexualized Pop Star answers. "I can barely keep food down but I've never been this thin in my life," she jokes. "Chemo is way more effective than a gluten-free diet . . . though I wouldn't recommend it." I can't help but laugh when I overhear and Not-So-Innocent Oversexualized Pop Star smiles at me. "What are you in for?" she asks my mother.

"AML. You?"

"ALL," she answers. "What cycle are you on?" she inquires.

"This is my third. You?"

"Fourth. I'm getting better but leukemia feels like it's harder to get rid of than a bad boyfriend or bedbugs." It's almost unfathomable to me not only that the biggest celebrity in the world is sitting feet away from me but also that while she is getting secret chemotherapy, she has any interest in my mother's journey.

"I'm Joan and this is my daughter Ella."

"Nice to meet you." Not-So-Innocent Oversexualized Pop Star and my mother have bonded in less than five minutes like war buddies. Not-So-Innocent Oversexualized Pop Star scrunches her face as the medicine begins to infiltrate her body. She looks over at me. "It's nice that you're here with your mom. I wish my family would come with me instead of sending bodyguards, but the only thing my parents are around for is to discuss my brand," she says, looking as if she is trying to hold back both tears and nausea.

Oh. My. God. It all makes sense now. I can't believe that I hadn't put it together before this. Hell, I can't believe nobody else has put it together. I know it's invasive but I can't help myself. The wheels are turning in my head and they won't stop.

"You didn't really have a breakdown, did you?" I ask. Not-So-Innocent Oversexualized Pop Star bites her lower lip and simply shakes her head. I've just stumbled upon the biggest celebrity story of the year—possibly even my lifetime.

"*Not-So-Innocent Oversexualized Pop Star Fakes Breakdown to Hide Cancer.*"

She created this entire facade to hide her illness and protect her brand. It all makes perfect sense in the most twisted but logical way. It's actually brilliant.

"Perception is everything." She shrugs. I know this all too well. "It's better if the world thinks I'm crazy instead of knows I'm sick," she continues. Not only has her ruse protected her brand, but it's even helped it. Her iTunes sales have gone through the roof since her first trip to the "psych ward" and she's been offered book deals, prime-time sit-down interviews, and any other kind of endorsement deal she could ever want.

Not-So-Innocent Oversexualized Pop Star and her team planned the most elaborate of celebrity stunts. Everything was calculated. She went to Ambiance and acted like she was out of control to make it more believable that she was losing her grasp on reality. The head shaving was to preempt possibly losing her hair from chemo and minimize speculation about her wearing wigs. The 5150 was necessary for her father to get conservatorship to handle her financial and medical matters in case at some point she was unable to make her own decisions. Her public cancelation of her upcoming tour . . . It's insane but it worked.

With people like me running around, she had to go to extreme lengths to protect her privacy and the best way to do that was to create a more scandalous story.

"Please keep this our little secret," she implores.

"Of course." This isn't gossip or salacious news for public consumption.

No matter what I've told myself or convinced myself of, my job was never harmless. There was always a victim even if I didn't realize it or didn't want to see it. There's no way I'm breaking Not-So-Innocent Oversexualized Pop Star's confidence and breathing a word of this to Victoria. This poor woman had to manufacture a meltdown on top of being sick. I couldn't live with myself if I divulged her health problems to the world. Within minutes it would be international news. Everyone has been telling me that I need to make choices, and right now I choose not to be that person anymore. Not ever again.

I'm so consumed with thinking about all Not-So-Innocent Oversexualized Pop Star has been doing to hide her illness that I don't even notice Dr. Jacobs come in.

"How are you feeling, Joan?" He looks at her chart, keeping his signature prickly persona intact with his monotone question.

"I don't know. I'm still feeling very tired. I know the new dosage is working but I don't know how much longer I can take it. I barely want to get out of bed in the morning and that's no way to live."

"I've put way too much time and work into you for you to give up on me now. You understand?" This is Dr. Jacobs's attempt at encouragement. My mom gestures with her head that she does.

"How about you?" He looks to Not-So-Innocent Oversexualized Pop Star.

"I feel like how I look in the tabloids." She laughs. Dr. Jacobs, whom I can't imagine reads celebrity gossip magazines, gives her a perplexed look before reviewing her chart.

"I want to do a new round of blood work on you," he tells her, making notes without bothering to look at her. "You will both be good to go in a few hours. I'll see you soon." He exits and the bodyguard resumes his stoic stance on the other side of the door.

My mom picks her magazine back up and when she opens it, I realize who's on this week's cover—it's Not-So-Innocent Oversexualized Pop Star. I swiftly glance at her to see if she's noticed and she has. My mother hasn't realized her faux pas yet but I'm mortified.

"It's okay," she assures me. "That's not me. It's my picture but it's not me. I'm so disconnected from the character of Not-So-Innocent Oversexualized Pop Star that the media perpetuates that it really doesn't affect me anymore."

My mother, confused by her comments, flips the magazine around to take a peek at the cover. She brings her hand to her mouth and after a few moments says, "I'm sorry. I completely forgot you were on the cover." Not only is she on the cover but she's also being bashed for her postbreakdown makeunder style. I now realize her baggier clothes are to hide her port. "I'm not going to read that article about you," she assures her.

"Honestly, Joan, it's fine." She gives us a devious smile. "Just don't believe everything you read." She winks.

My mom returns the magazine to the table. The silence is uncomfortable. I don't want to ask her anything because I don't want her to think that I'm prying, but sitting across from her and ignoring her is rude, too. Luckily, my mother takes the initiative.

"You know what sucks most about cancer?" Not-So-Innocent Oversexualized Pop Star asks rhetorically. "The food. I'm not able to appreciate food anymore."

"I know exactly how you feel," my mom adds. "Ella took me to Spago and I loved the experience but I couldn't muster up enough of an appetite to really enjoy it. Food is now just fuel for my body. I miss cravings and food being an experience. Now when I eat either my appetite isn't there, I take three bites and I'm done, and when I do have an appetite I'm nauseated after I eat. So I don't look forward to food now. There's nothing I'd love more than to have a voracious craving for fried chicken."

Not-So-Innocent Oversexualized Pop Star raises her hands in the air, as if the messiah had just come down from the mountain. "Yes! I miss friend chicken, too," she laments. "And I didn't appreciate it when I was able to eat it. I was on a stupid diet seventy-five percent of the time. If I knew I was going to get leukemia I would've gone gangbusters on all my favorite foods the past few years. I mean, fried chicken. What's not to love? It's breaded meat!"

"And the sides," my mother adds.

"Those are almost better than the actual chicken," Not-So-Innocent Oversexualized Pop Star points out. We all break into a fit of laughter and they continue to reminisce about all of the foods they wish they could enjoy. The next few hours fly by and I'm a little blue that this chemo session is coming to an end when Nurse Richards returns. She removes the medicine and gets them all cleaned up. Not only did my mom bond with one of the world's most iconic pop stars but it was also nice for her to have someone to vent to who actually understands the frustrations of what she's physically and emotionally been going through.

"Could you help me with this?" Not-So-Innocent Oversexualized Pop Star asks me as she places her wig on her head. "Make sure it's straight?" I can't even recognize all of the feelings and emotions I'm experiencing right now because they're all happening simultaneously. I feel sorry for Not-So-Innocent Oversexualized Pop Star and she makes me feel grateful for everything in my life, the good and the bad. She's brought so much joy to my life and I hate that she has to go through this, seemingly alone even though the entire world would say a prayer for her if they knew. I give her wig a light tug for adjustment.

"Maybe I'll see you gals around again," Not-So-Innocent Oversexualized Pop Star says hopefully.

My mom takes Not-So-Innocent Oversexualized Pop Star's hands, and her security is about to leap into action, but her look tells them to stand down. "Focus on yourself, dear," says Mom. "I know the public thinks we deserve a piece of you, but there's nothing more important to your fans than your health." Not-So-Innocent Oversexualized Pop Star is going to have a for-real breakdown now and hugs my mom.

"Mom, Robin had an emergency and won't be able to drive us home," I tell her as I check my phone.

"My other daughter, Robin, she's an ER doctor here," my mom proudly explains to Not-So-Innocent Oversexualized Pop Star.

"I'll call us an Uber."

"That's ridiculous. I'll have my SUV drop you off after they take me home," Not-So-Innocent Oversexualized Pop Star offers.

"We're in the Valley, are you sure?"

"Absolutely. You're lucky," she tells me, slightly envious of our relationship and support. "I would give anything to trade places with you." My mom grabs my hand. If only she knew what it took for us to get here.

"Car's here," her lead bodyguard tells us. We all follow him and meander through secret tunnels as if we are in the White House, and we are bombarded by paparazzi as we file into the SUV. I wonder how they got in here? I guess once Victoria got her source at the hospital the paparazzi followed. How did all of them sneak in? Or were they allowed in by someone who struck a deal with them?

The cavalcade of photographers is more intense than anything I've ever seen, and the shouting and name-calling, calling her a nutjob and a wacko to try to get a reaction out of her, is excessive. I can't imagine living with this 24-7, especially under her current circumstances. The bodyguards get Not-So-Innocent Oversexualized Pop Star in first and then I assist them in getting my mom into the backseat with her, which is difficult due to the paparazzi crowding around the SUV with a lack of care for our personal space. Once my mom is safe and settled in her seat, I hop in the passenger seat. Not-So-Innocent Oversexualized Pop Star is lying down in the last row behind me to hide from the cameras as best she can.

"Sorry about all this," she says as we try to part the sea of paparazzi with our Cadillac Escalade. The photographers continue flashing as we move at about two miles per hour even though the only shots they are getting are of the driver and me. Their tenacious nature won't allow them to let up and they stay in front of our vehicle until they are mere centimeters from being hit.

We arrive at Not-So-Innocent Oversexualized Pop Star's gated community trailed by at least fifteen cars of paparazzi. Once we are behind the gates she finally sits up.

"It must be exhausting being you," I tell her.

"You have no idea," she tells me. "I have a great life, though, even with cancer. It would just be nice to have a little more privacy and not have to orchestrate these theatrics. I mean, the media has their story about me. It's just not the real story. It's the story we fed them." We pull up to her gorgeous Mediterranean mansion. "This is me," she says before opening her door. "It was really nice meeting you ladies. I kinda felt like you let me be a part of your family for a few hours."

"You're welcome to join us anytime," my mother offers. "We can be chemo companions if you like."

Not–So-Innocent Oversexualized Pop Star nods her head. "I'd like that. Have your doctor call my doctor." She winks and closes the door and we're en route to Robin's.

I kept my phone in my purse the entire treatment and car ride so Not-So-Innocent Oversexualized Pop Star didn't have any reason to be suspicious of me texting even as a fangirl to her friends. I wait until we arrived at home just to be extra safe and I see another alert from *The Life*.

The Life: Sexy Indie Film Actor Dropped From 2 Upcoming Movies

My stomach churns and I check my e-mail. Something from Victoria marked Urgent. I've already given her everything I have on Sexy Indie Film Actor so I don't know why she's pestering me. Once I open the e-mail, I wish that's who she was bothering me about.

Ella,
I was looking through the hourly batch of paparazzi photos of Not-So-Innocent Oversexualized Pop Star at the hospital and noticed you getting into a car with her! GOOD JOB! Tell me everything. I don't know how you managed to pull this off but I must say, I'm impressed. Remember, no detail is too small but with her I want to hear it even if it's microscopic. Was she lucid? Did she smell hygienic? What did you discuss? This is a fantastic get. I'd like you to work for The Life full-time and be a part of our staff, effectively immediately. E-mail my assistant to set a meeting so we can discuss all of the particulars. Again, GREAT job.
Victoria

Oh. My. God! She knows. Of course she knows. Victoria scours every celeb photo that's taken daily and has sources everywhere. I feel like I'm holding the detonator to a bomb in my hands. I am. I know what happens if I reply to this e-mail. Hell, in a half hour the world will know. I also know what happens if I don't.

Jess, can you come to Robin's ASAP? It's an emergency.

Jessica knows that despite my flair for the dramatic, I wouldn't use the word *emergency* unless I meant it. She replies in under five seconds.

Leaving in 5 xo.

I gently place my phone on the kitchen island and slowly take a few steps back, with my hands extended in front of my chest, as if not to rock my world's equilibrium with any sudden movements. I retreat to the couch and stare at the TV, which is off. I want to shut my mind down until Jessica can help me figure this out. Thirty-five minutes of quietude later, and with my mind in a vegetative state, the doorbell rings. I open the door to find my friend flustered and out of breath. She stretches her arms out to their full span before squeezing me with them before I can close the front door.

"Is everything okay?" she inquires. "What's wrong?"

I break free from her arms and lead her into the kitchen without saying anything. I can tell that she's biting the inside of her bottom lip, waiting in anguish to hear my latest dilemma. I show her the e-mail on my phone.

"Holy shit," she concludes when she finishes.

"I know. That's why I asked you to come over," I agree.

"Before we get to Victoria we need to back it up for a sec. You and your mom got a ride with Not-So-Innocent Oversexualized Pop Star?" I nod. "Totally inappropriate but I'm *so* jealous. How many Thursday nights did we get sloshed and sing her songs at Mulligan's karaoke night in college?"

"You don't even understand," I explain. "You would've died. You're even less starstruck than I am and I had to resist every natural urge to ask her to break down all of her choreography for me." We giggle at our brief moment of levity. "But she has some serious shit going down."

"Uh, yeah. I live on this planet. I've seen and read the news. How did you end up with her?"

I want to tell Jess that Not-So-Innocent Oversexualized Pop Star isn't

having a battle with psychosis but with cancer but I can't. It's not my secret to tell and I refuse to make the same mistake twice. I gloss over her
question and reintroduce the issue at hand. "I can't say anything to Victoria," I tell her. "She is so nice and has so little interaction with people
in the regular world. I can't betray her like that and say a word to Victoria. She doesn't deserve it." She needs someone to protect her who doesn't
have anything to financially gain from doing so.

"I agree," Jess replies. "But you know you'll be fired if you don't tell
her," she postulates. "Are you okay with that?" She quickly continues, "I
think this is the right decision. But I want you to be prepared for what
happens. When you reply to this e-mail, whichever way you choose to
reply, you can't take it back. Remember, once is a mistake, twice is a
choice. This is where you need to decide who you are going to be for the
rest of your life."

I never would've believed that Not-So-Innocent Oversexualized Pop
Star would be tied to my existential crisis, but she is. "I know what I need
to do. I just didn't want to do it alone," I mutter.

Jess nods, proud of me, and I open my left palm, requesting she hand
me the device. After all of the actual hard work I did trying to keep my
job at *The Life* and impress Victoria, I finally have her approval. I respond
to her e-mail.

Hi, Victoria,
Thank you so much for the offer but I quit.
Ella

Twenty-five

· ·

"Thanks for driving me," I tell my sister.

"I figured you could use some moral support."

I lean my head against the car window. "Well, you should buy stock in Uber because with my license suspended the value of the company is going to double."

"Jeff and I will help drive you as much as we can." She's trying to help but she's only making me feel worse.

"What a mess." I wish I could bang my head through the window.

"It sucks but this is what happens when you get a DUI. Court-ordered AA, alcohol education classes, fines . . ."

"Keep going, twist that knife a little deeper," I beg sarcastically.

"Sorry. I am proud of you for pleading guilty and accepting the responsibility. I need a coffee," she says as she pulls into The Coffee Bean in her neighborhood.

"Me, too." I follow her inside dressed in my conservative secretarial black pencil skirt and white button-down shirt. The line of customers in front of us has every archetype of person you find in an LA coffee shop midday and it hasn't changed since I used to work here. Each customer has a very specific and complicated coffee order. The Real Estate Mogul who doesn't look up from his iPhone while he orders would like an Americano that is exactly 160 degrees. The Twentysomething Trophy Wife whose breasts are on full display and is carrying her dog as an accessory would like an iced blended with half no-sugar-added powder and half regular powder so the calorie count doesn't exceed 120. Normally I'd mock her but right now I wish I could *Freaky Friday* with her . . . or even the dog.

"Hello, welcome to The Coffee Bean & Tea Leaf, what can I get for you today?" The barista in his late thirties has long curly hair cascading over his black plastic-rim hipster glasses.

"I'll have a large Americano," Robin answers.

"And for you, miss?" he asks me. Something comes over me.

"I'd like to speak to the manager."

He rolls his eyes and intentionally lets out an audible sigh before disappearing through the swinging doors.

"Ella, what are you doing?" Robin has no idea what's going on and I didn't either until I asked for the manager.

"I'm going to work here again," I tell her. "You said it yourself. I have fines, I have to pay for alcohol education classes, I want to try to pay you back for my lawyer, living expenses while I'm at your house—"

"You have good intentions but you don't have to do this. What you'd make here wouldn't make a dent and you've been such a big help with Mom and Marianna. It's been really nice all being under one roof again. And you need to figure out what you want to do with the rest of your life."

"I haven't worked since I quit *The Life*. Being unemployed for thirty-plus days is getting to me and hasn't given me any clarity, and I can walk here. I want to work here," I reaffirm.

The barista returns with the manager, who is introduced as Spike. Spike, I would come to find out, is in no uncertain terms the last person you'd ever want to be able to exert any ounce of authority over you. He's the living, breathing definition of a pretentious man-child. Though in his twenties he claims to have an old soul (he does not). He's a little chubby, has a bad haircut for his sandy-brown locks, and is still sporting a soul patch, even though that trend went out in the 1990s. Spike is obviously in a "band" and thinks he's far more attractive (and probably far more talented) than he actually is. Regardless of my immediate disdain for Spike, I implore him to return me to my barista status.

"Please. I really need this job. And you won't have to train me. I remember all of the recipes." Believe me, I've tried to forget them.

"I actually do need another barista. Are you okay working nights?" The Coffee Bean doesn't stay open anywhere near as late as Ambiance. Those "nights" will feel like afternoons for me.

"Yes. Absolutely! Nights, mornings, weekends, holidays. I can be available whenever." It's not like I have a social life anyway . . . that is, unless you count my ill mother, workaholic sister, four-year-old niece, and occasional night with Jessica.

"Welcome back to The Bean, Ella. You're hired." I'm so overjoyed that

I hug Spike before I realize I'm doing it and can tell from the look on his face that he's slightly turned on, and even though I'm grossed out, I don't care.

. . . .

Thanks for coming over," I tell Jess when she arrives at Robin's.

"Are you kidding? I wanted to see how court went this morning. I was going to bring a bottle of wine but I wasn't sure if that was inappropriate, since you're telling me about your DUI sentence."

"As long as I'm not operating a motor vehicle, it's okay," I say. "Come on, I have champagne in the kitchen."

"Are we celebrating?" she wonders.

"Sort of. Champagne is always the perfect way to start a new beginning." I pour us each a glass. "To probation, fines, alcohol education classes, and AA," I toast. Jess laughs.

"It could have been a lot worse. You're lucky," she reminds me.

"I know. I know. It's just that it would be nice if I were still toasting to glamour and love. Come on, let's sit in the living room." She follows me and I plop down on the couch and turn the TV on but keep it on mute.

"So what's your new plan?" she asks.

"I don't have one."

"Oh my God, are you okay? Ella Warren without a plan?" she says, sarcastically.

"My plans haven't exactly worked out for me recently. I think I might be better off with spontaneity for now. Keep things simple and—" Out of the corner of my eye I notice Holiday on TV. I shift my attention away from Jessica and turn up the volume.

"Holiday Hall's man Tristan Bailey stood by his woman through her cheating scandal but will he stay when he learns that the coffee company she posts ads for on her verified Instagram was just linked to a dangerous cartel? More on that after the break." I mute the TV again in disbelief.

"She's been crucified everywhere lately," Jess remarks. "It's unbelievable."

"I know. I just wish there was something I could do."

Twenty-six

· · · · · · · · · · · · · · · · ·

L ook at it as free therapy," Robin advises when she drops me off at my first court-ordered AA meeting. "Even if you're not an alcoholic I'm sure you can learn and get something out of it. I'll see you later," she says, driving off.

Ironically, I'm assigned to the AA meeting on Robertson Boulevard, because Holiday's house was my registered address when I was arrested. This AA meeting happens to be informally known as celebrity AA. It's the only building on that block the paparazzi don't stalk—we all have a line somewhere and that's theirs. Because of that, I'm not exactly sure *who* comes to this meeting, but I've long heard girls joking that they would attend meetings or "happen to be walking by when a meeting let out" to try and score dates with celebrities.

The only thing running through my mind is that I hope I don't have to speak. I walk in and I realize that it's one of the only settings that seems to be accurately portrayed in the movies. The foldout metal chairs are banged up. People are huddled around the coffee, and it's the one public place I've actually witnessed people eating doughnuts in LA. As I pour my not-so-latte, a tall bearded man in a flannel shirt who looks like he's come straight from a catalogue shoot approaches the podium.

"If we can all settle in and take our seats, please. I'd like to begin," he announces. All of the women immediately adhere to his request and the seats on either side of him are taken faster than H&M's designer collaborations are scooped off the shelves. It's as if he was the celeb in the group. Once I see the faces taking their seats I realize this is very much not the case.

It wasn't just a joke that this is the celebrity AA. Maybe if I had come here before I wouldn't have had to blurt out my secret about Holiday. I would've been the worst person ever, though, so I suppose I dodged that land mine. The group is comprised of the usual suspects, aka famous people who have openly admitted that they are addicts, but there are quite a few (that shall still remain nameless—hence the anonymous) that I'm shocked to see. I take the seat closest to me and put my phone on silent and cross my arms.

"Welcome, everyone," says Flannel Shirt Man. "For those of you who are returning I applaud you on your efforts to maintain your sobriety and for those of you who are new, I want to tell you how proud of you everyone in this room is for focusing on your sobriety. Meetings are a critical step to recovery and we all know that beginning is the most difficult part. This is a safe space for you to share and heal.

"My name is Wade Abrams. If any of you would like to speak to me privately after the meeting I'll be hanging around for an hour or so after we finish. Let's start today, as we always do, with our serenity prayer." When I hear his name I realize this is the It AA not so much because of the Robertson Boulevard location. It's the AA everyone wants to come to because of Wade. He's like the sobriety guru. Celebrities with substance-abuse issues have long tried to hire him as their sober companions but he's not tempted by the money. He's about service. It's ironic that he's a celebrity himself in this microcosm. It seems almost impossible to escape fame anywhere in this town.

I look around the room as everyone recites the mantra and as I'm taking in my new surroundings I catch eyes with none other than Sexy Indie Film Actor, who must've slipped in. He mouths "hi" to me and I lightly nod back at him. Here they say that secrets keep you sick and almost everything about my life was a secret. I was always trying to lie to someone.

As I listen to people tell their stories, I find myself closing my eyes. Not because I'm tired or bored but because it's hard to look at people as they share. I'm paying attention while they speak but find myself wandering into my own head. Tuning in to their voices and catching snippets of each of their stories is making me immensely grateful. The mistakes I've made in my life have all been mine and thank God they haven't done much other than superficial damage to others. I'm heartbroken hearing how addiction has torn apart the lives of these people, who aside from this are no different from me. This is not scripted. It's real life. These people are open and honest and, most of all, accountable. My life is a mess, but after listening to these stories about how people with a lot less support were able to turn their lives around, I know that I have the power to change mine, too.

When the meeting ends, I make a beeline for Wade as the crowd disperses.

"Excuse me, Wade?" I tap his shoulder.

"Yes?"

"Hi, I'm Ella Warren."

"It's nice to meet you, Ella." Wade is warm. "What can I do for you?"

"Can you sign my form for court to prove to the judge I was here?"

"Sure."

I pull the form out of my purse and don't need to give Wade any further instructions. It's clear he's done this more than a few times.

"Next time I hope you will share with us."

I'd like to, but since I've probably screwed over a quarter of the people in this room I'm scared that this recovery meeting might turn into a lynch mob. I feel a tap on *my* shoulder.

"Bella. Hi." It's Sexy Indie Film Actor. My heart jumps. This is my chance. He's right in front of me. It's time for me to be accountable and take responsibility for my actions.

"Hi. Actually, it's Ella. Not Bella."

"Really? That's embarrassing. I've been calling you the wrong name the whole time I've known you. Why didn't you ever say anything?" He gives me a sexy smirk and it's hard to believe looking at him that he has any troubles in life, although there's no question he does.

"It's not your fault. I told you my name was Bella," I explain.

"Why?" He looks at me quizzically. Why would I do that? That is the question of the moment and the one that I most need to, but most dread, answering.

"I know . . . it's complicated. Do you think we could go for a walk or something?"

"Who am I to say no in the name of recovery?" He places his hand on the small of my back and we exit the building. I make sure to steer us north on Robertson Boulevard to avoid what's known as paparazzi alley. "I was surprised to see you. You've never seemed like an addict to me, although being an addict myself I realize what an ignorant comment that is to make."

"I'm not actually an addict. I was having a bad day and drank way too much and got a DUI. Mandatory AA is part of my sentence."

"Been there," he tells me with a smile and a laugh even though we both know it's not funny.

"It actually happened the night we made out in the bathroom at Ambiance."

He stops. "We made out at Ambiance?" Sexy Indie Film Actor racks his brain to try to find the memory that matches my story but the data isn't computing for him. "Fuck, Ella. I'm sorry. I don't remember. I'm an asshole." He shrugs his shoulders.

"It's okay. Neither of us was exactly sober and I knew what I was doing. I'd just run into my ex and I was craving attention and you were giving it to me.

"I thought I would hate AA," I admit. "But things started making sense listening to everyone speak. Everyone's stories are powerful and it makes me realize how selfish I've been and that I have to be held accountable for my actions and I need to make amends, starting with you." I stop and Sexy Indie Film Actor does as well. "I've lied to you since the first time I met you."

"You gave me a different name. It's not a big deal. Trust me; of all the lies girls in this town have told me, yours is innocuous. I forgive you."

"It's not just that . . ." His curiosity is piqued, wondering what other misleading information I intentionally gave him. "I was an undercover club reporter for *The Life*. I close my eyes again because I am dreading the look on his face.

"What does that mean?" He's calm but looking me directly in my eyes, and I have to come completely clean, not just for him but for myself as well.

"It means that every time you saw me I was working. The Chateau, clubs, all of it. I observed what you and all of the other celebrities were doing while they were out at night and I gave that info to *The Life*. When you read an article and it says 'according to a source,' that was me. I quit a month ago." My voice trembles as I notice the expression in his eyes. "I'm the one that told them about you doing drugs." His mouth tenses up and I feel like I have X-ray vision and am watching his brain run through a host of scenarios before determining which one to respond with. "If I hadn't seen you at the meeting today I don't think that I ever would've told you, but afterwards it didn't seem like I could see you again and talk to you if I'm keeping this secret. I know that making amends is a long way off for me in this whole process but here it is. The first time I'm being honest with you. I, *Ella* Warren, am truly sorry."

I'm waiting for him to scream at me. I'm waiting for him to do an about-face and walk in the other direction. But he stands in front of me with no reaction for a good twenty seconds, which feels like an agonizing hour.

"Ella—" I'm ready for my reaming. "I was mad at the magazine at first, but honestly, you helped save my life." Okay, so apparently I'm delusional, because the first words I hear come out of Sexy Indie Film Actor's mouth after my confession are gratitude.

"I saved your life?" Now it's my turn to stare.

"Yes. You saved my life. Or you helped save it."

"How?" That's not what I expected.

"You exposed me. You made my drug use public and I couldn't hide it or lie about it anymore. That and Twentysomething CW Bad Boy Heartthrob's overdose were the catalysts for me going to rehab and getting clean."

"That's great. I mean, not that your friend lost his life, but I'm glad you're in a better place. Are you okay? I know you guys were close." I place my hand on his shoulder to comfort him even though I'm the last person he'd probably want to seek solace with.

"Thanks. I mean, looking back on it I'm not sure how close we really were. We were always fucked up. It wasn't real life. Who knows if we'd be buddies if we were sober? I can't think of anything we ever talked about other than partying, acting, or girls. But in those circumstances he was my friend. I still can't believe he's gone and I'm still here. I'm still trying to make sense of it." He pauses. "Don't you see? You're part of the reason I was at that meeting today and why I also go to NA." I want to discredit his theory and not be all hippy-dippy but I know he's being truthful. "You leaking that information to *The Life* and my being fired from movies and having my agents drop me forced me to be honest with myself. Doing blow in the bathroom at Ambiance and making out with you and not even remembering . . . that's not why I became an actor."

"So you're not angry?" I check.

"No. I'm a little paranoid but I'm not angry. These were all my decisions. You're disappointed?"

"God, no. I just feel like I'm being let off the hook too easily or something."

"You said that you got a DUI?"

"Uh-huh."

He puts his arm around me. "Well, then I think you've paid your penance."

"The fact that you're thanking me . . . I feel like I'm hallucinating or something. It's bizarre."

Sexy Indie Film Actor playfully slaps my shoulder blade. "I said you helped save my life. I never said thank you." He winks playfully. "You did have a hand in killing my career," he adds. "I mean it was mostly me . . . but a little you." I can't stand having to look him in the eye. "I hate to contradict Andy Warhol, since he's one of my favorite artists, but sometimes measuring in inches what they write about you doesn't matter, because no matter how long it is everyone else is actually reading it."

Any positive feelings I was taking away with me from AA are now dashed. I had a hand in ruining Sexy Indie Film Actor's career and his dreams.

"After I was fired from the first movie I was dropped by my agent. Right now I would have to get on my hands and knees to beg to even be considered for the next season of *Dancing with the Stars*. Turns out not all press is good press."

"And it all stemmed from that one story. . . ." Right about now I want to wring my own neck. I'm sort of shocked he's able to stand in front of me and be so calm.

"Your story, to be exact."

The butterfly effect that I set into motion when I exposed someone's innermost secrets and demons is incalculable.

"It would be nice if I could send my public image to rehab, too. Fixing myself is easy compared to fixing the perception of me." He chuckles at his comparison but there's actually nothing funny about what he said.

Usually I get my best ideas in the shower. I've heard that it's one of the few places where we allow our minds to relax and their capacity to think and create expands, but right now I'm having a brilliant idea in the middle of Robertson Boulevard.

"What would you say if I told you I could help your image and your career?"

Sexy Indie Film Actor glances at me skeptically. "I'd say I'm listening."

"I know how the celebrity world works. The gossip. The sensationalism. The damage control. The spin. I was on the inside. I promise you. I can help you fix this and help you put your career on an even better trajectory than it was before."

Sexy Indie Film Actor raises his eyebrows.

"What do you want?" I ask him.

"I just want to be able to act again. To be given the chance to act again," he says, docilely.

"Let me help you," I say again, appealing to his lack of other options.

"I probably can't be any worse off than I am right now," he figures.

Maybe confessing to Sexy Indie Film Actor isn't how I'm supposed to make amends. Maybe I'm supposed to help him get his career back on track. Not just him but everyone I've hurt. And there's a certain British heiress who's on the top of that list.

"What the hell? I'm in."

"You keep working on your sobriety every day and take care of yourself. Eat well, go to the gym, stay away from the usual paparazzi spots, and get plenty of rest. You're going to need it. I will take care of everything else. You'll be back at work before you know it . . . and maybe even on the road to an Oscar."

"Great. What's the plan?"

I haven't formulated the full plan yet, but I have the first step.

I throw my arms around him and squeeze him tight. A tingle shoots through my body. Nothing sexual. I left those feelings for him in my holding cell at the police station along with my pride. This tingle is a feeling of gratitude. Through helping him, he's helped me realize what *I'm* supposed to do.

"Just leave it to me. I'm going to start this right away. Will you be at the meeting on Friday?"

"Yes."

"Perfect. I'll give you an update then." I kiss him on the cheek and grab my phone as he walks away.

I may have done some shady things when I worked for *The Life* but I was good at my job. My mom was right. With all of my connections I should be able to help Holiday . . . and Sexy Indie Film Actor, too. If I put my particular set of skills to good use I can salvage their reputations and careers. I know what I need to do but I can't do it alone . . . and I just happen to know who can help me.

Twenty-seven

. . . .

Jess, Maggie; Maggie, Jess." The two smile at each other, trying not to let their confusion and apprehension show. I return a keen one, being the only one aware of my plan.

"So what are we doing here?" Jess asks as she sips on a cup of coffee that, thank God, I didn't have to make, and skillfully snags a second guava pastry that my mother insisted on getting from Porto's Bakery to entice my friends into assisting me. Maggie leans her back into the sofa, silently reiterating Jess's question with her eyes. It's only been a day since I conceived my brilliant idea, so I don't have all of the details worked out yet, no devil in this plan, but I want to get the ball rolling ASAP and figure out the rest as we go.

"It's my new plan!"

"I thought you were done with plans," Jess reminds me.

I ignore her comment. "I invited you both to come here to ask if you'll help me." They pause their answers, waiting to hear what I'll require of them before they agree or not. "Obviously you're both aware of my situation with Holiday." Jess scoffs and a look washes over her face letting Maggie know I've just made the understatement of the year. "I was at my first court-ordered AA meeting yesterday and ran into someone else I'd done something similar to."

"The Robertson one?" Maggie jumps in. I nod my head, yes. "Who?" she wonders, with her eyes lit up like white twinkle lights on a romantic restaurant patio.

"Mags, I can't tell you that."

"Sure you can," she urges.

"The second *A* stands for anonymous. It would be like breaking the only rule they have."

"I'm just curious, Ella. It's not like I work for a gossip rag anymore."

My smile shifts to a smirk. "Well, actually . . ." I say, moving on, "I want to start a new gossip Web site."

Jess also sinks into the couch and closes her eyes, and from that sentence alone and her not-so-subtle gesture it's not difficult to determine her gut reaction.

"It's not what you think," I assure them. "I want to start a site that promotes positivity." They both lean in to me. Sheryl Sandberg would be proud. "The site is called *Compassionate Celebrities* and we only post photos and stories about celebrities doing good."

"*Compassionate Celebrities*," Maggie repeats. "It has a nice ring to it."

"Right?" I agree.

"Tell us more," Jess asks.

"So my vision is we follow the same structure as the other celebrity gossip sites. We run photos and daily items, but everything we write will be about celebrities who've done something kind or compassionate. We help promote the charities they support and help raise awareness about their charity events or when they've done something altruistic on their own."

"Well, that's certainly different," Jess says.

"Yeah. This would be the first site of that kind," Maggie reiterates. "Actually the more I let it noodle around in my head it's kind of brilliant. Plus it would be like us making social reparations for all of the reporting we did for *The Life*."

"Exactly!" I'm ecstatic that they are getting it. "Not only will it be an inspiration for the readers *but* it will also be a way for me to help rebuild any of the celebrity images I helped tear down . . . we helped tear down," I say as I lock eyes with Maggie.

"It does seem like it would help me atone for my stalking sins," she says as the idea continues to percolate. "I'm still in contact with the majority of my sources. I can try and dig up a few scoops to launch with."

"That's perfect!" I blurt out. I already feel the momentum building. "Jess, here's where you come in. I need an awesome writer to help me with the daily stories and someone who knows their way around Web layout, since I'm more 'I need a job' than Steve Jobs." I shrug my shoulders in a bid to cajole her.

"Are we getting paid for this?" she wonders.

"That's where *your* compassion comes in," I tell them. "If we end up making any money, of course, but for right now this project is going to be funded by the kindness of our hearts. Does that work for you?" My mind is pacing since my body can't while I wait for my make-or-break answer.

"Yes. Of course I'm in," Jess tells me. "I need a new project to help me diversify my writing portfolio. Never know, someday I may need to go corporate."

"Do you really think this will help?" Maggie asks.

"I don't know if we will be able to drown out all of the negative gossip, because there's so much of it, but I have to try." Besides, this is only Step One of my plan.

Maggie becomes distracted typing on her phone.

"What are you doing, Mags?" I ask.

"Making a list of all of the celebrities I need to include in this. My body count is much higher than yours. I've got Ethnic Actress-Writer with Her Own Show and Keen Fashion Sense, Stuck-Up Broadway Star Turned TV Queen, Hard Body B-List Actor Without Much Range, Gold Digging C-List Actress with a Wealthy Beau. And that's just the beginning."

Twenty-eight

. . . .

H i. Ella Warren to see Nick Williams," I tell the new model-
esque receptionist at Epic Agency. It feels like a lot longer than
three months since the last time I was here, distraught. The re-
ceptionists turn over faster than paleo banana pancakes. The new one is
wearing a cocktail dress in the middle of the day and looks like she'd give
her right eye for an M&M. She calls Nick's assistant and stares me down
as she's receiving information about me.

"Can you just tell them that I need five minutes, please?"

"She says she just needs five minutes," she repeats to Nick's assistant,
as if I've inconvenienced the receptionist by asking her to do her job.
"Okay." She rolls her eyes and hangs up. "Melanie will come out for you
in a minute. Take a seat."

"Hi, Ella, it's good to see you again," Melanie greets, with no hint of
judgment about what happened between me and Nick, or between me
and Holiday for that matter. I wonder how much she knows.

She escorts me to Nick's office. "Thank you for squeezing me in last
minute."

"Go on in," she tells me and gives me a small smile that indicates that
against all odds she's on my side. I go through the formality of knocking
on Nick's door to let him know I've arrived instead of barging in. His
feet are on the desk and he's leaning back in his chair reading a script,
which he places on the desk when I walk in.

"Ella, this is a surprise." He doesn't mean one of those surprises like
when your significant other tells you to pack a bag because you're going
to Palm Springs for the weekend or like you've won a million dollars from
a contest you never even knew you entered. He really means nuisance,
not surprise. I know that I have to be professional and I came here to help
Sexy Indie Film Actor, but I'm also feeling slightly selfish. This is the first
time I've seen Nick since he broke up with me and I'm fantasizing about

leaping over his desk and jumping into his lap like he's Santa Claus and squeezing him (not like Santa Claus). I'd give anything to nestle my head next to his neck and smell his cologne and feel his heartbeat against my chest. He sneaks a quick glimpse at his watch, subtly letting me know he has more important places to go and people to see and is definitely not giving off the vibe that he's feeling reminiscent about our romance.

"Thank you for seeing me." I take a seat in one of the chairs in front of his desk and hope he didn't notice my legs shaking as I walked in.

"What can I do for you?" he asks, getting right down to business.

"I'm here because I have a proposal for you." He places the script on his desk to indicate that he's listening but not invested. While I know that there's no precedent for me telling him or any other agents which clients they should sign, I know I have a great idea. I just hope he's willing to put our personal relationship aside long enough to give me a real chance. "I want you to sign Sexy Indie Film Actor."

"Ella—"

It's okay. I was prepared to be met with some resistance. "No, wait, before you answer, hear me out first. Please."

He interlaces his fingers behind his head and reclines in his chair, ready to listen.

"He is a hundred percent sober. You're the best agent in this town and you know it. You're the only guy who can turn his career around. You know how talented he is. If you represent him, he can be the biggest movie star in the world. You can get him an Oscar and a superhero trilogy."

Nick moves his elbows to his desk and leans forward.

"He has the talent. He needs the agent. He needs Nick Williams."

Nick squints at me as he considers my idea for about twenty seconds, long enough to be polite. "Let's say for a second I am interested. Why are you taking up his cause?"

I can't tell if he's curious or prying to find out if we're sleeping together. It doesn't matter either way. "I'm the one that leaked the info about him doing drugs with Twentysomething CW Bad Boy Heartthrob the night that he died. I was assigned to cover Ambiance that night, so his career stalling is my fault. He didn't deserve that and I'm trying to make it right." Nick ruminates on the information. "This isn't just for him. It would be good for you, too. He can be a movie star again. With you on his team, an even bigger movie star! And you will get all of the credit for reviving his career." I take a brief pause. "You know the Web site *Compassionate Celebrities*?"

"Yeah, the posts on that site are what saved Holiday's part on *Benedict Canyon*," he says.

It did? My body feels ten pounds lighter now that it's shed part of the burden of my mistakes. Even if Holiday never speaks to me again, knowing that I did whatever I could to repair the damage I caused her will help me move forward. I feel euphoric knowing I've been able to create a positive impact as strong as the negative impact I've had on her and other celebrities.

"It's a good thing that came out when it did. The producers were strongly considering recasting her role midseason after the scandal broke, but once *Compassionate Celebrities* hit and the positive press was balancing out the negative press, they agreed to keep her."

The site served the exact function I wanted it to. If I was right about *Compassionate Celebrities* being able to save celebrity careers I am, without a doubt, right about this.

"I started that site," I blurt out.

"You did?" He stares at me, first with relief then with intrigue, like the night we met at Holiday's party.

"Yes. I quit *The Life* and started it with some friends."

Nick rubs his lips together and for a brief moment looks at me with the same spark that he used to.

"I'm impressed." His demeanor shifts and his energy is more amiable. "You're doing a great job."

"Thanks. I'm not trying to get back into that world as a career or anything. I'm just trying to do the right thing and help make amends with all of the celebrities I hurt, the ones I know and the ones I don't." Without realizing it I fall back into my habit of fluttering my eyelashes and biting my bottom lip. As soon as I catch myself I return to business mode. "Sexy Indie Film Actor is the number-one male search on *Compassionate Celebrities*. His fans still want to see him in movies. This isn't even a gamble for you. It will just take a little creativity and hard work, two things I know you're phenomenal at." He's still hesitant but knowing Nick, coercing him more right now won't do my cause any good. I need to let him warm up to the idea on his own for a bit.

He raises an eyebrow. "I'll consider it." I know Nick well enough to know that if I put him on the spot he'll say no, but if I let him come around to the idea on his own my chances are considerably better. If he does it on his own, he will build enthusiasm for this pitch and sign Sexy Indie Film Actor. So in actuality, his "I'll consider it" means yes.

"Thank you." I get up to leave and hold my hand out for him to shake. He stares at it with bewilderment for a moment before shaking it. As I walk out of the office I have butterflies in my stomach. Not only from possibly pulling off a work-related coup but also because the chemistry between Nick and me is still there. I may have been hiding it and he may have been fighting it, but while sitting in his office I felt an actual gravitational pull toward him again. I poke my head back into his office. "It was really good to see you again, Nick." I dip out as quickly as I popped in. I have work to do.

Twenty-nine

· · · · · · · · · · · · · · · · · · · ·

know Holiday is back in town because I've been keeping tabs on her for *Compassionate Celebrities*. Her paparazzi pictures are splashed across the Internet. My only consolation is that she wasn't fired from *Benedict Canyon*—unbeknownst to her, at least partially because of my efforts. At some point I plan on apologizing to her in person but I'm caught off guard and not prepared for what I would've liked to have been my perfectly planned mea culpa when she walks into The Coffee Bean today.

She's the one person who will be able to recognize me no matter what kind of cotton-blend clothing I'm wearing. Besides, this uniform was her first impression of me. My flight response usurps every ounce of fight response in my body as soon as I see her Birkin bag swing through the entrance. Before I flee to the employee back room I catch a glimpse of Tristan following her. Unfortunately I'm not alone in my respite as my boss, Spike, is on his break, reading the latest issue of *Rolling Stone* when I explode through the door.

"It's not your break time yet," he reminds me without looking up from the magazine. "Twenty more minutes."

"I know. Please, cut me some slack. There's a customer out there that I don't want to see."

"Too bad, kid." I hate it when he calls me *kid*. It's not a term of endearment when he uses it; it's purely condescending since we're the same age.

"Spike, please," I beg. "It would be really bad if this customer recognizes me."

"You owe her money?" He maneuvers his tongue around his mouth as if he's searching for a piece of abandoned food.

"No." I scrunch my nose, trying my hardest to hide my nausea from both him and seeing Holiday.

"You steal something from her?"

"Not exactly." Just her privacy and good reputation.

"Then get your ass back out there," he orders after completing a lap of his mouth.

I peer through the small window on the door and notice Tristan paying for their order. My overzealous coworker, Julie, is manning the espresso machine, and due to her brisk service, I estimate that I only need to stall about two minutes for her to make their drinks and then they can leave. I've always found Julie's self-appointed employee-of-the-decade attitude as annoying as Spike's personification of coffee, but right now I'm internally praising her speed. She has a predilection for telling me everything I'm doing is wrong. While I stall, Spike is trying to convince me to get out there by threatening to garnish my tips, but I won't budge. I can't face them. Not here. Not like this. I take another peek outside and quickly formulate my stall tactic.

"So how's your band?" I ask. Spike places the magazine on his lap and starts to proselytize.

"The music is more alive than ever," he says, eyes wandering, as if he's staring out into the vast universe. "The thing is, I really think we need to change our name. Swallow's Rage doesn't describe who we are or our sound anymore." I fold my arms and nod my head to make him think I care so he will continue. "My bandmates are hesitant about changing it because they don't want to confuse our fans. We've recently gone through a period of maturation."

I've got to give it to Spike; he has the LA concept of "fake it till you make it" down cold. Right now I need to fake my interest and keep my gag reflex in check to handle all of the garbage he's spouting.

"I've evolved as a lyricist and I want our name to be more of an homage to us as storytellers than punk rockers."

I glance out the window to determine what stage of their exit Holiday and Tristan are currently engaged in. I don't see them and my eyes are glued to the window, searching. I haven't noticed that Spike has realized that I'm neither paying attention nor could I care less about his band until I feel his hands on my back pushing me back onto the floor. I unsuccessfully try to dig my heels into the ground like a celebrity mistress that refuses to give up her fifteen minutes of fame, but he is too strong for me and I'm unwillingly thrust back into the store and into reality.

"Back to work," he orders. "Your break isn't for twenty minutes, Ella."

As he says my name, my vision zooms in on the back of Holiday's and Tristan's heads and I see her turn her head in slow motion. Without thinking I collapse to the floor to hide behind the counter and start counting my Mississippis. Spike and Julie are too baffled by my behavior to stop me and by the time I get to my sixth Mississippi I realize that I'm making this much worse and have no choice but to get up and face the music, or the gossip in this case.

"So the rumors are true," Holiday jeers as I sheepishly rise. She couldn't be more smug. "You *are* working here again."

"Hi, Holiday."

She's relishing my downfall and isn't trying to hide that she's ecstatic that I've gotten exactly what she feels like I deserve. "I'm thrilled I was able to confirm the chatter with my own eyes." She folds her arms, satisfied and vindicated.

"Hi, El." Tristan nods his head at me. Holiday glares at him with fury for speaking to the enemy.

"Hi, Tristan."

"It's—"

Holiday doesn't let Tristan finish. She's got her social homicide ammunition and doesn't want either of them fraternizing with me any longer than necessary. "Let's go," she instructs him. Tristan gives me another neutral head nod so as not to upset her further. I wasn't prepared for this ambush but I can't let Holiday walk out of here like this. I don't know if I'll ever see her again. She slides the Ray-Ban aviators that were resting on top of her head down to shield her eyes, places all of her weight on her left foot, and pops her hip out to make a grand exit as she turns toward the door.

"Holiday! Can we talk? Just for a second?" I implore. She stops but doesn't turn back to me. "Please?" I'm giving her the verbal equivalent of begging on my hands and knees. I notice her left fingers dangling at her side curl and begin to form a fist as she takes a sip of coffee. I know her well enough to know that she's about to tell me that I'm high if I think she'll talk to me, but between her deep exhales and coffee to help soothe her anger, Tristan jumps in.

"Give her a minute, Hol," he requests.

Holiday's fingers release and she rips her sunglasses off her face with them so he can see her befuddled eyes. She's ready to argue but Tristan isn't going to be a willing participant.

"Just listen to what she has to say. I'll be here, and if it goes poorly we can leave," he says.

Holiday glares at him again.

"You owe it to her."

"I owe it to her?" Holiday gasps. I can see where her forehead wants to break past the Botox and wrinkle itself to show Tristan how wrong she believes he is, but the Botox wins that battle and her forehead stays smooth while her words cut. "You can't be serious?"

"I am. Ella was your best friend for a long time and even if things are fucked up now you owe it to what you two shared together." Tristan turns to me and I mouth "thank you" to him. "If you don't owe it to her, you owe it to me. I agreed to hear you out when this whole thing went down and I had no reason to."

Holiday rolls her eyes and reluctantly mumbles "Fine" after releasing an audible sigh.

I move to the nearest table and take a seat while she unenthusiastically follows. Tristan hangs back but still has a visual on us in case he needs to jump in and save us from ourselves.

"First, let me say again that I'm so sorry, Holiday!" I begin.

"Yes, you've said that before." Her icy exterior remains uncracked. I have a better chance of Holiday bursting into an a cappella verse of "Let It Go" than I do of her warming up to me, but this is about me apologizing, not her forgiving me.

"I know that you don't believe me, but telling your secret is the biggest mistake I've ever made in my life. I will never forgive myself. I lost everything that was important to me. I'm not talking about being able to live in your mansion or any of the material things you were generous enough to share with me." She sits looking through me and I'm trying to penetrate her gruff exterior and reach her heart. I know there's still a place for me in there, albeit small; I just have to get to it. "I lost you and I lost Nick." My lip quivers, and even though I'd usually be embarrassed and try to hide it, I want her to see it so she knows my sense of loss is genuine and not just lip service. "I miss you both every day. Even if you hate me for the rest of your life, I want you to know that."

Holiday raises her perfectly plucked eyebrows, pleased that I'm hurting. "Okay, I've heard you say what you have to say. Good-bye, Ella." She rises from the table and dominates me with her eyes again.

"Wait," I plead. "Since it happened, I've been trying to make it up to you."

"Oh, really, have you?" She puffs out her mouth and cocks her head to the left to patronize me. "Another lie from a professional liar."

"No, it's true." I reach into my pocket and grab my phone. "Have you seen this?"

"Seen it? Nick says *Compassionate Celebrities* is what saved my job on *Benedict Canyon*."

"It's *my* Web site," I tell her. "This is me trying, the best way I know how, to make amends with you and with Sexy Indie Film Actor and all of the other celebrities that I hurt. I helped expose your darkest secrets to the world and now it's time for me to make sure I shine a positive light on you."

She takes my phone and scrolls through the site, puzzled and amazed. "I can't believe you did this."

"It was the least I could do," I tell her.

She continues to peruse the site. "Who's this one about?" she asks in the excited curious voice she used to use with me before I entangled us in this mess. "A-List Sitcom Star Who Has Had Bad Luck With Men buys apartment building for homeless families to stay in."

"That's for you to guess," I tell her. "I try to make it fairly obvious but I've learned my lesson—even if it's something positive, my mouth won't confirm anything."

She lets out a sound that can almost be distinguished as a laugh while she keeps scrolling. "This one is me!" she exclaims. She holds the phone in my direction so I can see the screen. It's the item about her donating all of her clothes she hasn't worn in six months to Dress for Success.

"There are a lot about you," I tell her. "In fact, about fifty percent of all of the items are about you."

Her eyes dart back to the phone and I can tell she's trying to hold back tears. "It says here the site is run by a former industry insider who calls herself Hollywood Know-It-All."

I raise my eyebrows.

All traces of her bitchy demeanor disintegrate and I sense a slight bit of warmth radiating from her in my direction.

"You did this for me? After all of those horrible things I said to you?" she wonders.

"I hated myself for possibly taking away something you love. I couldn't let that happen," I assure her.

She returns the phone to me. "Thank you."

Tristan approaches us, noticing that our threat alert status has gone from red to green. "Are we okay here?" he asks.

I look to Holiday to give the response.

"Yes, darling. We're okay," she tells him.

"Good. I'm glad." He has a twinkle in his eyes, proud that he helped reunite us and that it didn't end with one of us in police custody or in the hospital. He places his hand on Holiday's shoulder and gives it a small squeeze. "I hate to break this reunion up but, Hol, we have to get going if we're going to make your meeting." He broadens his eyes and emphasizes the word *meeting*. It must mean she's meeting with Nick.

"Right." Holiday stands up, trying to play it cool and not mention his name. She again puts her Ray-Bans on.

"I'm glad he forced us to chat," she says, nudging her elbow at Tristan.

"Me, too." I take a deep breath.

"His thinking he's right all the time gets on my nerves but I'm not upset about him being right this time."

"In that case—"

Holiday cuts him off again. "I think I can handle it from here, darling." Holiday gives Tristan a quick peck on the cheek and he wraps his arms around her. "I think what Tristan was trying to not-so-subtly suggest is maybe we can do it again before I go back to Canada," she offers.

"I'd really love that," I tell her.

"We are here for the next few weeks on hiatus before we go back to shoot the rest of the season." She winks at me and the two of them finally move to make their exit.

"I'll text you," I shout as she reaches the door. She hastily turns around and waves good-bye to me. As the door swings open, I'm almost blinded by the sea of flashes and screams that commence in rapid succession asking about her scandal, relationship with Tristan, and her tips for the perfect blow out. The paparazzi really are following her every move now.

The afterglow from my rekindled friendship is interrupted.

"That didn't look so bad," Spike remarks, sidling up behind me. I take a deep breath and release all of the fear and anxiety I had when she walked in the door, and I think I even feel a smile creeping on my face.

"It wasn't," I answer.

"See. Sometimes it's best to face your fears."

"That is very insightful, Spike." I glance at him with a little more respect and a new set of eyes.

"By the way, I'm considering that your fifteen-minute break. Get back to work!"

Thirty

· · · · · · · · · · · · · · · · · · ·

This is my new favorite restaurant," my mom announces. "I loved it when Ella brought me here and now that I have some of my appetite back I love it even more—especially because we're all here together this time." Wolfgang Puck should hire her as the official Spago spokesperson.

"You deserve it, Mom," Robin tells her as we both watch my mother finish a meal for the first time since she started chemo. "We're all so proud of you. You didn't give up hope and you're showing signs only of improvement. You're going to be okay."

"We aren't out of the woods just yet but I am feeling better."

"Mom, you're in remission, that's huge." Robin wants her to acknowledge that she stood up to cancer and won.

"Sweetheart, you're a doctor. You of all people know that remission doesn't mean I'm cured. If I was your patient you'd make it very clear, just like Dr. Jacobs did, that I'm not cured."

"I'm not your doctor, though, I'm your daughter and I'm allowed to be optimistic, especially when your counts continue to improve."

"I'd like to propose a toast," I say, raising a glass of champagne. My mom can only have sparkling water since she still has a lower dose of chemo to finish as outpatient treatment, but what's in our glasses or on our plates doesn't really matter.

"My go-to toast is 'To glamour and love' but that doesn't feel right," I tell them.

My mom and Robin and Jeff look confused. Marianna doesn't care what's going on around her. She's devouring her pasta, and tonight we've learned that she likes truffles. She's going to be a handful and will no doubt make her teenage years hell on her parents. Talk about karma for Robin.

"What does feel right?" my mom asks.

"To Dr. Jacobs," I salute. The adults raise their glasses with me. My mother wants to get in on the toasting action as well. She raises her glass again.

"And to my two perfect daughters—"

"Mom, Ella and I are far from perfect. Perfect doesn't exist," Robin interrupts.

"So smart and you still don't understand." She nods her head at us, waiting for the answer to click but it doesn't and she flashes a smile, amused. Neither of us gets it. "You're right. Perfection doesn't exist because it's fluid." She eyes us both individually so we pay attention. Robin first, me second. "Perfect is now. It's the present. It's doing the best you can and appreciating everything and everyone in your life. So I'd say I have two pretty perfect daughters. Cheers!"

"Cheers," we all repeat.

"I love you, Mom," I say, kissing her on the cheek.

"I love you too, my sweet pea." The smile fades from her face and her stare is making me uncomfortable.

"Mom, what's wrong?" I ask.

"Nothing, dear. Nothing is wrong. I just want you to be happy."

"I am happy."

"Are you sure?" she presses. "What ever happened with that man you were seeing; Nick?" she asks. "You seemed to like him so much."

I look around for a waiter, hoping I can get a refill of my beverage, but sadly there are none in sight. "Mom, I told you, it's over between Nick and me." He signed Sexy Indie Film Actor as a client, but I haven't heard from him since that meeting.

"Do you want it to be over?"

"I don't really think I have a choice."

"All I'm saying is he seemed to make you happy. Sometimes in life you have to fight for the things and people who are important to you."

"Mom, there's a name for people who continue to try to date people who have broken up with them—stalker."

"I just think you should put yourself out there and give it another shot," she continues.

I nod my head, since it's easier to do that than explain my unfavorable decisions, which were behind the demise of my most recent relationship. I turn to Robin for an exit out of this conversation. My mom refocuses her energy on Marianna and helping her pronounce the foreign names of all of the dishes we consumed tonight.

"Thanks for dinner."

Robin checks the bill one last time to make sure it's accurate before signing.

"I was happy to do it. Was nice to have a fancy family meal out on the town," Robin says. "I hope we can do it more often."

"Me, too. Tonight was really fun." I smile.

"It was," she agrees, finishing her one glass of champagne from the evening.

"I kinda don't want it to end. What do you say? Stick around and have a sister drink at the bar with me? Just the two of us," I offer.

Before Robin says a word I can tell that she's going to give me ten excuses about why she shouldn't have more than one drink and why she shouldn't stay, so I decide I won't let her talk. "Come on, Robin. It's only eight thirty. I won't take no for an answer, and you know that I'm going to bother you until you agree." She sighs. "It's so much easier to just say yes and not go through the whole song and dance."

"But—"

"No. No buts. Just let go so we can have fun together," I urge.

Every natural instinct Robin has is fighting my request but tonight it will be a losing battle for her. "Jeff, will you get Mom and Marianna home? Ella and I are going to hang back and have a drink at the bar."

"Sure, sweetie," he replies. My mother clasps her hands together, overjoyed at our newfound sibling bonding.

"Have fun, my darlings," she says as she gets up from the table. Jeff and Marianna come over to kiss Robin.

"Good night, my lovebug," Robin says, pulling Marianna onto her lap. "Mommy isn't going to be home to tuck you in tonight but Grandma and Daddy will make sure you get your story and tuck you in."

"What about Kiss, Hug, Squeeze?" she asks.

Robin's face radiates with joy. "You're right. How about we do it here?"

"Kiss. Hug. Squeeze!" Marianna squeals.

"Good night, Marianna." Robin gets up and passes her back to Jeff.

"'Night, Mommy."

"What time will you be home?" Jeff asks.

"In about an hour or so." He kisses Robin good night as well and the three of them hug. As I watch them my mother comes over to me.

"Kiss, hug, squeeze," she says as she does them all, almost making me feel like I'm Marianna's age again—in a good way. "Good night, Ella."

"Good night, Mom."

We leave them for the bar as they make their way out to valet. I've never been "out" to have a drink with my sister before, so this bonding social experiment should be interesting.

"What'll you have?" the bartender who's from the Armani billboard on Highland Avenue inquires.

"A glass of champagne, please," I reply.

"Macallan Eighteen on the rocks for me," Robin adds.

"Whoa, going for the hard stuff tonight. Watch out, world, high-school Robin is in the room."

"Actually I was more of a vodka, gin, whatever-Dad-had-in-the-liquor-cabinet-when-he-forgot-to-lock-it kinda girl." We both crack up and can't stop laughing. "See, once you get me out of the house-and-work mode I'm fun," she insists. Our drinks come and she raises her glass.

"I'm proud of you, El. The last few months you've really stepped up. Especially with Mom." She points her glass toward me and drinks in my honor.

"Thanks. That really means a lot to me. I was really scared for a bit. I'm glad she's turned a corner in her treatment." As she continues drinking I notice the alcohol hitting her. She is definitely not high-school Robin anymore but she's not stick-up-her-ass ER-doctor Robin either. She's just being fun and my older sister.

"Can I get you ladies another round?" the bartender asks, noticing our empty glasses before we had.

"Yes!" Robin tells him without even checking to see if that's what I was thinking. "I needed this," she says.

"You did. You're not just a mom, a wife, or a doctor. You are allowed to have some fun and let some steam off and maybe—gasp—make a mistake every once in a while," I tell her playfully, masking the truth in what sounds like a joke to make it more palatable.

"You've been making the mistakes for us both," she jokes back, using my tactic against me.

"Ouch."

"Sorry. You're right, that was too far. I really am not used to more than two drinks now. I guess this stuff is really hitting me," she says as the bartender places our fresh drinks in front of us. She can say that again! "I want to be cool and do your toast," she whines. She is definitely more buzzed than I realized but I'm having fun with her.

"Okay, raise your glass." Robin follows my instructions. "To glamour and love," I say, clinking her glass.

"To glamour and love," she repeats as she looks down at her glass and takes a sip.

"Robin!"

"What? Did I do it wrong?" she asks nervously.

"You're supposed to look me in the eye or else it's seven years of bad sex," I warn her.

"Oh, that's not possible with Jeff," she says nonchalantly. Her cheeks are flushed. "You only really see the dad side of him but once we get in the bedroom—"

"Okay! That's enough. Any more and I'll have to find a therapist first thing in the morning. Just clink my glass again and look me in the eye."

Robin lets out a drunken laugh and toasts me again. "El."

"I swear, if you start telling me about some sexual fetish right now I'm going to pour my drink on you," I warn.

"No. I'm not *that* drunk. Two o'clock," she says, lightly tapping my thigh.

"Huh?"

"Two o'clock," she repeats. I turn my head and see Male Half of A-List Hollywood Power Couple on the opposite side of the bar. "Your job couldn't have been that hard," she jokes.

Thirty-one

· ·

You can do this, Ella. You're an adult. Just press Send.

> Me: Hey Hol, it's Ella (in case you deleted my number). Wanted to see if you're up for lunch this week?

I hit Send on the text message and feel more nervous than I did at court. Waiting for Holiday to reply feels like how she must've felt waiting for the results of her pregnancy test.

> Holiday: Wednesday 12 pm, the usual place?
>
> Me: Sure. See you at Mauro's.
>
> Holiday: No. I mean our other place.

What other place? She can't be talking about . . .

> Me: Chateau? Hol, you know I'm not welcome there.
>
> Holiday: You didn't hear???
>
> Me: No, hear what?
>
> Holiday: Pixie Haircut Hostess was fired! Apparently she was feeding gossip to one of the magazines! You're free to return!!!
>
> Me: No way!
>
> Holiday: I don't think they'll give you any problem but if they do I can handle it.
>
> Me: See you then!

I try on no fewer than ten outfits when Wednesday rolls around. I'm not exactly sure what one wears to a lunch with your ex-BFF that you're just trying to be F with again. Something inside me directs me toward some AG jeans. They've been lucky for me before so I throw them on, and even though seasons change, they never go out of style. I'm hoping it's an analogy for our friendship. I'm not sure what to expect. Our relationship as of late has been bipolar, rightfully so, but I'm hoping that today is the first step to us finding our equilibrium again.

As I enter I feel like I just ate bad Mexican food. A new brunette clad in a black T-shirt dress now mans the hostess stand. I clear my throat.

"I'm meeting Holiday Hall for lunch."

She checks her list and smiles. The attitude change in the hostess is noted. "Yes, right this way, please." She grabs two menus and I follow her . . . into the garden. I'm only waiting a few moments before Holiday is escorted over to me.

"Hi, darling," she says, leaning down, surprising me by giving me a double kiss. I wasn't sure we were back at the double-kissing stage. She sits down and removes her sunglasses.

"Hi, how are you?" I ask, still slightly hesitant and careful about everything I say.

"I'm doing well. Relishing my time off. How are you? How's your mom?" she asks after a few moments of us quietly staring at each other and the landscaping.

"She's been getting better. Right now everything is looking really good for her. Thanks for asking."

"I'm glad to hear that." We are both nervous. "This is so awkward," she finally admits.

"I know, I just keep thinking about how much history we have together and then being estranged during such a stressful time in both of our lives. It's really bizarre."

"That's not what I mean, Ella. I mean it's weird being out with you, here of all places, and your eyes aren't darting around looking for your story. You're here and present. I'm just not used to it yet." She picks up a menu and peruses it to give herself a task. We both know she knows it better than the waitstaff.

"I feel like we're exes or something." I sigh.

"We sort of are," she says. "Well, not so much exes. We're separated and trying to reconcile."

"Like our relationship had a midlife crisis and a one-night stand with a twenty-two-year-old," I joke, continuing the metaphor.

"Exactly. The first step is forgiveness and now we can try to heal and move forward."

"I have to be honest; I didn't think you'd ever forgive me." The busboy brings us water and I take my glass from him before he can set it down on the table.

"For a long time I didn't think I would either. But when you told me that you started *Compassionate Celebrities*. I knew that you were sincere about being sorry. I said such horrible things to you and even if my anger was justified, instead of telling me to bugger off you tried to help me. You didn't just apologize, you tried to make things right. And you did." She pauses and looks down briefly before continuing. "Besides, I was the one sleeping with a married man. I couldn't blame you for everything. I had to take responsibility for my part, too." I must look like I've been tased because it feels like my eyes are bugging out of my face. I desperately want to say something but I'm speechless. I couldn't find the words if I wanted to, so she continues. "I think that part of the reason I was so angry is because when the story came out everyone was saying I had no talent and I never would've gotten the part if I hadn't slept with the director, and I was scared that maybe they were right. As horrible as it was, I suppose it gave us both some perspective and direction."

We are two drastically different people than we were a few months ago, sitting across from each other at lunch, but I'm excited to see where these two people end up.

"Even when I hated you, I missed you," Holiday confesses. "Which made me hate you even more. Something would happen on set or Tristan and I would have a tiff or there'd be another new horrible story about me in the press I'd want to vent about and I'd want to text you and then I'd remember what happened and ugh, I didn't like it." The waiter comes around with the bread basket and Holiday shakes her head midconversation and he retreats with the carbs.

"I missed you, too! Jess is great but my friendship with her will never be what ours was. Robin and I are closer but I'm not ready to cry about Nick to her."

"Since you brought him up . . ." She snoops. "What's going on with you guys?"

"Nothing," I tell her matter-of-factly. "I went to his office to discuss him signing Sexy Indie Film Actor and he was polite but otherwise indifferent toward me."

"Really?" She seems surprised. "I find that hard to believe."

"Believe it," I advise her.

"It's just that he—"

"Hol, it's okay," I interrupt Holiday before she can continue. I don't want to drag this out. Talking about Nick sends me into an overanalytical tailspin and I can't keep obsessing about him or what we had or what we were or what I thought we could be. "I just need to keep moving forward. Of course I wish it was with him but it's not so . . ." When I glance down at the table to grab my mimosa, I realize we don't have them. If memory serves me, this is the first dry lunch Holiday and I have ever had. She tries to recover from the uncomfortableness of the Nick topic.

"What do you have going on the rest of the day?" she asks.

"I have to meet Jess and Maggie. They both help me with the site and we have to touch base about stories for the week since it's my day off from The Coffee Bean."

"About that, El. Even though all of this was a huge mess I'm sorry you got fired from *The Life*. I know you loved that job."

I jump in to correct her assumption. "Holiday, I didn't get fired. I quit."

Her jaw drops like a cartoon character. "You did?"

"Yeah. Victoria actually offered me a better job but only if I gave her info I had about Not-So-Innocent Oversexualized Pop Star. So, I quit. I'm glad I had all of those experiences. I'm certainly not going to be lying on my deathbed regretting that I never had any fun times or didn't live my life to the fullest, but the price just got to be too high. I didn't want to risk losing myself again, and if I stayed I was almost certain to."

The waiter finally comes to take our order. "What can I get you ladies?"

"Two mimosas," Holiday answers.

"Hol, I don't—"

"No bloody way, Ella. After everything we've been through you're not going to let me drink alone."

. . . .

How was lunch with Holiday?" Jess asks as soon as she opens her door. She and Maggie await my answer like they're waiting for me to announce the final number of the Powerball when they already got five matches.

"It was so weird," I tell her, plopping onto the couch.

"Weird? Weird how?" she presses.

"Weird in that it was so different but so familiar," I continue. "It was like I was having déjà vu but they were someone else's experiences, if that makes any sense."

She has a puzzled look on her face, so clearly it doesn't. "So are you guys all good?" she asks.

"Yeah. I think so. We will be. I hope. The friendship will never be exactly the same and I think it's going to take some time to get back to a place where we are as comfortable with each other as we used to be but I think we might end up being even better." I honestly believe that. "Let's get down to business," I request.

"Maggie, any pitches for this week?" I ask.

"My source confirmed that Singer with a Dramatic Love Life Who Plays Guitar is going to make an unpublicized visit to Children's Hospital this week. He's going to visit with the kids and play for them. I think that has the potential to be our feature of the week."

"I agree! That would be amazing!" I tell her.

"The source is going to send me a list of the songs he sung after he leaves," she informs me. "I also have a lead on Veteran Sitcom Star with Personal Problems renting out the El Capitan theatre for a week for private screenings for inner-city kids in after-school care programs. I'm still waiting on details about that one, though."

Jessica has a look on her face that means she has something to say that is either very good or very bad.

"In other news, we're now averaging five hundred thousand users a day!" Whoa, that's amazing. At this rate we'll be beating *The Life*.

"I don't know what to say. I couldn't have done this without you girls. Thank you."

"Apparently in our case, two wrongs do make a right," Maggie realizes.

"Well, maybe a little more than two," I tell her. But I agree.

Thirty-two

. . . .

After our Chateau lunch date went smoothly, Holiday invited me over for a girls' night.

"We're getting the band back together!" is what she said, and I didn't want to lose momentum by insulting her and pointing out that we're more of a duo. Walking into her house was bizarre. I felt like I was having another out-of-body experience inside my own body. I closed my eyes and let go of all of the negative thoughts before she leads me to the conservatory, where she's set out cheese and charcuterie. Before we can pop a champagne cork and start bonding she gets a text message and passes me the bottle, deflated. Something's up; Holiday almost enjoys popping the cork more than drinking the champagne.

"What is it?" I ask her.

She clenches and releases her fist five times to mollify herself. "I have a text from Nick. He told me there's an interview coming out with an ex-boyfriend of mine in London claiming that he was in a relationship when we got together and I seduced him away from his girlfriend." She's frustrated and wounded. "It's not true, but you know that doesn't matter. People are going to believe it anyway because they want to and it's salacious. He's trying to capitalize on the Seth affair and get his fifteen minutes of fame." She places her phone on the table facedown. This isn't what I want to be known for," she vents.

"You can fix this," I tell her.

"I can?" Some color flushes back into her cheeks. "How?"

"Here's what you do. Text Nick back and tell him to warn all of the publications that anyone who runs it won't get an interview with you when it's time to do press for *Benedict Canyon*. If you come out playing hardball now, they'll know you're serious and will fuck with you less because they'll want your cooperation for bigger stories."

"Thanks, El. How do you know all of this stuff?"

"File it under things I picked up from working at *The Life* for too long."

"Well, I'll use it to my benefit. I wish you could run interference for me all the time."

It dawns on me. "Holiday, I can."

"What are you talking about, darling?"

"I could be your publicist."

She's looking at me, like I pronounced Chanel "channel."

"Well, what if *that* was my job?"

She stares at me, waiting for me to explain in more detail.

"PR. You yourself said I'm great at it . . .," I remind her.

"You want to be my publicist?"

"You're going to need to have someone watching out for you and your image. You're only going to get bigger once the show premieres. Just think. If I could rehab your image and get the producers at *Benedict Canyon* to reconsider firing you, I can take care of any media crisis."

"Ella, I don't know. We just returned to nonviolent speaking terms. What if it affects our friendship?"

"I think it will help our friendship. You'll know that I'm always working to protect you. First of all no one knows where all of your bodies are buried better than I do. As long as I don't blab, which I swear I won't ever, they will stay hidden." She's actually contemplating my suggestion, so now it's time to go in for the kill. "You have to admit that no one knows the celebrity journalism game like I do. I know how they get their info, who their sources are, what places to avoid; we can create your image to be whatever you want it to be. Nick is going to be too busy to take care of anything other than your deal memos to help you with that."

Holiday knows that I'm right.

"We can even do it on a trial basis. Give me a test as your publicist, and if I do a good job, we'll make it permanent."

"What if it doesn't work out?"

"If we could make it through what happened with *The Life,* we can make it through anything. Besides, now I'm using all of that insider info to your advantage."

She ponders the offer. "And you're okay with a test?"

"Absolutely. One hundred percent. Anything."

"Okay, get Gwendolyn Ross to promise me the cover of the September issue of *Style & Trend Magazine.* You have one week."

The cover of *Style & Trend Magazine*? The September issue, no less. Holiday isn't fucking around. She wants to see if I can make the impossible possible. Every good publicist needs to be able to pull a white rabbit out of a top hat even if all they have available is a guinea pig and a Von Dutch trucker hat circa 2003. But Gwendolyn Ross? Her inner circle is notoriously impervious. Holiday isn't even in it. Getting through to her is as high on the difficulty scale as converting the pope to Judaism. I'd believe she didn't exist if I hadn't seen her with my own two eyes. It may be a long shot but instead of focusing on how difficult this is going to be I need to devise a plan . . . a good one. That's just what I do with my next day off.

Step Number One: Align *Style & Trend Magazine* with Holiday.

I am able to use my basic Photoshop skills to cobble together a collage of images of Holiday that looks more like a recap of Versace, Marchesa, Dior, and Dolce & Gabbana's greatest hits from New York Fashion Week.

Step Number Two: Assess Holiday's marketability.

Cover models have to be women who can move magazines off the newsstands. I compile her social-media data into a chart on my computer that makes it look like I put a lot more effort into it than I actually did and makes it look official. Next I check the visitor hits from *Compassionate Celebrities*. Every Holiday post has a minimum of twice as many visitors as other posts.

Step Number Three: Attempt to contact Gwendolyn with this information.

I scour the deep, dark corners of the Internet and feel like it's easier to find redacted government documents on Area 51 than a pipeline to Gwendolyn. After countless hours in a black hole online I recognize that her assistant's contact info is the closest I'm going to get. Even Gwendolyn's assistant's e-mail address is so difficult to find I'm beginning to think it's a myth, like the fountain of youth. I fire off my pitch to her assistant and use the law of attraction to manifest her assistant passing on the information and Gwendolyn saying yes. At this point it can't hurt. Two days later, no response. I will never understand how people can just not answer an e-mail. It takes two seconds to type a sentence. I send a follow-up e-mail. On the third day, when I still have nothing, I know that it's time for a backup plan. The window Holiday gave me to achieve this goal is beginning to close and I can't waste another day of waiting around. If I can't get past Gwendolyn's assistant I will have to go straight to Gwendolyn somehow.

The stress of having gotten nowhere with this task is giving me a head-ache. I need to get a coffee—one that I didn't make—to help take the edge off. I decide to up my vitamin D levels and take a calming walk to Robin's neighborhood Starbucks. It feels nice to be a customer again.

"I'll have a grande iced latte," I tell the barista, who is almost a mirror image of me, except for the fact that she's smiling.

"That'll be three dollars and seventy-five cents," she says without any contempt in her voice.

I reach into my wallet and grab my last remaining tip dollars and I notice it. I'd completely forgotten I have it. It's my membership card to Doheny Circle. With everything going on, Doheny Circle hasn't been on my radar recently, and even if it had been I'd be too scared to go there—I might run into Nick. But it's the last place I saw Gwendolyn, so it's my best shot at talking to her about Holiday. I wonder if he removed me from his membership when he broke up with me, but there's only one way to find out. I grab my iced latte and sprint home. It's time for me to get dressed up and be Bella one last time.

As I enter the lobby of Doheny Circle I feel my stomach tingle. *Breathe. Namaste.* I present my card to the hostess, who looks me up and down. She squints one eye at me. Fuck. Am I busted? Chateau part *deux.* I'm about to place my hands in front of me to save security the trouble while escorting me out when she speaks.

"Will Mr. Williams be joining you?" she asks.

"Not today," I reply back as icily as she'd asked. I normally wouldn't be so rude, but to the people at Doheny Circle, kindness would be con-sidered weakness.

"Enjoy," she says without so much as a smile. I let out a huge breath when I reach the elevator bank and head to the penthouse. I arrive at the bar area and park myself at a stool. It's only 3 P.M. but that doesn't mean it's empty by any means.

"Can I get you something to drink?" the nonmodel but career bar-tender asks.

"Just water for me."

He rolls his eyes with the confirmation he won't be receiving a large tip and begrudgingly slides me a glass of water. The people trickle in and out as the hours pass. We've moved on from ladies who lunch to men who make conversation with their mistresses, but no Gwendolyn. I check my phone. Shoot! I have to leave in ten minutes. Marianna's school play is tonight and I promised her I'd be there. I think about how two months ago I'd have canceled on my family because I would've wanted to wait until the end of the night to see if Gwendolyn showed. Ten minutes ticks by and it's time to wave the white flag. I leave twenty dollars on the bar as a fuck-you to the surly bartender and order an Uber. As the elevator doors open, who do I literally run into while I'm trying to enter and she's exiting but the elusive one herself, Gwendolyn?

"Watch where you're going," she snarls without looking up. I feel a lump develop in my throat. Without even saying a word, I blew it. I swallow and muster up some inner strength somehow. No! I'm not going down this easy. I abruptly turn around and chase after her and I reach her before she can be seated for cocktails.

"Excuse me, Gwendolyn, we met at Holiday Hall's house. I'm Ella." I extend my hand and she merely stares at it.

"Yes?" she asks, although she obviously wants me to scram.

"I'm Holiday Hall's publicist. I want to pitch her for the September issue of *Style & Trend*."

She stares at me blankly. "Holiday Hall?"

I nod yes.

"As the model for the September issue?"

"That's correct."

She looks me up and down, I'm sure finding fault with every piece of clothing and accessory that catches her gaze. She reaches into her pocketbook (Gwendolyn Ross doesn't carry a purse. It's most assuredly a pocketbook) and hands me a card.

"I like it. Here's my direct contact information. Call me to discuss details." Did I just pull this off? Could it have been that easy? I mean, it wasn't easy. I was resourceful, but did I somehow hit defrost on the ice queen?

"Thank you, she will be great for the cover!"

"The cover?" She cackles. "What did you say your name was?"

"Ella," I answer.

"Ella. There's no way I'm putting Holiday on the cover—of the September issue, no less. I enjoy her socially but I need star power for the cover. Call my office and we'll talk about a four-page editorial spread." My neck sinks. "Trust me. Even that is a gift." She turns toward the dining room and doesn't bother looking back.

I call Holiday from my Uber. With each ring that passes I'm hoping she won't pick up. I'm not sure how she's going to react.

"Hi, Hol."

"Hi, darling."

"I . . . I . . ."

"Are you alright, El?"

"I called to tell you that I can't get you on the cover of the September issue of *Style & Trend Magazine*. I did my best, I promise. But a four-page editorial layout is all you might get. So you don't have to hire me as your publicist. I—"

"Will you stop talking for a minute, Ella? You're hired."

"But I failed," I tell her.

"It was never about the cover of *Style & Trend Magazine*. I just wanted to see if you would tell me the truth and accept responsibility. I needed to know if I could give you my full trust again, and I can," she declares.

"I don't know what to say." I'm perplexed.

"Say that you'll start next week," she offers. "I have to go back to Canada to film the rest of the season and I'd feel a lot better knowing I have someone watching out for me here," she says. "Darling, listen, I have to go. I'm late to meet Tristan. We'll talk about all of the details tomorrow, okay? Ciao!"

I hang up the phone and text Spike my two-week notice. He tries to call me but I can't answer. My Uber has stopped.

I arrive at Marianna's school just in time.

Thirty-three

....

Since I've become a publicist I've completely immersed myself in work. Even more so than when I was at *The Life,* but my
boundaries are set much better. Unless I have to be at an event with
a client I'm off limits after 6 P.M. weeknights and on weekends. For a
brand-new publicist I've assembled quite the client list in such a short period of time. Not-So-Innocent Oversexualized Pop Star hired me after
consistent coinciding chemo treatments with my mom and her secret is
still as safe today as before I met her.

Because of Dr. Jacobs, both she and my mother are in remission, and
I've helped Not-So-Innocent Oversexualized Pop Star launch the comeback of the century. The only thing Hollywood loves more than a scandal
is a grandiose comeback. Then, of course, there's Sexy Indie Film Actor.
With the help of his superagent, Nick Williams, and *Compassionate Celebrities* his schedule is fully committed for the next two years . . . including
the lead role in that reboot of the huge comic-book franchise. Yes, *that*
one.

And of course there's Holiday. Though she's shooting in Canada most
of the time she's the client I have the most to do for day to day. Her still-
colorful life leads to me fielding calls from reporters to confirm or deny
rumors, arranging photo shoots and interviews, and making sure that
every word that I can control that's written about her is flattering. I've
fully restored her image and I intend to make sure that no job of hers will
ever be in jeopardy again.

The time has finally come for the premiere of *Benedict Canyon* and
Holiday's official debut. There is, of course, a huge party, and Holiday and
the rest of the cast and crew are flying back to Los Angeles to attend. This
will be the first time we walk a red carpet together as publicist and client.
My body is jittery with excitement—so much so that I can barely reply to
the hundreds of e-mails I'm receiving.

I arrive at her house that afternoon to organize her wardrobe options and review potential interview answers while her glam squad gets her ready.

"You're going to look perfect," I tell her when she emerges in her head-to-toe look. "Tonight is all about you, my dear." I pat her shoulder.

"You *are* a brilliant publicist."

My iPhone buzzes and I check my texts. "Hol, we have to hurry up. The SUV is here." The doorbell rings. "And that must be Tristan. Give your hair one more spritz of volume spray before we leave," I command.

"Bossy, bossy!" She gives me her soon-to-be-famous wink.

"That's what you pay me for, superstar," I quip as I make my way out of her room. I take the very familiar route to the front door, and when I answer, Tristan is on the other side holding a bouquet of roses.

"Wow. You look great," he says as he enters the foyer.

"Thank you. But wait until you see Holiday."

She emerges that very second as if we'd choreographed her grand entrance. Tristan almost loses his grip on the flowers when he sets his eyes on her and is in such a trance he can't speak. Holiday retrieves the flowers from his hand and inhales their scent.

"These are beautiful!" She fawns over the bouquet as if it was the Hope Diamond.

"Babe, you're stunning," he finally manages to get out, and she inches toward him and gives Tristan a long passionate kiss that's giving no indication of ending anytime soon. I clap my hands to break up their make-out sesh.

"Alright, lovebirds, we have a schedule. We need to get moving to stay on track."

"Are your mom and Robin meeting us there?" she asks.

"They are. But enough with the dawdling. We only want to be fashionably late, we don't want to miss the red carpet entirely."

. . . .

We pull up to the red carpet and Tristan exits first, then helps us get out of the SUV without flashing or falling in front of the cameras. He escorts himself to the entrance of the carpet, but I pull Holiday's hand and hold her back to have a brief bonding moment before we hit the mob scene.

"You ready for this? Your whole life is going to change when you get out of this car," I warn.

Holiday sarcastically applauds me.

"Those theatrics, Ella . . . are you the actress or am I?" she jests.

"I'm serious. I want you to remember this moment . . . and I also want you to remember, publicist or not, I'll always be there for you and look out for your best interest." I open my purse and take out a perfectly wrapped Cartier box and present it to Holiday.

"What's this?" she asks, even though she's received so many gifts from Cartier over the years she could put her ear to the box like a conch shell and tell me exactly what's inside down to the weight and metal details. That doesn't stop her from meticulously unraveling the ribbon from on top of the box. She opens it and when she sees its contents she lets out a slight gasp. "A pink gold Cartier love bracelet!" She's genuinely touched and I can see the tears welling up in her eyes. "Ella, you didn't have to do this." Upon further inspection, she notices the engraving and gives me a smile. "Well, well, well, Miss Moneybags. I can see you've been holding out on me," she jokes through the genuine moment to attempt to prevent tears from running down her face.

"You know how it is. I grossly overcharge my clients," I tease. I retrieve from the box the small matching accompanying screwdriver, also made of pink gold, and Holiday holds her wrist out for me to lock the bracelet onto her.

"Thank you," she says, staring at the bangle. "For this and for everything."

Holiday hugs me and a tear cascades from her cheek and lands on my shoulder.

"Don't you dare start crying and ruin your makeup before you're photographed," I reprimand. She takes a deep breath and grabs my hand as we walk to the red carpet to meet Tristan.

Holiday barely has both stilettos firmly planted on the carpet when the photographers start screaming her name like she's an athlete and they're cheering her on in the big game.

"Holiday! Over the shoulder!"

"One over here, Holiday! One more!"

"Blow a kiss to the camera, Holiday!"

"Put your hand on your hip! Beautiful! Gorgeous!"

"You're beautiful, Holiday! Over here!"

"Thanks, guys. That's enough," I tell them after three minutes of her uninterrupted professional posing, which feels like a lot longer than it sounds. They continue to scream for more shots of Holiday but she dutifully follows me as I lead her down the carpet for interviews.

"We make a great team," she says.

"We always did."

"Ella," I hear my mother call. She and Robin are on the other side of the red carpet near the reporters, and they wave excitedly. I wave back. Holiday marches over and unhooks the velvet rope for them to join us on our side.

"It's okay, they're with me," she tells security. My mother is in awe of the scene of a real premiere and I catch a look of whimsy in Robin's eyes, too. I hand my phone to Holiday.

"Can you take a picture of us?" I ask her. My mom and Robin snuggle in tight with me, and three of the four Warren women pose in front of the step and repeat while the lady of the night snaps a few photos so we will always remember it. None of us take memories for granted these days, and the fact that we can all stand here happy, healthy, and healed is better than any fame or fortune.

"Now do a funny one," Holiday instructs. We all instinctively duck-face for the last shot. Holiday returns my phone and we look through the photos.

"They're beautiful," my mom says.

"Will you send them to me? Marianna is going to love them," Robin gushes.

"Of course. You know, we do look pretty amazing here. Maybe we should look into getting our own mother-daughter reality show?" I joke. We all burst out laughing and say "nah" at the same time. Never in a million years. I screenshot the photo and make it my phone's background.

"Congratulations, Holiday." My mother hugs her even though this is the first time they've ever actually met.

"Thank you, Mrs. Warren. I'm glad you were able to make it."

Holiday puts her arm around me as we walk in with Robin and my mom right behind us.

"Before you start to mingle let me get a picture of you in front of your poster for your social-media feeds." Holiday marches over to the wall and quickly emulates all of the poses she just ran through on the carpet.

"Ella, stop working! We are supposed to be celebrating," she reminds me.

"As your publicist I never stop working."

She rolls her eyes. "Fine. I'm going to find Tristan. Can you at least work your way over to the bar and get us some champagne?"

"Of course."

"What can I get you, beautiful?" the bartender asks. This one is the Gucci model from the billboard right in front of the Chateau Marmont. I'm about to make my request, but before I do a familiar voice chimes in.

"She'll have a glass of champagne." The hairs on the back of my neck stand up. The voice belongs to Nick.

"And a scotch for the gentleman," I add. "Hi."

"Hi." Nick places his hand on the bar and leans toward me. "Of all the gin joints, in all the towns, in all the world, you walk into mine."

He hugs me but I'm jarred by his unexpected gesture and we are not in sync. He weaves while I bob and when I try to bob he weaves. After two failed attempts he takes the matter into his own hands, literally, and pulls me toward him. I've always loved how he takes control. I find myself grinding my teeth to calm my nerves and I'm afraid I'm going to whittle them down to a point by the end of our embrace.

"Ella—"

"Nick," I interrupt. Once I say his name I lose all of the control I had over my body. My voice quivers and my limbs instantly go numb. The bartender hands us our drinks just in time and I take a large gulp. The bubbles haven't finished tingling in my throat but if I don't say this now I'm scared that I never will. "I know that you hate me but I really am sorry. For everything."

"Is that what you think? That I hate you?" he asks. The usual sparkle in his eyes looks like it might turn into tears.

"Well, yeah. I never heard from you after that day at your office."

"Ella, I don't hate you. I could never hate you. I was angry. Disappointed. But most of all, heartbroken. I felt like you used me."

"I never meant to hurt you and I understand why you ended things and I really did . . ." I stop myself from finishing that sentence.

"Me, too," he says, understanding exactly what I meant to say. "You seem to be doing great, though. New career, *Compassionate Celebrities*."

"I'm just trying to make it up to everyone I've hurt the best I can," I tell him.

"I know you are. When you came to my office and told me about the site and asked me to represent Sexy Indie Film Actor I knew you had

changed." He can't stop staring at me. "I miss you." Our reunion or rec-
onciliation or whatever this might be is interrupted by Holiday skipping
over to us.

"I have the most brilliant idea," Holiday says, out of breath. Whatever
moment Nick and I were having immediately diffuses.

"Uh-oh," Nick whispers to me.

"Oh, bugger off, Nick."

"What's this idea?" I ask.

"Let's all go to a club!" she shrieks. Nick and I shoot each other a
glance that we are both on the same page and would rather slit our wrists
than do that. In that brief moment we feel like a team again.

"Come on! I know that look. Ella, have you even been to a club since
you stopped working for *The Life*?"

"No. Thank God," I blurt out.

"I promise, they can actually be fun. You said it's my night, and since
both of you are on my payroll I'm going to be a demanding client and
insist."

I attempt to wiggle out of her request. "What about my mom and
Robin? I don't want to leave them."

"Bring them along," she says. "They can really have the Hollywood
experience if they come."

What can I do?

"I'm only going if Ella goes," Nick disclaims.

I wave them over and pitch Holiday's plan.

"I think we're going to pass, honey," my mom tells me. "But you
should go." I turn to Robin.

"You should. You've earned this," she agrees.

"Are you guys sure?" I check.

I notice my mom staring at Nick, recognizing him from his photo,
and I suppose now is as good a time as any for their belated introduction.

"Nick, I'd like to introduce you to my family. This is my mom, Joan,
and my sister, Robin." He shakes Robin's hand and kisses my mom's as
he greets them.

"Well, it's about time. It's nice to finally meet you, Nick. You are *the*
Nick, aren't you?"

"Mom!" I playfully tap her shoulder and immediately use my hand to
hide my embarrassed face.

"I sure hope so." Nick and my mom both look at me for an answer and I nod that yes, this is *the* Nick and now I'm mortified. "Wonderful to meet you ladies." With that he has mesmerized them. "I'm glad to see that it looks like you're feeling well, Joan." She blushes and I can tell Nick has her seal of approval.

"I am starving," my mom announces. I never thought hearing her say those words would mean so much to me. "Robin, shall we make our way to the buffet?"

"Yes. Go have fun, El," Robin insists as she and my mother make their pilgrimage for food.

Holiday rushes to grab Tristan and I survey the room. You can take the girl away from the reporting job, but . . .

"I think our client is staking her claim in Hollywood. Everyone is here," Nick marvels.

Yes, *everyone*. Who happens to meet my gaze but Victoria Davis, who is in my immediate sight line. A few months ago I thought she had ruined my life but she probably saved it. I take a deep breath as I watch her as she approaches me.

"Hello, Ella. It's nice to see you." She pretends like no unpleasantness happened and ignores Nick. "I'm glad I bumped into you. You are a publicist now, correct?"

I nod. "Word travels fast."

"You of all people know that." She cracks a duplicitous half smile. "I want to talk to you about doing some interviews with your clients. Especially an exclusive on Holiday for *The Life*. Can I take you to lunch?"

I return her devious smile. Never again will I allow Victoria to mince my words or my clients'.

"No comment" is all I have to say to her.

. . . .

The impromptu seating arrangements in our car just so happen to have Nick shoved in right beside me. His leg scrapes mine and his virgin wool pants feel like sandpaper rubbing against my freshly shaven leg but I like it. I'm finally close enough to smell the scent of Nick's cologne and it's intoxicating. My heart is beating faster and my hormones are making me sweat in lady places I haven't sweat in for a long time, which I'm trying to hide.

"Where are we going?" I ask. I'm so out of the club-scene loop I don't even know what the hot spots and the has-beens are at the moment.

"Celestial Circus. It's supposed to be the best spot in town right now," Holiday says, trying to convince us.

I send a few text messages en route and when I finish with my phone I feel an unexpected squeeze on my shoulder. Nick moves his hand lower and it engulfs mine. I look down and stare at our hands together and then back up at him and lean my head to rest on his shoulder. Holiday and Tristan spend the ride responding to the hundreds of congratulatory texts they're receiving and I spend it in silence, happy to be present in this moment where all feels well.

We arrive at the club and Holiday emerges from the car first. She's instantly swarmed by a group of overzealous paparazzi. Tristan follows and the photo op intensifies.

"Your doing?" Nick asks, smiling, referring to the photographers.

"Normally I wouldn't tip them off but it's premiere night. Want to make sure their faces are everywhere so people remember to tune in on Tuesday night." Nick lets out a sigh and looks away and my heart once again splinters. I'm ready to launch into my expository defense when he turns back and kisses me. I melt into the familiarity of Nick's kiss. We come up for air after what feels like forever but also feels like not long enough. I smile and thrust my lips back toward his. I don't want to stop kissing Nick again and I don't, until Holiday prances back to the car and knocks on the window, interrupting.

"Are you two coming?" As soon as we hear her voice our lips repel like opposite magnets, but it's too late. She's spotted us smooching. "Never mind. Carry on," she says with a wink and the flicker of a devious smile in our direction before retreating to the club's entrance.

"We should probably . . ."

"Yeah," Nick agrees.

"Wait—" I interrupt. "Before we go in there together . . . before we start anything again, I have to tell you something." He looks at me quizzically. "Full disclosure, I used your Doheny Circle membership a few months ago," I confess. I continue before he has the chance to speak so he knows I wasn't trying to take advantage of him just to hang out at the swanky spot. "Holiday had told me she would hire me if I could get her on the cover of *Style & Trend Magazine* and after I exhausted all of my other options I used the membership to make it look like I haphazardly ran into Gwendolyn Ross." I'm eyeballing Nick, anticipating his reaction, but he gives me nothing and makes me sweat it out for some of the longest fifteen seconds of my life.

"I know," he says with his bewitching eyes, which are full of compassion.

"You do?"

"Of course. Doheny Circle e-mails the primary member every time the membership is used." I look away from Nick, part embarrassed but mostly too vulnerable to continue looking into his eyes. He takes his forefinger to my chin and swivels my face back around to his. "It's okay." I nod, not sure what I would say if I were to speak. "I appreciate you telling me, though," he continues.

"I have a confession to make too," he announces. I covertly cross my fingers on my far hand near my hip, hoping he isn't about to tell me he wants to do this but then lists the reasons why he can't.

"That day you came to my office . . ." He pauses, and I want to scream at him to spit it out! "It took everything inside of me to keep our meeting professional and not grab you and kiss you."

"Really? You were so distant until I told you about *Compassionate Celebrities* and quitting *The Life*."

"It was all an act. I was overcompensating." He smiles. "I was a child star, remember? And I couldn't help but stare at your ass when you walked out."

"I knew it!" I'm about to give him shit but he leans into my ear.

"I love you, Ella Warren."

"I love you, too," I whisper.

Nick kisses me again and our necking continues until we are interrupted by the bright flashes from the paparazzi. We remove our lips from each other's.

"Here's looking at you, kid," he says as he helps me out of the car. When I exit, I realize that we are at Ambiance. Well, what used to be Ambiance. It really is true, the more things change, the more they stay the same.

We catch up to Holiday and Tristan just in time to zip past the doorman—a new guy I've never seen. I wonder if he'd let me in if I were coming to work and not Holiday's guest? I'm beyond grateful I don't have to find out.

A cocktail waitress leads us through the club and I gasp. Visually, it's as if Ambiance had never existed. The interior was gutted, remodeled, and revamped, and it being a metaphor for Bella isn't lost on me. On the way to the VIP section I spot my nemesis from *The Life,* the snobby girl that was my competition . . . and she's with Pixie Haircut Hostess from the Chateau Marmont! The two girls trade sipping their cocktails for sneering at me as I waltz through the club. They are here together? And are friends? It dawns on me . . . now it all makes sense. The snobby girl and I had been neck and neck in points the whole time and she wanted to dispose of her competition. She must have been the person who was leaking gossip to Pixie Haircut Hostess and who ratted me out. Any hint of anger I would've had is replaced with gratitude. The snobby girl thought she was ruining me when in fact she helped save me. I give them an enormous fuck-you smile as I'm escorted past them.

We reach our table in the VIP section and I instinctually slide into the reupholstered banquette. Nick scoots next to me. Our waitress opens a bottle of Ace of Spades champagne and hands us each a flute.

"No Veuve or Dom?" I ask Holiday.

"New start, new champagne." She winks.

I look around at the other tables in our roped-off section. I guess you can take the girl out of the job but in some ways it will always be with me. The VIP area is full of the usual suspects but it seems like all eyes are on Holiday tonight. As I continue glancing around my eye catches a table kitty-corner from ours. It's Anaeliese, the woman who threw herself at Nick during Holiday's dinner months ago, and she's shamelessly hanging all over Older Multi-Oscar-Winning Womanizer. She's pulling from her usual repertoire, kissing his neck, whispering in his ear, and letting her hands explore every inch of him that's appropriate in public. His gaze happens to land on me and his face softens. He recognizes me. Then he spots Nick and gives me a reverent nod, an acknowledgment he was wrong about us. I nod back at him with a grin and raise my glass toward him. Anaeliese is frustrated that he isn't fawning all over her for thirty seconds and looks my way to learn what's distracting Older Multi-Oscar-Winning Womanizer from her. When she notices it's me she gives me major side-eye then returns her attention back to Older Multi-Oscar-Winning Womanizer. She doesn't even bother to come over and offer Holiday any congratulations on her success or well wishes for her new show. Her only concern is continuing her social climbing.

"I'd like to propose a toast," I announce. I raise my glass. Everyone follows my lead and moves in closer to hear me over the music. "To Holiday, the only woman who can drink like a fish, fuck like a man, swear like a sailor, and still be the classiest lady in the room." Holiday purses her lips as Tristan puts his arm around her and kisses her on the cheek. We're about to clink glasses and drink but Nick chimes in.

"And to the success of *Benedict Canyon*!"

We clink again and Nick places another soft peck on my lips. We rest our backs on the banquette and I snuggle into the nook between his shoulder and his neck that I've longed for since we split. Neither of us can stop smiling, as if tonight is our first meeting. And in some ways it is. We've never been out together when I could be only Ella. Our lovers' daze is interrupted when I blink my eyes and notice Holiday pick up the champagne bottle, ready to take a swig. I return to publicist mode and leap from my seat to rip it from her hands.

"Ella, what are you doing?" she grimaces.

"My job!" I lean in to her ear and whisper. The snobby girl from *The Life* has made her way to the perimeter of the VIP section alone and I point her out to Holiday. "You want to be on the Internet tomorrow morning but not with the headline 'British Heiress Turned Hollywood It Girl Was a Lush Chugging Champagne.'"

"But I am a lush," she cheekily protests.

"I know and I love you for it. But not tonight and not on my watch, sweetheart."

"I'm starting to regret paying you to boss me around." She smirks.

I shrug my shoulders. "That's the girl that got me kicked out of Chateau," I tell her. Holiday's eyes widen and she looks like she's about to pull her earrings off and leap out of her seat to give her a beatdown. "It's okay, let's just make sure we don't give her a story. That will be our revenge. As long as you keep your behavior to a playful celebration, she won't have anything." Holiday takes a breath to calm herself down and reluctantly pours the champagne into a flute. Nick whispers in my ear.

"What if we leak another, better story to the club reporter so she stays away from us?" I raise an eyebrow in anticipation. "What do you think of the headline 'Hollywood Superagent and Publicist to the Stars Give Relationship a Second Chance'?"

"If you want to get technical it's a little long for a headline . . . but I've always enjoyed breaking the rules," I add mischievously.

Nick playfully scoffs. "Let me try that again." I clear my throat.

"Sounds like the industry's perfect power couple to me." He leans in and kisses me and then rests his forehead against mine. Holiday interrupts our happy ending.

"One last toast tonight. This one is just for me and Ella." The men obey her instruction and continue to sip their beverages in silence to give Holiday her moment. She glances at the bracelet I gave her and her face plumps with pure joy. I swear being truly happy is the best beauty secret in the world. She and I once again raise our glasses, and I stare at my flute as if it is the Holy Grail. In a way it has been. I may not have always realized it, but I've had both parts of our toast all along. I clink Holiday's glass.

"To glamour and love!"

THE END

ACKNOWLEDGMENTS

To my mom and dad, the most concise way to say this is that this book simply wouldn't exist without you. If I said nothing other than "thank you" to you for the rest of my life, it still wouldn't be enough or accurately express the deep thanks and gratitude I have for all of your love and support. Thank you for always believing in me, even when I didn't believe in myself. I love you both wider than the whole solar system.

To my agent, Dan Lazar, I don't know where to begin. You were the first person in the industry to believe in me, and I will never forget that. You have fought for me since day one and have never once reprimanded me for the slew of neurotic e-mails I've sent you at completely inappropriate hours. Thank you for seeing something in me in your slush pile, holding my hand throughout this entire process and being so patient with me. Your keen editorial eye helped make this book so much more than another superficial Hollywood story. You taught me the art of nuance. Without you, this story would have no heart. Thank you from the very bottom of *my* heart. I owe my career to you.

To Torie Doherty-Munro, thank you for always being so helpful. I know there is so much you have done on my behalf behind the scenes that I'm not even aware of and I want you to know that it's greatly appreciated.

A huge thank you to everyone at Writers House, who have made me feel so supported as an author. I am thankful for the hard work everyone has put in to help make my dream a reality.

To my phenomenal editor, Laurie Chittenden, I can't imagine having worked on my first novel with anyone but you. Thank you for believing in me and this book. You have gotten it since day one. I can't thank you enough for making this the best book it could possibly be. Every single note you gave me made this book better. Really, every single one. I've always felt like you have been on my side, and I'm eternally grateful for that. I look forward to sipping many, many glasses of wine with you in the future.

Thank you, Lisa Bonvissuto, for all of your help and for being so kind about answering my incessant questions. Thank you, Karen Masnica. Your enthusiasm for this book from the beginning has been such a blessing. Thank you to the amazing Tracey Guest and Jessica Lawrence, for your PR prowess. Thank you to David Rotstein for designing the book jacket, which I couldn't possibly love more. A big thank you to Jeremy Pink, MaryAnn Johanson, and Shelly Perron. And thank you to everyone else at St. Martin's Press, for all of your hard work.

To Josie Freedman, thank you for taking a chance on me and on selling Hollywood to Hollywood.

Thank you Alex Schack and Charlene Young, for seeing the big picture and for your vision. I knew I had to work with you as soon as we met, and I couldn't be more thrilled. You ladies are the best of the best. This is only the beginning!

Dennis Jacobs, to say thank you for everything wouldn't suffice. Thank you for the support and encouragement you've had for this book when it was nothing but a Word doc on my computer that was rejected more times than either of us can count. Thank you for always offering to read every new word throughout this process no matter the time of day or night or whatever else you had going on. Thank you for always letting me bounce ideas and dialogue off you and for taking the ramblings of the numerous nervous breakdowns I've had throughout the years in stride. Let's be honest; without you, this book would be a smattering of words sandwiched between Xanax references and the repetition of "namaste." I hope you know how much I appreciate all of your help and, more important, your friendship.

Thank you to all of my friends who have loved and supported me throughout this entire process. Thank you for remaining my friends after I consistently flaked on our plans so I could write. Thank you for texting me to check in when I was MIA for long periods of time. Thank you for telling me you believed in my talent and not to give up. Thank you for getting me cocktails to take my mind off things when the going got tough. Those of you near and far always let me know you were there for me. Your friendship means the absolute world to me. A sincere thank you to: Jamie Beck, Diné Butler, Amanda Champagne-Meadows, Kiley Cristiano, Angie Dobrofsky, Robin Freni, Serra Garcia,

Keegan Killian, Katherine Klick, Alex Kurucz, Sara Lavoie, Megan Phelps, Tiffany Phelps, Lauren Pomykala, Jelena Rajic, Nate Reeves, Crystal Salazar, Eva Scheiringer, Erin Searcy, Melissa Shamberg, Tatiana Steelman, Andrea White, and Angela Wu.

Thank you, Rebecca Maizel, for mentoring me. You graciously gave me your time and the benefit of your experience. You made me a better writer. Forever will the phrase "show, don't tell" help and haunt me. I can't thank you enough for being the kind of mentor that all writers should be lucky enough to have.

A large thank you to Dr. Gary Schiller who graciously answered my medical questions for this book (and a disclaimer: He's not responsible for any inaccuracies).

An extremely heartfelt thank you to Leila Kenzle.